"We will not leave those clouds alive," Doc warned

Ryan drew his blaster and started firing, the red-hot rounds easily punching through the tough polymer and deflating the balloons.

"Water!" Krysty called out, pointing ahead.

There was a wide break in the stygian forest, a calm river that traversed the valley floor. Their target was a slim area of flat mud between the rocks, impossible to hit at their current speed.

"That's our best chance," Ryan shouted, slashing at the side ropes. "Wait for it.... Now!" In unison the companions dived from the pallet, and a split second later the *Pegasus* rammed into the trees and was torn apart by a thousand sharp branches.

Only the babbling of the shallow river disturbed the heavy silence. Then swatches of light bobbed through the darkness, and armed men stepped from the bushes along the riverbank to approach the still figures sprawled in the bloody mud.

Other titles in the
Deathlands saga:

JAMES AXLER

DEATH LANDS®

Shadow Fortress

THE SKYDARK CHRONICLES
Book III

A GOLD EAGLE BOOK FROM

WORLDWIDE®

TORONTO • NEW YORK • LONDON
AMSTERDAM • PARIS • SYDNEY • HAMBURG
STOCKHOLM • ATHENS • TOKYO • MILAN
MADRID • WARSAW • BUDAPEST • AUCKLAND

To Rich Tucholka, a good friend, and a good man

First edition September 2001

ISBN 0-373-62565-0

SHADOW FORTRESS

Printed in U.S.A.

Storm'd at with shot and shell,
While horse and hero fell,
They that had fought so well
Came thro' the jaws of Death,
Back from the mouth of Hell,
All that was left of them...

—Alfred, Lord Tennyson
1809–1892

THE DEATHLANDS SAGA

This world is their legacy, a world born in the violent nuclear spasm of 2001 that was the bitter outcome of a struggle for global dominance.

There is no real escape from this shockscape where life always hangs in the balance, vulnerable to newly demonic nature, barbarism, lawlessness.

But they are the warrior survivalists, and they endure—in the way of the lion, the hawk and the tiger, true to nature's heart despite its ruination.

Ryan Cawdor: The privileged son of an East Coast baron. Acquainted with betrayal from a tender age, he is a master of the hard realities.

Krysty Wroth: Harmony ville's own Titian-haired beauty, a woman with the strength of tempered steel. Her premonitions and Gaia powers have been fostered by her Mother Sonja.

J. B. Dix, the Armorer: Weapons master and Ryan's close ally, he, too, honed his skills traversing the Deathlands with the legendary Trader.

Doctor Theophilus Tanner: Torn from his family and a gentler life in 1896, Doc has been thrown into a future he couldn't have imagined.

Dr. Mildred Wyeth: Her father was killed by the Ku Klux Klan, but her fate is not much lighter. Restored from predark cryogenic suspension, she brings twentieth-century healing skills to a nightmare.

Jak Lauren: A true child of the wastelands, reared on adversity, loss and danger, the albino teenager is a fierce fighter and loyal friend.

Dean Cawdor: Ryan's young son by Sharona accepts the only world he knows, and yet he is the seedling bearing the promise of tomorrow.

In a world where all was lost, they are humanity's last hope....

Chapter One

Slithering through the jungle brush, the huge cobra reared its head and hissed loudly at the sight of the approaching humans.

Both of his hands splayed wide to force a path through the tangled vines, Ryan Cawdor didn't pause at the sight of the reptile, but instantly stomped down with his combat boot, pinning it. Struggling furiously, the cobra uprooted small plants as the man pulled a panga from its sheath on his belt and sliced downward with all of his strength. The blade neatly severed the head, pale blood spraying from the neck stump as the long body thrashed madly about in the leaves.

But as the snake head hit the ground, its eyes flared wide and the mutie spit out a long stream of greenish fluid. Ryan bent out of the way and the poison hit a tree, the bark turning white almost instantly. Stomping harder on the reptile, the one-eyed warrior felt bones crack, but the creature still struggled to get free. Muttering a curse, Ryan kept his boot in place and drew his 9 mm SIG-Sauer blaster from the holster at his hip. Racking the slide to chamber a round under the hammer, he lifted his boot and fired twice, the soft chugs of the sound-suppressed weapon lost in the rustle of the trees overhead from the ocean breeze. The soft-nosed slugs punched through both of the cobra's eyes, blowing its head apart, bones and brains splashing across the stubby grass under the papaya plants.

Three feet away, the hanging cluster of flowery vines burst apart and out stepped a short wiry man with a pump-action shotgun in his callused hands. The newcomer was wearing a fedora hat and wire-rimmed glasses. An Uzi machine pistol was slung across a shoulder, and a bulging canvas bag hung at his side. His leather bomber jacket was stained with sweat, and his clothes were discolored with quicksand and dried blood.

"Centipede?" John Barrymore Dix asked, the maw of his S&W M-4000 blaster sweeping the area for possible targets.

"Just a snake this time," Ryan grunted in reply, stabbing the panga into the moist soil to clean away any possible trace of the venom. "Nothing serious."

On the ground, the headless body of the mutie reptile still wiggled about as if unwilling to accept its unexpected demise. Ryan kicked it aside.

"Well, anything's better than those triple-damn leeches," J.B. said with a scowl, easing his stance.

Holstering his blaster, Ryan grunted in agreement, then ripped a leaf from a breadfruit tree to wipe the soft dirt off the steel before sheathing his blade.

Ryan towered over J.B. Long curly black hair framed a humorless face covered with a network of scars, an old leather patch masking the puckered ruin of his left eye. A 7.62 mm bolt-action Steyr sniper rifle was slung over a powerful shoulder, and a heavy canvas pack rode easily on his back. A coat lined with ratty fur was tied around his waist from the stifling jungle heat, his shirt was unbuttoned halfway, exposing a muscular chest with more knife scars and the dead-white dots of old bullet wounds.

Taking a small drink of water from his canteen, J.B. then offered the container to Ryan, who gratefully took a sip, sloshing the precious fluid about in his mouth before swallowing. Fresh water was merely one of the many things the companions were drastically running low on. This gamble to reach the crashed plane had better payoff, or they might find themselves in chains before Lord Baron Kinnison, a lunatic infamous for giving prisoners his terrible rotting disease before torturing them. That way, even if somebody escaped, he or she still died in screaming torment. It was a serious threat that few dared to risk.

"Which way?" Ryan asked, brushing back his wild crop of hair.

Reaching into a pocket, J.B. checked the compass in his hand and watched until the needle trembled only slightly. "Left."

Nodding in agreement, Ryan headed in that direction, using his bare hands to push aside the thick vines and broad banana leaves. The weight of the panga was a tempting reminder of how easy it would be to cut a path through the bushes. But that also left behind a trail so clean any feeb could follow. And on this nameless island, being discovered meant death.

Swatting a buzzing skeeter, J.B. let the tall man get a few yards ahead, then followed in his wake, trying to put his boots in the other man's prints to minimize the trail. Close behind the wiry Armorer came a ragged line of five more people, each moving quietly through the dense foliage: a tall redhead armed with a Smith & Wesson revolver, an albino teenager hobbling along on a homemade crutch, a stocky black woman with beaded hair who was hugging a predark med kit, a young grim-faced boy brandishing a sleek Browning semiautomatic pistol and, lastly, a thin old man with silver hair, sporting a huge revolver and an ebony walking stick with a silver lion's head on top. The group stayed three yards apart, the old man judiciously scratching the ground in their wake with his ebony stick to rearrange the leaves and try to hide their passage.

Slow miles passed, and Ryan checked with J.B. twice more on their direction as the group penetrated deeper into the heart of the island jungle. Soon the moss-coated trees were growing so close together that walking between the trunks was becoming difficult, and the branches overhead crisscrossed each other, effectively blocking out the sun. Midnight ruled the forest, but the travelers dared not light their sole oil lantern. The fish oil smelled awful, and they were much too close to the enemy ville of Cascade. The slightest mistake now, and it was all over.

Finally, Ryan reached a grove of massive banyan trees, the hanging vines so thick with leaves and orchids that the group could see nothing in the branches above. The only illumination came from a peppering of sunlight streaming in through a hundred tiny breaks in the foliage. It was like a rain of sunbeams.

As his vision adjusted to the dim lighting, Ryan gestured at J.B. The short man checked his compass, counting to twenty until he saw the needle quiver again, but it no longer seemed to be pulling to the left or right.

"This looks like the spot," the Armorer stated, tucking the predark device into his munitions bag. "We must be right underneath the plane."

"Can't tell a thing from down here," Ryan stated, studying the overhang of leaves and flowers. "We need Mildred's flashlight. I'll call in the others."

Stepping backward, J.B. put his back to a tree and leveled the shotgun. "Got you covered," he said, snicking off the safety.

Cupping both hands around his mouth, the man trilled a soft whistle three times. The signal was repeated so low Ryan almost couldn't hear it, but he answered with one short whistle. A few moments later, familiar faces started easing from the bushes on every side with loaded weapons in their hands.

"Hey, lover," Krysty Wroth whispered, her animated red hair splaying outward in anxiety. To those who knew the woman well, the movements of her hair betrayed her every emotion.

The tall woman was wearing a khaki jumpsuit with the front partly unzipped to expose a wealth of tan cleavage. Instead of combat boots, Krysty wore blue cowboy boots with steel-tipped toes and a spreadwing-falcon design emblazoned on the sides. Her bearskin coat was tied around her hips to keep the garment out of the way. An old police gun belt with ammo loops circled her shapely hips to support the open holster for the S&W .38 revolver. A sloshing canteen and U.S. Ranger knife were clipped to her regular belt, a bulky backpack riding high on her firm shoulders.

Glancing at Krysty for a moment, Ryan once again realized just how truly beautiful she was. Sometimes it was as if he were seeing her for the first time: the high cheekbones, emerald-green eyes and animated red hair that flowed past her shoulders. Krysty was the most beautiful woman Ryan had ever seen.

Ryan felt the usual rush of blood to his loins and forced his attention back to counting the shadows emerging from the jungle. He had to make sure it was just his crew, and that nobody was trying to sneak among them under cover of the shadows. When he was satisfied there was nobody else in the small clearing but the companions, he reached out and gave Krysty's slim hand a brief squeeze. She squeezed back with surprising strength almost equal to his own.

"Any trouble?" Ryan asked. He knew Krysty had some mutie blood, which gave her an ability to sense danger. More than once, it had saved their lives.

Leaning against a banyan tree, the woman breathed in the strange perfumes of the exotic flowers. "All clear," Krysty answered. "Not a sound of folks for miles."

For the first time in a day, the Deathlands warrior allowed himself to relax the tiniest bit. "Good. You're on guard. Let me know if anything starts coming our way."

Stepping away from the tree, Krysty nodded.

"So this is the location of our aerial El Dorado, eh?" Dr. Theophilus Tanner rumbled in a deep voice. The silver-haired man placed his walking stick on a tree root so it wouldn't sink into the soft earth, and leaned heavily on its lion head ferrule. "Well, we are indeed pilgrims in the valley of the shadows. Most appropriate."

Although only thirty-eight years old, Doc appeared to be more than sixty, with his heavily lined face and a wild shock of silvery hair. The alteration of his features was merely one of the side effects Doc had suffered at the hands of the ruthless scientists from Operation Chronos.

Ripped from the bosom of his family in the late 1880s, Doc was trawled forward in time to the late 1990s as a test subject. However, Doc proved to be an unruly and uncooperative specimen and was sent forward in time to what had become the Deathlands. Unfortunately, the trawling scrambled some portions of his mind, and Doc sometimes drifted away, reliving prior events or just dreaming aloud while wide-awake. But in a fight, the gentle scholar from Vermont became a deadly fighter and was a valuable member of the group.

Refusing to relinquish any hold on his past, Doc wore clothes of his day, including pin-striped pants and matching vest, a frilly white shirt with a string bow tie and a long frock coat, now with several bullet holes in the twilled fabric. A U.S. Army backpack was carried effortlessly on his shoulders, and around his waist was a cracked leather belt lined with ammo pouches for his gigantic .44 Civil War blaster.

"Pipe down, you old coot," Mildred Wyeth muttered, using handfuls of grass to try to wipe the residue of quicksand from her clothes. Once it dried, the stuff came off easily. It was only the high viscosity and depth that made the bog dangerous.

Short and stocky, the physician wore loose Air Force fatigues, with a Czech-made ZKR target pistol holstered on her left side for the cross draw she favored. Before skydark Mildred had gone into a hospital for a simple operation, but there had been complications, and a hundred years later she awoke in a cryogenic freezer, a new Gulliver trapped in a frightening world forged from atomic nightmares.

"Might as well set off a gren if you're going to

talk that loud,'' Mildred stated, tossing away the filthy grass.

''My humble apologies,'' Doc muttered in a wry apology, then continued in the same volume.

''So where is our arboreal harbor located, John Barrymore?''

''Straight up,'' J.B. said, jerking a thumb at the impenetrable ceiling of the jungle. ''From here, we climb.''

''Indeed,'' Doc said, studying the dense weaving of vines and creepers. ''How antediluvian for us.''

Standing her post, Krysty ignored the conversation, forcing herself to listen to the distant sounds of the forest, the chattering of a distant monkey, a flowing stream, birds in flight and the constant hum of the insects all around them. There were a lot of bugs in this jungle.

''I'll take the lead and cut us a path,'' Ryan stated, tightening the straps on his backpack. ''Just remember to put any loose branches or leaves in your pockets. Don't let anything fall to the ground and mark the spot.''

''Easy,'' Jak Lauren grunted, wincing slightly as he accidentally put some weight on his sprained ankle.

The bus crash at the quagmire had almost chilled the lot of them, and it was just chance that a barrel of shine had fallen on his leg. Thankfully, it was empty and he only received a sprain, not a break. Mildred was a good doctor, but there wasn't really much a person could do for a broken leg.

A true albino, Jak wore his snowy hair long, and often leaned forward so it fell across his scarred face to mask his pale red eyes from enemies and preventing them from detecting which way he was going to charge. Deception was the Cajun's favorite weapon.

In spite of the humidity and heat, Jak was still wearing his camouflage jacket, the lapels and collar decorated with bits of razors, special hidden surprises for anybody foolish enough to grab him by the jacket. At least a dozen leaf-bladed throwing knives were hidden on his person, and a big .357 Magnum Colt Python pistol was tucked into his belt.

"How are you doing?" Mildred asked, coming closer. "Feeling okay?"

In the gloom, Jak scowled. "Fine," he muttered through clenched teeth. "Nothing but pain."

"Crap," Mildred replied, and rummaged about in her med kit until unearthing a plastic film container. Snapping the top, she poured out three aspirins and gave the teenager two.

"Take them," the physician ordered in a no-nonsense tone of voice. "If we're going to be climbing trees, you'll need these."

Although hating to ever appear weak, Jak was no stupe and took the pills with a swig from his canteen. "Thanks," he said, wiping his mouth on a sleeve.

"No problem," Mildred replied, tucking away her meager medical supplies.

Boots softly crunching on the carpeting of leaves as he walked through the crowd of adults, a boy strode to the biggest banyan tree and briefly inspected the trunk. The branches were low and thick, vines everywhere for easy climbing. To anybody but the wounded, it was an easy climb.

"Want me to do a recce?" Dean Cawdor asked, holstering his blaster to free both hands.

Almost twelve years old, Dean was already the spitting image of his father.

"I'll go this time," Ryan stated, and reached up to grab a branch.

Suddenly, Krysty snapped her head to the left and raised a clenched fist. Instantly, the group froze, hands poised on their assorted weapons. Long minutes passed before the sound of engines could be dimly heard, then the voices of angry men. The noises came closer, the voices soon loud enough to hear clearly over the struggling engines of several vehicles. The companions tensed as the volume grew, then in ragged stages, the sounds of the wags and sec men began fading into the distance.

"Are they gone?" Mildred whispered tersely.

"No. There are more wags to the north and east," Krysty said, her green eyes half-closed to concentrate on the task of listening. "There's an army combing the jungle looking for something."

"Us," Ryan stated, holstering his piece. Mitchum wanted them aced; Glassman wanted to capture them alive. He wasn't about to let either event happen.

"No sounds of plants being crushed under tires," Mildred said thoughtfully as the tiny beams of sunlight streaming across the clearing flickered from the passing of a cloud overhead. "Must be a road close by."

"Too close," Jak stated, keeping his .357 Magnum blaster pointed at the greenery. He was down to four rounds, and was going to make each one count before he took the last train west.

"Think it was Mitchum?" Dean asked anxiously, his young face tense and serious. They had befriended the sec man, saving him from the stew pot of cannies, but somehow that had gotten turned around and now the sec man was hell-bent for revenge.

"I do not believe so, lad," Doc rumbled. "To the best of our knowledge, the good colonel did not have access to any motorized transport. Horses were his sole venue."

Carefully, Doc set the selector pin on his huge hand cannon from the shotgun barrel to the .44 cylinder. The LeMat was a Civil War antique, but in the old man's steady hands the LeMat struck like the wrath of God.

"Must be his new associate, Glassman," Ryan said, pulling the panga from its sheath and sliding it into his belt for easier access.

"Here fast," Jak said slowly.

"Those steam-powered PT boats of his are mighty quick," J.B. agreed, tilting back his fedora. "He must have swung around the island and gotten fresh troops from Cascade ville, trying to catch us between him and Mitchum."

A distant rattle of a machine gun shook the jungle, the animals going quiet, the birds screaming loudly and rustling the trees as they launched for the sky.

Frowning deeply, Krysty turned in a circle. "Gaia save us, there are Hummers everywhere."

"Trying to flush us out," Jak said, awkwardly shifting his stance on the crutches.

Reaching high, Ryan grabbed a branch and pulled himself off the ground. "Wait for my signal to follow," he said from the blackness above. "Don't do anything until I come back. If I get aced, head for the mountains. We passed a cave there you can use to hide in until things cool down."

"Get going and find that plane," J.B. growled irritably, balancing the shotgun in his grip.

Digging in his boots, Ryan started shimmying up the tree and soon disappeared from sight in the thick foliage. A few minutes later, a brass cartridge fell to the ground, bouncing off the branches until it hit the ground. Dean scooped it up and saw the cartridge was intact, and not a spent round ejected from his father's blaster.

"Live," he reported. "Dad found it."

"Get moving," J.B. said, and started up the tree himself, moving slower than Ryan because of the Uzi on his back. The little branches kept sticking into the weapon and slowing him.

Grabbing a vine, the Armorer tried climbing that instead of the tree and made much faster progress. The vine was thicker than a gren, and the wide leaves provided good bracing for his boots. As the vine ended, he shimmied along the branch until reaching the trunk. He stabbed a knife into the wood, drawing himself up as he kicked footholds in the rough bark with his boots.

The higher he climbed, the cooler it got and the brighter the sunlight. Soon J.B. emerged from the canopy of leaves to find himself blinking in direct sunlight. Ryan stood nearby with a boot resting in the fork of two branches, looking through the curtain of vines.

"There she is," he said, indicating the direction with his chin.

Pulling himself onto the stout branch, J.B. could only marvel at the titanic machine sprawled in the treetops before them. It was gigantic.

More than a hundred feet long, the incredible aircraft supported two huge engines with six propellers on each wing. Vines and creepers covered the plane, only the glass of the cockpit and the tail rudder clearly visible amid the flowering creepers. It was a wonder Dean had spotted it from a mile away.

"That's a Hercules," Ryan said, swaying to the wind. It was a lot stronger up there and carried a strong taste of salt from the nearby ocean. "Saw a picture of one in a redoubt, pinned to the wall like a girlie poster."

"Yeah, I know," J.B. replied. "I spent a month living in a crashed wreck once. Good planes."

Carefully, Ryan glanced downward. "Any chance the sec men could see us up here?"

"No way in hell," Krysty replied, crawling into view. Then the woman paused at the sight of the huge plane. "That flew?"

"Like an angel," Mildred said, pulling herself along a vine and stepping onto a branch. "The Hercules C-130."

In a short while, the rest of the companions arrived, Jak and Doc last, the elderly man assisting the wounded teenager to a fork in the trunk. The Cajun gave the old man a nod in thanks and settled his aching back against the trunk of the tree.

"No way this thing flew," Dean stated flatly. "No way."

"Big mother," Jak agreed, massaging his throbbing ankle.

Careful of his footing, Ryan walked along the branch and experimentally rested a boot on the tip of a wing. It didn't move, so he put on more and more weight until he was standing fully on the leafy metal. Nothing moved. He chanced a jump, and the leaves shook a little, but the plane remained firmly in place. There was no way anybody could have moved such a colossal machine into the treetops to make a hidden ville. The aircraft had to have crashed here during a storm, and the branches grew around the trapped plane over the decades, trapping it forever.

Moving to a more secure position, Ryan brushed away the vines to see a smooth expanse of green metal. There was no sign of rust. He rapped it with a knuckle and heard nothing. Too solid to echo. Good enough. If it hadn't fallen in a hundred years, there was no reason it should this day.

"Okay, it's safe," Ryan said to the others over a shoulder. "She's solid as a rock, moored in place by over a dozen trees. Couldn't move the damn thing if we wanted."

Curiously, the rest of the companions started warily closer, with Jak staying behind to guard their flanks. The aspirins had helped ease his pain, but not a lot.

"Yeah, this should be okay for a temp shelter," J.B. said, adjusting his glasses to glance at the fiery storm clouds overhead. The metal hull would protect them from any acid rain. If they had to stay somewhere until Jak healed, this was as good a place as any.

"Certainly be a triple-bad bitch to attack," Krysty agreed, placing one boot carefully ahead of the other as she crossed the wing.

His long hair blowing in the steady wind, Ryan scowled at the pronouncement. Proceeding very slowly with a hand hovering near his blaster, the man surveyed what he could of the downed behemoth. There was no sign of anybody using it as a home. The cockpit windows weren't broken, the side hatch was still in place and the aft cargo hatch appeared to be sealed shut. He relaxed with the knowledge that they were the first to discover the predark wreckage.

Warily, the Deathlands warrior eased along the network of branches between the wing and the front of the plane to reach the cockpit windows. A layer of dust covered the plastic, and he used a handful of leaves to brush the transparent material clean. The sun was at the wrong angle to illuminate the interior, so Ryan cupped hands around his face to try to see inside. After a few minutes, his eye became adjusted to the darkness. The pilot and copilot were still strapped in their chairs, their skeleton hands on their throats. Their uniforms were mixed; the pilot was Air Force, the copilot Army, the navigator Navy. There were blasters in flap-covered holsters at their sides, and he thought there was another skeleton slumped over a radio set just aft of the cockpit, but it was too dark to tell. But the major factor was the complete lack of vines, spiderwebs or even cobwebs inside the vehicle. The hull hadn't been breached over the long decades.

"Hull is still intact," Ryan stated to the others. "There are skeletons inside."

"How are the seats?" J.B. asked.

"Never been touched."

"Dark night, our first good luck in weeks." J.B. sighed.

Careful of his balance, the man traversed the tangled vines to reach the side door and ran a finger along the seam. There was a light coating of moss and some windblown seed pods, but nothing serious. J.B. started pulling out tools from his munitions bag and got to work releasing the ancient catch.

"No structural damage in sight. Doesn't look like

it hit bad enough to chill the crew,'' Krysty commented. ''So why didn't they leave?''

It was a good question and Ryan quickly checked the rad counter on his lapel, but saw only the usual background count. There had been ''clean'' nukes used in the war that didn't leave lingering rads. Maybe that was what happened here. An airburst caught the plane and threw it into the trees with the crew already dead from the rad burst.

Or perhaps whatever the soldiers were carrying as cargo had burst open on the rough landing and chilled the crew instantly.

Spinning, Ryan started to shout a warning when J.B. stepped away from the aircraft. The Deathlands warrior could only watch as the door dropped open and out billowed a dry metallic wind tasting of ancient death.

Chapter Two

Dust rose in tiny clouds around his shuffling boots and sweat dripped off his haggard face, but Cal Mitchum forced himself onward, raw hatred fueling his every step.

Using his longblaster as a crutch, the chief sec man continued along the jungle trail, pieces of predark asphalt appearing now and then from under the layer of windblown dirt. For some unknown reason, the jungle stopped at the side of the roadway, only the tiniest of creepers daring to grow across the old road. Perhaps it was some ancient science that held off the plants, or maybe it was simply that there was no nourishment in the soil atop the hard black macadam. He had no idea. The world was full of unanswerable questions, and a man would go futz-brained if he tried to solve them all. Mitchum found a simplified view of life was sufficient for him: stand by your baron, keep your word, treat your sec men like children and get revenge in any way possible.

Ryan had betrayed the chief sec man and shot him in the shoulder and thigh, leaving him for dead after Mitchum warned Ryan of the arrival of Glassman. The son of a bitch had said they were flesh wounds and would convince the baron of his story of the companions jumping him. But Mitchum didn't believe a word of that bullshit. Ryan had tried to ace him to cover his escape, and simply fucked it up. The outlander would pay for that, if Mitchum had to walk every trail to every ville in the Thousand Islands. He would find the one-eyed bastard, cut out his beating heart and make him eat it raw.

Every step was torture, but Mitchum kept moving. His almond skin was turning light gray from the accumulated dust, and his bandaged shoulder stung from the sweat seeping into the wound. His thigh throbbed like the pounding surf. But pain could be controlled. He'd suffered worse defending his ville, and still been alive to watch the crucifixion of the attackers. Pain made you strong.

An odd motion in a bush made Mitchum jerk alert, and he drew a flintlock pistol from his belt with lightning speed. Pushing the weapon across his chest, he cocked back the hammer and leveled the blaster ready to fire when two hands rose above the greenery and waved in surrender.

"Don't shoot!" a man's voice called, and out stepped a young sec man in unfamiliar garb. "Damn, you're fast with a blaster, sir."

The stranger was in ragged clothes made from beaten hemp fibers. He had a spear in his hand, a bow and arrow strapped to his back and a flintlock pistol tucked into his rope belt.

"Who the fuck are you, boy?" Mitchum growled, the gaping maw of the .75 black powder weapon never wavering from the stranger's stomach. He normally went for a chest shot, but in his weakened condition, Mitchum wasn't sure he could ride the recoil of the hog-leg enough to keep the miniball on target. Best to aim for the belt buckle and let the lead hit the other man in the face. Anything above the waist was a clean hit. Afterwards he could cut the kid's throat and steal his ammo.

The youth started to answer when the sound of engines filled the air and Mitchum dropped the longblaster to painfully draw and cock the other flintlock pistol. Adrenaline pounded in his veins, giving the exhausted sec man the needed strength to stand and watch the convoy of Hummers appear around a curve in the road. The wags were badly dented and streaked with dirt, the grilles filled with clumps of vegetation. But long .30-cal machine guns rested on fancy supports, the back seats filled with armed sec men. And more importantly, Captain Glassman was in the front wag, his hands on the windshield to keep standing. His light brown hair was pushed off his grim face, exposing the flares of gray at his temples. Liver spots dotted his hands, and he was unshaved.

"Full stop," Henry Glassman yelled, and the convoy braked to a ragged halt.

The thin commander of the lord baron's navy was dressed in loose gray clothing and sandals, the standard wide leather belt around his middle serving as a tool belt and holster for his flintlock and an even bigger predark revolver. A machete hung handle down in a shoulder holster. The navvies, as his sec men liked to be called, were heavily tattooed, displaying their ranks on their faces, and dressed in a similar way, making them easy to spot among the others in the wags. Old and young men, their crude homemade uniforms were identical to that worn by the man in the bushes.

As the engines were turned off to save juice, Captain Glassman looked over Mitchum and could readily tell the bad news. The big sec man was battered and bruised, his crew of twenty armed riders nowhere in sight. Glassman could guess what happened; Ryan and the others had ambushed the patrol and aced the riders with only Mitchum surviving—probably from sheer stubbornness. The sec man was stronger than an armored tank, nearly unkillable. Everybody in his ville was terrified of the man, and most considered him a mutie of some sort. But nobody had ever dared to say that aloud.

"This idiot yours?" Mitchum sneered, gesturing at the youngster still standing in the bushes.

"A scout," Glassman answered. "We sent out a dozen. Private, get your ass in the wags. Campbell!"

"Yes, sir?" the sergeant rumbled from behind the wheel of the first wag. Campbell had a smiling face and laughing eyes. He always seemed amused, even as he sliced off a tongue or testicle. His face was a mask of tattoos, showing his rise, fall and subsequent rise again in the navy of Lord Baron Kinnison, ruler of the Thousand Islands. Unlike any of the others, Campbell was armed with a sleek bolt-action long-blaster, and a bandolier of long brass shells was slung across his chest. He was both the top kick for the captain and his executioner should the officer fail to recover the outlanders.

"When we get back, give this feeb ten lashes with the whip for this failure," Glassman ordered, climbing from the Hummer.

"Done," Campbell said and smiled pleasantly.

"B-but, sir!" the private said, fighting his way out of the thorny plants to stand on the roadway. "I was sent to find Colonel Mitchum, and I did!"

Checking his blaster, Glassman snorted in disdain. "Seems more like he found you. And now it's ten lashes with a whip soaked in salt water. Any more objections, and I'll make it twenty."

Silently, the sec man stumbled toward the rear of the convoy to be as far away from the sergeant as possible.

Leaving the rest of the troops behind, Glassman walked over to Mitchum and softly said, "Okay, tell me."

"They live," the man replied simply, easing down the hammers of both his blasters. "Caught us in a boobie and fried my men alive."

Glassman scowled. Alive was all he cared about. Kinnison was going to exchange his family for the outlanders, but only if they were still breathing. Briefly, he considered chilling Mitchum right there, then realized that was stupe.

"Don't worry, we'll find them," the captain said, patting the man on his good shoulder. "Do you have anything that was worn by one of the outlanders, or better, has their blood on it?"

"You got dogs?" Mitchum asked suspiciously, glancing at the wags.

"Something close enough."

There was only one other possibility. "Hunters!" the sec chief gasped, backing away a step. "Are you mad?"

"No Hunters," Glassman snapped. "The local baron had one that he claimed was tame as a gaudy slut. Even did tricks, and such. Shot it dead in its cage. There is no such thing as a tame Hunter. They just act whipped until that door is open, and then rip off your head."

"Smart move," Mitchum said, sagging a little as his thigh trembled with weakness. For a moment, he gazed at the wags longingly, then stood tall once more.

The captain tucked his thumbs into his wide belt. "We've got a dozen hunting dogs trained to track escaped slaves. You give us anything with their smell, and those beasts will track them through fire and water."

"Lots of bloody clothing at the wreckage," Mitchum said, jerking a thumb over his shoulder. "Most of it is burned, but mebbe something is still usable."

"Good," the captain said, turning to the wags. "Corporal Yantar! Take a squad and check over the wreckage of a wag down the road. I want anything stained with human blood. Anything at all. If these dogs are any damn good, they should be able to track the scents of a dozen slaves with no trouble."

The corporal grinned, displaying badly stained teeth. "We'll have those outies in chains by nightfall! I'd bet my life on it!"

"Accepted," Mitchum grunted. "Find them by darkness, or we leave you staked out for muties."

Going pale, Yantar scrambled from the Hummer to join the sec men walking past the officers and headed for the wreckage.

"Better get in a wag, Mitchum," Glassman ordered. "Have the healer check those wounds. Should put some shine on them, and a little in you to ease the pain."

"I'll walk," Mitchum replied stiffly. "Can't show weakness in front of my men."

"They aren't your sec men," Glassman stated coldly. "All of your troops are chilled. These are my navvies, and some of the local baron's grunts. They obey only me. Now, get in the bastard wag. You're the only person alive who has seen the faces of the outlanders, and I may need that in case they try to slip through us to steal a boat. I'm gonna keep you alive at any cost, so get in or get dragged in like a chained slave. I don't care. Your choice.''

"How about we try this instead, ya skinny fuck. Tell them I'm your new chief," Mitchum growled softly, "or I blow you in half."

There was a jab into his gut, and Glassman looked down to see a blaster pressed against his stomach, the hammer pulled back and ready to fire. The barrel was warm, but it sent a chill down his back. Unfortunately, Glassman was blocking the view so there was no way the sec men in front, or behind, could see he was in danger.

"Decide fast," Mitchum ordered, touching him up a little with the barrel. "Share the command or die. Your choice."

Glassman could feel sweat forming on his face, but kept his voice level and forced out a soft chuckle. "Black dust, I'm impressed. Always need men good as you. But the lord baron wants the outlanders alive. Agree to that, and you're my new top kick."

The blaster moved forward an inch. "No."

"Then do it, gimp," Glassman spit, pressing his body against the blaster, forcing a surprised Mitchum to back up. "Shoot me and watch my men take you apart as I drop."

Temporarily outmaneuvered, Mitchum clenched his teeth, fighting the pain of his wounds and the burning desire to seek revenge. Few men would face down a weapon to their guts. Glassman had to be a fanatic, or Kinnison had a hold on him more frightening than death.

"I get to ace Ryan, you get the rest," he offered hatefully.

"Agreed," Glassman stated, then bellowed over a shoulder. "Sergeant Campbell!"

"Sir?" came the prompt reply.

"Mitchum here will be assuming your duties as my second in command. You're the new top gunner."

Looking around the dirty windshield, Campbell stared at the two men talking down the road. Something was going on, but since he had no idea what it was, he'd best just obey orders for the present.

"Yes, sir!" Campbell shouted, stepping into the rear of the vehicle to take a position at the big machine gun.

"Satisfied?" Glassman asked, staring the man in the face.

"For the moment," Mitchum said, jabbing the sailor with the muzzle of his flintlock one more time, then holstering the piece. "But remember, I took you face-to-face, while surrounded by your stinking troops, and I can do it again whenever I please."

"Mebbe," Glassman muttered.

"Try me anytime," the wounded man growled, shuffling for the lead Hummer, then bitterly added, "sir."

"Count on it," Glassman whispered, but only the ocean breeze heard the words.

AS THE LONG EXHALATION of stale air ceased flowing from the inside of the plane, the companions stopped holding their breaths and took a tentative sniff. The interior of the craft still reeked faintly of rotten flesh, kerosene and dust, but the smell was quickly fading as the fresh clean air of the jungle poured into the ancient cargo bay.

His blaster leading the way, Ryan walked inside and waited for his vision to adjust to the dim recesses of the giant aircraft. J.B. and the others were right behind him, with Doc staying at the open hatch and Jak remaining in the tree.

The scant light coming in through the open hatchway of the C-130 was barely sufficient to see anything, so Krysty and Dean lit candles, while Mildred dug a small flashlight from her med kit. Pumping the handle a few times to charge the ancient batteries, she flicked its switch and out came a strong white beam that soon faded to a soft yellow. The hundred-year-old device was slowly dying, and there was no way the physician could ever replace it. But the weak light filled the cargo bay of the aircraft, outshining the dancing flames of the tallow candles.

The ceiling was twenty or so feet above them, and heavily padded with some sort of insulation material. Pieces of ventilation conduits, wiring and fuel pipes showed here and there for maintenance. Directly in front of Ryan was a row of seats filled with the bones of dead crew members. To his left, a door was set into a metal wall that led to the front ammo bunkers and the washroom. Alongside that was a short flight of stairs going to a veined door with multiple hinges, the access to the cockpit. J.B. went straight up the steps and checked the door.

"Give me a sec, it's locked," he announced, pulling tools out of his bag.

Moving deeper into the behemoth, Ryan saw the main body of the aircraft extended for yards and yards, with huge canvas lumps filling the central passageway, the mounds of cargo resting on thick pallets and firmly lashed into place by a dozen ropes and chains. The distant rear of the craft was lost in shadows. Dean headed that way along the left wall, and soon came back along the right.

"Nothing else but these things," the boy said, nudging a pallet with his boot. "No more bones or doors."

"Careful opening those," Krysty warned, lifting her candle high to follow the path of some power cables. "The gov often booby-trapped important cargo."

"Gotcha," Dean said, moving away from the canvas mound. He made a mental note to ask J.B. to start teaching him about traps and locks. It was an important skill these days.

At the open hatch, Doc stomped on the deck, crushing something with a lot of legs under his boot. "Begone, Visigoth!" he snorted, and kicked the dead millipede onto the wing. As it landed on the leaves, the vines twitched and a flower bent over it to close its rainbow petals about the pulped insect and start eating.

"A sylvan glade, indeed," Doc muttered, holstering his LeMat.

Going to the wall seats, Ryan inspected the desiccated skeleton of paratroopers still strapped in place. Their uniforms were only rags now, the fresh air making them crumble apart. Each man and woman was armed with an M-16 carbine and a side arm. But all of the weapons were so heavily rusted salvage was impossible. Only the plastic stocks of M-16s and the rubber grips of the handblasters were still in pristine condition. The rest of the steel had been corroded by acid, eaten clean through in spots. The weapons had been fired just before the plane crashed, the cordite exhaust gas mixing with the moisture in the atmosphere to make carbolic acid that destroyed the weapons slowly. He checked the clips and found them full of lumpy green brass and loose lead rounds. Placing the rapidfire aside, he tried the automatic blasters and found they were in the same condition. Had to have been a hell of a firefight somewhere. He studied the sheets of insulation lining the hull and saw no signs of bullet holes. Perhaps the troopers had seized the craft by force to escape the nukestorm. He would never know, but it seemed a logical guess.

Inspecting the collection of uniformed bones, Krysty discovered that one of the officers was a woman with a large military chron on her wrist. Krysty removed the timepiece and wound the stem to see if it worked. The watch started ticking without pause and continued steadily. Thank Gaia! She removed her own wrist chron smashed in the bus crash and slid on the new chron. It fit fine, and hopefully was a lot tougher than her old model.

"How are the blasters?" she asked, adjusting the strap on the mechanism.

"Pure junk," Ryan stated, shoving the rusted lump of metal that had once been a 10 mm Colt back into its dusty holster.

"I see something," Mildred said, retrieving a briefcase from under the wall seats. A handcuff dangled from its steel handle, but there was no way of knowing which of the dead soldiers it had once been attached to. Setting her flashlight on an empty seat, Mildred tried to open the case but it was firmly locked. However, her belt knife swiftly cut through the leather flap holding the carrying case closed. Inside were hundreds of papers bearing government seals, but the printing was so faded with age it was impossible to read in the dim light.

"Probably just a duty roster," Krysty said, holding her candle dangerously close to the yellowed paper.

"Most likely," Mildred agreed, watching some of the faxes crumble into dust at her touch. "I'll take these outside and see if I can read them there."

As the woman left, Krysty started going through the remnants of the uniforms, and Ryan went to the base of the stairs. "How's it coming?" he asked, his voice echoing slightly in the confines of the great vessel.

"Almost through," J.B. answered, both hands busy with lock picks.

Stepping out of the forward hold, Dean glanced at the two men working on the door to the cockpit. "How's it coming?" he asked.

Ryan allowed himself a brief smile. Like father, like son. "Almost through," he said.

"Well, I checked the front blasters," the boy said. "See if we could salvage anything. But they're rusted solid, the barrels full with bird nests. Lots of 40 mm and 20 mm ammo shells in the ammo bunkers, but the brass is covered with corrosion."

Mildred walked back in and tossed the briefcase back under the seats. "Krysty was right, just a cargo manifest."

"Nothing useful, then?" Dean asked hopefully.

"No weapons or food."

"Damn."

"Got it," J.B. said, the armored door to the cockpit swung aside on creaking hinges.

There was another rush of stale air, and after it passed, Ryan and J.B. stepped into the cockpit, their faces tense with anticipation. The sunlight streamed in through the leafy-edged windows, casting odd shadows. The remains of the command crew were in the same positions, but now their clothing was starting to visibly decompose at the invasion of clean air. Ryan gave the skeletons a fast glance, while J.B. took out his compass and went to the dashboard. He flipped several switches until the needle stopped jerking.

"It was their emergency beacon," he said, tucking away the compass. "The nuke batteries were almost drained. Another couple of months and we never would have found this plane."

Lying on the deck, Ryan was looking under the pilot's chair. "Seals are unbroken," he announced, running his fingertips along the undercarriage of the pilot's seat.

"Same here," J.B. said, doing the same to the co-pilot's chair. "We might just be in luck here."

Both men got busy with their knives, removing service panels, and then slicing through the nest of wiring inside the seats. They knew the sequence, blue, green, red, and each man did the job carefully. Ejector seats were tricky. Ryan remembered when Finn tried to take one apart too fast and it launched straight through the top of the plane, damn near taking his head along with it for a ride. And the fiery blast of the launch nearly aced the Trader.

Soon, they had the ejector rockets disassembled and toppled the seat to extract a sturdy plastic box shaped like a lopsided arch.

The boxes were sealed airtight, but J.B. made short

work of the lock. Lining the inside was some form of clear plastic wrapping that knives wouldn't cut. But Ryan found a ring tab on the side and gently pulled it along the seam, the plastic parting sluggishly to expose a layer of gray foam. Tossing away the plastic, Ryan removed the foam cushion to finally uncover an assortment of supplies, each neatly nestled in a shaped depression in the gray foam. It was the wealth of the predark world in perfect condition.

"Good stuff?" Dean asked curiously, craning his neck to see.

"The best," his father replied.

"This is a pilot's survival kit," J.B. said, grinning in triumph. "An emergency pack for a crashed pilot to grab as he ran from a burning plane, just enough supplies to keep him alive for a few weeks until a rescue team could arrive."

"Haven't seen one in years," Krysty said, watching the proceedings eagerly. "They are almost always taken after the crash."

"Not this time," Ryan said, and began laying out the contents in a neat row.

J.B. freed the copilot's survival kit and then started defusing the navigator's chair. Soon the five seats were in pieces and the precious kits splayed open wide.

There were five 9 mm Heckler & Koch blasters, vials of oil, fifteen empty clips, ten boxes of ammo. Survival knives with whetstones, fishing line and hooks, dye markers, Veri pistols with colored flares, signal mirrors, water-purification tabs, gold coins, MRE packs, spools of wire, bundles of rope and med kits.

J.B. called Mildred in from outside, and the phy-

sician eagerly went through the collection of pills and
capsules, throwing away most of the drugs. Even
sealed in an airtight container, a lot of the chemicals
would lose their potency over the long decades, and
a few would turn lethal. Everything else she placed
in her battered shoulder bag: bandages, bug-repellent
sticks, elastic bandages, methamphetamines, barbitu-
rates, sulfur powder, antiseptic cream—as hard as a
rock but reclaimable—sunscreen, toothpaste, three
hypodermic needles, sutures, surgical thread, iodine
tablets and silver-based antibiotics.

After taking inventory, the companions divided the
supplies, each taking what he or she needed the most.
Ryan and J.B. split the 9 mm ammo, the Uzi getting
the lion's share. Ryan, Krysty and Mildred each took
one of the fancy two-tone H&K blasters to replace
their depleted weapons. Neither woman cared for
autofires, the things had a bad tendency to jam just
when you needed them the most. However, fifteen
shots of maybe was better than two rounds of definite.

Since his Browning had a full clip, Dean took the
Veri pistol and studied the single-shot blaster until
figuring out how the 30 mm breechloader worked.
The catch was very simple. Satisfied, he tucked away
the blaster and filled his pockets with the flares. The
stubby gun could throw a flare three hundred feet into
the air, where it would detonate into brilliant colors
to help searchers find a lost crew member. But the
device could also fire horizontally and punch a sizzling flare straight through a man at fifty feet.

Nodding in approval, Krysty took the other Veri
pistol and the rest of the signal flares.

"Be right back," Mildred said, checking the elastic

strength of the bandage. "I'm going to wrap Jak again. This will get him back on his feet."

"Good. Give him this, too," Ryan said, tossing her an extra H&K pistol. "No spare ammo, but it's something."

"Right." She made the catch and disappeared down the ramp to the broad wing.

"Here's your share, Doc," J.B. said, placing a pile of food packs, soap, razor blades and other assorted small items next to the man sitting on the ramp. Amid the salvage was the last of the H&K pistols.

"Thank you," Doc said solemnly, reluctantly lifting the blaster for examination. The LeMat was on its last reload. Nine shots and he was defenseless.

Awkwardly, Doc worked the slide of the blaster, chambering a round, and experimented dropping the clip, then inserting it again.

"Think he'll take it?" Dean mumbled around a mouthful of cherry-nut cake, the other envelopes scattered on the floor around his boots. He had been starving, but then he was constantly starving these days.

Weighing the weapon in a palm, Doc made his decision and clicked on the safety of the sleek blaster to tuck it away in his frock coat.

Just then, Mildred rushed into view. "Great news," she said, clambering into the airship.

"Jak can walk now?" Ryan said as a question. "Good."

"Better than that," she said excitedly. "Remember those cargo manifests I was looking at? Couldn't read them at all, until Jak smeared the paper with gun oil. Damned if that didn't bring the words out nice and clear."

"What were they carrying?" Krysty asked, glancing at the six huge canvas lumps on their stout pallets. "Hovercrafts?"

"Weather-sensing equipment," she said in a rush. "Balloons to carry computerized pods high into the sky to check on the pollution levels from the old nukes. See if the air was any better."

"Stop using the nukes," Dean said bluntly, wiping his face with a moist towelette. "Then the air would get better."

"Amen," Doc agreed roughly.

"Weather balloons," Ryan repeated slowly, then stood and walked over to the first pallet. It was the triple-craziest idea he had ever heard. "Big ones?"

"Thirty feet across."

"How many?"

"Hundreds," Mildred said eagerly. "A year's supply for the testing station. Don't know the lift-to-drag ratio. So we just make it as large as possible. Always best to err on the side of power."

"We'd need something for a basket," Ryan said, nudging the shipping pallet with his boot. The honeycomb plastic was a good foot thick, and more than ten feet wide on each side. Designed to airdrop supplies to troops in the field, the pallets would make perfect bottoms. "These should work fine. They're light and very strong. Just no sides."

"We can tie extra ropes around support ropes," Krysty said quickly. She finally realized what they were discussing. "Weave a basket around the pallet. And we can use the ropes lashing down the canvas to hold it all together. The cargo netting is plastic and should certainly be strong enough."

"You folks firing blanks?" J.B. asked skeptically, thumbing the last round into a clip, then easing the magazine into the Uzi. He worked the bolt, chambering a round, and slung the weapon over his shoulder. "We're going to fly to Forbidden Island?"

Standing, Doc wet a finger and held it outside. "The wind is blowing in the correct direction," he announced. "Well done, madam. An exemplary idea! There is no way Mitchum could follow us aloft."

"Fly the Hercules?" Dean asked, frowning. "Hot pipe, this thing will never eat clouds again. It's completely aced."

"We're not going to use the plane," Mildred told him, crossing the deck to the first canvas mound. She ran a hand over the rough expanse of material. "We'll fly the cargo."

"Worked once before. Why not again?" Ryan mused.

"How can we steer?" Dean asked bluntly.

"We'll wet blankets and hold them over the side," Krysty explained. "That'll give us some drag, and as we slow down to the left, to drift to the left."

"Crude and dangerous," Doc rumbled. "Yet, alas, we don't really have another choice."

"Anybody want to row across fifty miles of open sea with those steam-powered PT boats hunting for us all the way?" Ryan asked brusquely.

There was a long moment of silence.

"Didn't think so," Ryan said, cracking the knuckles of his hand. "Okay, we start with the ropes."

Chapter Three

Dean was surprised how easily the craft was constructed.

The sun was hovering just above the horizon by the time the balloon was ready to launch. The cargo netting barely proved adequate to contain the weather balloons as they were filled with helium from the pressurized tanks. With each balloon, another rope had been tied to the plastic pallet to keep the craft from soaring away, and the companions ceased adding balloons only when the overhead net was completely filled, the anchor ropes creaking from the strain of containing the lighter-than-air vehicle.

"These will help," Krysty said, tying a lumpy bag to the pallet. Trousers from the dead paratroopers were tied off to make crude sacks, and then filled with broken pieces of electronic equipment from the cockpit. The counterweight would give them a hair more control over the flying craft. Not much, but every little bit helped. But the balloons didn't descend in the slightest until six more of the heavy bags were lashed into place.

"She's got more than enough lift," Mildred said, beaming in pleasure at the buoyant craft. The bobbing net filled with the taut balloons nearly blocked out the stars it was so large. "We'll ride like kings on the wind."

"Till crash-land," Jak added grimly, standing guard over the pile of their backpacks. They had all removed their packs to work faster, but wisely didn't toss them into the rope basket of the flying machine until ready to launch. If a rope broke and the packs soared away with all the food and ammo, they would be good as chilled.

"She needs a name," Dean said, studying the huge thing, then glanced at the airplane. "Did Hercules have a kid?"

Checking the anchor ropes, Doc paused to scratch his head. "Indeed, he did. Three sons, but I cannot recall any of their names."

"Don't need a name, long as it works," Ryan said, zipping up his pants as he stepped from the plane. "Remember to use the washroom before we go. And throw away anything not needed. Weight is at a premium." The craft had plenty of lift now, but not with seven people in its basket.

"Never thought we'd leave the island this way," J.B. observed, placing a cigar in his mouth. The pilot had been carrying a pocket humidor of the best quality, and two of the cigars inside were in smokable condition. The Armorer was trying hard to quit, but sometimes the urge simply couldn't be denied.

Reaching in a pocket, he pulled out a butane lighter and Doc rushed forward to snatch the device from his grasp.

"Are you mad, John Barrymore?" Doc whispered urgently, brandishing the lighter. "Hydrogen is extremely flammable! One spark and we'll be blown to pieces."

"Not filled with hydrogen," J.B. replied curtly. "Helium."

Doc paused in confusion. "Helium," he repeated slowly. "The word sounds familiar, but I fear its meaning eludes me."

Refilling the canteens from a lotus flower that bled water, Mildred gave a start and stared at the man askance, then slowly recalled that the element was discovered around 1870 by Sir somebody or other. Damn, she couldn't recall the name. Maybe helium wasn't in wide usage by the time Doc was trawled.

"Trust me," Mildred said, topping off a canteen and letting the excess water flow onto the broad wing. "We're completely safe. Helium is a noble gas, totally inert."

"Really, madam?" Doc exhaled deeply. "In truth, I had been deeply worried about an aerial conflagration. The Army of the Potomac constantly had their observation balloons destroyed by flaming arrows from Lee's rebels."

"Can't happen here," she stated confidently, screwing on the last cap and slinging the heavy container over her back.

"How delightful to know." Doc said, then passed back the light. "Yours, I believe."

"Thanks," J.B. drawled, pocketing the lighter. For some reason he no longer had an urge to smoke, the image of the airship exploding into flames filling his mind.

"We are gonna fly," Dean said excitedly, swatting a skeeter and lifting his head to look at the darkening sky. The fiery storm clouds weren't bad, lots of distant thunder, but very little sheet lightning. Plus, there was no smell of rotten eggs, so the chances of acid rain were zero.

"I say we wait another hour until night," Ryan

suggested, squatting on the wing. He pulled out a stick of gum from an MRE pack and started chewing. "We disappear in the darkness, then Mitchum and Glassman can search the nuke-shitting jungle for us till they chill as wrinklies."

"Sounds good," Jak said, walking carefully up the ramp into the plane. The predark bandage on his ankle eased most of the pain. Running was out of the question, but at least he could walk again without gritting his teeth.

"Mebbe we should leave now. The wind is right," Krysty announced, her animated hair moving with the tangy sea breeze. "With any luck, it'll carry us straight to the next island."

"Mebbe," Ryan muttered thoughtfully.

"How about the *Jules Verne,* or better, the *Papillon,*" Mildred said out of the blue. "That's a good name. She's not a war wag, after all, just an escape pod."

"The *Papillon,*" Doc said, arching a snowy eyebrow. "And if I recall my French correctly, why should we christen it, the *Butterfly,* madam?"

Before Mildred could explain, from somewhere in the growing darkness came the long drawn-out howl of a hound dog. Immediately, the companions pulled blasters and waited, listening hard. His boots softly tanging on the metal deck, Jak appeared at the hatchway, his belt partially undone, both knife and Magnum blaster at the ready.

The barking of hounds grew fainter, then came back strong until it seemed the beasts were directly under the plane. Seconds later came the roar of Hummer engines, and the voices of men.

"Look at the dogs, sir!" a man cried. "They must be in the trees!"

"Shut up, you damn fool!" a deeper voice snapped. "Now they know we're here."

"Open fire!" a third voice commanded, and a fusillade of blasters cut loose, the big .75-caliber miniballs from the flintlocks peppering the tree branches and ripping the flowers apart. A stray shot punctured one of the lower balloons of the airship, and with a long blubbering hiss it began to deflate.

"Stop firing!" another man shouted angrily. "Glassman wants them alive!"

There came the sounds of grunting from below, and the companions knew that armed sec men were climbing the trees. Fast and silent, Mildred grabbed a backpack and heaved it into the rope basket. Jak joined her efforts, and when the airship was loaded, he awkwardly climbed in himself.

Standing on the wing of the great plane, Ryan felt hot blood pumping through his veins and fought to control his terrible temper. He hated to run from a fight, but if the balloons got damaged they would be trapped there. It was now or never.

Getting into the basket, he accepted the handful of canteen straps from Doc, who climbed in, closely followed by J.B. and Krysty. Holding his knife to an anchor line, Ryan whistled softly, but his son ran to the edge of a wing and drew the Veri pistol. Taking a balanced stance, Dean fired the magnesium charge straight down. The flare hissed away, and seconds later there came a blinding flash of light from below, followed by numerous screams. Dean fired twice more, changing the angle of the shots, and there came a large explosion, bitter smoke fumes rising into the trees. He had to have hit a Hummer.

Turning, the boy started for the balloon when a sec man appeared amid the gently waving leaves of a nearby banyan tree. Blaster in hand, the soldier paused for a moment, startled at the sight of the bizarre floating craft, and that split second of indecision was all Ryan needed to ace the man with the SIG-Sauer blaster. The sleek weapon gently coughed twice, and the sec man's eyes disappeared, instantly becoming bloody holes. The lifeless corpse released the branch and plummeted into the foliage below.

"Black dust, it's Jimbo!" a voice cried.

A second replied, "Screw Glassman! Let's ace the fuckers!"

Suddenly, a .50 cal burped into life, the bottom of the plane rattling with incoming rounds, the skeletons in the jumpseats shaking apart as if dancing. Holes were punched through the wing, the flowers exploding into tiny sprays of juice and petals. Dean remained motionless until the barrage stopped, then he raced to the airship. He barely got a leg over the ropes when another sec man swung into view on a vine and landed on the wing of the plane. Jak jerked his arm forward, and the invader staggered backward, blood gushing around the knife jutting out of his throat. As the man dragged the flintlock pistol from his belt, Ryan fired his SIG-Sauer once more, the 9 mm slug spinning the man off the wing. His scream lasted for brief seconds, then abruptly stopped.

More rounds peppered the hull of the craft, and another balloon was punctured as the companions rapidly cut through the anchor lines. Another face appeared in the leaves, and Doc had no choice but to trigger the LeMat. The massive blaster thundered flame at the invader, the soft-lead miniball blowing away half of his face. But even as the mutilated corpse fell, two more men swung out of the trees holding on to vines. Both landed on the wing of the plane and dropped flat, opening firing with their flintlock pistols. One sec man fired at the Hercules, while the other turned his attention to the waving balloon and basket. A miniball hummed past Ryan as he returned fire with the barking H&K, but the smoky discharge from the black-powder weapons effectively masked the position of the prone invaders.

From the jungle below, the crackling of the flames steadily became louder, and it was soon apparent that the trees were on fire. Extending his arm as far as he could reach, Ryan managed to slash another anchor rope. The other ropes would have to be cut by whoever was near them. The companions were packed like sardines in the little basket, and it was difficult to move.

Their rifles spent, the sec men pulled pistols and fired again. While they hastily reloaded, the companions shot blindly into the smoke, eliminating both. But with the wing directly beneath them, the companions were unable to shoot at the sec men until they peeked into view from the trees. Sniper fire erupted from the shadows, but most of it was concentrated on the Hercules. The darkness worked both ways, and it was obvious that the ville sec men thought the companions were hidden in the plane.

Tongues of flame lanced from the treetops, the miniballs peppering the hull of the huge aircraft and punching straight through, the stressed aluminum no match for the heavy wads of rolled lead. Unexpectedly, an explosion shook the Hercules.

"By the Three Kennedys, that was a helium tank!" Doc thundered, firing the LeMat again. A sec man fell from the trees, hitting another and they both dropped out of sight. A voice cried from below, sounding more surprised than in pain. "The gas may be inert, but those pressurized tanks burst apart like a bomb when hit!"

"How many left!" Ryan demanded, tracking the muzzle-flashes in the trees and firing back just slightly above. Almost every time he was rewarded with a scream.

But the sec men were learning that trick and starting to fire back at the people in the rope basket. J.B. grunted as a miniball hummed by so close he felt the heat of the lead. An inch to the left would have aced him on the spot.

"Too damn many!" Mildred spit, working the slide to clear a jam. "If a chain reaction starts, with the helium tanks damaging each other, the wave of shrapnel will tear the Herc apart, and us along with it!"

"Don't worry about it," Dean told her, slashing through the last anchor rope with his bowie knife. Instantly, the balloon began to drift leisurely across the wing as it followed the gentle evening breeze, heading straight for the sec men in the trees.

"Too heavy!" Jak started to saw at the tough plastic ropes holding the weighted bags. The loss of the two weather balloons may have grounded the airship before its maiden flight. The first bag dropped away and nothing happened.

More sec men appeared in the foliage, firing their

handcannons in a cacophony of blasts, a stray round nicking one of the plastic ropes holding the overhead netting in place. Swinging up the Uzi, J.B. cut loose with the subgun in a stuttering spray and emptied nearly a full clip into the trees, wounded sec men slumping over branches, the dead falling away like overripe fruit.

Screams filled the night, black smoke was pouring from the ground fire and flintlocks threw hot lead everywhere. Holstering her piece, Krysty went to slash the next weighted bag, but it snapped before her blade could touch the plastic rope. Instantly, the balloon and its crew bobbed straight into the air, their velocity increasing with every second.

"Hot pipe," Dean whispered, watching the wreckage of the Hercules and the jungle dwindle below them.

As the strange craft cleared the trees, the evening wind took hold and they swung away from the crashed plane and over the treetops. Continuing to shoot, Ryan could see the sec men swarm over the smoking Hercules, several managing to climb on top to send a unified volley toward the escaping airship. Another balloon in the net noisily deflated. Their craft slowed its ascent, and Mildred frantically dropped one of the few remaining bags in response.

"Not enough," Krysty said with a frown, holstering her blaster. Drawing the Veri pistol, she took careful aim and sent a blinding flare directly into the open cargo door of the Hercules. It ricocheted off the metal floor and disappeared into the cargo hold. Moments later, the interior of the plane became violently illuminated with the hellish red light from the sizzling magnesium charge. The woman sent in a blue flare, then a yellow, in an effort to set off the huge stacks of old ammo. Even a small explosion could damage the helium tanks and stop the sec men from shooting at them. She had no idea if guncotton lost its ginger over the decades the way black powder did, but the C-4 plastique sealed safe inside the airtight warheads of the big 40 mm Bofor rounds should be strong as ever. Hopefully.

Shifting position, Dean joined her and the two sent more incandescent flares into the ship before Ryan stopped them.

"Save it," he directed sternly. "May need these to get out of here."

"Flares?" Krysty demanded as she tucked away the stubby blaster. Then comprehension filled her face. "Right. Hadn't considered that."

The blasterfire from the sec men became sporadic as the airship rose high into the night, and then without warning a gout of flame belched from the open hatchway of the Hercules as the entire vessel shook. Then the hull split open lengthwise as the craft disappeared in a blinding thunderclap. The concussion of the staggering blast savagely rocking the balloon, causing Jak to lose his grip on the ropes and fall to the pallet, grabbing his bad ankle.

Incredibly, the tandem-mounted Bofors chattered into action as the corroded shells in their breeches cooked off from the heat, kicking the cannons into momentary life. Four stuttering streams of tracer shells flew in every direction, the ancient 40 mm warheads detonating randomly.

As the rumbling mushroom cloud spread outward, the wave of shrapnel arrived, burning bits of wreckage soaring across the sky. A burning motor went straight by the companions to arch gracefully over the jungle and head back down like a meteor toward the nearby ocean. Then the partially dismantled ejector seats launched from the flaming wreckage, propelled high and wide by the rocket engines built into their stout titanium frames. At the apogee of flight, two of the rockets unexpectedly detonated, but the rest disengaged and white parachutes blossomed from the backs of the chairs. Then the ancient silk ripped apart under the weight of the empty seats, and the predark safety mechanism fell into the dark greenery to crash out of sight.

A roiling gout of flame washed over what little remained of the Hercules, and then the airplane simply vanished in yet another strident detonation of ancient ordnance, the windows finally shattering, the propellers spinning madly away.

Drifting ever higher above the burning rain forest, the companions watched as the remains of the destroyed aircraft began to slowly sink out of their sight. Distorted by the distance, the wreckage hit the ground in a muffled crash, the sec men and dogs trapped underneath screaming briefly then going utterly silent.

"We did it," Mildred said softly, a touch of disbelief in her voice. "The damn thing actually works!"

"Fare thee well, Glassman and Mitchum," Doc muttered, looking at the battle zone, his face ruddy from the flickering lights. As if in harmony with the destruction below, the ever present storm clouds rumbled threateningly above.

"We're free and clear," Dean said, the salty wind blowing back his unruly hair and making him squint.

"For the moment," Ryan corrected him, rubbing a

hand over his unshaved jaw. "Better start checking for damage. Still have a long way to go tonight, and we have to figure out how to land this thing without going into a rad pit and chilling ourselves."

"Or landing in a volcano," Krysty added, cracking open the Veri pistol to dump a spent shell and slide in a live round. "Forbidden Island has a lot of those."

"Yeah, I know."

"Any ideas?" Jak asked.

"Working on it," Ryan said grimly, tightening his grip on the topmost plastic rope.

SILHOUETTED by the cold moonlight, something flew above the convoy of Hummers tearing along the jungle road, but Mitchum paid it no attention. Probably just a cloud or a bird. Nothing important. They were heading toward the sounds of battle, naturally assuming that one of the recce squads had found the outlanders. Soon, Ryan would be dead at his feet. The thought filled him with an almost sexual pleasure, and he chuckled softly.

But suddenly, the .50 cal in one of the war wags started chattering loudly and men began shouting, cursing and screaming.

"Close ranks, volley fire!" Glassman shouted in an automatic response, hastily glancing around for any sign of their attackers. It had to be Ryan and his crew of coldhearts. Nobody else would dare to challenge an armed convoy. However, nothing was in sight but the cool jungle and the long empty road. What the hell was going on here?

"What in nuking hell is that?" a sec man gasped, staring at the nighttime sky in abject horror. As others looked in the same direction, some went pale, several screamed, more dropped their blasters from trembling hands. One weeping man bolted from the Hummer and dashed madly into the thorny bushes alongside the old road, uncaring of the deep gashes and rips he received.

Unnerved by these reactions, Mitchum glanced up from the wheel and savagely braked the Hummer, almost losing control. The other wags did the same, narrowly missing slamming into one another.

The collection of sec men and navvies stared into the sky without speaking. Floating high above them was something that resembled a bunch of huge balls caught in a fishing net, with a sort of basket slung underneath.

"Plane. It's a bastard plane," Campbell said hoarsely, backing into the .50 cal and sitting impotently atop its polished brass gimbal. The machine gun in the other wag continued firing until the barrel grew hot and it jammed.

"Nukes from above," someone whimpered.

"Rad me..." Glassman whispered, instinctively drawing his revolver and pointing it skyward. He could tell the object was out of range for the weapon, but the feel of steel gave him a much needed boost of courage. A flying machine. He shuddered. The very thought made his blood run cold.

"S-skydark," a sec man croaked, barely able to speak.

Another trembling man slipped from the wag and ran away.

"Ryan." Mitchum cursed. So the big bastard had some sort of a predark flying machine, eh? That explained a lot. Marooned on the island chain, just trying to find a boat so they could leave. What a crock of shit. The outlanders had to be invaders from the mainland, spying out the local villes. Lies, everything Ryan had told him were now obviously lies!

Even as he raged at the sight, Mitchum fought back a shiver at the thought of a fleet of dozens of air wags filling the sky and dropping bombs onto villes. Even the lord baron would be defenseless against such an attack. It would be no more of a fight than clubbing a chained slave to death.

"Sergeant Campbell, shoot that thing down!" Glassman roared, stepping from the wag and firing his revolver at the flying object. The cracks of the .38 seemed lost in the immense jungle.

There was no reply.

"Sergeant, shoot the fifty!"

"Y-yes, s-sir," Campbell managed to say, fumbling with the arming bolt with sweat-slick hands. Twice he lost his grip, then dried his hands on his pants, worked the bolt and started pounding lead at the bobbing aircraft.

"Stop wasting ammo! They're too far," Mitchum stated furiously, leaning forward to press his face against the windshield. "Launch a Firebird!"

"S-sir?" someone asked, turning to the captain.

"Belay that! Too many trees in the way," Glassman countered, holstering his useless piece. "We need a clear shot. Back to Cascade! We'll strike from the beach."

"We're heading north," Mitchum snapped, starting the engine. "Only a few miles from here there's a cliff that juts over the breakers. They're following the wind, so we can outmaneuver them on land."

"Get moving!" Glassman ordered. "And prepare

a Bird. One warning shot and they'll surrender quick
enough.''

"Ryan will never surrender," Mitchum stated in a
growl, throwing the wag into gear. "We ace the bastard, or he escapes. There is no other choice."

Visions of his family before a firing squad, Glassman opened his mouth to speak, then shot a glance
at the thing in the sky. Desperately, he tried to cook
up any kind of a plan to capture the flying machine,
and nothing came to mind. He was down two men
already. How could you trap a bird in flight? The only
way he knew was with another flying machine. Lacking that, all he could do was chill the outlanders.

A great and terrible calm flowed over the officer as
he realized this failure meant the death of his wife
and child. Then his temples pounded with the knowledge that if they had to die, then so would the accursed Ryan and his crew!

"Prepare every Firebird we have," Glassman
stated, feeling oddly detached from the world, as if
he were watching this happen to somebody else.
"We'll blow them out of the bastard sky and feed the
fish their bones. Now move these wags!"

"Aye, aye, sir," the navvy replied hesitantly, and
commenced readying the entire pod of deadly missiles.

"Time to die, traitor," Mitchum said, baring his
teeth in a feral snarl as he began racing down the
cracked length of predark asphalt.

Chapter Four

A cool breeze wafted from the wine-dark sea over the aerial craft, the ropes creaking as its speed remained constant.

The balloon, now called *Pegasus,* as Mildred finally decided to name the craft, had leveled off at four hundred feet and sailed effortlessly along with the thick jungle spread over the landscape below like a lush green carpet. Here and there a craggy rise of bare rocks broke the cover, and to the west was the shiny flat expanse of the nameless lake, edged by the quagmire full of muties.

The churning ribbon of blue cut a path through the trees, and as the *Pegasus* sailed above the river, it abruptly descended to merely two hundred feet, and angled away from the winds to unexpectedly begin to follow the rushing waters. Disturbed by this, Ryan started to cut away another weighted bag, but Mildred stopped him.

"Not necessary," she explained. "The cool air above the river forms a low-pressure zone that makes us drop a little. Nothing to be concerned about. Once we reach the sea, the *Pegasus* will go right back up and catch the high winds again."

"Hope so," Ryan replied curtly, holding on to the support ropes. "Because Cascade is built on a waterfall, this river could feed that."

"Heading in the right direction," J.B. added, checking his compass.

"Better do a recce," Krysty suggested, trying to listen for any hints of men or machines. But the endless rustle of the leaves masked sounds coming from the ground.

"No prob," the Armorer said, reaching into his shoulder bag to extract a short, fat, brass can.

Sliding the antique telescope to its full length, he swept the landscape. The storm clouds were thin in the sky, admitting a wealth of silvery moonlight, the jungle turning black in the reflected illumination. No birds were in flight, no campfires visible. Other than the burning wreckage they had left behind, the entire valley was peaceful.

Then tiny jots of yellow flickered into existence to the south. Following the river, J.B. adjusted the length of the telescope and brought into focus the outline of a predark bridge with a small ville built on top. The shore at one end was sealed off with some form of bamboo wall, tiny figures moving along the top. Beyond the bridge was more forest, partly masked by great clouds of mist.

"There's a ville dead ahead," he reported, struggling to hold the telescope steady against the rhythmic rocking of the rope basket. "Seems to be a waterfall just beyond. Must be Cascade."

"How picturesque," Doc rumbled in amusement. "A city on a waterfall."

Mildred added, "Pretty slick if they know anything about building waterwheels."

"Fireblast," Ryan cursed, throwing his weight to the left to try to stop the rope basket from turning. The trick worked and the craft settled. "No wonder there are so many bastard wags in the area. Cascade was only a few miles away from the crashed plane. We were right on top of the baron's troops.''

''Yeah, but do they know we're coming?'' Dean asked urgently, drawing his bowie knife and holding the blade to a plastic rope.

''Don't think so,'' J.B. answered slowly. As the *Pegasus* moved steadily toward the ville, more details were coming into focus, but the balloon was making him queasy with its crazy motions. His guts felt watery and cold.

''There are—'' he swallowed hard and tried again ''—there are some sec men moving along a defensive wall. But they're smoking cigs, and one guy is taking a leak in the river.''

He lowered the brass scope and compacted it down in size. ''The ville is way too quiet. I'd say they have no idea we're coming.''

''Good,'' Ryan said, drawing the SIG-Sauer. ''Mebbe we can sail by and they never know it.''

''We're going to be dangerously low as we pass,'' Krysty reminded him, easing out the clip of the H&K blaster and counting the rounds she had remaining before sliding it back into the grip. ''Mebbe we should drop another bag.''

''Only six left,'' Mildred warned. ''Best we save them for emergencies.''

As the ville swelled closer, J.B. tucked away the telescope. Now they could see the lit windows of brick houses, cooking fires scattered about on the ground and sputtering torches moving along the concrete streets. They heard the sounds of drunken singing and the crack of a whip followed by yowls of pain.

"Backpacks on the flooring," Ryan ordered, sliding his off and stepping onto the canvas bag. The companions copied his action, but withheld shooting at the small figures of the sec men, knowing they were out of range.

In graceful majesty, the *Pegasus* silently floated over the wall of the ville, and a sec man screamed loud enough to be heard by the companions.

Calmly, they watched as the guards frantically dashed about waving their arms, and several dived into the river to escape from the horrifying sky machine. Then a cannon roared, throwing a smoke ring across the ville square, and a bonfire grew bright and strong to cast harsh light across the ville as a bell began to ring in strident urgency.

"Get ready," Ryan said, tucking away the SIG-Sauer and drawing his H&K blaster. If silence was no longer important, he'd rather use the autofire. The sound suppressor on the SIG-Sauer cut down muzzle-blast, and he might need those few extra foot-pounds of pressure to accurately hit a target two hundred feet away.

Suddenly, a flight of arrows shot up from the ville to arc across the dark sky and impotently fell away, completely unable to reach the balloon.

"Thank God. These people have never heard of the longbow," Doc muttered, one hand holding his H&K, the other resting on the checkered grip of the LeMat snug in its holster.

Directly above the settlement, they could see gardens planted on every rooftop, and a row of corpses hanging from nooses thrown over the side of the wall. Then a gasoline engine sputtered softly into action, and an electric light stabbed onto the shoreline, then angled upward to sweep across the sky.

Before the beam reached them, Ryan worked the bolt on the Steyr SSG-70 and fired a shot. The searchlight shattered into darkness, and a wild barrage of assorted blasters banged away from every roof in the bridgetop ville, the miniballs humming past the *Pegasus* by the dozens.

The companions returned the fire, and sec men fell from the walls. But more took their place, and tiny puffs of smoke from the ville announced further incoming rounds. Then a backpack on the floor jerked from an impossible hit.

"Fuck that," Ryan growled, and pumped half a dozen rounds at the guards. Two dropped their blasters, clutching red bellies, another grabbed a limp arm and a fourth toppled over the bamboo wall falling onto the hard city streets.

Without warning, the *Pegasus* was past the wall and over the river once more, the dim lights of the ville fading into the distance. As the companions checked the vessel for damage, the balloon built speed, heading down the waterway straight toward the thundering falls only a hundred feet distant. A huge cloud of mist rose from the torrent flowing over the jagged cliff, effectively hiding whatever was beyond.

"Anybody hurt?" Mildred demanded, hugging her med kit.

"Only an MRE," Krysty said, lifting the dripping backpack, red fluid oozing from the bullethole. "Spaghetti, I'd say."

"Scorch! Don't talk about food," J.B. muttered huskily, mopping the sweat off his pale face. Dark night, he felt awful. What the hell was wrong with his guts?

As the craft entered the cool spray, the *Pegasus* lost height and was seized by a cross current, abruptly changing direction to race directly for the southern shore, a solid line of tall trees looming ahead.

"The branches!" Mildred warned, fumbling for her belt knife.

But Ryan already had his in hand, and cut away a weighted bag, just as Dean did the same on the other side of the rope basket. Instantly, the *Pegasus* flew higher and missed the row of trees by less than a yard. A flight of birds exploded from the branches at their passing, cawing angrily at the aerial invader.

Doc muttered something in Latin, and Mildred nodded agreement, thinking that had been much too close for comfort. Maybe the balloon hadn't been such a great idea. Only an hour in the air, and already they had been nearly aced a dozen times.

Leaving the waterfall in its wake, the *Pegasus* caught the western winds once more and sailed away, free and safe again.

Looking behind, Ryan could see the trees along the edge of the cliff mixed with the misty cloud of the waterfall to perfectly hide the ville from any passing vessel. The layer stone of the ridge was only a couple of yards high, no more then three or four, and the sides sloped gently to a sandy beach. Jutting into the ocean waves, smooth spurs of volcanic rock formed natural docks for fishing boats and visiting ships.

Slinging the Steyr over a shoulder, Ryan grunted in approval. Mighty good location. Under the right hands, it could be quite a formidable settlement. Too bad it was under the control of some spineless futz brain who was loyal to Lord Baron Kinnison. He would never willingly bend a knee to a fool, no matter how much power and arms some baron wielded. The Deathlands warrior would rather die as a man than live as any form of a slave.

"Have at thee, stout hearts," Doc announced, staring straight down. "And let loose the dogs of war!"

The companions looked in the same direction and saw that moored to the stony jetties were several of the lord baron's PT boats, the decks full of men staring in fright at the balloon passing by overhead. Several raised their blasters, but none fired, some of the navvies taking refuge behind the pod of Firebirds, the smokestack of the engine or the big .50 cal machine gun.

"They're no danger," Ryan said in some satisfaction. "Too damn scared of us to try anything."

The two groups stared hard at each other as the *Pegasus* moved over the open sea. Beyond the cooling influence of the falls, the airship steadily rose and built speed once more. Soon the peteys were left behind, far beyond blaster range.

Majestically, the balloon continued along the ragged coastline, following a volcanic peninsula of broken lava spurs that formed the eastern boundary of the large harbor. To the west was a vague palisade of forest and boulders forming a barrier to blunt the crushing waves and killer winds of tropical storms.

Yanking off his hat, J.B. stuffed the beloved fedora into his jacket, then did the same with his glasses.

"Hot pipe, I like flying." Dean beamed in delight, holding on to the woven sides of the rope basket with both hands. "Makes my stomach feel like I'm steadily falling. Kind of tickles."

Krysty smiled at the boy; there was still a lot of child left in the young warrior. Hopefully, that part of him would never die. She loved Ryan with all of her heart, but the man had dark places buried down deep inside that she'd never reach. Ryan was a steel blade, forged in emotional fires that would have melted most men. He survived, but would forever carry the scars of his own brutal creation.

"I say, John Barrymore, are you quite all right?" Doc rumbled in concern, studying the trembling man. "You seem rather pale."

"Catch round?" Jak demanded, checking the man's clothing for any signs of blood.

"Worse," J.B. mumbled, then leaned over the top rope of the woven basket and proceeded to lose everything he'd recently consumed. Jammed next to the man, the others did their best to ignore the event and give him some privacy. Luckily, he was standing downwind of them at the rear of the basket.

After a few minutes J.B. lifted his face, a string of spittle hanging from his slack lips. "Dark night," he gasped. "What the hell is wrong with me, rad poisoning?"

"Nonsense," Mildred chided, placing a palm on his forehead, then checking his pulse. "You're not dying, John. It's just airsickness. The adrenaline rush of battle must have held it off until you relaxed. This happens to a lot of people."

"Not me," Dean announced, deeply breathing in the clean salty air. "Hey, look over there! It's a whale!"

"Shut up," J.B. muttered weakly, then started retching again. As a kid he had envied the birds in flight, sailing effortlessly over the deserts and rad craters. Never again.

When he was eventually finished, Mildred fumbled in her med kit to extract a small battered tin canteen. "Here, try this."

Hawking and spitting to clear his mouth, J.B. took the canteen and drank a healthy swig of the contents in the canteen. The Armorer waited nervously to see if his churning stomach would keep the fluid, then greedily drank some more.

"What was that?" J.B. asked, passing back the container. He felt much better, his stomach calm and steady as if they were back on firm ground.

"Some of my jump juice," she replied, screwing the cap on tight. Half the precious contents were gone, but this was what she had made it for. "I figured that if it helps with the nausea we get taking a jump in a mat-trans chamber, it should work for airsickness, too. Did it?"

"Some," he muttered hesitantly, then stood a bit straighter and slid on his glasses. "Yeah, it did. Thanks, Millie."

"Any time, John." She smiled, closing the straps on her med kit. This mix promised to be her best batch yet. Boiled tobacco leaves, menthol cough drops, honey, mint leaves and whiskey. Maybe she had finally found the right combination to keep them from puking out their guts after a bad jump. Some were easy as a nap in bed, but others were pure hell with nightmares and physical sickness.

"We've attracted attention," Ryan said, pointing with his H&K autoblaster.

Large birds with tremendous wingspans were starting to circle the cluster of balloons. The shadows of the clouds blocking the moon disguised their features until one flew close and Ryan saw it was a condor. Exactly the same as the giant muties that attacked them on Spider Island. Doc said they were normally that size, but Ryan didn't believe it. The triple-damn things were too fast and strong. Intelligent killing machines.

"Here they come!" Krysty shouted, pumping a round at the winged giants.

But instead of heading for the companions, the flock of condors dived straight for the cluster of weather balloons, clawing and pecking at them. The resilient plastic netting resisted their attacks, and the balloons themselves, designed to survive the worst tropical weather, proved too tough.

Defending their territory, the enraged flock now circled the cluster of balloons, screaming a challenge. A small condor dived straight through the ropes, its talons extended to rip apart the soft human flesh. The companions opened fire in unison, the barrage of lead blowing holes through the wings and forcing it back. Only wounded, the mutie charged again while another appeared, walking along the ropes with its claws, and dropped into the rope basket.

As the first dived into the ropes, the bird caught a wingtip in the complex rigging. With a gesture, a knife slid from Jak's sleeve into his waiting hand and he stabbed upward, slit open its belly, then blew off its head with the .357 Magnum blaster.

Caught reloading his blaster, Doc slapped the second bird with the long barrel of his weapon, shattering its hard beak, then, while the creature was momentarily stunned, he tossed it overboard.

Leaving a contrail of blood, the condor struggled

to spread its wings and catch the wind, but the bird plummeted straight down onto the sharp rock spurs, where it burst apart in a gory spray of guts and feathers.

Cawing in rage, a condor sailed under the basket to land on the pallet, its claws clinging tightly to the plastic. Shoving the barrel of the Steyr through the open spaces in the flooring, Ryan fired the longblaster at point-blank range and the bird exploded in a spray of feathers. But the corpse stayed there, the claws locked tight in death.

Using three rounds, Mildred took out a condor flying by, Krysty got another, Dean missed twice, then J.B. triggered the shotgun and two more were ripped apart by the ferocious blast of stainless-steel fléchette rounds. Moving hastily away from the *Pegasus,* the remaining flock whirled about, screaming in rage. Then they started to fly away, returning beaten to their nests in the rocky crags of the congealed lava flow.

Curiously, there was a flash of light from a cliff at the very end of the peninsula, and a high-pitched whistle sounded from the oceanic rocks as something streaked toward the *Pegasus* on a skylark tail of fire. The invisible object slammed directly into a condor and violently detonated, the concussion rocking the rope basket with savage force.

"Firebird!" Ryan growled, firing his weapon blindly down into the dimly seen distance. It had to be Mitchum. He had to make the sec man duck for cover, or else they'd be blown out of the sky!

"More coming," Jak said, coolly aiming his .357 Magnum blaster at the fiery exhaust of the rockets and carefully squeezing off shots. If they hit, there was no reaction.

Dropping her revolver, Krysty yanked out the Veri pistol, thanking the forces of the universe that she had reloaded. Holding the signal device in a two-handed grip, she held her breath and forced everything else from her mind but the approaching Firebird. The trajectory was impossible; the Firebird was arching up from the ground, the balloon rising and drifting away, plus the wind was blowing in gusts, not a steady breeze. There had never been worse conditions for a shot, and they had only a half-dozen flares.

Gently, she squeezed the trigger, and the colorful blue flare streaked toward an empty patch of sky. A split second later, the Firebird rose to meet the wad of burning magnesium and violently detonated.

A couple of .50 cal machine guns began to chatter from the darkness, then another Firebird launched. The fiery back-blast silhouetted the sec men and Hummers parked on the approaching cliff in stark clarity.

While the others maintained a steady fusillade at the war wags, Dean took Krysty's empty weapon and passed her the second flare gun, loaded and ready. Sweat trickling down her face, Krysty shot at the second rocket and made a hit. But then three Firebirds rose from the cliff, with two more close behind.

J.B. triggered the Uzi on full-auto, throwing flame at the receding sec men. As her H&K blaster clicked empty, Mildred grabbed a reloaded Veri pistol from Dean and shot off a flare. The sizzling green round punched through the leading rocket, making it explode, the blast damaging the Firebird alongside and throwing the rocket wildly out to sea.

Slamming in his last clip for the Steyr, Ryan fired as fast as he could work the bolt. Another Firebird

altered course and shot straight upward to disappear
into the stormy clouds. But despite the amount of copper-jacketed lead going their way, the last two rockets
bore straight in at the companions.

Her hair a wild corona, Krysty released a green
flare, but the windsheer threw it away from the incoming missiles. As J.B. slapped in a fresh clip, Ryan
fired again and a rocket tore itself apart. As he worked
the bolt, the spent shell jammed in the breech. Dropping the blaster to the plastic floor, Ryan drew his
SIG-Sauer and started banging away. Meanwhile,
Mildred and Krysty sent off a double charge of flares
from the painfully hot Veri pistols. The signaling devices weren't meant to be weapons and were overheating from the constant use. The flares were sticking to the barrel from the accumulated heat, along
with the women's burned fingers.

In a gorgeous mix of colors, the flares curved toward the incoming missile when one abruptly died in
midflight. The other erupted in a blinding purple flash,
and the missile shot right through the display completely undamaged.

The companions concentrated their attention on the
last rocket, but it was horribly close. J.B. abandoned
the Uzi and used the last few shells in the shotgun to
send off a hellstorm of fléchettes. Incredibly, the companions could see the damage it inflicted as the missile appeared to be slowing, and for several breathless
seconds it seemed to hang motionless in the sky behind them. Then the flame of its rear exhaust sputtered away and died, the reserve of black-powder fuel
gone. Rendered powerless, the lethal Firebird fell
away and disappeared into the night.

As the companions relaxed, a salvo of rockets was

launched from the Hummers on top of the jagged cliff. But the passengers of the *Pegasus* withheld shooting and merely watched as the swarm of deadly missiles climbed ever higher into the dark sky, only to slow as their tail flames weakened and died, the dreaded Firebirds tumbling helplessly into the cold sea.

"Finally out of range," Ryan said, flicking the dead brass from the Steyr over the ropes. As if in reply, thunder rumbled from the clouds so very close overhead.

"Sons of bitches want us bad," J.B. added, clearing the breech of the empty shotgun.

"Hopefully, that is the last we see of them," Krysty said, flexing her singed gun hand.

Glancing at the floor, Mildred saw the ejected brass had fallen through the holes in the plastic pallet and couldn't be gathered for repacking. Great, they were low on ammo, attacked constantly from every direction and riding a makeshift helium balloon mostly held together by spit and baling wire. The situation could only make the physician snort a bitter laugh.

"What funny?" Jak asked, startled at the noise.

"Remember the condors?" Mildred replied, holstering her piece. "Those were an endangered species in my time."

"So?"

The salty wind blowing her beaded hair, Mildred turned to face the featureless horizon of the east.

"Now we are," she finished somberly.

HOBBLING TO the edge of the crumbling cliff, Mitchum roared defiantly as he emptied his blaster at the departing airship.

"No! Not again!" Mitchum raged, cocking the hammer and dry firing the spent weapon several times. As his fury ebbed, the man turned toward the line of Hummers parked nearby.

"You there!" he shouted, pointing. "Launch another Bird!"

"Belay that shit," Glassman stated grumpily, stepping out from behind the rocket pod. His face and clothes were streaked with black from the multiple launches, and he angrily tossed aside the glowing piece of oakum he had used to light the fuses. Privately, the former healer wondered what the hell had the outlanders used to stop the Firebirds.

"We failed, Colonel," Glassman continued, pulling a rag from a pocket to wipe his face and hands. "They're gone."

"The hell they are. We're going back to Cascade," Mitchum snapped. Limping to the wag, the sec man climbed behind the steering wheel and started the engine.

"Get in!" he ordered brusquely. "We can race after them in the PT boats. Those are a lot faster than that floating soap bubble! If we use the coal-oil fuel instead of wood, we can easily get them back into range again and finish the bastard job once and forever!"

Reluctantly, Glassman had to admire the sec man's blind determination. It was either that or his lust for revenge had driven the man mad.

"Sergeant Campbell," Glassman said, going to the lead Hummer, "any more Firebirds on the boats?"

"Yes, sir," the sailor replied with a salute. "Sixteen more in the arms trunk of each petey."

"See?" Mitchum retorted, gunning the engine. "More than enough for another attack!"

"Only if we don't encounter any Deepers on the journey back home," Glassman countered, taking a seat in the war wag.

"Tomorrow's problem," the sec chief growled as he spun the steering wheel, driving the Hummer back and forth as he hurriedly turned on the narrow crag. A rear tire went over the cliff, but the wag didn't tilt and he fought it back onto firm ground. Time was against them. Every minute put Ryan that much further out of his grasp.

"We'll need to leave the Hummers behind," Mitchum said, leading the convoy of wags along the narrow trail of the peninsula to the island. There was a sheer drop into the sea on both sides, but the predark headlights gave enough illumination to keep him from driving into the abyss. "Dropping the weight will give us better speed."

Holding on to the door and windshield, Glassman scowled before answering. He was sick of this man's private blood feud, and the baron's threat against his family was lessening with every hour he was away from them.

"Too risky," he decided. "That leaves us on foot if they go inland somewhere."

"We'll take that chance."

"No, *you* will," Glassman stated coldly, bouncing in his seat as the racing wag bounded over the rippled surface of the lava flow. "Because if we lose the outlanders again, I'll personally bring you alive to the lord baron as payment for costing him so many men and weps!"

"Yeah?" Mitchum snarled, a hand going for his

flintlock. Only the weapon wasn't in its holster, and the cold barrel of a blaster was pressed to his neck from behind.

"Do as the captain says," Campbell growled hatefully. "Or I'll be delighted to pull the trigger. Your call, lubber."

Furious at being trapped for the moment, Mitchum started driving faster. Suddenly, more than just mere revenge depended on his success in chilling the accursed outlanders.

Chapter Five

As the *Pegasus* floated away on the evening breeze, the companions shifted their backpacks to make some room and settled in for their flight. With no way to calculate airspeed, they didn't have any idea how long the journey to Forbidden Island would take. Maybe only a few hours, but it could be much longer.

Time passed slowly, the moon traveling across the starry sky while the companions took turns catching short naps. There was little room in the rope basket, but they had lived in cramped quarters before and knew how to make do.

After the weapons had been cleaned and checked, the MRE envelopes were carefully ripped open, and the chow eaten cold. It was edible, but no more than that. Mildred tried to make coffee in a tin cup, and while the brown crystals dissolved satisfactorily, neither the sugar nor the powder cream would. She experimented with her butane lighter to no success and in the end poured the sodden mess overboard.

Pulling out a plastic safety razor, Jak dry shaved while standing guard duty, the scrape of the twin blades becoming fainter as he successfully removed his snowy beard.

Hoping nobody was watching, Dean rubbed a palm along his own chin but found only smooth skin. Nothing yet. Standing guard, Ryan caught the furtive motion and held back a grin. He remembered his first shave, and the bushy mustache he sported for a while as a teen.

Just then, something in the darkness caught Ryan's attention. He studied the open sky until he caught the reflection of moonlight off leathery wings. The soft flapping grew steadily louder, and when Ryan was sure the creature was coming their way, he waited until the clouds parted, catching it in plain sight, and snapped off a shot with the SIG-Sauer. The blaster coughed, and the flying creature gave a piercing squeal, promptly identifying it as a bat. Gushing blood, the mutie spiraled down out of control to splash into the smooth expanse of the shimmering sea.

The discharge of the blaster made Dean stand and draw his own weapon. "What was that?" he demanded.

"Just a bat," Ryan said calmly, holstering his piece. "Already aced. Everything's green."

A bat? Curiously, Dean looked over the rope sides of the makeshift basket and watched the dying creature flounder in the water, sharp fins already circling the bloody carcass. Then huge white figures rose from beneath the waves and began tearing the wiggling corpse apart.

"Those sharks?" Dean asked as the balloon drifted over the struggling creatures.

"Great whites, yes, indeed. But not those," Doc said, gesturing with a waggling finger. "See the difference in the dorsal fins? Those are dolphins come for the kill."

"Dolphins eat sharks?" Dean asked, shocked. The

dolphins were so much smaller than the great whites it was hard to believe.

"No, they eat fish," Mildred replied, looking at the moon. There had been too much death already today; she had no interest in watching the aquatic battle. "Dolphins kill sharks on sight. The two species hate each other."

"Ace, no eat?" Jak said with a frown, running a whetstone along the blade of a knife in slow strokes. "Triple stupe."

"Not if you're in the water with sharks coming after your ass and a bunch of dolphins show up," Ryan said, unwrapping a foil envelope to expose cherry-nut cake. Fireblast, was this the only dessert the Army ever fed its troops? He broke off a corner with his teeth and found it dissolved easily. Okay, not bad.

"They're one of the few good muties that are friendly to norms," he finished with a full mouth.

"Not a mutation, my dear Mr. Cawdor," Doc rumbled. "Since time immemorial, dolphins have been the friends of humanity. Although God alone knows why. We have certainly treated them poorly enough."

"How chill?" Jak asked, mildly interested. The dangers of the deep were important things to know.

"A dolphin will ram a shark in the belly with its nose," Doc explained, watching the event occur. "See? They die almost instantly."

"Hot pipe." Dean sighed. "Dad, didn't you say it's possible to chill a man that way, too?"

"Requires a hell of a kick," his father said, tossing away the wrapper. "But it can be done."

"Smack in the belly?"

"Just under the rib cage," Ryan said, moving a

hand to the spot on his chest. "Right here, and slightly upward."

The boy nodded studiously, filing away the info for future use.

"Enough of that, land ho!" Mildred cried out, breaking into a smile. "There she is, people! Forbidden Island!"

Majestically rising over the horizon like a green dawn was a wide island of hills, cliffs, mountains and volcanoes, everything covered with a lush growth of tropical plants. Silly thought, but to Krysty the place almost looked like two or three islands rammed together.

The *Pegasus* started to accelerate toward the island as a fresh wind blew over the companions, forcing the balloon onward. The twin volcanoes rumbled softly, sounding like distant thunder, their ragged tops lit from internal fires, wisps of yellow sulfur fumes rising to the sky. The firelight actually reflected off the thick layer of storm clouds. Two volcanoes so close to each other seemed unlikely to Mildred, and she postulated they were simply the planet trying to clean itself from deadly residue of multiple nuke hits.

"Found them," J.B. announced, holding the brass telescope to his face. In a valley set between the volcanoes were the ruins of a large predark metropolis sitting on top of a short mesa. The buildings were only silhouettes in the ambient light, black shadows as still and dead as the ferro-cement from which they'd been built.

As they continued closer, details came into view, a huge waterfall rushing off a tall cliff to their left, the smashed wreckage of a Navy yard to the right, the buildings and rusted hulks of warships partly swamped in a bay full of violently swirling water. The whirlpool made more noise than the waterfall, as it raged out of control.

Something large winged across the dark ruins, and Doc rubbed his eyes to see clearly, but the apparition was already gone. Tightening his lips, the time traveler wondered if he had just actually seen a pterodactyl, a winged lizard from the Jurassic period. No, quite impossible.

"May I be so bold as to strongly suggest that if we encounter anything exceptionally large," Doc said, checking the load in his LeMat, "shoot only for its head? Nowhere else."

"See something?" Krysty asked in concern, staring at the approaching land. Seemed rugged and wild, but ordinary enough.

"I do not know for sure, dear lady," Doc muttered, frowning. "And that is what quite worries me."

"Rad pits coming," Ryan announced as the ebony night thinned about the island showing reddish-green glows dotting the landscape, and completely covering the Navy base. Quickly, Ryan checked his rad counter and saw the readings steadily climb toward the danger zone.

"Fireblast! It's hotter than Washington Hole," he stated, shifting his arm about. The clicks of the device seemed slower to the left, toward the valley that cut through the mountain range. That was the location of the mesa. But this was no place to make a guess.

"J.B., check my readings," Ryan said urgently.

"Yeah, valley seems okay," J.B. added, his own rad counter out and sweeping for danger. The sides of the mesa were sheer vertical stone. A bitch of a climb to make, but no problem to reach from the air.

"Okay, start wetting those blankets and try angling us toward the mesa," Ryan directed, sliding on his backpack.

"No need," Mildred replied. "The wind has shifted again, and we're heading straight for it."

"The volcanoes are making a current for us," Krysty said, frowning slightly. "Taking us right there."

Tucking away his sharpened knives, Jak scowled. "Somethin' wrong."

Mildred shuffled around the rope basket and checked the weight bags. Each was tied firmly in place.

"Millie?" J.B. asked.

"We appear to be rising," she answered slowly. "Nothing serious yet, but we better let out some helium."

"My job," Doc said, pulling the sword from his stick. Reaching high, he stabbed the lowest weather balloon and it noisily deflated in a blubbery rush. But the *Pegasus* didn't lose any height. Puzzled, Doc stabbed another, then another, and incredibly the airship began to rise.

"How's this possible?" J.B. demanded, trying to see above the makeshift craft. Did something have a hold of them and was dragging the balloons skyward?

"Goddamn it, we're caught in an updraft from those cross currents!" Mildred said, drawing her blaster and blowing away the largest balloon. It burst as the hot round tore through, but their speed didn't slow.

Steadily the *Pegasus* streaked for the storm clouds overhead, and Ryan briefly considered dropping all of their excess weight to get above the clouds. Unfor-

tunately, the sheet lightning filled the sky and they
would be fried rising through the wild storm—if the
rads and chems didn't ace them first. But if they shot
out too many balloons, they would plummet from the
sky and crash on the rocks below. They had passed
the ocean several minutes ago and were now moving
over bare soil studded with boulders and rusty predark
junk. The companions would be torn to pieces even
if they survived the brutal landing.

As they rose still higher, Krysty cried out in pain,
then the rest rubbed their arms and faces, skin prick-
ling from the deadly proximity to the heavily polluted
clouds. Just then, both of the rad counters began to
wildly click ever faster.

"If we enter those clouds," Doc warned in a sten-
torian tone, his eyes painfully tearing, "none of us
shall ever leave it alive!"

With no other choice, Ryan drew his blaster and
started firing, the spent brass kicking over the side of
the basket. Fireblast, he thought, the problem with
balloon wags was supposed to be keeping them afloat,
not getting them to come down. Just one solution for
that. The red-hot rounds from the SIG-Sauer easily
punched through the tough polymer sheeting, deflating balloons far out of the sword's reach, and the craft
instantly slowed. Then it began to descend, and soon
the itchy crawling feeling of radiation was fading
away. Only now the island was rushing toward them
with nightmare speed as the *Pegasus* descended out
of control.

"Too fast!" Jak stated, slashing through the ropes.
The heavy bags fell, and the *Pegasus* continued to
drop.

"Shitfire, we've slipped out of the thermal!" Mildred warned. "Now we're too heavy. Toss everything overboard!"

The companions slid off their backpacks and heaved them away, but the reduction in weight made no real difference. Too many of the balloons had been destroyed in their efforts to avoid the death clouds. But the airship was also still moving inland. The moonlight heralding their way, the terrain became grasslands, then a forest with a stone arch extended across the valley, connecting one mountainside to the other. A natural limestone bridge flew by.

"Get ready to jump," Ryan ordered, climbing the ropes.

The others copied his actions, but the *Pegasus* swung past the bridge moving way too fast, the bottom of the plastic pallet scraping across the limestone for the briefest instant before they were past the obstruction and over the trees again.

"Fireblast!" Ryan spit, falling back into the rope basket.

Incredibly, from somewhere below an alarm bell began to ring, and blasters crackled from the dark trees as cannons roared from hidden bunkers on the shadowy mountainsides, their discharges throwing tongues of flame that illuminated the valley.

"It's another ville!" J.B. snarled as a cannonball rushed by, buffeting them with the wind of its passing.

"Water!" Krysty shouted, pointing ahead.

There was a wide break in the stygian forest, where a calm river traversed the valley floor. Unfortunately, the river was narrow, with sharp rocks lining both shores, with more trees returning on the far bank.

Their target was a slim area of flat mud between the rocks, impossible to hit at their current speed.

"That is our best chance!" Ryan shouted, slashing away the side ropes, open air directly before the man. "Wait for it... Now!"

In unison the companions dived from the pallet, and a split second later the *Pegasus* rammed into the trees and was torn apart by a thousand sharp branches.

Only the babbling of the shallow river disturbed the heavy silence of the muddy banks. Then swatches of light bobbed through the darkness, and armed men stepped from the rushes along the riverbank to stealthily approach the deathly still figures sprawled in the bloody mud.

THEIR BLACK PLUMES trailing across the starry sky, the four PT boats steamed across the ocean, their engines thumping loudly.

A number of dolphins swam alongside the lead petey, occasionally lifting their bottle-nose heads to give a stuttering squeal. With both of his wounds stiff and aching, Mitchum slid the longblaster off his shoulder, pulled back the heavy hammer and shot one. The creature moved sideways from the impact of the .75 miniball, human-red blood spraying from the gaping wound. The entire pack dived out of sight instantly, and as the chugging fleet left them behind, the dolphins returned to circle the dying mammal, gently nudging it with their stubby noses. Then a female gave a long howl as if in mourning as the gut-shot male rolled onto its back to expose its pale belly to the air. The rest of the pack circled their dead friend once more, then swam away, leaving the lifeless meat to the endless scavengers. But more than one of the dolphins turned to stare at the noisy dead thing that thundered over the water, watching the two-legs with intelligent eyes full of raw hatred.

"What was that?" Glassman demanded, lowering his plate of beans and dried fish.

"Some kind of baby shark," Mitchum said, purging the longblaster before refilling it with powder, lead and cloth wad, then carefully tramping down the fresh charge with a blunt nimrod. "Who cares? Just a fish. Ain't got no brains or human feelings."

With a shrug, Glassman returned to his meal.

"Ahoy, the captain!" a sailor called out from an aft PT boat, a hand pointing to the sky. "Two o'clock high!"

"It's them!" Mitchum snarled, lifting his longblaster, but withheld firing. The weird air wag was bobbing along in the sky without a care in the world. The sec chief trembled with the urge to kill, and had to mentally force his hands to lower the flintlock.

"Well, don't stand there gawking like virgins in a gaudy house!" Mitchum snarled, stalking along the deck. "They're getting away! Load the .50 cals! Ready the Firebirds!" Nobody moved to obey the command. The sec chief fumed in his impotence, and bit back words he knew would only get him aced.

"Land ho!" another called in warning. "Breakers at our noon!"

A corporal backed away from the sight. "That's Forbidden Island!"

"What?" a sec man gasped, spinning in shock.

On the horizon was a long landmass with two live volcanoes. There could be no doubt as to which island that was.

"Nuke me, it is!" Glassman shouted, throwing away his plate. "Emergency stop! Cut all engines!"

The crew rushed to the tasks, and soon the boats were anchored relatively motionless in the waves. Reaching into an equipment box, Glassman pulled out binocs while Mitchum limped to the forward bow.

Illuminated by the silvery moonlight streaming through the rumbling clouds, the men watched as the distant air wag abruptly rose high into the sky, then dropped toward the ground, narrowly rushing over a stone bridge. Cannons roared at their passing, and the air wag disappeared into the darkness beyond.

"Did you see those cannons?" Mitchum growled, fighting a wild mix of emotions. "This must be a pirate base!"

"No," Glassman corrected, lowering the binocs. "It has to be their main base. This is the home of the pirate fleet!"

"Where are the ships?" a young ensign asked, bewildered.

An older navvy grunted in reply. "Don't be stupe, ya feeb. Think they'd leave the fleet in plain sight? It's probably anchored on a nearby atoll where we can't see them."

"Which means," Mitchum said, grinning and cracking his knuckles, "that they can't see us, either." For some reason, that seemed important to the sec man.

Just then the island trembled slightly and seconds later a wave lifted the ships yards high, then lowered them undamaged. The navvies paid it no attention. Just a quake wave, and they rode them out all the time. Nothing to be concerned about.

"Skipper, the outlanders are pirates?" a navvy asked.

"Looks like. Must have been testing out their air wag before starting a war," Glassman said, tucking the binocs away. "On the other hand, lads, we just found their home dock. We're rich! Kinnison will make every one of us a baron for finding this!"

"But Ryan escaped! They're on the island!" Mitchum raged, gesturing with a clenched fist. "We have to land immediately and run them down!"

"Without wags?" Glassman reminded him harshly.

Breathing raggedly, Mitchum said nothing. He had taken a gamble and lost.

"Besides," a navvy said knowingly, resting a boot on a coil of rope, "they're dead by now from the rads."

"Ass, the pirates live here," Mitchum retorted with a sneer. "So the outlanders will be fine."

"Mebbe," the other recanted unwillingly.

Which raised an interesting point for Glassman. The air wag gave the outlanders a ride over the rad pits, but how did the pirates manage to do it every day?

"There's got to be some kind of safe passage through the craters," Mitchum stated, obviously following the same train of thought. "But how the hell can we find it?"

"First we lift anchor," Glassman said, taking the captain's chair and settling into place. "Bosun, take us back to Cascade. Best speed."

"Aye, aye, sir!" the navvy replied, and got busy at the control board. Soon the engines were thumping alive once more.

"You're leaving?" Mitchum demanded furiously. "Well, put me on the beach. I'll stay."

"Can't. I need you to help oversee the handling of the slaves. You've done it before—my sailors haven't," Glassman said, waving over a young sailor. "Donovan, send off a messenger falcon to Kinnison. Tell him what we've found and request the entire fleet. Every ship we've got that can carry cannon or Birds."

"Aye, aye, sir!" the man said, hurrying below-decks at a run.

Mitchum limped closer to the captain. "Slaves?" he asked in confusion.

"All they have," Glassman answered grimly as the petey began to turn a slow curve in the waves. "And if the ville hasn't got enough, we'll also take every citizen and sec man. I'd say a hundred should be enough."

"Enough for what?" Mitchum asked, frowning.

"To use as a key," Glassman said cryptically, studying the compass to check their course. Straight ahead, dawn was starting to tint the eastern horizon with rosy light. Behind them, night still ruled in absolute authority.

But not for long.

Chapter Six

Ryan's dreams were wild nightmares of falling, then suffocating, loud noises, pain, laughter, bad smells and now endlessly rocking....

The Deathlands warrior awoke with bright sunlight shining in his face, and he sat up to see where they were only to slam his head against something hard. Trying to rub the spot, Ryan found his hands were bound with ropes. He tried to break the strands, then realized it was some of the plastic rope from the *Pegasus*. Fireblast! So those dreams had been real. They lived through the crash, only to be taken prisoner.

Gathering his wits, the one-eyed man saw he was in an iron cage on the back of a wooden cart, the steady sound of horse hooves on stone coming from the front. As his vision cleared, Ryan saw he was traveling through a ville full of people. Streams of men and women were moving past the cart on both sides, children were playing in the mud, barking dogs running about, farmers selling produce from wheelbarrows and in the distance he could hear a muted work song from slaves. Then the cart rolled by the bloated corpse of a woman hanging from a rope, *Disobeedeant* scrawled on a placard hung around her swollen neck.

Ryan checked his clothing, but his blaster and gun belt were missing. Along with his backpack, panga and everything else. Even his eye patch was on backward and his clothes in disarray. He'd been searched, and anything that could possibly be a weapon was gone.

Surreptitiously, Ryan checked the laces of his combat boots and was pleased to note the laces were still tied with the double knot he regularly used. Okay, not completely unarmed then. But nothing he could reach fast.

The thick bars of the cage cast most of the interior into shadows, so Ryan crawled across the cramped quarters to check the other passengers. Rolling over a man, he saw it was J.B., with everything gone but his glasses. That was odd. It had to mean something important, but what?

Lying nearby were Doc and Dean, in a similar state of disarray. They had each been stripped clean; even Doc's walking stick was gone. Fireblast, they had to have found the sword inside.

But the rest of the companions were missing. A flood of blood pounded in his temples, and Ryan fought to control his terrible temper. Whatever was happening to his other friends, there was nothing he could do about it at the moment.

Going over to J.B., Ryan placed a hand on the man's mouth and shook him awake. Instantly, J.B. flicked open his eyes and reached for a blaster, his hands jerking to a stop by the ropes binding his wrist to his ankles.

"Stay quiet," Ryan whispered into his ear. "We've been captured."

J.B. nodded in understanding as Ryan scooted around for Doc, but the scholar winked at him and slowly sat upright.

"I, too, am alive," Doc rumbled softly, wincing as if with a terrible headache. "But only technically, I assure you."

Patting the man on the back, Ryan checked Dean and found his son also awake, only pretending to be unconscious.

"How are your boots, Dad?" he said eagerly. "Mine are okay!"

The man shot the boy a stern look, and Dean blanched at the stupid mistake he'd just done. What a feeb! They were in a cage and the unseen driver could probably hear everything they said. Hot pipe, he might have already given away their only chance at escape!

"They're both okay," Ryan said, pointing overhead, then pressing a finger to his lips.

Awkwardly shuffling to the bars, J.B. studied the lock, then turned away in disgust. There was no lock, just a length of steel chain bolted in place. No way he could open that from the inside, even if he had a wrench big enough to do the job.

Looking at the passing ville outside, he saw the houses were predark, rebuilt into decent condition. The road was paved, broken sections patched with pieces of sidewalk giving the roadway an odd checkerboard appearance. Chained slaves were everywhere, small children whipping a crippled old man who was trying to sweep a dirty floor with his bare hands. A squad of sec men marched a badly bleeding man toward a hangman's gallows. In a tavern, a young girl stood silently weeping with her serving tray held high as the drunken customers pawed at her budding breasts.

"This isn't Cascade," J.B. stated, fumbling in the

shadows to check his boots. The laces were still tied. He glanced at Ryan and they nodded. A moment of privacy was all they needed.

"Indeed not, John Barrymore," Doc agreed, tucking his legs together in a yoga position. "And if we had been taken by Mitchum and Glassman, they would surely be standing alongside to gloat. This must be some unknown ville on the island."

"A secret ville on Forbidden Island," Ryan muttered thoughtfully. Then loudly said, "Could be throwbacks, or even pirates."

"We're pirates!" boomed a voice from the front of the cage. "The true rulers of the world! Now shut up."

Going to the front of the cage, Ryan reached through as far as he could with his tied hands and tugged on the dangling coat of the unseen man driving the horse and cart.

"Hey!" a voice called out. "Do that again, and I'll use the whip! The baron wants you alive, but he never said undamaged. So be still!"

Alive, eh? "Fuck that crap," Ryan snarled, attempting to check the man's reactions. "Tell me where you're taking us, or I'll rip out your guts with my bare hands!"

"Ain't telling you shit," the driver snapped, and lashed down with a whip.

Ryan yanked his hands away from the bars just in time to miss losing flesh. The man was fast, and serious. A dangerous opponent.

"We can pay," J.B. said from the other side. "I know the formula for—"

"Nukeshit," the driver interrupted. "You know shit, and you got shit, so don't give me no shit. You belong to his nibs, and that means you're dead. What can a dead man give me?''

Then he roared in laughter and pulled out a 9 mm Heckler & Koch blaster. ''Besides, I already got your blaster!''

Retreating to the center of the cage, the companions rode through the bumps as the cart rolled up a short flight of stone steps and onto an older street made of cobblestones, the granite pegs worn smooth by the passage of the years.

Suddenly a mob of children shrieked in delight at the arrival of the cage and started pelting the prisoners with stones. The men moved quickly into a huddle to protect their faces, and grunted with the impact of every hard-thrown rock. The driver allowed it for a while, then whipped the brats away.

As the men released one another, they could now observe that this was a much nicer section of the ville. The houses were bigger, and many had glass in their window frames. There were no more farmers selling in the street, and the men and women slowly walking by were dressed in fine clothes with no patches, boots polished, faces well fed. Only the men wore the wide leather belts of a sailor, but both sexes carried blasters on their hips. Often they had liveried servants carrying parcels, or holding umbrellas to keep the sun off their fancy masters.

''Officers' quarters,'' Ryan said.

The horses whinnied as the driver took them up an inclined road, to crest onto a higher level. Here the road was made of redbrick, and the cart wheeled past a yard-tall stone wall lined with heavy cannons, mounds of cannonballs and bags of powder placed close nearby. The gunners stared at the passing prisoners, laughing and making crude comments. Each man wore a wide leather belt with a short sword thrust through. Many were barefoot, with rags tied about their heads to keep the wind from blowing hair into eyes. No lacy dandies here—these were fighting men, the defenders of the ville.

Rubbing a rock bruise on his shoulder, Ryan guessed it was these guards who fired cannons at the *Pegasus* when it arrived. He looked them over carefully, but saw no signs of recent scratches on their faces. Maybe Krysty, Jak and Mildred slipped free and were safe in the jungle. But there was no way of telling without giving away their presence on the island fortress. He would have to play this very carefully, or they'd all go under the yoke.

More buildings moved past the companions, sturdy structures of brick and concrete, most with sandbags lining the roofs as protection from incoming cannonballs. No children were in sight here, no peddlers, or dogs, and Ryan knew they had reached the heart of the ville. The baron's fortress.

As the cart rattled to a halt in a small courtyard, a dozen men surrounded the iron cage with blasters in their hands. Most were muzzleloading flintlocks, but a few were predark revolvers, and one tall bald man with small ears carried a Thompson machine gun. Ryan marked him as the sec chief.

Burly men walked forward with wrenches and released the chains only after a lot of grunting and a few bleeding knuckles. J.B. reasoned this wasn't standard procedure for prisoners, and wondered what made them special, and how the info could be used to their advantage.

As the door swung aside on squealing hinges, the

companions exited one at a time, the pirates keeping them covered with several blasters. Each had the ropes on his feet cut away, but they were lashed together again by chains around their necks. In single file, the companions marched along the brick street, unable to do more than study their surroundings.

The fortress rising before them sported iron grilles on the windows and a massive double door thick enough to stop any blaster round. Inside, the floor was smooth marble, predark lighting fixtures adorning the high ceilings, the walls decorated with faded pictures and recently added gun racks. Doc reasoned this abode was formerly a museum for the tourists visiting the paradise of the Marshall Islands.

"Stop searching for a way out," a bearded man snarled, and lashed Ryan across the back with a strap. "If the baron didn't want you alive, I'd flay you till your bones dropped out for such insolence!"

So the pirate baron really did want them alive, eh? Good. Spinning, Ryan slammed the toe of his boot into the man's gut with all of his strength, the tip hitting just below the lip of the rib cage. Going livid, the pirate staggered backward and dropped his whip, then toppled over.

"Stop your gaffing," a sailor snorted, nudging the big man with a longblaster.

There was no response.

"Pete?" the sailor asked faintly, kneeling by the fallen man to check for a wound. "Nuke me, he…got no breath. Lieutenant Pawter, the fucking outlander aced him!"

"Aced him with a kick," the tall man with the machine gun said, working the bolt on the ancient blaster. "Most impressive."

''Pete was me mate, you modderfucker!'' another snarled, cocking back the hammer on a flintlock and pointing the blaster.

''Belay that!'' Pawter ordered, and the rest stopped advancing toward the prisoners.

The lieutenant then shifted the aim of his rapidfire toward the chained men. ''Nobody goes near Blackie anymore. That bastard is dangerous. Keep your blasters on him at all times. Next move he makes, wound the boy and castrate him on the spot.''

Saying nothing, Ryan locked eyes with the lieutenant, and they exchanged a private conversation. Then Ryan eased his stance and started walking along the corridor.

''Yes, very dangerous I see,'' Pawter said, keeping a clear field of fire between himself and the outlanders. ''Mebbe you are exactly what we need.''

''Try that move again, One-eye,'' the first sailor snarled, drawing a second blaster, this one with a dozen tiny barrels like a honeycomb, ''and this pepperbox will show your guts the ground.''

Ryan ignored the guard, keeping his attention on the lieutenant. It wasn't only that rapidfire that made him the most deadly enemy in sight.

Marching along some branching corridor and up a grand flight of stairs, the guards stopped the prisoners before an ornate door covered with delicate carvings and intact human hides, the skin perfectly tanned and complete in every detail from the scalp to the genitalia. Doc muttered something in Latin and received a slap to the head that made the man reel.

''No talking,'' the sailor grunted, raising a hand to deal another blow.

Doc raised himself to his full height and glared defiantly at the other man when Pawter spoke.

"Boss said alive," the lieutenant reminded, the barrel of the Thompson shifting away from the prisoners to point at the angry sailor.

The man noticed the action and lowered his hand, stepping away. "You're mine, prick," he muttered threateningly.

Uncaring, the big guards at the door watched the events, but did nothing. Both were armed with big-bore revolvers, the ammo loops in their police gun belts full of fat rounds. The men were scraped clean and smelled faintly of perfume, their clothing sharply pressed and meticulously clean.

Almost as if they were women, Ryan noted mentally, suppressing an expression of disgust.

Stepping close so nobody else could see, Pawter gave the guards some kind of a complicated hand signal. They responded, then drew their blasters and pushed back the heavy doors, admitting the prisoners into the next room. The barrels of their blasters never wavered from the passing outlanders.

A short antechamber led past what resembled a ticket booth and then opened into an auditorium filled with rows of chairs. At the far end was a stage with a single huge chair on a raised dais. An older man was sitting in the simple throne while a group of frowning men studied the wreckage of the *Pegasus*. A long table nearby held their backpacks and weapons laid out on display.

Shuffling his boots along the ratty carpet, Ryan almost smiled at the sight, but again withheld comment.

"Yes, I can have my girls patch these bags," a

young man said, fingering the cloth of the weather balloons. "But what do we fill them with?"

"We'll ask them," Baron Withers said, rising from his throne.

The man stood big and broad, at first looking fat to the newcomers, but under closer inspection there was only hard muscle showing. Long curly hair was braided into a ponytail and tucked inside his pants, and every inch of exposed skin was a dark brown, but whether naturally or from decades under the tropical sun, there was no way of knowing. The baron wore military fatigues, clean but rumpled as if put on in a hurry. Matching revolvers were tucked into his wide leather belt, the hands turned inward for a cross draw, and an Uzi submachine gun hung over one shoulder. J.B. didn't recognize it as his blaster. Same make and model, but then Millie had told him that the Uzi was one of the most popular rapidfires before skydark. Only made sense he'd encounter another someday.

As the guards moved away from the prisoners, Pawter kept them covered with the rapidfire.

"This them?" the baron demanded, walking to the edge of the stage.

"Bruised, but alive," the lieutenant replied.

"Thought we'd lose at least one," Withers said, almost sounding disappointed. "Okay, who are you and what are you doing on my island?"

"You the baron here?" Ryan asked.

Frowning, Baron Withers pointed at Dean. "Him," he ordered.

With a roundhouse swing, a guard punched Dean in the side of the head and the boy dropped. He held his face in both hands, blood dribbling onto the floor.

Barely controlling his rage, Ryan wasn't surprised at the results, although Dean was strong for his age, he was still a boy, not a man yet.

"You were talking to me," Ryan said gruffly, taking a step forward.

"Then answer my bastard questions," Withers replied, glowering at him. "And the next time you answer a question with a question, Andrew will remove an ear."

A guard drew a wicked knife, the curved blade deeply serrated, made for sawing through bone. "Aye, sir." He grinned, displaying broken teeth.

"I know the formula for black powder," J.B. stated loud and clear.

The guards chuckled at the announcement, and Withers broke into a laugh. Their reactions startled the companions, the formula had been an ace in the hole. Black powder was the backbone of the lord baron's wealth and power. Nobody alive knew what it was made of.

"Do you now?" the baron stated. "How nice. Well, so do I. Forced it from one of the lord baron's barrel boys four seasons ago. That won't buy you anything here, outlander."

"Name's Ryan," he stated. "That's Doc, J.B. and Dean."

"Better," Withers muttered. "Now tell me about your flying machine."

"I think it's broken," Dean drawled through bleeding lips as he climbed back to his feet.

A snarling guard rushed forward, but Ryan blocked the man's way with his body.

"Harm another one of us and you're dead in the water," he stated. "This isn't something simple like black powder. You'll never get the air wag to fly again without our help."

Ryan turned to face the baron. "Our willing help," he added gruffly. "Or else the blast will level this bastard island."

It was obviously a lie, but how much was bullshit, how much the truth? Buying time, Withers filled a brass mug from a crystal decanter. He slurped the homemade beer, trickles running down his cheeks, then slammed down the brass shell and beamed a smile.

"Fair enough. We'll cut a deal. Pawter, remove their chains."

"My lord?" the lieutenant asked askance.

"Do it!" Withers commanded. Then softly added, "After all, we have their three friends, and at the first lie…" He drew a thumb along his neck while making a guttural noise.

Ryan felt hope flare deep inside and tried his best not to show any emotion. They were alive!

The chains around their necks were removed, but the ropes around their hands stayed in place. Ryan didn't mind. It was the metal that had been holding them back. Now they could make a move.

"So tell us," a fat, bearded man on stage demanded gruffly. "What are these bags filled with?"

Rubbing his chafed neck, Ryan scowled. "You want that here?" he said to the baron. "With all these ears present?"

"Stop stalling," Withers growled. "These are my private council. What I know, so do they. Now start talking."

"Doc invented it," Ryan said.

A sailor scowled. "The old man did?"

"Indeed I did, sir. And I will elucidate, if I may," Doc rumbled in his best schoolroom manner, and started up the stairs leading to the stage.

"Talk English," Withers demanded, swinging the Uzi around to lay it on his lap. "Last chance, old man."

"But of course, your noble highness."

The baron roared with laughter. "Highness, that's a good one. I may keep you around, old-timer."

Which meant the rest would be killed as soon as the secret of the balloon was revealed. Doc had a terrible flashback to being captured by Cort Strasser, who tortured him horribly every day. The old man shook his head. Never again would that happen. Doc would rather die than suffer such ignoble torment once more.

"Do you have any chalk?" he asked. "I need to draw a picture."

"Chalk?" the baron said as a question. The other men on stage shrugged in ignorance.

"It is a soft white stone used to make pictures," Doc explained to their blank faces. "No chalk, eh? Never mind, I can use a knife and scratch a picture on the floor."

The old man went to his knees and ran hands along the veneer of the old wood. "Yes, this will do nicely."

"No knives," Pawter said.

"But I need something," Doc complained, looking helplessly at the baron, then at the table full of their equipment.

"My cane," he said gesturing at the table laden with their belongings. "That has a steel tip. I can use my cane. Surely that is not a danger, and I need something.''

''I can go outside and get a sharp piece of coral,'' Pawter suggested.

Doc felt his bowels run cold. That damn man would ruin everything.

''Give him the stick,'' the baron directed impatiently. ''Let's get this going.''

A sailor took the stick and, holding it by the shaft, offered it to the scholar. ''Here, now get writing!''

Casually, Doc seized the lion's head of the stick, gave it a twist and stepped away with bare steel in his hand. Before anybody could react to the sight, Doc lunged forward and slipped the point through the neck of the guard before him. The man tried to yell, but only gargled from the red blood pouring out of his destroyed throat.

Doc swung around and Ryan was already on the stage, his hands as far apart as the ropes would allow. The razor-sharp steel sword sliced easily through the plastic, and Ryan slammed both of his fists into the faces of onrushing sec men, teeth and bones breaking from the powerful blows. As they crumbled, Ryan grabbed a blaster from the fallen man and fired a round at the baron, who was fumbling with the Uzi. The miniball impacted into the wood of his throne, missing his head by the thickness of a hair. But the startled pirate dropped the rapidfire to the stage floor.

''Chill them!'' Baron Withers roared, drawing both revolvers from his belt, when the spent blaster arrived, hitting him hard in the throat. Withers dropped his weapons and clawed at his neck, fighting for air from his crushed windpipe.

''Save the baron!'' Pawter shouted, leading a rush of guards.

Knowing this was their only chance, J.B. threw himself to the floor and rolled into their path. Two dodged out of the way, but two more tripped over the Armorer and went sprawling. Punching one in the groin, J.B. buried his teeth into the other guard's throat, ripping free a ragged gobbet of flesh, veins and ligaments stretching horribly from the ghastly wound.

A sec man was drawing a bead on his father, so Dean spun and kicked the guard directly in the stomach. The man doubled over coughing, but didn't drop his blaster, so the boy slammed a knee into his face, crushing the nose in a bloody spray. Then Dean wrapped his tied hands around the man's throat and tried to throw him over a shoulder. The sec man jerked from the attempt, his neck making a loud snapping sound, and then he crumpled to the floor with a broken neck.

Grabbing his blaster, Dean fired at Pawter just as he reached the throne, blowing off the back of the lieutenant's head. As the corpse toppled, the boy rushed forward for the Thompson still held in the twitching fingers. But another guard got there first and started fiddling with the rapidfire, trying to make it work.

Dodging incoming lead, Doc abandoned killing strikes and stabbed his sword stick among the sec men, wounding as many as possible. A shot was fired that tugged on his coat, death avoided only because he was constantly in motion. But he had expected as much. Black powder was rare and valuable in these islands, which meant that target practice was virtually nil, and thus not many were marksmen with a blaster.

Reaching the throne, Ryan grabbed the twin Webley .44 revolvers from the retching baron and blasted a path to the weapons table. But a dying man bumped into it, knocking the backpacks and weapons everywhere. Tossing away the spent revolvers, Ryan grabbed the first thing in sight and turned to fire the Uzi at an onrushing guard. He was gambling all of their lives on the belief that the sailors might have pulled the clip, but wouldn't think of working the bolt to eject the round in the chamber. The Uzi roared, and the shrieking man clutched his ruined face, eyes and teeth flowing between his blood-smeared fingers.

Spinning away, Ryan dodged a thrown knife and grabbed a clip for the rapidfire. Slamming it in, he jerked the bolt and cut loose, the stuttering machine pistol spraying copper-jacketed 9 mm rounds into the startled sailors. A round hit the table alongside him, spraying out splinters, and he winced as several stabbed into his bruised leg. Those damn rocks had done more damage than he first thought.

Ignoring the minor pain, Ryan thumbed the selector switch to auto and rode the rapidfire into tight groupings, the barrage of hot lead knocking down the sailors. The bolt kicked back when the clip was spent, and Ryan went around the table to grab the LeMat. Remembering Doc's lectures on the oddball blaster, he clicked back the hammer before pulling the trigger and unleashed thunder, the last sailor slammed off the floor as he rushed up the aisle for the exit. The slug hit him in the back, blood splashing onto the wood in front. But incredibly, the sailor still fumbled with the latch. Holding down the trigger, Ryan fanned the hammer and put a barrage of miniballs into the man before he finally surrendered and slid to the floor in a crumbled heap.

"Tough son of a bitch," Ryan growled, tossing Doc the LeMat and taking the Steyr and SIG-Sauer.

"Good work, Doc," J.B. said as the old man cut away his ropes.

"Violence is the last resort of the thinking man," Doc said in a singsong manner that meant he was quoting somebody. "But only a fool refuses to face the fact when it becomes the option for life."

Dean limped to the table. Ryan cut the boy's ropes, he briefly inspected his face, which was already turning purple, but it was only a bruise.

"You okay?" Ryan asked.

"Been better," he mumbled through puffy lips. "Give me a blaster."

Just then the doors slammed open and guards rushed into the throne room, waving blasters. Taking cover behind the rows of chairs, J.B. mowed them down with the Thompson. The ancient blaster chattered a stream of .45 rounds at the startled men, tearing them apart.

As the last man fell, J.B. and Doc raced to close the doors and dropped a heavy locking bar into place, only moments before something heavy hit the doors from the other side.

"Reinforcements are here!" J.B. announced as he and Doc started piling benches, chairs and anything else they could find in front of the double doors as a barricade.

"This will hold for a while," Doc stated, busy hands already purging the spent chambers of his weapon. "But I fear not for long."

Riffling the still living baron for spare ammo, he

found several shells for the Webleys and reloaded the blasters. Roughly hauling the baron off the battered throne, Ryan fired a round right next to the man's ear, the muzzle-flash washing over the appendage. Writhing in pain, Withers gurgled incomprehensibly, clutching the blistered flesh.

"Where's your escape route?" Ryan demanded as the main doors thudded again across the auditorium. There was no response, so he shook the man hard. "Show me!"

Weakly, Withers pointed, still unable to properly breathe, much less talk with his ruined throat. Ruthlessly, Ryan dragged the dying man along to show the way. He didn't like torture, but it was the baron's life or their own. No contest. Desperately, Ryan wanted to ask about Krysty and the others, but since Withers couldn't speak, there was no point.

A heavy red curtain covered the wall behind the throne, and hidden under a second tapestry was a small door made of old steel, pieces of metal bolted into place for additional armor.

"Found it!" Ryan announced when Withers got loose in a burst of strength and managed to pull a derringer from his shirt. The baron shoved the tiny blaster into the outlander's face, just as Ryan triggered both Webleys at point-blank range. The double blast literally blew the man in two, his face a rictus of shock as the derringer harmlessly discharged toward the ceiling.

Shoving the warm body aside, J.B. rummaged in his munitions bag and got busy with his lock picks on the door, while Ryan stood guard, Dean and Doc dragging over the table and the throne for protection. Minutes ticked by and the main door remained quiet, which only meant that the pirates were trying something new.

"Got it," J.B. said, and Ryan leveled the twin Webley blasters while the door opened.

The brick room beyond was small and dark, lacking even a window. Doc flicked a match into life on the wall and the tiny flame revealed an arsenal of blasters: flintlocks, revolvers, longblasters, shotguns, pepperboxes and a dozen huge barrels of black powder. There were even a few cases of grens.

As they filled their pockets with ammo, Ryan paused for a moment at the sight of a bolt-action longblaster, a Weatherby .460 Nitro Express. The bullets looked even bigger than the man-stoppers used by a Barrett 1A. He debated the matter for a precious moment, then grabbed the Weatherby and passed it to Dean.

"Try this," his father suggested. "We'll need the extra firepower."

Without a word, Dean slid the longblaster over a shoulder and raided the boxes for the bulky ammo. The balance of the heavy Weatherby was odd, but the boy was sure he could handle the recoil.

"This must be the treasure trove of the pirates," J.B. said, keeping a watch out the door. "Stuff they got off all the ships they raided and sank."

"Take the grens," Ryan directed, stuffing his pockets. "Then find a fuse. We'll need a diversion to help us get out of here and find the others."

"No prob," J.B. said, leaving the door to rip the top off a wooden crate to reach the HE grens packed in soft straw.

"Old friend, I fear to offer the suggestion," Doc rumbled hesitantly, accepting a few of the checkered globes. ''But the others may already be across the River Styx. In the arms of Morpheus eternal, as they say.''

Grimly, Ryan worked the bolt on the Steyr, slamming in a fresh rotary clip. ''Mebbe,'' he admitted. ''But I'll need to see their dead bodies before leaving.''

There was a small explosion near the double doors, and through the swirling gray smoke charged a swarm of men who began to climb over the smashed barricade with sharp knives held in their teeth.

''Let's go,'' Ryan ordered, and walked from the armory firing at every step.

Chapter Seven

A chill took Krysty, and she instantly awoke to find herself stark naked and strapped spread-eagled on a hard bed.

The room was large and well lit, golden sunlight streaming in through the open windows. Old faded decorative paper with flowers and grapes covered the walls, the ceiling a rough stucco popular with rich civvies for some unknown reason. Nude centerfolds from girlie mags had been pasted into picture frames here and there. A large armoire with hinged doors stood near a small table with a wash basin, a stoppered jug of water and several bottles of homemade shine. The only door in sight was closed and bolted shut.

Krysty tested the ropes holding her to the posts of the canopied bed and found them much too strong to break. Sniffing, the woman realized the sheets were old and used, reeking faintly of rancid sweat.

Across the room, Mildred was also stripped naked, and tied up in a heavy wooden chair. The physician seemed unharmed.

"Awake, at last," a silky voice purred. "Good. I much prefer it when my sluts know what's happening to them."

In a shadowy corner of the bedroom, a short woman rose from a wingback chair and padded over to the companions. The newcomer was beautiful; there was no denying that. Wavy ebony hair hung down to her trim waist, and firm breasts pushed against the front of her flower-print dress, making the fabric gape between the taut buttons. Her face was oval, with a pointed chin, her arms and long legs smooth and evenly tanned.

"Where are we?" Krysty asked softly, glancing at the closed door. "No, tell me later. Cut us free and we'll help you escape."

The young woman laughed in an easy manner.

"I don't want to escape," she said, going over to the bed and sitting on the mattress. "I'm the madam here and run this gaudy house, and you're my new sluts."

"Never," Mildred spit, struggling against her bounds, but the ropes were good, and the chair seemed to be nailed to the floor. Almost as if it were built in place for just the purpose of holding an unwilling woman helpless.

"I will attend to you later," the madam said in a voice of stone.

Turning back to Krysty, the woman reached out to cup the redhead's left breast and gently squeeze, savoring the delicious flesh. Krysty recoiled from the unnatural contact, which only made the madam chuckle.

"Don't like it, eh?" the madam purred. "Get used to it, bitch. We service both men and women here. A lot of men will ride your peach before the fuzz wears off. An' I will earn a lot of gold and blasters before I toss you to the drunken sailors on a ship to be their barrel girl. Know what that is, red? Let me tell you."

Crawling over the naked woman, the madam whispered horrid and obscene things into her ear.

Suddenly, there came the sound of water hitting the floor, and the madam looked over a shoulder and smiled at Mildred, strapped to her chair in a puddle of urine.

"Wet yourself in fear?" The madam chuckled, climbing off Krysty onto the floor, not caring where her knees stabbed into the prisoner. "And we haven't even kissed hello."

"Fucking psycho!" Mildred spit. "Perverted freak!"

"You may call me Sophie," the mutie said, grinning and walking closer. "And soon that mouth will be pleasuring me, one way or the other."

Sophie grabbed Mildred by the hair and pulled her head back. The physician grunted from the pain, but still managed to spit at the woman.

"Fight, yes, that's good. Struggle all you want," Sophie said, licking the bound woman along her cheek, then stepping back and brutally slapping her face with two resounding cracks.

Her nails raked down Mildred's spine, leaving bloody furrows.

Unable to help her friend, Krysty thrashed about in the bed, frantic to get loose. Slamming back and forth in the chair, Mildred tried to avoid the touch of her tormentor. Finally, the madam walked away, and tiny droplets of blood trickled down Mildred's back to mix with the fluid on the dirty floor.

Weeping uncontrollably, Mildred started banging her head on the chair, her shoulders shaking with shame and rage.

"Now the fun begins," Sophie announced, laughing happily, fumbling in the closet to extract a set of long leather whips.

"Now, which slut to tame first?" Sophie said thoughtfully, chewing a fingernail. "Red, or shorty, both look so nice. Oh, I cannot wait to hear your screams for mercy. Speak up, who'd like to taste the lash first?"

"E-eat sh-shit, bitch," Mildred taunted, her splayed fingers clawing the air.

Sophie contorted her features into a hideous scowl and strode toward the helpless physician. "Get ready, my pretty," she growled, clawed hands reaching out for her prisoner.

Unexpectedly, Mildred screamed in defiance, and her hands came free from the broken arm of the chair, which she had been working on all this time. Sophie stepped back, and Mildred expertly swung her arm about to drive the splintery end of a dowel directly into the kidney of the woman.

Gasping in shock, Sophie fell to the floor, blood gushing from the wound. Snarling in anger, Mildred leaned over and beat the mutie on the temple with the solid chair arm, the skull bone audibly cracking.

Throwing away the makeshift club, Mildred went to work on the rest of the knots. When the last rope yielded, the doctor rose from the chair and shuffled over to Krysty. At the bedside table, the physician poured some water on her hands from a ceramic mug to clean away the filth, then smashed the jug and used the sharp shards to cut her friend loose.

"How...?" Krysty began to ask, her hair flexing wildly on the stained pillows.

"I pissed on the plastic rope to make it slippery," she explained, finishing one arm and starting on the other. "Got one hand free while she was amusing herself, then broke off the arm of the chair when I was banging my head. Come on, let's find our stuff."

"And where the others are," Krysty said, walking to the closet where the madam had stored her whips.

Inside hung a collection of sexual devices the likes of which Krysty could only guess about. It also held their clothes, and knives, but not their backpacks or blasters. Dressing quickly, they searched the bedroom and found a stash of flintlocks and pouches of black powder in a bottom drawer of the mahogany armoire.

"Have to make do," Mildred grumbled unhappily, hefting the muzzleloader and checking the spring that drove the flint onto the flash pan. "Damnation, this piece of crap is going to misfire half the time. The flint is as blunt as a baron's wit."

"New flints," Krysty said, and brought over a cardboard box of the sharpened stones.

The women easily repaired the blasters, and armed themselves with as many as they could comfortably carry: two in their belts, one in each boot and one at the small of their backs. Fully armed, they listened at the door and heard only the sounds of muttering voices and soft cries of pleasure.

Going to the window, they looked at the ville below—winding cobblestoned streets, red tile roofs and swimming pools now used to store drinking water.

"This was a resort hotel once," Mildred declared, a blaster in hand as she peeked out the shutters. "I know the chain."

"Appears to be a pirate base now," Krysty added.

"Maybe their main base?"

"Could be. But if it is, then Ryan and the others will be with the baron."

"There," Mildred said. "That fancy place on the hill. It's got to be the baron's mansion."

"Quiet," Krysty whispered, leaning into the ocean wind.

Mildred tried to hear what had caught her attention, but could only discern some faint cheering. Glancing around, the crowd noises seemed to be coming from a crumbling sports arena with raised bleachers and a grandstand.

"Is it Ryan?" Mildred asked, knowing that J.B. would be with him. The men were brothers in everything but name.

"No, it's Jak." Krysty frowned. "I can faintly hear something about the albino outlander going up against Big Mike."

There sounded a large roar from the crowd.

"Local fans like the idea," Mildred said, furrowing her brow, knowing that arena fights were never fair and always deadly. All of the companions had fought their share.

Looking down, she saw the ground was only two stories below. An easy climb, even as sore as the women were. She ached in places that had never ached before, and her back felt stiff from the drying blood of those scratches. Mildred only hoped the abrasions didn't go septic. Her med kit wasn't in the room.

"We've got to try to help him," Mildred said, closing the shutters. Going to a side window, she found that one overlooked an alleyway. Perfect.

"Better hide our trail first," Krysty advised.

Going back inside, Mildred saw the madam try to rise from the crimson-stained floor and collapsed back down, the floorboards shaking from the impact.

"Might get some folks checking on her soon," Krysty said.

"Get that jug of shine," Mildred stated, taking the armoire and shoving it in front of the door. The cabinet wasn't that heavy, but it should buy them some time.

Already, Krysty was pouring the shine on the floor and walls. Mildred yanked the dirty sheets off the bed and ripped them into long strips, which she then knotted into a crude rope. Meanwhile, Krysty poured all of the excess black powder on the floor and removed the corks from the unused bottles of shine and placed them carefully on top of the loose powder. Tying one end of the rope to a bedpost, Mildred tossed the other end out the window and started climbing down into the alley.

Close behind her, Krysty placed a closed bottle of shine on the window ledge and shimmied down next. Reaching the ground, she lit the rope with her butane lighter and it promptly caught, the flames licking up the rope to reach the sealed bottle of homebrew. After only a few moments, it burst apart, sending pieces of glass and burning shine everywhere. There was a brief pause before there was a whoosh, and blue flames began to lick out the open window. Mildred nodded. Good enough.

Moving quickly, the women darted down the alleyway, trying to keep out of sight as they headed for the arena. But turning a corner, Krysty and Mildred found themselves facing a squad of sec men lounging against a wall and smoking hand-rolled green cigars.

"And who the fuck are you two, strangers?" the sergeant demanded, glaring suspiciously over his smoldering stogie.

ONLY A FEW BLOCKS away, the line of chained slaves moved through a short dark tunnel toward death, step by grueling step. For Jak, the throbbing of his sprained ankle was worse than ever since the pirates had removed the bandage to see if it was hiding a weapon.

The curved walls of the concrete passageway were battered and in disrepair, water stains edged with black mildew and greenish-blue molds, with tiny yellow flowers. One of the slaves before him plucked a flower and sniffed its delicate perfume. Poor bastard. If he survived these contests, or whatever they were heading for, he'd be sorry he touched that flower. It was wart rot, nasty stuff Jak had encountered in the bayou. The mold consumed human flesh, invading your entire body until the victim fell to the ground and burst apart, a loose flap of crumbling skin jammed full of greenish-blue mold. As the line shuffled past a particularly dense patch, Jak held his breath, then breathed through his shirt. Hopefully, that would be enough.

''Next!'' a gruff voice called out, and the line of old men, blind teenagers and crippled children surged forward once more.

One of the first things Jak noticed was there were no women in the group. But then, old, blind or cripple, the pirates had a use for any woman.

Chained at the neck and ankles, hands tied, there was little Jak could do about escaping until it was his turn at the head of the line. His blaster and knives were gone, and while he had something in his boot, it would take forever to get it out with tied hands. No, that old trick of the Trader would be of no use to the teenager this day. He wondered if it would be single combat with an armed opponent or a simple execution? But he didn't hear any blasterfire, so the entertainment was most likely not a firing squad. That was both good and bad.

There was a commotion ahead of him, the crowd roared in approval and the line moved again. Stepping forward, Jak moved from the shadows into the sunlight. Blinking against the brightness, he could see it was high noon, and the predark arena was mostly in ruins, whole sections reduced to piles of broken concrete and twisted steel. Teams of slaves were working in the rubble, effecting slow repairs. But the rest of the place was packed with dozens, maybe even hundreds of people spread across the levels seated at tables, waving bottles of shine, eating snacks, drunkenly cheering and making bets with the local jack.

A lot of the folks in better clothes were spooning a purple powder to their faces, and Jak recognized it even at this distance as jolt.

An old word that Doc used occasionally came unbidden to his mind: decadent. The teenager nodded to himself. Yeah, a bunch of feeb druggies getting their jollies watching folks get snuffed. Ever since his wife and child had passed away, Jak had prepared himself for the day when he also would go into the great blackness. Krysty talked about the spirit of the world, Mildred of the human soul. Jak only believed in honor and a warrior's dignity. If he was going on the last train west, he would make it something the freaking pirates would remember for years.

"Next!" that same voice called out.

Jak shuffled forward, and through the crowd of armed guards he could catch a peek at the arena below. The playing field had been divided into four unequal areas by stout brick walls topped with iron spikes, the churned soil in each puddled with red blood. In the first was a pack of wild boars stomping a headless corpse, their tusks ripping out huge gouts of flesh with every strike. In the next a huge lionlike cat was mauling a youth with its claws until the screaming ceased, then the beast tossed away the body with a head shake. In the third pit were stickies, hooting insanely as the crowd actually tossed handfuls of jolt into the air, and laughed as the drug drifted down onto the humanoid muties. The fourth contained only bones, with something moving below the soil out of sight, only the disturbances on top of the ground marking its passage. The teen nodded. Fair enough. If he had any say in his destination, Jak certainly knew which of these he'd choose. No question about that.

"Next!" the voice called.

"Here, motherfucker," Jak snarled, and held out his wrists.

"Ah, a mutie!" A pirate chuckled as a slave undid the albino teen's neck chains, then released his wrists.

Jak rubbed his wrists while the lead restraints were removed. He walked through the crowd of guards and looked over the crowd. The people laughed at the albino, and bets were placed, handfuls of live ammo exchanged across the grandstand.

"Nice jacket. Give it to me," another grunted, holding out a tiny knife, the blade no more than three inches, "and I'll give you this knife."

Jak considered it. "Fair deal," he said, and slid off his leather jacket, then slapped it across the face of the guard.

The sec man screamed, the razor blades and bits of

barbed wire sown into the collar and lapels ripping apart his flesh and removing an eye. Jak tossed the jacket at the nearest guards, and they recoiled from the garment, unsure of exactly what had just happened. Spinning, Jak kneed another in the groin and took his blaster, firing over the falling body at the next sec man. The flame from the muzzle covered the man's head, the miniball exploding his skull, sending a grisly rain over the closest attendees.

The teen grabbed a chair and turned to find a score of blasters pointing his way. He hesitated for a moment, then lowered the chair, his bid for freedom gone.

"Tough little bastard, ain't ya?" a pirate roared, and slapped the teenager across the face.

Jak filled his mouth with bloody saliva and spit it back at the sec man.

"Lord Baron Kinnison says hello," he said, sneering, hoping they might think he had the same disease as the dying master of the islands.

It seemed to work, because the sec men moved farther away, their hands no longer quite so steady with their blasters.

"Chill him!" the bleeding man on the floor cried, his face horribly disfigured. "Set him on fire! Give him to the worms!"

"Aye," the big sec man muttered. "It's been long enough for them to be hungry again. We'll toss him to the worms."

The word was relayed across the grandstand, and the viewers shifted their seats for a better view of the fourth arena.

"Like worms," Jak snarled. "Eat them for breakfast."

The sailors laughed at the show of bravado, and Jak shifted his plans. Maybe he could earn their respect and get enlisted. That would give him the chance to help his friends. If they were still alive.

"That buys you a drink," a sec man said with a chuckle, passing over a greasy bottle.

Jak took a sniff and forced himself to recoil. "What is?" he demanded. "Horse piss?"

The big sec man lost his grin and shoved a blaster into the teenager's side. "Shut up and drink," he ordered, obviously angered that the gesture had been rebuked. "And for every drop you miss, off comes a toe. Eh? How's that, gimp?"

"Fair," Jak told him, taking a long swig. Then sprayed the bitter brew into the pirate's eyes.

Momentarily blinded, the sec man fired his blaster, but Jak had already moved, the .44 miniball slamming into the guard behind the teenager. Clutching his chest, the startled man stumbled backward and fell into the nearest pit.

Kicking another man in the knee, Jak felt the bone break. As a guard rushed forward, the teenager smashed the bottle over his head and stole the guard's knife. With half their number aced in a few moments, the remaining guards scrambled for distance to safely use their blasters. Meanwhile, the crowd roared its approval as Jak buried the broken end of the bottle into the face of a bearded pirate, twisting the shards in deep. The mutilated sailor howled in agony, falling to his knees on the suddenly bloody floor. With lightning-fast hands, Jak grabbed his blaster and a second blade, then started for the tunnel, the only escape route available.

But the guards were already rushing toward him

with raised chairs as shields. Shifting plans, Jak fired the blaster, catching the slave with the keys in the belly. The man slumped over in pain, the keys clattering as they fell to the ground. The line of slaves stared in wonder at the sight, then dived upon the keys, insanely fighting among themselves to get loose first.

A guard rushed Jak with an ax. The teen blocked the strike with the spent blaster and grabbed a fresh weapon from his attacker. Then the others swarmed over him, and the teenager was forced off the grandstand and fell into a pit himself.

The crowd redoubled its yells of delight as the wild boars raced upon the sprawled teenager, blood from their last chill dripping off their razor-sharp tusks.

Chapter Eight

The trembling slaves stood in a bunch on the deck of the PT boat, staring in open horror at the island only a hundred feet away. Most were people dragged from the hovels outside Cascade, beaten and chained as slaves, then herded onto crude rafts of lashed timbers and hauled behind the four petey boats across miles of ocean until reaching this horrid destination. Forbidden Island. To many the words were synonymous with hell.

"You first," Mitchum ordered, grabbing a skinny man by the shoulder and shoving him off the boat. The man hit the water splashing and yelling.

"Swim for shore, idiot!" a sec man shouted angrily at the floundering man. "And when you hit the beach, walk straight."

"But I'll die!" he replied, kicking madly to stay afloat. "The air is poison! Muties everywhere!"

"Convince him otherwise," Glassman ordered from the wheelhouse of the boat.

"Aye, sir." Campbell lowered his longblaster and fired. The slave shouted as the miniball punched into the water near his chest, the tiny geyser splashing onto his face.

"Swim or die," the navvy ordered, another sailor passing him a loaded blaster.

The chained crowd whimpered and muttered

among themselves as they watched the man dogpaddle for the nearby shore. The waves were gentle along that section of the beach, and if there were any riptides that far from the deadly whirlpool, none seized the man and hauled him underwater.

Mitchum scowled from the vessel's bobbing wheelhouse. The crew had dropped anchor, but it did little to smooth the rough waves. Hopefully, it was merely the advance notice of a coming storm, and not the herald of a Deeper arriving.

After delivering its load of people, the petey had swung away from the rest of the boats and assumed a defensive position in the deep waters off the landmass. The pirates couldn't fail to see their arrival, and once they figured out what was going on, they would hit the navvies with everything they had. Against that eventuality, Glassman had given the sec chief a predark revolver from the captain's armory: a .357 Magnum Ruger Redhawk. As a precaution, he tied the blaster to his belt, so it couldn't fall overboard. The blaster weighed a lot, but he had been assured that it hit harder than a .44 flintlock. Mitchum was eagerly looking forward to seeing if that were true.

Battling to stay on the surface, the slave stared at the beach he was heading for. Big rocks that looked like molten glass studded the beach, and the trees beyond were oddly stunted, their trunks twisted and gnarled as if in pain. He flinched as something brushed against him under the water, and he rushed forward to gratefully touch the sloping sand of the shallow shoals, the sand squishing between his bare toes.

Rising timidly from the sea, the man eyed the nearby bushes and wondered for a moment if the sailor could accurately shoot that far, when a blaster sounded and a glass rock on the beach exploded into shards, one of the pieces scoring a bloody scratch along his ribs.

"Keep moving," a voice shouted. "We'll tell you when to stop!"

Swallowing hard, the slave began to shuffle forward, moving around a gaping hole in the ground that seemed to be filled with small pieces of the glasslike rocks, the air about it hazy with a greenish hue. Almost immediately, a wave of weakness flowed through his body, and the slave shivered with unexpected cold. It was becoming hard to focus his vision, he felt dizzy, the taste of metal filled his mouth and every step was becoming more tedious, his legs wobbly as if they were melting. Sweat poured down his face as his teeth chattered, and a ragged cough took his chest. Wiping his mouth, the man saw flecks of blood on his hand. Suddenly, it was impossible to breathe, his lungs laboring to draw in the smallest sip of air. His teeth began to ache, and blood poured from his nose. He coughed again, and his teeth fell to the ground, along with a sprinkling of his hair. What was happening to him? Unable to think clearly, he turned and started back for the ocean, thinking in a wild delirium that he would be okay again if he could just get back on the petey.

The waves washed over his feet, the salt stinging like acid, when there came a puff from the boats moored offshore and something hit him very hard in the chest. The pain became a warm numbness, and he fell backward into a black pit without a bottom.

"Was that necessary?" Campbell asked, lowering his longblaster.

"Yes," Glassman said, reloading the flintlock. "If the slaves know that we'll ace them when it gets too bad, then they won't dash about madly and ruin the chart."

"Makes sense, sir," the sailor reluctantly agreed.

"You're next," a navvy ordered, grabbing a young woman by the arm and shoving her into the water.

Far away, Mitchum eagerly watched as she swam to shore, then walked along the beach, about fifty feet to the left of the corpse sprawled in the sand. She made it a lot farther before collapsing, fighting to breathe.

"Starting to look good," Mitchum said with a cold smile. This was a good idea. Use the slaves to walk along the rad-hot beach and find the pirate's safe passage to the interior. He had thought it a long shot at best, but that damn plan seemed to be working. Soon, they could land the Hummers and drive into the jungle after the outlanders.

"Sir?" the pilot asked from the till.

"Nothing," Mitchum scowled. "Pay attention to your job."

"Aye, aye, sir," the pilot answered sheepishly.

Leveling his weapon, Campbell fired and the girl on the beach jerked once, then went still. Grabbing another slave, a navvy tossed the teenaged boy into the ocean.

"Go fifty feet to the left of the girl," Glassman ordered.

Splashing about, the youngster nodded, then pulled in a lungful of air and dived out of sight.

"Fucking bastard." The sergeant sighed and gestured at the crew. In oft practiced ease, the armed men went to both sides of the foredeck and aimed their blasters. In the mob of slaves, an old woman began to cry. After a few minutes, the teen bobbed into sight about sixty feet behind the PT boat. The sec men opened fire in a rough volley, the barrage of miniballs tearing into the boy, blood spurting high into the air as one round smacked him right in the heart. Gurgling horribly, he sank from sight, leaving a crimson wake that slowly thinned away.

"Damn fine shooting there, Donovan," Glassman said with a smile. "Been practicing?"

"In my spare time, aye, skipper." The navvy grinned, preening with the praise. "A sailor that can't shoot, ain't nothing but ballast to his shipmates."

"Damn right," Campbell said. "Skip, we need a new bosun."

"You're it, Donovan," the captain said with a wave. "Consider that longblaster yours to keep."

"Yes, sir!" the man said, grinning from ear to ear.

Just then a sharp whistling cut the air, and Donovan's head disappeared. A split second later, something slammed into the water beyond the boat as a rumbling boom echoed from the mountains of the jungle island.

"Cannonfire!" Campbell cursed, rushing to the anchor and yanking the release lever. Instantly, the chain slipped free from its ratchet and snaked into the drink.

Set loose, the boat began to move with the choppy waves, and two more cannonballs slammed hard into the ocean exactly where the craft had been only seconds ago.

"They found us!" a navvy shouted in warning, firing his flintlock longblaster at the distant mountainside bunkers. As if in response, a series of white smoke rings silently shot out from the trees on the mountainside, the twenty-pound lead balls arriving long before the sounds of the discharge could reach the sea.

"Start the engines!" Mitchum commanded, brandishing his revolver. "Get us the fuck out of range!"

"Too late!" the pilot cried as the cannonballs slammed into the water amid the peteys, a round crashing into a floating raft packed with slaves.

Timbers and human arms flew skyward from the strike, the mortally wounded slaves shrieking for a few moments as they tried to swim away, but the heavy chains linked to their ankles dragged the helpless people down and out of sight. The bloody water bubbled madly from their submerged death screams.

Even as the vessel sputtered into life, black smoke blowing from its short flue, Glassman bitterly lamented the terrible loss of human life. That was the last of the slaves. Now he had less than a dozen slaves to find the safe path through the rad craters. After that, he'd have to use his men. What a waste.

The hidden mountain cannons blew more smoke, the balls whistling past the moving ships to hit only water. Then the first of the Firebirds launched from PT 181 with a muffled roar and a cloud of gray exhaust fumes. The rocket streaked toward the dense greenery, spiraling once in the air as the tiny pilots in the warheads had been taught by Kinnison to confuse enemy gunners, and then it angled sharply to the left and shot into the trees. Almost immediately there was a tremendous explosion, bodies and cannons carried skyward on a column of flame from the combined detonation of the Firebird and their ample store of black powder.

On the sea, the navvies cheered as a second rocket

was set off, this one heading deep into the valley only to be caught by an updraft and slammed directly into the granite bridge. In slow majesty, the arch began to break apart, cracks spreading along its length until pieces began to fall off. Then, in crashing thunder swallowed up by the distance, the bridge shattered and crumbled into the jungle, tiny geysers of muddy water forming as the mammoth stones plummeted into the shallow river.

"That'll put fear into their bones!" Glassman sneered in triumph. "Ready another Bird!"

"Aye, sir!"

"Incoming, nine o'clock!" a sailor shouted, pointing to their left.

Jerking his head about, Campbell growled in anger and raced to operate the big .50 cal as three tall pirate ships crested into view from around the quay of the islands, a row of smoke rings appearing along their sides as the pirates cut loose a full broadside of their heavy ship cannons. The lead hit everywhere around the boats, but did no damage, the range simply too great for an accurate strike.

But the sergeant knew that had been no warning shot. The pirates had tried for a fast ace and failed, that was all. Now the sailing ships raised every yard of canvas available to their masts and started charging forward at their best speed. Closing in for the chill. The windjammers were huge, more than ten times the size of the PT boats, and even at three to four, the odds were heavily in their favor.

"Orders, sir?" Campbell asked, turning to his captain.

"Prepare more Birds, fast," Glassman snapped, then drew his blaster and started firing.

Campbell spun about to see a slave going overboard and another dashing forward to grab the .50 cal, swinging it across the deck. The crew dived for cover, but nothing happened as the slave wildly yanked on levers and pulled the trigger out of sequence.

Moving from behind the smokestack, a navvy rushed forward and slashed out with a machete, the blade cleaving the slave from shoulder to waist. Ropy guts slithered onto the deck as the dying man tried ineffectively one last time to operate the big fifty, but the complex double safety was just beyond his comprehension.

The navvy pushed the corpse over the side and corrected the settings on the .50 cal, firing a short burst at the sky to make sure. Then he swung the massive weapon to cover the rest of the slaves and they cowered in fear.

"Clear the deck!" Glassman ordered, rising from behind his chair. "Ace the lot of them!"

Screaming, the slaves begged to stay on the boat. But the fifty cut loose, the heavy slugs slamming their tattered bodies past the gunwale and over the side. The slaughter was done in less than a minute, but the rebellion had bought the pirates precious time, and now cannonballs were hitting the ocean around the peteys from two directions.

"Ahoy, the 94!" Glassman shouted, then cupped hands to his mouth, as the spray of a near miss rained down on his craft. "We'll handle the mountains! You hit those fucking jammers, and send them to Davey!"

But the guard boat was already in motion, the hull of PT 94 shuddering as the gears of their trannies were thrown into reverse. The steam engine bucked in response as the propellers abruptly changed rotation, and forced the craft to awkwardly turn until the bow was pointing straight at the approaching windjammers.

"Full speed ahead!" Mitchum cried, a rope lashed to the captain's chair, held tight in his hand.

The pilot relayed the order via the speaking tube to the engine room belowdecks. In a gush of smoke, the steam engine surged with power. The petey rapidly accelerated to attack speed, the water foaming white as the bow of the nimble craft sliced across the rough water.

"Ready all tubes!" Mitchum shouted, the wind blowing against him so hard he was forced to sit in the captain's chair to keep from falling over. This was his first taste of a sea battle, and an almost sexual thrill was coursing through the sec man.

Behind them, the other three peteys were sending off salvos of Firebirds at the mountain bunkers, but not one rocket was aimed at the pirate windjammers. They were Mitchum's concern, do or die. Good, that was the way he liked it, to be his own master, answering to none.

"Ready all!" a navvy replied, scampering along the slick deck as if the vehicle were standing still.

"Give us the word, Skip!" another shouted.

Skip, eh? So he had finally been accepted by the sailors. For some reason that pleased him greatly.

"Give them hell, boys!" he bellowed, raising a clenched fist.

Switches were thrown, nuke batteries sparked brightly and the boat lurched as the wide tube on the left side of the deck threw out a blunt-nosed cylinder, its aft propeller spinning in a blur. The torpedo hit the water and skimmed away, steadily building speed. Then the right torp was launched and the two sped away. Operated by tiny alcohol engines, the predark machines shot through the salty waves moving ever faster until they were literally flying from one wave crest to the next.

Breaking formation, the sailing ships began to move away from one another in an effort to lessen the danger from the incoming torps. Then the surface of the ocean was peppered with cloth bags of shrapnel from the cannons on the foredeck as the pirates tried to stop the incoming weapons.

While the petey crew hastily reloaded both tubes, Mitchum nervously watched the torps head for the enemy vessels. Lacking the guidance systems of the tiny muties inside the weapons, this was purely a matter of aim and timing. Too soon and they would pass harmlessly in front of the ships—too late and they go behind.

"Ready all!" a sailor called, his hand on the firing lever.

"Wait for it," Mitchum commanded, grabbing the windshield of the low-slung wheelhouse. The wakes of the torpedoes were lost amid the rough waves, and it was impossible to see exactly where they were located.

Suddenly, the ocean jumped a hundred feet in front of the first pirate vessel, the water rising high in a steamy geyser. The pirates cheered the hit. Then the second windjammer broke apart as a strident fireball formed amidships, timbers flying everywhere as the sea poured in through the gaping hole in the hull. Immediately, the craft began to list and the crew started leaping off the deck, fighting the breakers and the waves in an effort to reach the shore.

Turning away from their sinking sister, the other windjammers brought their main guns to bear on the lone PT boat, firing salvo after salvo. A round shot across the deck, the wind of its passing knocking down sailors. Another clipped the smokestack, the glancing blow leaving a crimping dent and causing the steel flue to ring deafeningly, flakes of paint shaking off the vibrating metal.

"Full stop!" Mitchum shouted, and the anchor was dropped as the aft propellers were disengaged. Then as the boat slowed its progress, the sec chief quickly added, "Release the fish!"

The last two torpedoes were launched, both traveling for the first sailing ship. Both of the vessels opened fire with their cannons to smash the machines, the black smoke of the rapid discharges covering the sea battle like winter fog.

"Now, while they can't see, launch the Firebirds!" Mitchum commanded.

"How many, Skip?" a sailor asked, lifting a torch of greasy rags and lighting it from an alcohol lantern kept burning for just that purpose.

"All of them!"

Startled, the navvy blinked, then smiled. "Aye, aye, sir!"

Shouting a battle cry, the gun crew rushed to the pod, locked it into position and lit the line of fuses before backing away. Even as an explosion came from the other side of the smoke barrier, the rockets began streaking away to disappear into the gloom.

Masked by the acrid cloud, Mitchum could only hear explosions, and the sounds of splintering wood.

Cannons roared almost without stopping, then more explosions. An unnerving silence covered the sea, broken only by the sound of the waves lapping against the aluminum hull of the modified PT boat.

Mitchum rushed to the stern of the boat, his new blaster in hand and ready. His crew assumed firing positions along the gunwale, a shirtless sailor covered with tattoos manning the .50 cal. The four torpedoes and six Firebirds were all that had been allotted to the lord baron's gunboat. Instead of saving each weapon for a point-blank chill as he had been told to do, Mitchum instead gambled on a two-step barrage of high explosives. If it worked, the island would be defenseless once the mountain bunkers were taken out, and they could do that with sec men on foot if necessary. Then landing the Hummers with their .30-cal machine guns would be easy. But if even one windjammer sailed through the thinning smoke, the peteys would have only handcannons and longblasters to defend themselves from the thundering black-powder cannons, and that meant retreating to Cascade. Days would be lost rearming the crafts—valuable time the pirates could use amassing ships and digging in for the next attack.

"There she is!" a navvy cried out, as the bow of a windjammer sailed out of the swirling fumes.

Yet even as they started shooting, the rest of the vessel came quietly into view. The hull was on fire, the mast gone, the deadly cannons tumbling from the broken hull to splash into the water. There was no sign of the second sailing ship.

"She's dead!" the bosun cried, firing a burst from the fifty in celebration.

"Belay that mutie shit!" Mitchum ordered, hols-

tering his piece. "Pilot, get us some distance before
her magazine of powder blows!"

"Aye, sir!" the man answered and shouted directions down the speaking tube.

The steam whistle keened once to balance the
boiler pressure as the petey swung about and headed
back to the others.

Returning to the landing area, Mitchum grunted in
approval as his pilot expertly eased PT 94 alongside
Glassman's boat. Most of the Firebirds were gone,
and the windshield of the vessel was missing, the
deck littered with glittering shards, but it seemed otherwise intact.

"Well?" the captain demanded, glancing up from
a conversation with the pilot.

"Aced the lot of them," Mitchum gloated, then
jerked his chin at the distant mountains. "What about
the bunkers?"

"Nothing from them since our last flight," Glassman said, rubbing his arm. A piece of glass from the
smashed windshield had gone through his upper arm.
The wound was minor, but hurt like a son of a bitch
every time he moved. Easing his hand into a pocket,
he forced the arm to relax and the pain diminished.

"We're out of slaves," Mitchum said with meaning.

Releasing his arm, Glassman glared hatefully at the
shore and its invisible barrier.

"Yeah," he muttered. "I know."

Legs splayed to stay properly balanced on the
gently pitching deck, Mitchum crossed his arms and
studied the rocky beach. Blue crabs covered the
corpses sprawled on the sand, sharp pincers ripping
the flesh from their bones. There was a glowing rad

crater to the left of the shallow river, the body of the chilled girl about a hundred feet to the right of the waterway. If there was a safe trail into the valley, he would guess it'd be just to the right of the river.

"Only one way to find out," Mitchum said aloud. He was so close to Ryan, there was no way he'd stop now. Not even to save his own life. "Pilot, head for shore and drop me off."

"Sir?" the pilot gasped, releasing the till. "You can't do that. You're the captain! Send a mate, or the barrel girl we got in the bilge."

Damn, he'd forgotten all about her. "Get the slut," Mitchum commanded.

In short order, the woman was dragged to the deck and the colonel explained the situation. She was to swim to the shore at just that spot, or they'd bloody her up and drag her alive behind the petey until sharks arrived—then they would cut her loose.

Nodding dumbly, the bruised woman jumped into the water and swam to the shore. Rising from the gentle waves, she slowly walked along the right bank of the shallow river with her wet rags billowing in the wind. Twice she stumbled, the sharp coral in the sand cutting her feet. Each instance, she dared to glance backward and saw the longblasters tracking her every move. With little choice in the matter, she continued onward until reaching the bushes. She had done it! Walked past the beach! Then she darted into the greenery just as a flintlock spoke. The miniball ripped away a handful of green leaves, but she was already gone.

"She made it!" a navvy cried, and more took up the cheer.

"All boats, land the Hummers!" Glassman

shouted, sliding a longblaster over a shoulder and taking the binocs.

"Pilot, the boat is yours until I return. Stay a hundred feet offshore, and if any pirate ships arrive, you haul ass and come back at moonrise. We'll swim out to meet you. Got that?"

"Aye, Skipper," the man said, then trying to curry favor added, "Wish I was going with you!"

Strapping an extra ammo belt around his waist, Glassman glanced at the navvy. "Then you're an idiot," the captain said simply, and walked to the aft of the boat straightening his weapons.

With only some minor maneuvering, the PT boats sidled up the shore and reached the shallows. The wind was blowing their black exhaust into the trees, but Mitchum heard no coughing from hidden snipers as a result. Good.

Lowering anchors, each craft then dropped a heavy sheet-iron tailgate onto the shore. Releasing the chains holding the Hummers in place, the sec man started the war wags, while the navvies tossed in bags of ammo, grens and the small portable Firebirds. Wary of the lolling deck, the sailors drove the Hummers down the inclined metal into the shoals and then successfully onto the beach. The navvies and sec men followed next, and soon the lord baron's men were assembled on the rocky beach.

As the PT boats raised anchors and moved away, a flurry of blasterfire crackled from the mountainside. The gunnery mates of the peteys promptly responded with their .50 cals, the stuttering machine guns sending a hellstorm of flying lead at the unseen defenders.

"The pirates are ready for us," Mitchum stated, taking the passenger seat in the front of a wag. A box of grens was on the floor between his legs, the loaded revolver in his grip, the other hand holding a small hand ax to repel boarders.

"Nuke them," Glassman grunted, doing approximately the same. He knew this was going to be a bloody fight, but the prize waiting in victory was worth any risk. A ville of his own! "Okay, lads, let's get the bastards!"

"No prisoners!" Campbell added, waving a long-blaster.

With their engines revving, the armored war wags rumbled into the jungle, smashing the plants out of the way.

"Death to the pirates!" a sec man yelled, then sat back in his seat with an arrow through his neck.

Without any hesitation, the rest of the men cut loose with their weapons, blasters ablaze in every direction, ruthlessly chilling anything that dared to move.

"PIRATES?" Lord Baron Kinnison said, glancing up from his breakfast.

"Yes, my lord," the chief of the palace guards said with a salute. "Captain Glassman has found the home ville of the pirates and wishes reinforcements immediately."

"Does he now?" Kinnison muttered, narrowing his eyes to mere slits. Clean white layers of bandages covered his humongous body; the disease oozing from his sores had not yet seeped through the new cloth wrapped around him this very morning. Over the bandages, Kinnison was wearing a loose caftan of predark cotton, woven sandals and two gun belts.

Caught just once without a weapon handy, his empire had nearly toppled. Such would never happen again.

The dining hall was empty except for the baron, his elite cadre of guards, sec men who had remained loyal to the baron during the revolution, and the chancellor. The polished cherrywood table gleamed in the candlelight from the chandelier and the alcohol lanterns in wall niches, and heaping mounds of food filled the long expanse, platters of steamed crabs, savory fried fish, fresh young squid, bowls of clams, pitchers of beer and loaves of steaming fresh bread. As a platter was emptied, pretty young serving girls appeared to replace it with another, broiled chimpanzee replacing the crab, hot buttered ears of corn in place of the chilled clams. There was enough food to feed a ville, even though it was only for the handful of men and their obese leader.

Chained to the wall opposite the feasting people was a very skinny man, his clothes hanging loosely from his emaciated frame. The vile traitor hadn't been fed anything but thin broth for a week, and madness was starting to appear in his fevered eyes. Under threat of castration, the prisoner was forced to watch the baron and his cohorts consume huge meals three times a day. Formerly a sec man for the lord baron, the starving wretch was the last of the rebels who had tried to seize the baron's throne. As the very last alive, Kinnison was doing his best to prolong the man's death for as long as possible.

Studying the messenger, Chancellor Rochar Langford wiped his mouth on a cloth napkin, the only one at the table, and placed there solely for his use. The others made do with hands and sleeves. A small goatee was growing on his chin, but the second in

command of the island fortress was still clean shaved
from his navy days, when lice was a very real problem. Small scars marked his youthful face, and a gold
earring hung from the stubby remains of his left lobe,
the rest removed in a bar fight on a distant island ville.
With his short-sleeved shirt, the tattoos on the fore-
arms were visible to all, a striped tiger on the left and
a green dragon on the right. It was something he had
copied from a predark poster found in the ruins of a
crumbling city. He had instantly liked the effect and
had it copied, a process that meant months of pain,
but was well worth the inconvenience.

Langford still wore the woven canvas gun belt
given to him by his first captain as a reward, but the
flintlock was now replaced with a huge autofire called
a Desert Eagle.

"They plan to attack an entire island with only six
boats?" the chancellor asked pointedly.

The chief guard checked the message once more.
"Four, sir. At least, that is what this message says,"
he reported, squinting to see the tiny lettering. The
words were badly spelled, the paper old and badly
wrinkled from being tied around the leg of a falcon.
But there was no doubt about the contents. The pirates
had been found. Incredible.

Popping the leg of a kiwi bird into his mouth, Kinnison sucked the meat off the bone and chewed
thoughtfully for a few minutes before swallowing.

"Good for him," Kinnison said, picking his teeth
with a thumbnail. "However, the question is whether
we should commit more peteys as backup."

"Yes!" the sec chief stated, thumping the table
with a fist. "Destroy the pirates and we will rule the
Thousand Islands unopposed forever!"

"I will rule, you mean," Kinnison muttered in a dangerous tone.

Hastily, the pale sec man corrected his statement.

"Lord Chancellor, what is the minimum number of vessels needed to protect Maturo Island from attack?" the baron demanded, refilling his mug from a clay pitcher. No glass was allowed on the dining-room table, nor any mirrors in the hallway. The baron never wanted to be reminded how hideous he was from the black rot consuming his acres of flesh.

"None, sir," Langford replied instantly. "Our batteries of Firebirds can repel any attacking force. With your return to power, we are invulnerable."

"From outsiders," Kinnison stated softly, draining a cup of beer.

The others grew sweaty at the words, but Langford ignored the reproach. "My lord, we could send messenger falcons to the rest of the fleet hunting pirates and have them converge on Forbidden Island. That would give Glassman over fifty peteys and four windjammers to assist his invasion. Leaving us twenty more as reserves in the harbor, plus the Firebird batteries."

"Reasonable," Kinnison said, nibbling an ear of corn. "Lieutenant Kirkton, send the falcons at once. Include one for Glassman, telling him his family has been removed from the dungeon and have their own home in the ville. No harm will come to the kin of the man who found the pirates' lair."

"Of course, my lord." The sec chief grinned in amusement. "And meanwhile I will…" He left the sentence hanging, waiting for instructions.

"And meanwhile, you will do as your lord commands!" Langford bellowed, outraged at the implied discourtesy. "Release the woman and child from the dungeon and give them a good house, lots of foods, clean clothes and a couple of slaves."

"Yes, Lord Chancellor," Kirkton hastened to say, knowing the wrath of the young man was only marginally less terrible than the old baron's.

Spearing a potato with a fork, Kinnison growled in agreement. He didn't care for the idea, but if he didn't keep his oath to Glassman, then nobody would ever believe his offers of rewards again. Ruling was a balancing act between the carrot and the stick. If a ruler lost either one, he was doomed.

As the sec chief and the messenger departed to their assignments, Langford refilled his mug of springwater and took a sip. "My lord, do you think the outlanders are pirates?" he asked.

"No," Kinnison replied, savagely biting off chunks of a suckling baby pig, the rich gravy flowing between his pudgy fingers. "I don't know what they are, but no pirate carried their kind of blasters. Or built a flying machine."

The sec men at the table shivered again at the notion, and tried to force the image from their minds of air wags and falling bombs. The quartermaster of the palace looked as if he would be physically ill, then rushed from the room with a hand covering his mouth.

Openly, Kinnison scowled in scorn at the public show of weakness, but privately he agreed wholeheartedly. Death from above—the words brought visions of skydark, and that was enough to break the spirit of any sane man.

Just then a serving girl hurried into the dining hall and whispered something to one of the sec men in charge of the black-powder mills. The man gave her a small pouch of powder in return and noisily cleared his throat, then did it again.

"Lord Chancellor..." he began.

Puzzled, Langford stared at the man, then his face brightened in remembrance. Ah, she had arrived at last. Excellent.

"Since your health is on the mend, milord," the chancellor said, standing at the table with an unreadable expression, "I have found a special gift for you. Which I am sure you will enjoy."

"Really," Kinnison said noncommittally, a hand creeping under the table to finger the trigger of the shotgun hidden there. After the revolt, the baron trusted nobody and nothing fully. Nor would he ever again. There was an old phrase that his father had once used—"Fool me once, shame on me. Fool me twice, die screaming, motherfucker." Wise words, indeed.

Langford clapped his hands, and the doors were opened by armed men, who stood aside to let a fisherwoman from the ville walk into the room. The woman was old but not aged, thirty, maybe forty years of age, with a scattering of gray in her thick blond hair. She walked with strength, and a full womanly figure moved tantalizingly beneath her loose dress. Her clothing was worn and patched, but very clean, with no loose threads or ragged hems.

"Who is this?" Kinnison asked the men at the table. "Some new slut for me to bed? A small gift, indeed."

The woman stopped approaching at those words and smiled in amusement at the fat baron. "I will be the mother of your heir," she said simply.

Kinnison waited, but there was no more coming.

"You?" the baron scoffed. "I can mount ten women a day if it pleases me. Each more beautiful than you. Why should I mount you instead of throwing you to my dogs?"

Sipping his water, Langford waited, letting the woman speak for herself. In this matter, she needed no assistance.

"My name is Deirdra, and my brother stole a blaster," she replied, hands on her hips. "You lashed him for a day, then gave him your disease as a punishment. Fair enough, I suppose. But I tended to him for months before he finally died."

"Yes, I recall the incident," Kinnison said. "And you do resemble him, somewhat. So what do you wish? A quick death from a firing squad, or a supply of jolt to ease the terrible pain?"

Deirdra held out an arm. "Examine my skin."

The sec men in the room were alert as he waved her closer, and began to closely look at her face and arms. At first in contempt, but then in wonder. In growing astonishment, he lifted her skirt to see underneath; the condition of her feet would tell the truth. But she was wearing nothing underneath the loose dress and Kinnison saw every inch of the firm, clean body. Her lean legs showed no stretch marks, her belly flat without wrinkled folds of loose skin.

"I am a virgin," she admitted, not ashamed or proud, but merely stating a fact.

"And immune," Kinnison whispered, dropping the thin cloth. Then he turned on the other nobles. "Is this some sort of a trick?"

"Never, my lord!" Langford cried.

"Try me," Deirdra said, taking a small knife from

the table and cutting her forearm. She passed the baron the blade, handle first. "Do the same and smear your blood on my wound. Nothing will happen."

As if moving in a dream, Kinnison started to cut his arm, then dropped the knife.

"Everybody out," he commanded harshly. "Including you, Lord Chancellor."

Sensing his urgency, the men and serving girls quietly withdrew. Once the baron was alone with the woman, he stood and slid out a chair for her in unaccustomed courtesy. Nodding in thanks, Deirdra sat and turned to face him directly, with no evasion or sideway glances. A person was simply looking at him of her own free will. Kinnison could scarcely believe it was happening. His last reserves against her beauty crumpled at the simple action, and he leaned forward eagerly.

"What are your terms?" the baron asked, his heart pounding.

"I become the baroness," Deirdra stated, her hands folded primly in her lap. "But if the first child is sick or not a boy, then you may chill me."

He furrowed his brow. "That's all?"

"That is enough."

"Done," Kinnison said, extending a bandaged hand.

She shook it without flinching and began to remove her dress. "Shall we start?"

"What, right here?" Kinnison asked amused, and slightly shocked. He wasn't used to aggressive females. Normally, they wept and screamed, and often had to be raped while tied to chairs or even unconscious.

"The sooner we begin, the sooner I am with your

child,'' she responded, dropping the old dress to the floor.

Deirdra looked magnificent in the candlelight, her smooth skin glowing with health. With a dry mouth, Kinnison shuffled to his feet and began removing his own clothing, wiping the grease from his fingers on the material. Let the navy battle the pirates; which ever side won he didn't care anymore. This amazing woman was the answer to his prayers. Soon he would have a son, an heir! And his reign would continue. For Lord Baron Kinnison, the war with the outlanders was already over, and he was the absolute winner.

During the sweaty coupling on the tabletop, the fat man didn't once notice the flick of a forked tongue between the lush lips of the mutie female, even when she did it again in the most unusual of places.

Chapter Nine

Falling through the air, Jak angled the descent to protect his sprained ankle and landed heavily on his shoulders, the blow knocking the breath from his lungs.

Panting, he frantically rolled toward the wall and just barely avoided the rush from a small boar, its tusks so new the bone extended straight out from its jaw like slim daggers.

Scrambling over a corpse, Jak threw himself at the wall and drew the blaster, choosing a target, then he quickly shifted aim, and then again. Where was the big bastard?

Ah, there he was. A huge boar...no, a big sow, twice the size of the other hogs, her shiny black coat streaked with white from old scars, one ear half chewed off. But the monstrous animal radiated an aura of power. She was the baron of her brood, the absolute master.

Aiming the unfamiliar weapon, Jak fired, and the .44 miniball slammed into her side, knocking the big sow back, but not over. She squealed at the wound, sniffing at it with a twitching nose. Then she swung her head toward the albino and pawed the bloody mud, preparing to charge. With no reloads, Jak dropped the blaster and grabbed the headless corpse from the sticky ground. Holding it as a shield, he backed into the corner of the pit and drew one of his stolen knives.

The crowd shouted something unintelligible, and gold coins rained into the pit. A reward for being clever?

Snorting loudly, the big sow rushed at Jak, her tusks slashing open the legs of the corpse. Pulling free, the animal seemed confused at the lack of re-action from the victim and lurched forward again, only to stop halfway, as if trying to lure out the cornered two-leg. Then she did it once too often, and Jak slashed her across the snout, splitting both nostrils wide open.

The sow keened in shock and dashed madly about, slamming into her brethren and bouncing off the brick wall, the loss of smell affecting her more than blind-ness to a human. While the sow attacked a smaller boar, Jak rummaged through the filthy pockets of the chilled pirate, tossing aside the gold coins and cigs, but keeping the matches and a third knife.

Testing the blade on a thumb, Jak found the edge dull, the balance barely acceptable, but it would serve. Choosing a target, he stepped from the wall and threw hard. In the grandstand, a laughing dandy waving a bottle went still as the blade took him in the belly. Gushing blood, the man dropped his bottle and, stum-bling about, fell into the pit. He landed only ten yards away, but the boars converged on the body, stomping the flesh under their sharp hooves and goring it with their pointed tusks. Behind his shield, Jak had eyes only for the predark revolver in the gun belt of the aced pirate. The loops were full of ammo, maybe even enough for the teenager to blast his way out of the pit. Across the muddy field was a small wooden gate in the wall, painted to resemble bricks. That had to be how they let the boars into the pit. Which meant that was how he could get out. If only he could reach that blaster! Knife in hand, Jak started warily creeping forward, but the smaller boars drove him back into the corner, the flesh dangling off the legs of the corpse until the bones showed from within.

Angry noise came from the attendees, and most retreated from the pit, fearful of another attack by the prisoner. Then several voices demanded the immediate use of blasters. Knowing he stood no chance against those, Jak charged the boars, plowing through the smaller beasts until reaching the aced pirate. Ignoring the throbbing pain in his ankle, Jak heaved the headless corpse onto the tusks of the big sow, the obstruction keeping her busy for a moment while he dug in the mud for the blaster.

A movement to his left made the teen dodge and the small boar just missed goring his stomach. Cocking the hammer of the muddy weapon, Jak aimed and fired. The .357 Magnum blaster roared and the tiny male went motionless, then flopped to the ground, every breath squirting out a crimson arch.

The noise of the blaster clearly scared the animals, and they moved away from the Cajun warrior as Jak fumbled with the gun belt of the pirate and finally dragged it free. Draping it over a shoulder, he watched with dismay as several rounds fell into the thick mud, but he kept creeping along the wall toward the gate.

A guard shouted a warning about his plan, and now flintlocks did discharge, the miniballs ricocheting off the brick wall around the teen. Pumping a round at the boars to keep them at bay, Jak fired twice more, and a guard slumped out of sight, his arm gone from the elbow down.

Jak cracked the cylinder and dumped the spent shells. Keeping on the move, he reloaded a single round and aced another officer in the grandstand, starting a riot in the attendees. Removing the spent cartridge, he fully loaded the blaster and stuffed the two spare shells into his pants pocket. Turning for the gate, the albino teen cursed and flung himself sideways, the big sow only slamming into his sprained ankle, the impact sending lightning bolts of agony along his leg.

Landing in a heap, the teenager turned over and fired the .357 at point-blank range directly into the face of the wounded sow, the hollowpoint rounds tearing off a cheek and blowing away an eye. Her face dripping with blood, the animal shook her head, trying to remove the fluid, and threw herself at the hated norm. Waiting until the last second, Jak spun out of the way and buried a knife into the back of her neck, snapping the spine. Carried on by sheer momentum, the beast continued to walk several yards, then gently lay down and rolled onto her side as if going to sleep.

Limping to the gate, Jak aced two more boars, the rest moving away from the pale killer, a few of the smaller animals going to the dead sow and nudging her with their snouts as if trying to awaken her. Seizing the moment of freedom, Jak inspected the gate, trying to figure out which side held the hinges. He pumped two rounds into the left, blowing out huge gouts of wood, then did the same to the opposite side. Nothing happened. Bracing himself, Jak swung his good foot and kicked the portal. The weakened wood cracked, but neither side yielded.

Muttering curses, the teen thumbed in his last two rounds, then crouched low and used them both at the line of guards forming along the grandstand. Blasters boomed, throwing hot lead at the teen, but two of the pirates were already sagging, blood spreading across their chests from the deadly Magnum weapon.

Out of ammo again, Jak raced across the field and threw himself at the damaged gate. He felt the portal give a little, but still he didn't break through. Through the separating pieces of wood, he could see the heavy locking bar on the inside, keeping the barrier in place. There was no way he could get through without explosives or an ax.

Suddenly, a bell began to ring, and the pirates above lowered their longblasters, their faces twisted in surprise. The dim noise continued, and the guards turned and ran. In the grandstand, the attendees moved as if their clothes were on fire, dropping bottles and knocking over tables as they dashed from the grandstands shouting at one another.

Standing amid the carnage, Jak stared as the arena quickly emptied of people. In minutes he was alone with the boars. Dragging his bad leg, Jak grabbed the dead sow by her front legs and hauled the body to the base of the wall. The boars moved out of his way as the teenager gathered the chilled pirates, placing their bodies on the sow. Awkwardly climbing on top of the pile, Jak found the top of the pit was still beyond his reach. Stabbing his knife into the concrete between the bricks, he tried pulling himself higher, his fingertips brushing along the rough rim when a pair of different-colored hands grabbed his wrist and hoisted the young man over the top.

"You okay?" Mildred asked, crouching alongside the panting teen, checking for wounds. But thankfully, none of the caked blood covering the filthy clothes seemed to be his.

"Been better," Jak admitted, stiffly standing and limping to a nearby table full of toasted sweetmeats and sliced fruit and other delicacies. Grabbing a fresh bottle of shine, the teen pulled the cork with his teeth and liberally poured the alcohol over his face and clothes, washing away most of the crud.

"Know where the others are?" Krysty added, watching the empty grandstands, a flintlock held in each hand.

Somewhere in the background, the warning bell never stopped ringing, and now the sounds of long-blasters and cannons were added to the shouting of the pirates.

"Not seen," he muttered, smoothing back his wet hair. "What's happening ville?"

"We're not sure," Mildred answered. "But from the amount of cannons firing, I'd say a war just started."

"Good," he grunted. "Need blaster."

Krysty handed over one of the handcannons taken from the dead guards in the alleyway. Jak checked the weapon, then grunted in satisfaction as he tucked it into his damp belt.

"Stink," he muttered, wrinkling his nose. "Need bath bad."

"So do we all, my friend," Krysty stated.

"Can you walk?" Mildred asked, observing how he stood.

The youth tried a few steps, then frowned deeply. "No," he answered honestly.

"Sit," the physician commanded, gently shoving him into a chair. Untying the laces of his boot, she spread on the last drops of analgesic cream from her med kit, then rewrapped the bandage tight. He winced, but said nothing.

Mildred knew the ankle had to be agony. The flesh was swollen, with new bruises compounding the sprain, but none of those were life threatening. A tight bandage would hurt a lot but support the weakened ankle, allowing him to walk, and fight. That was enough for now. Later, if there was a later, she'd do more.

Washing off the reeking boot with more shine, she slid it gently on his foot and he did the laces. Good enough. Mildred knew about the material hidden inside the boots of the men, but there was no present need for the wads of C-4 plastique.

"Okay, let's get going," Krysty said, putting her shoulder under the arm of the teen and helping him to stand.

"Where first?" Jak said, testing his weight on the foot. The pain was much less, and he nodded at the physician.

"Slave quarters," Mildred replied. "Then the baron's fortress. They'll be at one or the other."

"This way," Jak said, heading along the rows of seats and finally into the dark tunnel. "Don't touch walls!"

"No problem," Krysty answered, staring at the deadly yellow flowers growing in such abundance. Did the pirates not know, or not care about the fungi thriving in their ville?

Proceeding to the end of the tunnel, they found an iron gate blocking the exit, the door held in place with a chain and heavy padlock. Waiting for the sounds of battle to peak, Krysty blew off the lock with her muzzle loader and cast away the chain.

Stepping into the street, the three crouched low as a squad of armed men ran by the arena, closely followed by a horse-drawn cart packed with straw and carrying a ship's cannon. As the wag rattled around a corner, a lone man scurried into view, his arms full of smoked joints of meat. Leaning against the iron grille, Jak flipped his arm and the man across the street cried out, clutching the knife sticking out of his thigh.

"Don't chill me!" he pleaded, crawling away on the seat of his pants, a hand raised to ward off the expected blow.

From his ragged clothing and demeanor, Krysty could tell he was no sailor or guard. His hands were rough, the knuckles swollen and she made a guess.

"Carpenter," the redhead stated, aiming her blaster.

"Ship's c-carpenter," he stammered, inching away. "Look, that meat is mine. A gift from a friend. I'm no thief!"

Not a good one, anyway. "Talk fast," Krysty ordered, cocking her piece. "Where is the baron's house?"

Badly frightened, the man pointed with a shaky finger. "Two blocks over and up a flight of stairs. Big place, lots of guards."

The two women exchanged glances. That description matched the fortress they had seen on the low hill from the window of the gaudy house.

Stiffly bending, Jak shoved the man's head against the side of the brick house, knocking him unconscious. Yanking off the knotted rope the carpenter was using as a belt, the teen gave it to Mildred, who tied a tourniquet around the man's leg. When she was done, he retrieved the blade. The Cajun had no objections to chilling an enemy, but the terrified worker was no threat to the companions. Even in the Deathlands, there were lines that couldn't be crossed if a man considered himself a man, and not a coldheart. The differences were small, but to the companions extremely important.

Just then, the sound of marching boots filled the street and the companions slipped into a tavern to hide. More troops passed by, the sailors loading their longblasters on the run. Clothing was disheveled, faces stubbly with beard, and it was painfully clear the men had been roused from their sleep.

"The battle must be going bad," Krysty said, peeking out the wooden shutters covering the windows, "if they're calling in the reserve troops already."

"Firebirds against cannons isn't a fight," Mildred stated, watching from the front door. "That's just a slaughter."

Jak could only mumble in agreement, his mouth stuffed with food from the abandoned plates on the score of deserted tables.

As the sailors hurried out of sight, the companions followed in their wake, heading toward the baron's fortress. Everywhere, people were running about in panic, and several homes had been broken into and looted, clothing and such scattered in the cobblestone streets.

Smoke was rising from something burning in the

distance. Cannons roared as Firebirds streaked across the sky, flintlocks discharging continuously. Half a dozen times, the companions were forced to hide rather than engage the squads of armed pirates, the sailors only seeming to travel in groups of ten or more. Then they found several chilled officers partially buried under the bricks and timbers of exploded buildings, the mashed gun racks and beds in the wreckage indicating this had been a barracks. Unfortunately, the longblasters of the officers were bent and useless, but their pepper boxes and shotguns were undamaged. The companions took the weapons, and the next group of sailors was ruthlessly cut to ribbons by the triple shotgun blasts, then the bleeding bodies looted of all the ammo they could carry.

Locating the flight of stairs, the women and teenager slowed and proceeded carefully up the hill. Cresting the ridge, they found a low stone wall dotted with cannons. Warily, they crept forward, the reloaded shotguns sweeping for targets. Even if most of the guards had gone to defend the ville, some would always stay at their posts. Fanatics and fools were the essential backbone of any baron's regime.

''There it is!'' Mildred cried out when the fortress came into sight. A sandbag wall surrounded the structure on the ground, the rooftop foamy with coils of barbed wire. Beyond the fortress rose the escarpment of the towering mesa, the ruins on top lost in the haze of sheer distance.

Oddly, no guards were in sight, and that made the companions suspicious enough to drop and take cover. Had everybody gone to the ville walls, or were folks already fleeing the ville to escape into the deadly jungle? Rad craters dotted the island, and without a rad counter, any journey through the dense foliage would end quickly in screaming agony.

Jak covered the women as they moved from the wall of cannons toward the front door of the somber fortress, when without warning, a strident explosion ripped the structure apart, tongues of flame extending from every window and doorway. The concussion brutally slammed the companions to the paved street, and as they watched with ringing ears, a growing fireball lifted the building and split it apart, throwing the broken debris and flaming corpses far and wide across the turbulent sky.

"Mother Gaia, no," Krysty whispered, staring in horror at the wide expanse of smoky destruction.

Suddenly, a machine gun stuttered from behind, and the three spun in time to see the missing men gun down a group of pirates taking aim at them from behind the low wall. Krysty and Mildred burst into grins as Ryan and the others joined them, brief smiles playing across their dirty faces.

"Glad to see you alive, lover," Ryan said, taking the redhead in his arms. They fiercely hugged, savoring the sheer existence of each other, then reluctantly parted.

"Same here," Krysty replied, her animated hair relaxing around her shoulders.

"Here, compliments of Baron Withers," he said, passing over her gun belt, blaster and a heavy box of ammo.

"Thanks," she said, tossing away the flintlock pistol and quickly checking the load in her revolver.

Meanwhile, Mildred pulled J.B. close and nearly suffocated the wiry man with a long fierce kiss.

"You okay?" he asked in concern over the unusual

display. The woman was normally much more reserved. Something was wrong.

"Tell you later," she replied softly, accepting her ZKR target pistol and a full box of live rounds.

Gratefully, Dean dropped his load of backpacks to the road, and they all took their bundles of possessions without checking the contents. There was no time for that now. Even with his ankle throbbing, Jak felt better with the pack in place. He always seemed slightly off balance with the backpack missing.

"What happened to the fort?" Krysty asked.

"Thought we could use a diversion," J.B. explained, shifting his grip on the heavy rapidfire. "After the alarm sounded, the guards rushed out to man the walls, so we raided the armory and lit a couple of fuses."

"Chaos is the shield of the lost," Doc rumbled, passing out grens. Each companion got four of the AP charges, and shoved them away into pockets and backpacks.

Just then, a crackle of blasterfire peppered the stone wall, and J.B. answered with a barrage of lead from the Thompson, the rounds punching a line of holes along the side of a house. Then Doc emptied his Webley, and a pirate appeared in a second-floor window to fall to his death.

"Nice shot," Dean complimented him.

"A necessity," Doc rumbled, cracking open the top of the Webley and flipping it over to pour out the shells. Tossing them away, the spent brass musically rang on the cobblestoned street as he started thumbing in fresh bullets. As much as the old man hated to admit it, the Webley was a better blaster in every way to the LeMat. More accurate, loaded faster, lighter, less recoil, hit harder, everything. Perhaps his adamantine decision to keep the ancient weapon was due for some serious thought.

Through the scope of the Steyr, Ryan swept the ville below them, checking the combat encircling the wall. Hummers raked the defenders with machine guns, the pirates replying with flintlocks, cannons and crossbows. But every time the sailors formed a group to concentrate their weapons fire, the sec men launched a Firebird and dozens of sailors were aced.

"Glassman and Mitchum," Krysty said, scowling at the faraway combat. Then she noticed the granite bridge was gone, and past the valley PT boats patrolled in the shallows off the beach.

"This is no recce or raid," she stated, "but a full invasion."

"With enough weapons to get the job done," Ryan agreed grimly, lowering the Steyr. "They came to get us, and found the pirates instead."

"Prob think we pirates," Jak stated, checking his Colt Python. The revolver was in fine shape, clean and oiled. The cartridges looked old, but there was no sign of corrosion. And for the first time in months, he had a full complement of ammo.

"Most definitely, my friend," Mildred said, frowning. "I think the sec men want the pirates first, but we're definitely number two on their hit list."

"I do not know who to root for," Doc muttered. "Glassman or the pirates."

"Doesn't matter," Krysty said unhappily. "Both sides want us aced."

"Better take this, Millie," J.B. said, easing the tension on the arming bolt and passing over the bulky

Thompson. "I can't operate it and my Uzi at the same time."

She holstered her revolver. "Chambered for .22 rounds?" the physician asked, accepting the heavy rapidfire. She was surprised by its weight. The thing had to be ten pounds, maybe more.

"Nope, .45APC," he replied, and began pulling rectangular ammo clips from his munitions bag.

"Can't imagine we'll need this to get out of here," she said, stuffing the extra clips into her pockets.

"Madam, we are going to require a blessed miracle," Doc said in a deadly serious tone.

Just then a Firebird launched from the Hummers, and arched over the wall to streak directly toward the companions.

"Incoming!" Ryan shouted, both of the Webley revolvers blazing away.

Chapter Ten

The companions cut loose as the rocket did a lazy spiral over the tumultuous pirate ville. Then it angled sharply and dived almost straight down to disappear behind a brick building. There immediately followed a tremendous explosion.

"Wasn't after us," Ryan said, lowering his blasters. A warm draft from the detonation washing over the companions, carrying the smell of sulfur and roasted flesh.

"Next time it will be," Krysty stated, watching the mushroom-shaped cloud rise into the sky. Any hot explosion could cause a similar cloud, but the shape still disturbed her slightly.

Across the settlement, the blasterfire continued unabated from the wall, but the cannons were sounding more sporadically. Probably running low on black powder. The nameless ville had been there for decades and never been attacked. The locals simply weren't prepared for a major battle against sec men armed with rapidfires and in war wags.

Screaming and pointing at the cloud, a group of terrified people ran out of the alleyway, clutching their meager possessions. The companions let them pass unmolested until some armed pirates ran into view. Both J.B. and Mildred dropped into a firing stance, and the Uzi and Thompson chattered briefly, mowing the men down.

Something slammed into the stone wall in front of them, and Dean spotted a sec man on a rooftop hastily reloading his longblaster. The boy raised the Weatherby, braced for the recoil and fired. The crack of the Nitro Express made heads turn across the ville, and it was a full second before the sniper flipped over backward. Without expression, Dean worked the bolt, levering in a fresh cartridge. At short range the massive rounds went straight through a man like a rock through glass, with about the same results.

Just then, a rickety cart loaded with barrels of black powder rattled by on the cobblestoned street, the driver cursing and whipping the sweaty horses. Dean raised the Weatherby, but Ryan stopped him from firing.

"We want the pirates to have the ammo," he explained. "The longer they fight with the sec men, the fewer can come after us."

"Gotcha," he replied, easing the pressure on the hair trigger.

"Mayhap it would be appropriate to terminate our visit," Doc rumbled, discharging the LeMat, then the Webley at pirates coming their way. One man dived for cover with a badly wounded arm, while the other went flat and stayed there.

"The mesa is only twenty miles or so to the west," Mildred suggested, fighting to clear a jammed round. Over near the arena, she noted that plumes of smoke were rising from a two-story building with wooden shutters. Good.

Pulling out his scope, J.B. swept the entire ville.

"There's a gate in the western wall," he said, collapsing the brass telescope. "Only a few guards."

"Horse cart came from over there," Krysty said, making a gesture with her smoking revolver.

Choosing his target, Ryan chilled an officer on the wall, but ignored the troopers. The more confusion in the ranks, the longer the battle would last.

"Okay, let's grab some transport," Ryan said, deliberately not looking at Jak. "Twenty miles is a long way to run."

Firing one blaster, then the other, the albino teen said nothing, but seemed vastly relieved.

"Let's go," the Deathlands warrior shouted over the growing din, and the companions took off at a run into a side street.

STRIDING ALONG the wide top of the limestone wall that sealed off the valley, Peter Tongamorlena shouted orders to the sailors under his command. The air tasted of black-powder fumes, and aced pirates lay everywhere, pools of their blood making the limestone slippery to walk on. Most he knew by name, shipmates and fellow officers, but every corpse built a rage for revenge against the invaders. How the fuck had the lord baron's sec men gotten past the rad craters alive? Nobody else had succeeded in getting off the beach in the past fifty years!

"Keeping firing!" Tongamorlena bellowed, discharging his blaster at the racing Hummers darting about in the jungle. Incredibly, he scored a hit, but the .44 miniball only ricocheted off the armored side of the military wag. The lord baron's sec men answered with a burst from their giant rapidfire blaster, the spray of .50 caliber slugs raking the wall and its handful of defenders.

Designed to withstand bombardments from rogue ships in the bay, the stout limestone blocks were holding against the Firebirds and grens. But the steel-plated front gate was beginning to weaken, the cold iron hinges sagging under the weight of the door. Rocks on the brick barbicon had been dropped to hinder the advance of the Hummers. And the tactic worked, but only for a while. The grens of the sec men were slowly clearing a path for the deadly war wags.

As Tongamorlena quickly reloaded, the pirates struck back with flintlocks and crossbows, the wounded reloading for the healthy. Then the few remaining cannons roared in a ragged volley, sending a hellstorm of seashells and rocks into the jungle. More than once a hidden sec man screamed and fell to the ground horribly mutilated from the razor-sharp barrage. But there always seemed to be more, and nothing stopped the Hummers. Even the tires seemed resistant to lead and arrows.

Behind him, chaos filled the streets of the ville, buildings burning out of control and the civilians looting like hungry jackals. The triple-damn cowards. There only seemed to be a couple of those PT boats in the bay, and the pirates outnumbered the attackers twenty to one. But those accursed Firebirds made the difference, even when they missed. The fallout from the explosions threw flaming wreckage about and spread the damage across HomePort ville.

Taking a pepper box from an arm without a body, Tongamorlena tracked the passage of a Hummer and squeezed the trigger. The forty-five tiny chambers of the honeycomb barrel simultaneously fired, the swarm of iron needles spraying the military wag. A sec man cried out, his face a bloody ruin.

In response, a sec man stepped from the bushes holding a fat tube and launched a Firebird. The rocket streaked past the limestone so low that its fiery exhaust washed over several men, igniting their clothes and hair. Shrieking, the pirates slapped at their crackling bodies, one going over the side, and the other dashing madly about until aced by one of his own men.

"Cannons, fire!" Tongamorlena roared, limping along the top of the barrier.

"Sir, we can't!" a dirty-faced ensign growled. A red-stained rag was wrapped around his neck, one eye partially closed from a cluster of burn blisters. "The metal is too fuckin' hot. The powder will blow if we try a reload."

"Then wash them with water first!" Tongamorlena bellowed.

The man spread his arms in reply, indicating the dozen empty buckets scattered on the wall.

Scorch! They were going to lose the ville because of water?

"We got any Firebirds?" Tongamorlena demanded.

The gunner scowled. "We've stolen dozens over the years," he answered, "but they won't launch at Kinnison's troops. Got no fucking idea why, but they just won't do it. It's like the bastard things were alive!"

A fifty chattered, and both men ducked for a moment.

"Okay, then launch them at the sky. When the

rockets run out of powder, they'll rain down on the attackers from above.''

"Yeah, might work," the gunner said grudgingly. "But the wind could shift to our side of the wall and—''

"Obey!" Tongamorlena raged, brandishing the spent pepper box.

The gunner saluted and limped away, shouting orders. He only got a few yards before a .50 cal cut the man in two.

Bellowing in anger, Tongamorlena aimed and pulled the trigger on the pepper box before remembering it was empty. Scorch! It was the only weapon they had that was harming the sec men, and it took half an hour to reload! With a hundred of these, Kinnison's troops would be feeding the fish by now. But there were only about twenty in the whole ville, and each had been used already.

Furious, the officer tossed the useless blaster away, and grabbed a flintlock and ammo bag from a headless man. As much as the officer hated to admit such a thing, it was starting to appear that they were going to lose this battle. Best be prepared for street fighting. Although with Baron Withers's fortress gone, he had no idea where the pirates could retreat to for a last stand. Maybe the slave quarters, or the armory? No, that was also gone.

Going to the edge of the wall, Tongamorlena whistled for attention. "Barricade the door!" he shouted.

"Aye, aye, sir!" the overseer yelled, then turned to crack a knotted bullwhip at his workers. "You heard the man! Get moving!"

Shoulders hunched against the expected lash of the bullwhip, the line of chained slaves began hoisting wreckage from the collapsed houses and piling it against the door to reinforce the portal.

But they had only a few pieces in place when somebody on the wall shouted a warning and a strident explosion ripped the massive doors off the weakened hinges. The ton of metal fell to the cobblestones, smashing the slaves and the overseer into crimson pulp. A Firebird flew through the black and gray clouds to strike a pair of cannons set behind a sandbag wall. The rocket hit a man and detonated, the blast setting off the bags of black powder. The resulting explosion sent the cannons in every direction.

A Hummer rolled into view through the breach in the wall, its .50-caliber blaster steadily firing to finish the task. The military wag bumped over the horizontal door and the human remains trapped underneath, ending their cries of pain.

"No prisoners!" Mitchum screamed, driving the Hummer through a crowd of startled pirates, the armored fenders smashing the bodies aside.

The long barrels of flintlocks extended from the open windows of nearby buildings, and miniballs slammed into the wags, bouncing harmlessly off the body armor. The .50 calibers spoke, the heavy slugs chewing a path of destruction along the facade of the buildings, and the sniper ceased.

"Find me the outlanders!" Glassman shouted, shooting a wounded man in the back as he ran away.

"Ace everybody else!" Mitchum corrected, pulling out his blaster and pointing it at the captain. This was the perfect chance to permanently settle the matter of who was in charge.

But Glassman had been expecting the sec man to try a judas strike, and already had his blaster out. The two men fired in unison, the smoky discharges of the black-powder weapons temporarily masking the results of the conflict.

WHEN THE ALARM BELL stopped ringing, Ensign Raynor feared the worst and got ready, laying out a line of clips from his predark blaster for easy access.

Even before the sec men arrived, he had been standing alone to guard the rear gate of HomePort. Only made sense. It was twenty miles to Deadman's Cliff, and nobody had ever been known to get more than halfway there before getting aced.

A movement in the bushes caught his attention, and Raynor blindly fired his weapon. The motion ceased, but that meant nothing and he stayed alert. The Hunters were tricky. Only the guard of the western gate was allowed to carry a bolt-action blaster, and never had to account for how much ammo he used on a shift. Baron Withers encouraged random shots to try to put some fear into the horrid muties. They were the reason the wall around the ville had been built in the first place. Sure, the Hunters normally stayed in the trees and merely watched the norms, but occasionally they ventured close and stole a horse, sometimes a whole family.

Even from here, the ensign could see pieces of the predark ruins on top of the mesa, and he licked his lips thinking about the loot that waited up there for the first man to reach the city. But the few who tried were never seen again. However, the Hunters would sometimes toss the gnawed bones over the wall, almost as if trying to give the pirates a warning. The mesa was forbidden territory, although the oldsters of the ville whispered that none of the monsters had ever been seen climbing the cliff, almost as if there was something up there that frightened them. Raynor shuddered at the thought, unable to imagine what in nuking hell could frighten a Hunter.

The strident detonations of the Firebirds seemed to become louder, and many structures were burning out of control. But the ensign refused to leave his post until relieved from duty by the sergeant of the guard, or the enemy came and chilled him. He'd given the baron his oath, and a man meant less than a slave if he didn't keep his word.

Just then, a rattling horse cart rolled out of an alleyway, a large canvas mound covering whatever was in the rear. Holding the reins was an oldster with silver hair, wrapped in a horse blanket as if bitterly cold. Instantly, the ensign suspected looters and worked the bolt on his M-1 longblaster.

"Keep moving," Raynor said, aiming the weapon. "Can't use this gate."

"But sir, I've got orders from the baron to haul these blasters outside," the old man whimpered, cowering slightly. "We're losing the battle, and I must get these blasters to our snipers."

"Snipers would have their own blasters," the ensign said with scorn. "Nobody leaves."

The old man rubbed his face. "I have a bag of gold," he stated.

The guard snorted a laugh. "Only we use gold," he snapped. "Kinnison uses black powder for jack. Now get going before I have you keelhauled for disobeying a direct order!"

"But—"

"I wouldn't open the gate for anyone other than

the baron himself,'' Raynor said, then fired a round that went wide of the canvas mound. "Now move!''

"As you say,'' the old man said in a sad tone. "Well, I tried. Goodbye, young man.''

Puzzled, Raynor scowled at the expression and a sharp cough sounded from under the tarpaulin. Searing pain took his chest, to be replaced with a numbing cold and then absolute blackness that reached forever.

"Krysty, get the gate,'' Ryan said, throwing off the canvas sheet with his blaster.

The redhead clambered from the cart and rushed over to the imposing portal. Grabbing the heavy bar, she tried to shove it aside, then had to use rocks to hammer the rusted metal bolts out of their positions. Even then, the gate itself proved to be rusted shut. This exit hadn't been used in years.

"No more games,'' J.B. said, the Uzi held by his side as he watched the ville streets. "That was a damn waste of time.''

Wrapping the reins around a hitch on the buckboard, Doc snorted in reply. "Attempting to not take a life is never a waste of time,'' he rumbled, buckling on his gun belt and stepping down to the ground.

"For once we agree,'' Mildred said. "Just wish the path to righteousness wasn't so well paved with land mines.''

"Again, madam, we agree.''

Trying not to grunt aloud, Jak took the old man's place at the reins, resting his hurt ankle on his folded camou jacket.

"Hey, lend a hand,'' Krysty grunted, throwing her weight against the door to no results.

J.B. stayed on guard while the rest of the companions joined the woman at her task. The gate required the combined strength of everybody to be slowly forced aside, and after Jak drove the cart through, they forced it shut again to confuse the trail. The bolts were still undone on the other side, the sentry aced, but hopefully nobody would notice for a while. Whichever side won the battle, the survivors would certainly come after them for payback.

Past the gate was an open field separating the wall from the jungle, stubbly grass and flowering weeds dotting the land showing it had been cleared by hand. But not for farming. There were no furrows or even irrigation ditches. Just flat open soil.

"A clear field of fire," Ryan stated, laying the Steyr across his lap as the cart rolled forward. "They expected to get attacked from this direction."

"Attacked by whom?" Mildred said, then added softly. "Or should I ask, attacked by what?"

"Neutral pronoun, dear lady," Doc stated, his hands busy reloading the LeMat. He had a lot more charges for the ancient revolver than he did bullets for the British-made Webley.

Nearly lost in the weeds was an old path of rain-washed ruts, the wheel gullies pitted with loose stones and potholes.

"Pirates don't use this much," Dean observed, studying the primitive road.

"Which raises an interesting question," Krysty said thoughtfully. "If they rule this island, why seal off the door that leads to the ruins? It's an easy climb."

"Nothin' there?" Jak suggested, shaking the reins.

"Mebbe," Ryan answered pensively, his fingers tripping the checkered grip of the powerful Webley. The front gate of the ville had been armed like a predark tank, but the back gate was merely locked with a lone sentry standing guard. More like they were trying to keep folks in the ville, rather than keeping an enemy outside. Strange.

"Watch for muties," he warned, feeling the hair on the back of his neck stiffen and raise. He'd felt the same thing a hundred times in the Deathlands and was hardly ever wrong.

In silent agreement, the others checked their weapons and turned their backs toward one another so they could watch the jungle better. Rambling along the crude road, the cart bucked and bounced as it entered the cool shadows of the overhanging branches. Thick vines hung in clusters, each heavily dotted with different-colored flowers. Fruit festooned every branch, the grass littered with rotting peels and chewed cores. A tiny squirrel leaped from a palm tree ripe with coconuts, the limp body of a baby tarantula in its mouth. Birds were singing in every tree, a python hissed at the passing cart and swarms of insects parted before the horse cart and its occupants, closing behind them. The companions began to feel as if they were riding a boat floating through a serene green lake of tall rushes.

Then the berry-laden leaves of a tall bush abruptly parted and something inhuman leaped out to dart across the road. Flinging itself airborne, the thing landed on the horse and grabbed hold of the reins. Caught by surprise, the horse whinnied at the attack and reared on its hind legs, trying to buck off the animal. Still holding on to the reins, the mutie reached out to start throttling the mare with its second pair of arms.

The humanoid creature resembled a silverback gorilla, the largest and most powerful simian species in the predark world. Only this animal was a deep chestnut brown, and its elongated fingers were tipped with tiny black talons.

In unison, Jak and Ryan fired their blasters, the heavy slugs slamming into the huge beast less than a yard away. The mutie gorilla roared at the impacts, but only small trickles of blood were oozing from the deep wounds.

Standing, Dean swung up the Weatherby, but his father was in the way, still firing the Webley. Pounding its chest, the mutie released the trembling horse and reached for the norms. Stoically, they kept firing, but even at point-blank range their blasters were doing almost no damage.

"Try this!" J.B. shouted, squeezing between the men and triggering the shotgun. The pirate armory hadn't possessed any fléchette rounds, but the double-aught buckshot blew off an arm.

Howling in pain, pale fluid squirting from the ghastly wound, the mutie abandoned the horse to dive at the companions. Dean, Doc, Ryan and J.B. fired again while it was in midair, the triple blast throwing it to the dirt road.

"Giddyap!" Jak shouted, yanking the reins, and the wild-eyed horse started galloping away at top speed.

Behind them, the gorilla rose and started giving chase in a peculiar loping sprint. Aiming for its belly, Dean tried a shot, but the moving cart made him miss. Going to the rear of the cart, Krysty pulled the pin on a gren and dropped the charge rather than throwing it. The metallic sphere bounced twice, then violently erupted between the cart and the mutie, throwing up a cloud of leaves and loose dirt. Covered with fresh wounds, and still losing blood from its missing arm, the creature fell, but still alive, it started crawling after the companions.

"Here!" Dean said, holding out his longblaster lengthwise.

Krysty grabbed the hot barrel, Mildred braced the Thompson on the stable platform of the rifle and pounded the giant mutie with a spray of .45 rounds. The barrage tore the creature apart and it finally dropped.

"Bastard mutie," Jak cursed, glancing briefly over a shoulder, then turning back to pay attention to the road. Tree stumps and large rocks threatened to smash the rattling cart apart. An instant too slow in a turn and they'd crash. But the teenager refused to reduce their speed and drove on, whipping the horse to go faster.

Miles flew beneath the shaking wheels, and another of the mutie gorillas attacked the cart as it slowed to splash through a shallow creek. Ready this time, Ryan fired a thundering round from the Webley directly into its snarling mouth, blowing out the back of its head. Dripping brains, the creature fell limply across the horse and almost got tangled in the reins before slipping off to the ground. The cart nearly toppled over as its wooden wheels jounced over the bulky corpse.

"Now we know why they had the gate locked!" Krysty said, firing her S&W .38 at something unseen in the shadows of the jungle.

"Tropical paradise my ass," Mildred muttered, yanking out the exhausted clip and slamming a fresh mag into the Thompson.

Tense hours passed as the cart raced through the lush greenery. A carpet of vines nearly stopped them at one point, and the companions had to get down and push the cart over the obstruction. A fallen tree completely blocked the road at a curve. J.B. and Mildred sprayed the tree and bushes with their rapidfires, while Ryan set a gren and blew the decomposing log apart. The panting horse reared at the explosion and tried to turn away, but Jak forced it onward through the blast crater. But over the next few miles the mare wasn't running as quickly as before, and the teenager worried he had pushed the elderly horse too hard.

"My dear Jak, why are we slowing?" Doc asked in concern.

"Not me. Horse is," Jak replied curtly, shaking the reins. "Giddyap!"

In spite of the desperate urging, the old animal began to trot instead of run, and soon even that slowed to a walk. Jak lifted the whip, then put it down. The mare was wheezing for breath, white foam dripping from her mouth. No amount of pain would restore the strength of lost youth.

"Cover me," Mildred said, hopping from the cart with her med kit. Water was what the poor thing needed, and God help her, she'd give the mare a massive dose of the jolt she stole in the arena. That would get her moving again, but the rush would wear off quickly and kill the beast. She had no choice. They needed the mare to haul them out of the jungle and to the cliff.

The companions maintained random fire into the greenery as the horse greedily accepted the water from her palm. Then she tried to give it the jolt and the horse refused, her nostrils flaring in disgust at the smell of the toxic chem.

"Okay, girl," she said in a soothing tone, dumping the powder out of her hand. "Can't really blame you."

"She take it?" Ryan asked, watching the trees.

"No. Just drive. We'll be okay."

Jak walked the horse for a mile to let her rest, then broke her into a trot. As long as the cart was rolling, they should be okay.

Minutes later, the overhead branches thinned and they could see the rising cliff only a hundred yards away.

"We made it!" Dean shouted in relief, pointing with his longblaster.

Startled by the cry, the horse started to gallop toward the tall cliff, when two gorillas hit the mare from either side. Burying their teeth into her neck, the creatures tore loose gouts of dark flesh, hot blood pumping from the wounds to wash their inhuman faces. With no reason to hold back, J.B. sprayed all of the animals with the Uzi until they fell as a group, friend and foes entangled forever in death.

"Looks like we walk from here," J.B. said, slapping in a fresh clip.

"Krysty, help Jak," Ryan directed, handing the woman one of his blasters. Her .38 would do nothing against these jungle behemoths.

The redhead accepted the Webley and a handful of ammo, then assisted Jak down from the cart. She grabbed him about the waist and they started moving, their blasters cocked and ready.

"Take our packs?" Dean asked, jumping to the grass.

A hooded cobra rose to hiss at him, and Doc blew it away with the shotgun charge of the LeMat.

"Just take the MRE packs and ammo," his father directed. "We need speed."

He nodded. "Yes, Dad."

Dumping his backpack, J.B. pulled the pin on a gren and snugly tucked it over the pile of packs. The first person, or thing, that lifted the packs would have its face removed by eight ounces of high-grade military plastique. That ought to slow down even these four-armed monsters.

Roars came from the jungle around them. Mildred put a few bursts from the Thompson into the forest, the leaves shaking under the chattering fury. A gorilla darted into sight, and she concentrated the rapidfire on the mutie until the clip was spent. Swaying, the ape dropped to the ground.

"Bullshit!" Ryan growled, and pumped a few rounds from the Webley into the creature.

Growling and slavering, the gorilla stood and rushed the norms, fresh blood on its massive chest.

"Knavery, eh?" Doc growled, discharging the LeMat and the Webley together. The double roar thundered in the trees, the reports bouncing off the stone wall to sound like a hundred blasters.

Rocking slightly, the hunting ape patted at the gaping wound in its belly, pale blood welling with every breath. Finally, the brutish head lolled and it lay down as if going to sleep.

Snapping the reloaded Webley shut, Ryan triggered the blaster and blew off a chunk of its hairy skull, pinkish-gray brains pouring out like warm grease.

"Head shots only," he ordered. "These bastards know how to play possum."

"Incoming!" Dean shouted, firing.

Snarling wildly, a dozen of the great apes charged out of the forest. Slamming their knuckles onto the ground, the muties swung their torsos forward, then grabbed the soil with stubby toes to swing their arms again. Even as he pumped hot lead into their faces, Ryan couldn't understand how they got any speed that way, but the beasts moved with amazing velocity across the open roadway.

J.B. emptied the Uzi once more, and the rest of the companions fired head shots into the wounded muties. They had a system now that worked, but used a lot of irreplaceable ammo.

Sprinting down the dirt road, more gorillas came from the jungle and were aced. But the next wave didn't charge at the humans, but stayed just out of range, and only charged when the companions turned their backs to leave.

"Fireblast!" Ryan cursed, stopping in the road and turning. "I'll hold them until you reach the cliff! Then cover me!"

"Done!" J.B. answered, and took off at a run.

As the others departed, the gorillas paused in confusion, then charged in a group. Shooting as fast as he could pull the trigger, Ryan emptied the Webley. Four of the gorillas fell with blood spraying from their faces, but the fifth took a round smack in the chest and didn't even pause.

Cursing the miss, Ryan threw a gren, and the ape caught the sphere to sniff at it suspiciously. The blast reduced it to a smoking stain, and Ryan took off after the others, fumbling to open the top of the revolver and thumb in fresh rounds.

Reaching the rock wall, J.B. turned and waited until Ryan was in sight, then emptied a clip in one stuttering volley into the forest behind the man. The 9 mm rounds ripped apart the leaves, and six gorillas fell wounded or dying. But they started after the companions again, crawling along the ground with their four arms, heading straight for the Armorer, their tiny red eyes staring hatefully at him. The sight chilled his blood, and J.B. had to force himself to stay and reload the Uzi, instead of starting up the cliff face.

"Get going!" Ryan ordered, dropping the Webley and drawing the SIG-Sauer. He hadn't wanted to use the silenced blaster because it had less of a punch than the booming revolver, but he was out of ammo for the big-bore top-loader. Krysty had the last of the .44 rounds, and she was completely out of reach.

J.B. started to object, when a hail of lead hit the ground around the gorillas as they crossed the little stream. Craning his neck, the man saw the others clinging precariously from the rock face, firing their blasters with one hand. Then there came the telltale thunderous boom of Doc's LeMat, and a wounded male stepped backward to fall over, showing the back of its head missing.

"Climb!" the old man shouted, sounding like Zeus on Mount Olympus.

Ryan swept the field with his SIG-Sauer, putting a round into each of the remaining six apes, then turned and threw himself at the rock wall. Both hands grabbing hold of a horizontal crack, the Deathlands warrior pulled himself up until his boots found purchase on the rough surface, and he extended his arms to find another crack.

Clawing for cracks, J.B. followed a few feet away from his old friend. Cold logic dictated that everybody climb alone in case they lost their grip and fell. They had no ropes, or pitons, only bare hands. There was no way to help each other now, except for not colliding into someone on the way down.

Dean and Doc were already ten feet off the ground, moving faster than expected, and Mildred was scaling the rocks as if she had done it her whole life.

As Jak slowly struggled along the crevices, Krysty snagged an outcropping on the side of the mesa and pulled herself higher. Ryan and J.B. followed, pausing when they reached a small ledge to shoot at the hunting apes below. More than half of the muties were sprawled on the ground, but the rest continued on, uncaring of the deadly lead flying past their stubby heads.

Checking below, Ryan cursed as he saw the huge apes pawing at the rock wall, leaning close to sniff the mesa, then tap it with their massive fingers. The bastard things were still trying to follow the group.

One gorilla reached up with an incredible long arm and pawed the rocks, pulling itself off the ground with the one hand. Their flexible toes worked as auxiliary hands that fondled the rocks to find any purchase, and the beast moved higher on the wall. Grunting among themselves, the rest tried to follow the first and soon the six were hot in pursuit, and moving faster than any of the companions.

A particularly large ape roared at the tiny humans, and Ryan tried to target the big male, but the angle of the sheer cliff prohibited that now. Reluctantly, he holstered his piece and proceeded skyward once more.

"Still after us," Ryan warned the others.

"Fuck that," Jak said, and fired twice at the creatures with his .357 Magnum blaster.

The apes flinched at the noise of the weapon, and one round ricocheted off the wall, spraying out rock chips and dust. The other creased the hairy shoulder of the bull male, and the beast sounded very human as it cried out from the pain of the wound. Then it locked its gaze on Jak, and the teenager saw the murderous intent in its face. He aimed again, and the mutie moved just as he fired, the round missing completely.

Unable to load without falling, Jak holstered the piece and concentrated on his climbing once more. But not able to use the hurt leg, his speed was pitiful, and the ape gained on the teenager with nightmarish speed.

There was a cry from Mildred, and J.B. saw her flail as the root in her hand came free from the wall, loose pebbles sprinkling downward. Instinctively, J.B. reached out a hand to help her, but she was yards away. He watched in horror as the physician struggled not to fall, then cheered as she stabbed a knife into the cliff and used that as an anchor to move to a more secure area.

Tense minutes passed as the companions did nothing but concentrate on their individual tasks. Fingers dug painfully into the smallest of openings, and boots slipped constantly as they tried to dig in for a purchase that would hold their weight, if only for a scant few seconds.

Pausing to catch his breath, Ryan shot at the hunting apes and scored a wound. The beast was still scaling the cliff, but much slower. Encouraged by this, J.B. pulled a jagged piece of cliff loose and let it drop at another gorilla. The stone fell straight for the mutie's face, but the creature reached out with an enormous hand and caught it, then lobbed the stone right back. J.B. barely had time to swing out of the way before the limestone slammed into the mesa where he had just been, exploding into powdery shrapnel.

"Son of a bitch is fast," he muttered, paying closer attention to his climbing and wisely deciding to not try that again.

Then a shout of surprise sounded from above and Dean fell away from the cliff, the end of a thick root grasped in his hands.

"Dean!" Ryan cried, reaching out for the boy, but Dean was completely beyond his father's grasp.

Chapter Eleven

As Mildred and Krysty fired at the muties below, Doc looked up at Dean's cry and saw the boy coming. Instantly, the old man dug in his heels and reached out to grab for Dean. He knew it was impossible to catch the lad directly—the impact would pull him off the cliff also. But there was another way. Maybe.

Doc got a hold of the boy's belt and pulled with all of his strength, the jerk almost tearing him off the rock face. A searing explosion of pain swelled in his shoulder. Holding on for dear life, the old man swung the boy inward and Dean hit the mesa with stunning force, his head cracking against the stones and going limp.

By the Three Kennedys, Doc thought. It had worked! He successfully neutralized the inertia by using the cliff itself. The boy could be dead from the blow, but he would have died anyway. At least the boy was given a chance at life.

Sweating from the strain, Doc could see the boy was unconscious and forced himself to start climbing again. There was no other way. His knuckles were white from tightly holding on to Dean's belt, and the pain in his shoulder grew into a white-hot agony worse than any bullet wound. It had to be dislocated.

As he had done many times before in his life, Doc blocked the world from his mind and thought only of the climb and holding on to his young friend. Find another crack, shift his weight, climb, brace himself, find the strength from within, tighten the grip on the belt. Now do it once more. Again, and again. There was no time, no sounds. Only the endless cliff and a universe of distant pain.

But then there was no more rock before his face, and familiar arms reached to take Dean under the armpits to try to lift him, but Doc refused to relinquish his ward.

"Let go, Doc," Mildred said softly. "I've got him. It's okay. Dammit, you old coot, let him go!"

The man tried to do as requested, but his aching body was moving with a will of its own. Sluggishly, he inched over the edge and crawled onto the top of the mesa, still dragging the unconscious boy. When he cleared the rim, Doc collapsed onto the bare soil, pulling in lungfuls of air.

In the background somewhere, Doc heard blaster-fire and the howls of wounded apes. He tried to rise and draw his LeMat, but somebody forced him back down.

"Rest for a sec," Ryan ordered, and Doc was too weak to even nod in response.

"Thank God, Dean is okay," Mildred announced, brushing the hair from the boy's face. There were no broken bones or fractures that she could detect. Oh, Dean would have a new scar under his hair, but that was a fine trade against having his brains splattered across the landscape.

Privately, Mildred still couldn't believe that Doc managed to catch the boy. She knew his appearance of being old was merely a side effect of time travel, but she had never truly appreciated just how strong the tall man was. Until today.

As the red fog of exhaustion left his vision, the old man saw Ryan crouched alongside him, resting on his boot heels. Gently, the one-eyed man was probing the swollen shoulder with his fingertips. "No breaks," he said finally. "Must be dislocated."

"I can fix that," Mildred said, kneeling.

"Doc, this will hurt bad, but only for a few seconds."

"Proceed," the exhausted man whispered.

Mildred placed her left boot under the Doc's armpit and the other on the side of his neck. Wrapping her hands around the man's wrist, Mildred gently rotated the arm slightly clockwise to align the bones, then savagely pulled with all her strength. Doc screamed, and the electric shot of pain flooded his body with cold adrenaline.

"Better," Doc said in an almost normal voice, then after a moment carefully lifted the arm and tried flexing his hand. "Much better. Thank you, my dear Dr. Wyeth."

In an unusual display of affection, she ruffled his crop of silvery hair. "No prob."

Nearby, J.B. was standing at the edge of the cliff, reloading the Uzi, while Krysty and Jak tossed grens at the gorillas. The dull thuds of the grens faintly shook the ground, and the muties briefly shrieked. Working the arming bolt, J.B. started firing short bursts over the side, and another ape howled, the noise quickly dwindling into the distance to abruptly stop.

"Two retreating," Jak stated, thumbing rounds into the Ruger, then switching weapons back to his Colt.

His Ruger Redhawk sported only a four-inch barrel, which made it a fast draw. But the six-inch barrel of the Colt Python made a difference in accuracy. Maybe he'd keep both; they made a nice combo.

"Nobody escapes," Ryan said in a voice of ice. Sliding the Steyr off his shoulder, the man went to the edge and swept the cliff face with the telescope mounted on the longblaster. When the crosshairs found a mutie, he centered the scope on its face and blasted its features with a 7.62 mm hollowpoint round. The other tried to flatten against the cliff to escape, but Ryan winged it in the leg, and, as it doubled over to grab the wound, he planted a round into its ear. Already chilled, the gorilla went sailing off the rock face and impacted heavily into the ground.

Ryan pumped a few additional rounds into any corpse that was mostly intact. He wasn't going to have the apes come back in the night to attack the companions in their sleep.

"See any more?" J.B. asked with a frown.

"Not yet," Ryan stated, slinging the longblaster on a shoulder. "But there's no way we wiped out all of them. I'll check on the others. You stand guard."

"Done."

Holding a wad of cloth to his head, Dean went over to Doc, a trickle of blood flowing from under his dark hair.

"Thanks," the boy said, extending a hand. "Owe you."

Gingerly, the old man took the hand and they shook. "Next time," Doc said with a smile, "you catch me."

"Done," Dean said seriously.

Suddenly, a hairy arm came over the edge of the

mesa and the big bull mutie rose into view. The companions drew their blasters, but Jak was first, the Colt firing as the barrel cleared the holster. Ryan was only a split second behind the teenager, and the men led the rest of the companions in hammering the beast with lead until it staggered backward and plummeted out of sight.

"That's six," Ryan said, working the bolt to drop in a fresh clip. He pocketed the spent mag and put his back to the cliff. "Let's get walking. I'm on point, J.B. cover the rear."

Moving away from the edge of the mesa, the companions wearily trudged along the bare ground. Ryan could see his friends needed rest and some food, but this wasn't the area for that. Once they put a few miles between themselves and the jungle, he'd find a secure spot where they could establish a campsite. Even he got tired after that much combat.

Lagging slightly behind the rest, Jak was shuffling along, trying to keep the weight off his foot. Doc slowed to walk alongside the teenager, then passed over his ebony stick.

"Just a loan," Doc said.

Jak nodded and, switching the Magnum to his other hand, levered himself along using the stick as a cane. Some of the tension eased from his face, and his speed noticeably increased.

The top of the mesa was a flat field of bare ground, stretching before them in an endless vista of rough ground that resembled black glass.

"Cooled lava," Krysty said, nudging a crystalline spire with her boot.

Squinting, Ryan looked at the two volcanoes on the

island. "Too far away," he stated. "Something else slagged this ground."

"Nuke?"

"Probably so." The Deathlands warrior checked the rad counter on his lapel and saw it registering only normal background activity.

"Clear," Ryan announced in relief.

The Uzi cradled in his arms, J.B. glanced at his own rad counter and nodded in agreement. The area was safe.

Tiny cracks were starting to appear in the smooth flow, and soon small weeds dotted the black ground, the tufts highly visible against the dark material. The greenery thickened until it carpeted the land. Ahead of the companions were trees and bushes, the beginnings of a small forest that appeared to reach all the way to the towering ruins of the predark metropolis. The gleaming towers of steel and concrete rose dozens of stories high, without any apparent sign of corrosion or blast damage.

A flock of birds nesting in the grassy field took flight at the approach of the norms, and Ryan jerked to a halt. The rest of the companions froze, weapons at the ready, when the man knelt and waved them closer.

"We're not the first to reach the top," Ryan said, lifting a human skull out of the weeds.

The object was clean, without a sign of flesh, but the bone was still white, not the dusky yellow of a skull long exposed to the inclement weather.

"How old?" Ryan asked, passing it over to the physician.

Mildred turned the skull and checked inside.

"Year," she stated, biting a lip. "Maybe two. But certainly no longer than that."

"Not a predark?" Dean asked, leaning in to see.

With a crack, Mildred removed the lower jaw and displayed the pitted yellow, teeth. "All these cavities, and not a sign of dental work?" she said as a question. "No way this man is from my era."

"Man?" Krysty asked curiously.

"You can tell from the size," Ryan replied, standing and brushing off his pants. Odd there was only a head in the middle of a field.

A few yards away, Jak gave a sharp whistle.

"More," the teenager announced, lifting a shiny femur from the grass. Other than the skull, the thigh bone was the most identifiable part of the human skeleton, with its double knuckles at the top and bottom. It also made a damn fine club.

"And over here," Krysty added, scowling, looking for pelvis bones. The bones were all mixed together, cracked open and chewed by animals, and some folks carried away skulls of their enemies as trophies. Counting the number of hipbones was the only way to get an accurate number of skeletons.

"Nine," she announced after a couple of minutes. "Could have been a hunting party. Or raiders."

Trying not to step on any bones, Mildred joined the redhead. "Yeah, they're all adult males, but... look there, some of these are white, some brittle and yellow." The physician lifted her head and pulled her blaster. "I think this is the dumping spot for the something that has been chilling folks for decades."

"The gorillas?" Krysty asked in concern.

Mildred vehemently shook her head. "I saw the

teeth of those muties. They were big, but herbivores. Meat eaters aced these men.''

''Found their weapons,'' Dean announced, standing and wiping the dirt off a broken knife. The metal was green with corrosion, holes eaten completely through the blade.

Ambling over, Ryan saw the scattered remains of carved bone and bits of plastic mixed together, the steel weapons reduced to mere ghostly outlines of rust. Lifting the largest piece of metal, Ryan studied it carefully.

''What is this, a matchlock? No, a pipe gun,'' he said, the cumbersome weapon crumbling under his touch. The primitive longblaster was merely an iron pipe with a hole in the top for a fuse, and a wooden stock closed off the rear end. That was it. Load the muzzle, light the fuse, aim and wait. The device was so crude it made a flintlock look like a nuke.

''Dark night, nobody on the islands would use these anymore,'' J.B. stated. ''This guy must have bought the farm a long time ago. A lot more than a couple of years.''

Mildred shook her head. ''This is new bones on top of old weapons. Layers of people died over the decades.''

Glancing at the field and forest, Ryan rubbed his chin to the sound of sandpaper. ''Folks must have been trying to reach the ruins for quite a while, and something always stopped them right here.''

''Or trying to leave,'' Dean added, observing the towering monoliths, their mirrored sides shimmering in the reflected light of the noonday sun.

''Welcome to El Dorado,'' Doc muttered, drawing both of his weapons.

Adjusting his wire-rimmed glasses, J.B. frowned. "Don't get you, Doc," he said. "I've been to Eldorado, big ville in south Tex. Nothing but bars and gaudy houses."

"I think he was referring to the old poem," Mildred said, also viewing the predark ruins. "A fabled city of gold that nobody ever reached alive."

"However, we've got a bastard lot better than matchlocks and wooden clubs," Ryan stated, leveling the longblaster. "Okay, I'm on point with Krysty. J.B. and Dean, cover the rear. We go slow and watch your steps. Whatever aced these folks could live underground. Anything appears, shoot on sight."

Warily, the companions assumed formation and crossed the field to enter the tall grass. These plants were green and alive, not dead weeds, the grass mixing with wild wheat and barley, almost as if this had been a farm long ago. The wind made a hushing sound as it blew over the waist-high crops.

"Watch for waves," Krysty warned, referring to the disturbances animals made when they moved through tall grass. From the top the patterns resembled ripples on a lake and gave away the predator's exact position as it closed for the kill.

As the grass became taller, the ground became mushy, and the shoulder-tall plants stopped at the bank of a rushing stream, the water so crystal clear they could see to the bottom. Knowing their canteens were low, Ryan called for a halt, but had J.B. test for rads and Mildred check for chems. They both pronounced it safe to drink. Happily, the companions rinsed out the canteens before filling them again, then took the opportunity to splash some of the water on their faces, doing a brief wash. The stream was cool and tasted faintly of mineral deposits. Best they'd had since arriving in the Marshall Islands.

When they were finished, the group waded to the other side. But Jak called a second halt and passed Dean several weapons before wading back into the middle of the stream and lying down. Rigorously, the teen began rubbing himself all over, trying to remove the mud of the area from his hair and clothing. The downstream runoff was black at first, then as the layers washed away, it turned brown and finally clear.

"Better," he grunted, wading to the shore and taking back his blasters. The teenager looked like a pale drowned rat, but nobody shifted position when he came near anymore.

"Damn pigs," Jak muttered, shaking his jacket.

"You're preaching to the choir on that, my friend," Doc growled.

Then surprisingly, Krysty and Mildred did the same thing, even though they didn't seem to be very dirty.

"Goddamn, that's cold!" the physician said through chattering teeth, both hands busy wringing the water from her beaded hair. "But I feel more like a human being now."

Making an inarticulate noise of pleasure, Krysty wildly shook her head, the animated filaments splaying out to facilitate drying, then slowly returning to the gentle crimson curls.

"This will do until we can find some soap," she said, squeezing the sleeves of her jumpsuit.

Greatly refreshed, the three companions dried as the group walked toward the forest, the formation of trees proving to be only a slim windbreak a few yards wide. Leaving the forest, they traversed a rubble-filled culvert, with half of a predark bridge high overhead, the span ending in the middle of empty air.

Reaching the top of the culvert, the group easily crawled under a heavy wire fence, braided with plastic strips that hid whatever was beyond. The companions found themselves standing on the gravel berm of a predark road, the smooth pavement extending out of sight in both directions. Across the road was a collection of warehouses, rusty cars with flat tires standing at ancient parking meters. Streetlights hung from power cables over every intersection, more cars stopped forever at the faded crosswalks. An assortment of houses lined the side streets, the front yards wild tangles of ivy and flowers, a few of the homes completely buried under the unstoppable advance of the resilient ivy. Not a window was broken, doors were closed and telephone lines were still connected to the poles. An unnatural silence lay heavy over the predark metropolis, and the companions fought a small shiver.

"Don't like this," Ryan said with a frown. "The damn place is in perfect condition. As if everybody simply stopped moving for a hundred years."

"Not quite everybody," Doc rumbled, pointing upward with the LeMat.

Rising above the factories and homes were the monolithic skyscrapers of downtown. Stretched between two of the high rises was a giant web, exactly like the one they had seen on Spider Island.

"Now we know where the bones came from," Ryan said.

"Gonna need some Molotov cocktails," J.B. stated, hefting his unusually light munitions bag. "Those worked last time."

"Sort of," Mildred corrected.

"There's a beer plant," Dean said, indicating a building down the street. "We can get bottles there."

"Keep your eyes peeled for a gas station," Ryan said, starting down the middle of the street.

"Need the soap powder from a laundry, too," Krysty added, the Webley feeling heavy in her hand. Her knuckles had been badly skinned in the rock climb, and the weapon was already christened with specks of blood.

HIGH ABOVE the silent streets, something watched the seven people proceed deeper into the heart of the city.

The newcomers were wounded and poorly dressed, but with good boots and very well-armed. This indicated a high probability that they were scavengers who had raided a supply dump. Thus additional weapons may not be in visual range. Grens were almost a certainty, and possibly even an energy weapon: a portable microwave beamer, or Bedlow laser. Such lethal armament was not to be taken lightly, and willful self-termination was authorized only as a last resort. More data was required to form a course of action.

Closing the blinds, the Walker moved away from the window, stepping off the ceiling and through the door to stealthily make its way down to the ground level. Clearly, further reconnaissance was necessary until it could decide exactly how and when to exterminate the humans.

Chapter Twelve

Walking down the middle of the street between the lines of dead cars, the companions tried to keep a watch in every direction and found it impossible. There were just too many windows, sewers and doorways in the metropolis. If somebody wanted to hide, there was no limit to the places where they could ferret.

"Creepy," Mildred said, fighting a shiver. "I've been in plenty of ruins, but this place, well, it isn't ruins. It's just old and empty. I keep expecting the traffic lights to click on, and the cars to start moving again."

"This was no nuke attack," Krysty said, watching the tattered remains of cloth curtains fluttering in the open window of a second-floor apartment, a red ceramic flowerpot balanced precariously on the sill. "Mebbe poison gas."

"Or a neutron bomb," J.B. said, watching the reflection of the passing companions in the plate-glass window of a millinery store. "Damn thing only aced people and machines but did no damage to the buildings. Got no idea how it worked."

Mildred started to explain about jacketing a tactical nuke with deutronium-rich water and tritium injectors, then stopped herself. The details weren't important. Only the results.

Going to a police car, Ryan studied the interior, then smashed in the glass with the barrel of his Webley. The green squares of the safety glass scattered underfoot. Reaching in, he took the pump-action shotgun out of the skeleton hands of the dead officer and racked the slide. A shell came out and he closely inspected it. The plastic was firm, not brittle, the brass bottom shiny and without any signs of age or corrosion.

"Looks good," he said, tossing it to J.B.

The Armorer made the catch. "Yeah, if the whole place is like this, we'll be ass deep in supplies."

"This city is so dead," Krysty said. "I can feel the death laying over these buildings."

There were skeletons inside almost every car with the windows closed, piles of bones behind the steering wheels, briefcases on the passenger seats, foam coffee cups still perched on the dashboards.

"You sensing anything alive?" he added.

"In every direction," the redhead said. "Plants, animals, things I can't describe, but no human life." She paused. "Or rather, nothing I call human."

"'For a thousand silent ghosts trod the ancient way, seeking a speaking to those warm and alive,'" Doc said softly in his singsong voice.

Rattling the handle of an ambulance, only to find it locked, Mildred turned at the quote and frowned. "Don't know that one. Is it Emerson?"

"One of my own efforts, madam," he answered, staring into the distance. "From when I wrote poetry and thought it a very important thing to do. A million years ago."

"You're a poet?" Mildred chuckled.

He offered a wan smile. "In due honesty I must admit my works were very poor things, indeed."

"Quiet. We're being watched," Ryan said, the hairs on the back of his neck stiffening. The man raised the Steyr and gently worked the bolt to chamber a round. This clip was the first of the ammo from the armory of the pirates, and he hadn't had a chance yet to check the cartridges. He was going to find out real fast if it was any good.

Using the Uzi to tilt back his fedora, J.B. said, "Yeah, I can feel it, too. Just like when we were traveling with the Trader, and the convoy would roll into a pass. There was nothing to see, but we could tell the bastards were there anyway."

"Gorilla or spider?" Jak asked, reaching for a knife and biting back a curse. Damn pirates took everything. He needed to get more soon. Had to be something in this city he could use or adapt.

Slowly turning, Ryan didn't answer, his eye staring hard at the alleyways and rooftops. That's where he could launch an attack from. And he had learned from experience to always consider what the enemy could do, not just what they might do.

With a cry, Dean turned and fired. A rat exploded into gory fur off the hood of a car, the .460 Nitro Express round continuing onward to slam into and punch a hole through a brick wall. The blast of the Weatherby echoed along the concrete canyons of the city, slowly fading into the distance.

"If the locals didn't before," Ryan growled, "they damn well know we're here now. Put away that long-cannon, Dean, and use the Browning."

"Sure, Dad," the boy said. He cleared the breech of the heavy rifle, then slid in a third round before slinging it over a shoulder. The .460 rounds of the big-bore longblaster were so huge, the breech could only hold two spare cartridges in the internal mag, plus a third up the pipe. Not a lot, put the thing hit like a bazooka.

Pulling out his Browning semiautomatic blaster, he clicked off the safety and jacked the slide.

"Ready," Dean announced somberly.

Ryan gave a nod, then continued scanning the multitude of buildings. Five, six, ten stories tall, the buildings stood in lines along the downtown like mountains reaching for the stars.

"First thing we need is to recce this burg," he said, annoyed. "Be here for years if we have to check every building."

"That seems to be the tallest," Krysty said. "We could see the whole island from the top."

"Not going to find a redoubt from above," Mildred countered, then added, "but we're not going to see people walking the streets, either."

The redhead frowned. That was true. Somewhere in this city there had to be a redoubt, or a gateway. But where could it be located?

"Check gov office," Jak stated casually. "Or base."

"And after that?" Doc inquired politely.

Unconcerned, the teenager shrugged.

There was a shattering of glass, and the companions spun to see Doc reaching through a busted car window to withdraw a map. Carefully, he unfolded it on top of the vehicle's hood, then crumpled the paper into a ball and tossed the wad away.

"Fiji," he said succinctly.

"Okay, top of the skyscraper it is," Ryan decided,

hoisting his longblaster. "Should be easy to spot the dome of the capitol building or a military base from there."

"Easy enough to get there," J.B. agreed, looking at the granite monolith towering above the metropolis. "We just keep making rights and lefts until we're there."

"Unless we pass a hardware store," Ryan said. "Army-Navy, camping outlet, anything like that. We need supplies."

"How much food does each of us have?" Krysty asked, patting the pockets of her bearskin coat. She had six MRE envelopes and a small can of soup. That was it—everything else had been abandoned in the horse cart.

"Combined, we have enough for three days," Mildred replied. She considered it part of her job in the group to keep track of the food. "After that, we hunt for cans."

"Or hunt," Jak said, leaning heavily on the ebony stick. Then he glanced backward at the stain and frowned. "Not partial to rat."

"Should be no shortage of food," Ryan said. "If it really was a neutron bomb that chilled this place, the stores should have tons of canned goods. Neutron blasts make cans last forever."

"Just watch for rust," Mildred reminded curtly. "Somebody gets ptomaine poisoning, there's nothing I can do to help."

"A feeb in swamp ate from rusty can," Jak said. "Saw it. Died screaming."

Instantly, everybody became alert as a warm wind blew down the street, carrying a faint whiff of sulfur. Nervously, they scrutinized the sky overhead. A flock of condors was lazily winging over the city, and endless sheet lightning was booming amid the fiery orange-and-purple clouds. But there was no sign of the dreaded acid rain coming. The smell of sulfur had to have been from the windward vents of the local volcanoes. Nothing to worry about.

"Let's get a move on," Ryan said, starting along the parked cars in the street. "And if a spider attacks, blow out a store window and get inside. It's too big to follow us through most stores."

As the group went along the city streets, the smell of sulfur got consistently stronger, then eased away just as fast as it came. Taking a cross street, they found no cars about, and the sightless eyes of the countless glass windows became a hall of mirrors reflecting their images against one another, forming a multiple of ever smaller companions. Ryan fought the urge to start blowing out glass, and gratefully left the visual labyrinth of the city block behind as they took another turn, getting ever closer to the skyscraper.

But then just for a moment, Ryan spotted a new reflection in a silvery window. It was a tall man with his silvery hair tied back, and wearing a fancy embroidered duster, with a long white eagle feather in his hair.

Ryan stared at the sight, feeling his guts twist and heart pound like predark artillery. It was the same man who appeared in the Deathlands just before Trader took the long walk to nowhere. Instinctively, Ryan started for his blaster, then thought better of it.

"Hey," he called out in a friendly manner.

The reflection turned and was gone. Charging forward, Ryan ran around the corner and found himself staring at a long empty street. A breeze blew some dust off the roadway into a ghostly cloud, and a lizard scuttled under a rusted-out mailbox to escape from the heat of the day.

"Ryan," a voice said.

The man spun with a finger tightening on the trigger of the Steyr, to see Krysty come about the corner.

"Hey," he repeated, the word sounding flat in the dry air. "Just saw the strangest thing."

Almost worried, Krysty studied his face for a moment. She had never seen him this way before. "Looks like you just saw death itself," she said, adding a smile to let him know it was a joke.

But the big man didn't laugh or smile. Instead, Ryan turned and stared hard at the empty street again.

"Mebbe I did," Ryan muttered, feeling as if he had just been given a warning of some kind. A damn important one, too. But whether it was to go, or stay, or what, he had no idea. Only one thing was certain; something terrible was about to happen. Right here and now.

Just then, a sharp whistle shrilled, and the pair rushed back to the others. The rest of the companions were gathered around the front doors of a four-story building, a dark neon sign stretching across its second-floor facade proudly proclaiming it a department store.

"Might be just what we were looking for." Mildred smiled, cupping hands to her face in an effort to see inside. But another set of doors stood a few yards away from the street doors, and the exterior light couldn't penetrate strong enough for the woman to be able to make out anything clearly—only vague outlines of display cases, racks of clothing and what she hoped were mannequins. Sure had a lot of them, though.

Lying on the sidewalk, J.B. was busy tricking the locking mechanism set into the bottom steel rim of one of the glass doors. "Stupid ass place for a lock," he mumbled, both hands full of probes and lock picks. Rattling the door, he tried again and this time was rewarded with a dull clank.

"Damn good lock," the Armorer said respectfully, getting to his feet and tucking away the collection of tools.

The next set yielded much faster and as they opened it, out flowed dry, lifeless air that seemed to suck the very moisture from the skin as it rushed into the street and was gone.

Moving through the wind break of the two sets of doors, the companions entered the department store. The interior was as dark as night, false walls blocked the sunlight from coming in through the window, the hundreds of electric lights in the white tile ceiling cold tubes and bulbs. Going to a rack of dresses, Ryan ripped the arm off a mannequin and wrapped a silky frock about the wooden limb. Then dampening the material with a few drops of gun oil, he flicked a butane lighter and the torch crackled alive, filling the area with bright illumination. The rest of the companions did the same, and soon everybody was carrying a torch. They began to prowl through the cavernous building.

Moving in their nimbus of firelight, the companions proceeded along the aisles with their weapons primed. For a moment, J.B. stopped at an eyeglass display set into a wall, and looked longingly at the hundreds of pairs of frames, then moved on reluctantly, knowing from past experience that the frames held clear glass. His glaucoma hadn't gotten any worse in the past while, and he forcibly reminded himself to stop worrying about things he couldn't change. If, or when, he started to go blind, he knew exactly what he would do.

Holding his torch away from the flammable clothing, Dean grabbed some fresh socks off a rack and stuffed them into his hip pockets. Nearby, Doc was doing the same in the men's section with underwear.

"Camping gear!" Jak reported, hobbling in that direction.

Converging on the area, the companions ransacked the shelves finding mess kits, rain ponchos and new backpacks. It was merely civilian equipment, not sturdy Army haversacks for soldiers on field maneuvers, but the canvas was camou-colored and better than nothing.

Krysty took an extra pack and loaded it with plastic packs of beef jerky and instant soup. Ryan located a display of field lanterns, and carefully drained a hundred partially dried-out bottles of oil to fill three reservoirs. Then he worked the attached pump to build the pressure inside the reservoirs and lit a steel gauze wick. It glowed like a red ember, but as he turned up the pressure flow, the field lantern gave off a wealth of brilliant white light. Quickly, the other two were ignited and the smoking torches stomped out underfoot on the terrazzo floor.

Rifling through a box of magnesium flares for making campfires, J.B. froze, a hand easing toward the Uzi. For just a moment, he could have sworn something moved away from the bright lantern light. But as minutes passed and nothing happened, he began to relax. It had to have just been the shadows flickering as the lanterns changed position. Yeah, made sense. But J.B. moved the selector switch on the rapidfire to full-auto, just in case. There was something disturbing about this store, although he couldn't quite put his finger on what.

Smashing open a locked case, Jak removed a dozen knives from the wide assortment. Using his teeth, the teenager ripped off the plastic-and-cardboard backing from the first blade, then used the shiny weapon to slice open the rest of the packs. Expertly, Jak tested each blade with an artful flip, tucking only the best of the leaf-shaped throwing knives into his clothing. Then he shifted his leather jacket a few times to get adjusted to being properly armed again. He had felt naked without steel up his sleeve.

Taking a pair of shoes, Doc replaced his old worn pair and stood flexing his feet in sublime pleasure.

"Any combat boots?" Dean asked hopefully.

"No, but lots of sneakers."

Disappointed, the boy walked away.

Closing the gun-rack case, Ryan turned and walked away in disgust. Some feeb bastard had put an open can of soda in the case, and the moisture of the soft drink had ruined every blaster in the case over the long decades. Underneath the case were multiple shelves filled with stacks of ammo, but most of the rounds were half-load wadcutters that would only foul a gun barrel if used too much, and anything live was the wrong caliber, .22 short and long, .32, .360, .45APC, .475 Nitro, 8- and 10-gauge shotgun shells, and a special order for 10 mm AP rounds—nothing they could use. There were several spots where other boxes of .38, .357 and 9 mm bullets had been neatly stacked, but those were gone. Typical. The predark world had to have been getting pretty rough and more than once he found a gun store with most of its weapons and ammo gone, sold off in a panic of a war that lasted only three minutes.

Regrouping, the companions exchanged some items, then moved toward the rear of the store. As they went past the housewares section, Krysty paused to snare a nonstick frying pan and stuff it into her new backpack. But Mildred stopped to examine sports bras and took two, stepping around a display of sexy lingerie to come out again adjusting something under her shirt.

Ignoring the toy section, they swept through the pharmacy. Mildred emptied shelves of aspirins, rubbing alcohol, bandages, antiseptic mouthwash and iodine, filling her med kit. The men took disposable plastic razors, the women passed by the perfumed soap to take only unscented bars and everybody grabbed a replacement toothbrush. Dentistry these days was a pair of pliers and a shot of shine, an event to be avoided at any cost.

Passing by the liquor store, the companions moved slowly up the powerless escalator, knowing the lanterns were revealing their advance to any onlookers. Ryan darted out first and took cover behind a rack of music boxes. He whistled when it was clear, and the others eagerly spread out, wondering what treasures they would find on this level. It was incredible that the city hadn't been looted to the walls by the pirates, in spite of the mutie gorillas.

This level of the department store was packed with useless items: more clothes, purses, jewelry, cosmetics, wicker baskets, towels and linens, beds and easy chairs. The companions prowled farther into the dark recess of the building, hoping for better.

Bypassing a hair salon, J.B. slipped inside a photo shop and returned with a half-filled plastic bottle, grinning as he tucked it away into the munition bags. Then pausing at a display of cigars, he lifted one from a humidor, and inside the plastic wrapping the leaves crumbled into dust. Sighing in resignation, J.B. wiped off his hands and moved on.

"Eureka!" Doc called out, removing a velvet rope from a brass stand. "We have located the dreams of To Chi!"

Situated prominently on a carpeted dais were half a dozen brand-new Harley-Davidson motorcycles on display. Huge placards from the manufacturer advertised the new model, with improved gas mileage, piston jets for a cooler engine and the old-fashioned chain linkage replaced with a state-of-the-art geared transmission.

"Just like those BMW bikes that Silas used," J.B. grunted.

"Think mebbe they'll run?" Dean asked, running palms over the chrome handlebars and leather seat.

"Tires are flat, batteries dead," Ryan said, working out the drain plug and feeling inside. The motor was slick with the residue of oil, only a few drops falling to the floor.

"Also needs lube," he said, wiping his hand clean. "But I don't see why these shouldn't run with some work. They burn alcohol, and there's liquor on the first floor."

"Saw lots vodka," Jak stated.

"Save us a week of walking," Krysty noted.

"That's a live round," Ryan agreed. "Doc, go with him and grab some wicker baskets to carry the stuff."

"Certainly, my dear Ryan," Doc rumbled, and, taking a lantern, led the way to the escalator with the teenager limping behind. The halo of their lantern receded into the distance and was gone.

"Probably need some ether to prime the carbs on these Twin-Cam 88s," Ryan continued, checking over the shiny chrome-plated engines. The big V-shaped motors were tough brutes. "Dean could check the electronics department for cleaners for computer equipment."

"I'll grab some oil from automotive, too," Dean said, and, taking the second lamp, he grabbed a wicker basket and disappeared into the darkness.

"I'll lend a hand," J.B. stated, adjusting his glasses and walking outside the circle of light of the last lantern.

"Anything else needed?" Krysty asked, squatting alongside the man.

"Not really. Everything else we can cobble together here," Ryan told her, starting to disassemble the machine.

"But check around for a repair kit. That'll have a hand pump to inflate the tires. If not, there'll probably be something we can use in the automotive section."

"On it." While Krysty got busy searching, Mildred stayed on guard. The redhead found the pump under the hinged seat and filled the first of the studded tires, when Doc and Jak returned with baskets full of vodka.

Soon, the second floor was filled with the sounds of mechanical repairs, mild cursing and then the sputtering cough of an engine struggling to life before settling to a smooth purr.

Chapter Thirteen

A few hours later, Dean cocked open the exit doors on the ground floor and the companions rode their bikes out onto the street one at a time.

Arching about, Ryan throttled down the 1450cc Twin-V engine and waited until Dean climbed on behind him, his shoulder bag clattering from the dozen Molotov cocktails. Most of the motorcycles were equipped with riding pegs for the drivers to rest their boots on for comfort, but a couple of the Harleys had floorboards to accommodate passengers. Those were the bikes that the companions doubled on. Ryan and Dean, Jak and Doc. Everybody else was solo, and loaded down with supplies and bedrolls.

The sky was turning gray, the shadows of downtown stretching inky fingers across the preserved city. A swarm of squeaking bats poured from a parking garage, and rats scurried from the sewer gratings as the nocturnal creatures left their nests to hunt for food in the starry night.

"Getting too dark to recce," Ryan said, gunning the engine. "We better find someplace to hole for the night. Hit the scraper in the morning."

"Not want fight spider at night," Jak agreed.

"We could camp in the store," Dean suggested, tapping his father on the shoulder. "Lots of big beds."

"And no security," Mildred stated, twisting the throttle, careful not to redline it. They were still breaking in the motorcycles and knew better than to push them too hard too fast, or they'd blow a ring. Machines were a lot like horses—a person had to stay in absolute control, but also give them lots of attention.

"If those hunting gorillas attacked," she went on, "there'd only be some window glass between us and them."

"Agreed," Krysty added, flicking on the headlight and checking the few gauges that worked. "Should we head for a jail or a bank?"

"Bank," Ryan decided. "Muties are strong, but they can't bust through six inches of Plexiglas."

"An excellent suggestion," Doc rumbled.

"Damn," Krysty said, staring at the rearview mirror. "Nobody turn around, but check behind us."

Trying to act casual, Ryan shifted his head to look into the mirror mounted on a chrome rod attached to the handlebars. At first he saw nothing unusual, but then a subtle movement on the third floor of the department store riveted his attention.

Some sort of a machine was slowly easing out of an open window. The device resembled a mechanical spider, even though it only had four impossibly thin metal legs. The jointed limbs attached to a tiny oval no bigger than a human head, with a video camera lens sticking out of the front, and some kind of a weapon swiveling about on a belly mount.

"Droid," Dean said softly, sliding the Weatherby from the gun sleeve strapped to the frame.

Surreptitiously as possible, the others started doing the same, but as small as the motions were the sec droid leaped off the side of the building. In a blur, Ryan drew and fired three times, the 9 mm slugs tracking the descent of the machine until it crashed in a riot of crunching metal and shattering glass on top of an ancient car at the curb.

But it straightened immediately and started toward the companions, the device hanging from its belly strobing with a hellish green light. A wave of heat swept over Ryan, and a sharp hiss to the right made him turn and stare at the molten crater in the granite cornerstone of the apartment building only yards away. A laser!

"Take cover!" he shouted, slipping off the Harley to hit the pavement behind a compact car.

Swinging up the LeMat, Doc triggered a round, and the machine recoiled from the impact of the .44 miniball, its legs stumbling for a few seconds until it righted itself. But now there was a dent in its armor.

Mildred stepped into view from around a minivan and fired the Thompson at the droid, the slugs making its legs buckle and pounding more dents in its armored skin. The Walker simply stood there and accepted the punishment, then the laser glowed as it charged. Mildred dived for cover and the energy weapons strobed rapidly, the condensed light stabbing a line of holes through the predark vehicle, nearly cutting it in two.

From the pavement, Krysty fired off the last two rounds in the Webley, as Ryan and J.B. both tossed grens. But as the spheres bounced along the street toward it, the droid scurried over a limousine. As the charge ripped loose, the resulting double blast gouged a jagged hole in the asphalt and sent out a corona of gravel as shrapnel. The stones hit cars, windows and signs everywhere, instantly turning the area into ruins.

Then a thunderous crack sounded and the Walker was slammed against the glass doors on the department store in a shattering explosion.

Working the bolt on the Weatherby, Dean darted to a closer car and tried another shot. But deflected by the thick glass, the .460 round missed the droid standing only a foot away. Stepping behind an undamaged pane of glass, the machine stayed motionless for a few moments, before crashing through the glass, its pulsating laser sweeping the line of parked cars.

Ryan hit the ground and rolled for safety, coming up behind a luxury car. If these had been working vehicles, that light show would have ignited the fuel in most of the wags, the resulting hellstorm of fire and shrapnel chilling the companions on the spot. But the dead wrecks gave no reaction as sizzling holes went through their engine blocks and fuel tanks.

Taking a step backward, the droid paused as if puzzled by the lack of reactions from the vehicles. Ryan knew there wasn't enough space in its body for a powerful computer and the power plant to run the laser. Its builders had made a decision, and now the companions were going to prove it had been the wrong choice.

Flicking his lighter, J.B. lobbed a Molotov at the droid. The bottle hit directly in front, the mixture whoofing into a huge fireball. Unconcerned, the Walker strode through the flames, as the glow around its laser slowly increased until the weapon fired again, the scintillating beam riddling the cars to no effect.

"Ten-sec recharge!" Krysty shouted, dropping the

exhausted Webley and shooting her S&W .38 at the video lens on top.

"Wait for it!" Ryan ordered, hunching low, switching the SIG-Sauer to his left hand and sliding the Steyr SSG-70 off his shoulder.

The laser flashed, and the store windows behind the companions violently shattered from heat expansion, thousands of shards of glass raining on them. Writhing in agony, Krysty screamed, clutching her glass-covered hair.

"Now!" Ryan shouted with blood trickling down his cheek. He stood, firing both blasters.

Rising into full view, the companions opened fire on the Walker with everything they had, the barrage of lead making a leg buckle, and then the video lens exploded into sparkling trash.

Blind, the machine began walking around in a small circle, firing the laser every ten seconds randomly.

"Some sort of autoprotect program," Mildred muttered, working the bolt to clear another jam in the breech of the heavy Thompson.

At her words, the Walker rushed at the wag, climbing over the vehicle, its legs stabbing through the thin decorative metal. Poised on top like a cougar on a rock, the sec droid remained motionless, its lasers glowing into full power, and then nothing. It simply stood there, waiting for another sound, the scrape of cloth on stone, a cough, anything to pinpoint its human prey.

With her back pressed to the granite wall, Mildred sat on the sidewalk, the Thompson held in both hands, the bent brass shell still sticking out of the ejector port. The laser was pointing right at the physician and her ZKR was tucked into its holster. Maybe it was only the coming darkness of night, but the glow emanating from the laser seemed to be increasing as if it were going to fire. With no choice, the woman licked suddenly dry lips, and began to sneak a hand toward the arming bolt.

Towering above her, the Walker shifted its stance a little bit from the evening breeze.

Covered with glass, Krysty froze in place, afraid to make any move or the falling pieces would announce her position. Moving extremely slow, Dean was trying to lower the Weatherby and draw his Browning semiauto blaster. Caught in the middle of slapping a fresh clip into the Uzi, J.B. started to swing the weapon toward the machine, aiming the lone round in the barrel start for the muzzle of the laser.

Silhouetted by the headlights of the purring motorcycles, Ryan tossed away his blaster and charged. At the sound of his boots, the Walker spun, then the weapon landed with a loud clatter on the hood of a police car. The machine paused for only a moment at the trick, then swiveled right back and fired the laser at the sidewalk. But that brief lapse was all Mildred had needed. She was already gone, and the beam merely vaporized a deep hole in the concrete.

Ryan leaped on the hood of the car, then on the roof. Grabbing the laser in a hand, he crushed the lens, then grabbed the sparking remains of the video camera and pulled with all of his strength. Both of the items broke loose from their weakened housings, and there was a brilliant crackle of blue light, writhing tendrils of electricity crawling over the Deathlands warrior.

The companions rushed closer as the Walker

limply slid off the roof onto the street and Ryan collapsed onto the roof.

"You okay, lover?" Krysty asked, brushing the black hair off his still face. Faint wisps of smoke were rising from his clothes, and there was the terrible smell of burned flesh.

"Mildred, get over here!" J.B. shouted as he felt for a pulse in the wrist. Nothing. Quickly, the Armorer tried the main carotid artery in the throat. There was no detectable beat.

"Is...is he...?" Dean started, unable to finish the sentence.

Even as Mildred sprinted toward them, a heavy silence descended upon the darkening street. Krysty bent over to cup the still man's face, and J.B. closed his eyes. As much as he wanted to speak to the others, he said nothing. There was nothing to say.

"No," Jak whispered, dropping the stick and walking closer.

"Yes, goddamn it, he's dead!" Mildred cursed, shoving the man out of her way.

But as the woman came around the vehicle, the damaged Walker rose into view on its telescoping legs. Her hands full of the medical bag, the physician fumbled to draw her blaster, when Doc strode toward the machine. A finger holding down the trigger of the LeMat, he fanned the hammer like a Western gunfighter. Six shots struck the Walker with trip-hammer blows, slamming aside the buckled armor to expose the delicate circuit boards inside.

Attacking from the side, Dean jammed the Weatherby into the guts of the droid and fired, the whole interior momentarily awash in flame. The .460 Nitro rounds blew out the other side of the hull and the

Walker crashed to the street. Working the lever to open the breech, Dean thumbed in another round and blew apart the largest piece of intact circuitry. Instantly, the droid burst into flames, black smoke pouring from every vent.

Only seconds had passed in the blitzkrieg against the Walker, but Mildred was already working on Ryan, her hands pressed to his chest and pushing hard three times, followed by a pause, then three more hard pushes.

"Keep giving him air!" she ordered.

Krysty didn't reply, but pressed her mouth against Ryan's and continued blowing into his lungs. The Deathlands warrior's chest rose and fell, but there still was no pulse.

"Strive to live," the redhead whispered between breaths. "Please, lover, live."

Straddling the man, Mildred began pounding on Ryan's chest with both fists clasped together. The thumps sounded hollow and empty.

"Follow my mark!" the physician commanded. "One, two, three, mark!" She punched as Krysty exhaled.

"Again!" Mildred commanded. "Again! Again!"

A minute passed, then another with only the sounds of the fists hitting flesh disturbing the silence of the dark street. The crackling light from the burning Walker cast bizarre shadows on the walls of the predark buildings.

"Give it up, Millie," J.B. said softly. "He's gone."

"Fuck that!" she raged, and slammed the man in the chest even harder. "Live, you son of a bitch! I've lost enough patients in this godforsaken hell. You're not gonna be one of them! Come on, you one-eyed bastard! Live, goddamn it! Live!''

Suddenly, a tremor shook Ryan's body and his eye fluttered open. He drew in a ragged breath. Krysty pulled back, as the man began to cough, then weakly turned on his side to lose his breakfast over the bumper.

"Motherfucker..." Ryan panted in a whisper, gasping for breath. "What...hit me?"

"Got electrocuted," Mildred said, grabbing his wrist to check the pulse. The beat was irregular, but getting stronger. "It, ah, knocked you out for a while."

Accepting a canteen from Dean, Ryan washed out his mouth and spit, then drained the container to fall onto his back exhausted from the effort.

Krysty took his hands and held them to her breast. "Glad to have you back, lover," she whispered.

"Thanks. Hurt worse than losing the eye," Ryan croaked, then impossibly slid off the minivan and stood on wobbly legs, one hand palming the damaged hood for support.

Astonished, Mildred couldn't believe the sight. Anybody else would need bed rest for a few days.

"I don't doubt it hurt like blazes," the physician said, massaging her hand. Punching the man in the chest was like punching a bag of potatoes. Solid muscle. "Back in my day, we used to kill criminals by electrocution until the folks realized just how horrible a death it was."

"Feeling okay?" Dean asked, handing his father the dropped blaster.

"Sure." It took him a few tries, but Ryan got the SIG-Sauer in its holster. "Kind of weak," the man admitted, wincing as if the sound of his own voice was causing him pain.

"That'll pass soon enough," Mildred said, rummaging in her med kit. "Here, take these aspirin and suck on this piece of C-4."

Not quite sure he heard that correctly, Ryan stared at the items lying in his palm. "You want me to do what?" he demanded uncertainly.

"Consume plastic explosives, madam?" Doc rumbled askance. "What voodoo is this?"

"Stuff it, you old coot." Mildred scowled and turned to Ryan.

"C-4 is mostly nitroglycerine. That's good for the heart and yours just had a hell of a strain."

Hesitating for a moment, Ryan dry swallowed the pills and tucked the whitish-gray lump of plastique in his cheek. Immediately, he made a face at the horrible taste, but a few moments later there was a rush of color to his cheeks and the man stood straighter with renewed strength.

"Nuke me," Ryan said, giving a rare smile. "I feel better."

"Using C-4 for a bad ticker," J.B. said, kissing Mildred on the cheek. "That's a new one on me."

"Only for an emergency," she answered. "It can kill as easy as cure."

Unexpectedly, Ryan pulled his blaster and jacked the slide. "Where's the Walker?" he demanded, looking around in the stygian blackness. The headlights of the bikes threw great swatches of light across the parked cars, the beams crisscrossing one another.

"Dean and I terminated its prime functions with extreme prejudice," Doc answered, busy reloading the blaster. Then he raised his head to grin. "And we did so with great pleasure, my dear Ryan."

"It's chilled, Dad," Dean agreed grimly, his long-blaster resting on a shoulder.

Stepping from the darkness into the beams of the headlights on the humming motorcycles, Jak nudged the physician. "He aced," the teenager stated. "You fix. How do?"

"The technique is called CPR," Mildred said, struggling to finally clear the jam in the Thompson. The bent brass sprang clear and flew away to land on a car with a metallic ring.

"And he was only technically deceased, not quite all the way there," she continued, easing the pressure off the bolt. "There were no wounds, or physical trauma, just had his heart stopped. Sometimes a doctor can fix that, if we get there soon enough."

"Teach me," Jak asked.

"Yeah, happy to." Mildred smiled. "Might need it myself someday."

Krysty touched the physician on the shoulder, her hair cascading in crimson waves. "That's two I owe you."

"You're my family now," the physician started, then turned away, unable to finish the thought.

Walking stiffly to the still running bike, Ryan climbed on and revved the 1450cc engine a few times to clear the carb. As expected, dark exhaust blew out of the mufflers, slowly clearing away to white fumes.

"Let's find that bank," Ryan said, a flutter in his voice. The man hawked and spit. "I'm on—"

"I'm on point," Krysty stated as a fact, pulling her bike alongside. "Stay in the middle of the street. Dim the headlights to low. Dean, with your father. J.B., cover the flanks. Mildred, the rear. That Tommy working again?''

"Last clip,'' she answered, rigging the sling so the rapidfire hung across her chest. ''But the breech is clear.''

"Good.''

"And I, dear lady,'' Doc espoused dramatically, "shall watch the windows above. Where once it rained a foe, again that can occur.''

Krysty started rolling forward. ''Be sure to use that fast-firing trick again,'' she said.

"That is indeed my full intention,'' Doc replied, tucking the mammoth blaster behind his belt buckle for a faster draw while astride the motorcycle.

In tight formation, the companions pulled away from the littered street, watching Ryan as closely as they did the surrounding darkness. The man was hunched over the handlebars, but operated the bike without any problem. Dwindling in their wake, the burning wreckage of the Walker flared brightly as something flammable ignited, then died away completely.

Heading for the downtown area, they found several banks and chose the financial institution set between two buildings whose roofs were lower than the bank's. This gave some degree of safety from above, and allowed them an escape route by jumping from the bank's roof to the lower structures. Not perfect, but it was acceptable.

Easily opening the locks, J.B. closed and locked the doors behind them, then drew the shades and lowered the venetian blinds to hide their presence. A brief recce showed the bank was empty of any hidden machines, the windows standard bulletproof Plexiglas.

The companions drove the bikes up the stairs and made camp on the second floor. Two of the pressurized lanterns were turned off to save fuel, the last lowered to a soft glow, barely enough to illuminate the office. Bookcases were moved in front of the windows, and the desk shoved against the door. Nothing could gain entrance without alerting them.

Taking a seat in the corner, Jak stood guard with the Thompson, while Doc formed a simple Bunsen burner from a bottle of vodka, the blue flame giving off little light or smoke to betray their position. It was Ryan's turn to cook a meal, but Dean assumed the duty over his father's objections, and started making coffee and stew, the contents of the MRE packs augmented with some beef jerky from the store.

While the food cooked, the companions took turns washing in the bathroom, the water tank on the roof giving only a tiny trickle of warm water before running dry. But it filled the sink and that was enough. Then they tended to their assorted cuts and bruises and cleaned their weapons—but with one of them always standing guard holding a loaded blaster.

The food was passable, and during the coffee wild animal screams sounded from the streets below. Briefly, something heavy strode across the roof, then was gone into the night.

"Good meal," Ryan said, placing aside his tin plate when finished. "I'll do double meals tomorrow."

"Fair enough," Krysty said, stacking the dirty metal plates for scrubbing later. "You want U.S. Army nut cake or a granola bar for dessert?"

"A cigar," J.B. said wistfully, tucking a toothpick into his mouth.

Knowing how difficult his struggle to quit smoking was for the man, Mildred patted him on the arm in solace and whispered a different suggestion.

"That beats a cigar any day, Millie." J.B. smiled, patting her hand.

"And you have no idea how much I need it tonight," she said, sharing a glance with Krysty.

The redhead understood and moved closer to Ryan. Mildred had warned her the electric shock always hit men hardest in the kidneys. Nobody knew why; it just did. And from the grunts of pain she had heard when Ryan went to the bathroom before, they would only be exchanging some body heat in the bedroll tonight, and nothing more.

"And now allow me to offer something special. A rare treat, indeed," Doc said, producing a dusty bottle bearing a wildly ornate label. "I found this in the locked cabinet of the store. The door was most stubborn, but I persisted to victory."

"Mother of God," Mildred gasped. "Is that what I think it is?"

"Quite so, madam."

"Incredible!"

"Shine?" Jak asked, offering his plastic cup.

"Ah, but this is no ordinary beverage," Doc said, using a small knife to cut away the wax sealing the cork in place. Switching to the screw attachment on his Swiss Army knife, the old man successfully opened the bottle with a loud pop.

"Now this should really breathe for an hour," he apologized, pouring a small amount in the plastic cup of his mess kit before passing it along. "But our circumstances being what they may, I think we can dispense with that custom just this once."

"'Napoleon brandy,'" Krysty read as the bottle came her way. "Good stuff, eh?"

"Absolutely the best," Mildred stated, pouring a splash into her cup. Crystal goblets were what this should be served in, but those were from another time, a different world. "Now don't gulp it down, take small sips."

Ignoring the advice, Jak drained his cup in a shot, and his eyes sprang wide. "Damn," he stated in appreciation.

"Indeed, Mr. Lauren." Doc chuckled, biting back a smile at the pronouncement. "Not even the genius of Tennyson could have better described three-hundred-year-old Napoleon brandy than in such a manner."

"Fucking grade-A hooch," Jak agreed, adding another inch and sipping the potent brandy. It filled his mouth with a magnificent changing flavor, and slid easily down his throat to fill his chest with warmth.

Feeling the liquor begin to ease her muscles, Mildred added another splash to her cup and raised it for a toast. This was something they had not done for many months, and somehow it seemed appropriate this night.

"To absent friends," Mildred said solemnly.

"Good toast," Ryan said, lowering his cup, the soothing liquor easing away the ache in his joints. "But we've got to do this right and give names."

"Trader," J.B. said without hesitation, raising his cup.

"My sweet Emily," Doc rumbled sadly, copying the gesture. "And dear little Lori."

"Finn and Flynn," Ryan added solemnly. "Rick and Michael."

"Rona," Dean stated.

"Christina and Jenny," Jak said softly, his hand tightening on the cup.

"Mother Sonja," Krysty whispered.

"Paddy," Mildred continued. "And Ellie, too."

Then Ryan stood and held his cup above the eerie blue flame. "Laurence," he said simply.

The rest of the companions rose and extended their cups. "Laurence," they chorused, and drank a sip, then poured the rest onto the flames, making the fire soar with a majesty that filled the office with a fleeting moment of heat and light.

After refilling their cups, little more was said for the rest of the night. The friends finished their drinks and took turns sleeping, listening to the silence of the huge city, feeling its million ghosts move by them in the darkness. But knowing that at least one of the unseen visitors would be forever by their side in any battle to come.

Chapter Fourteen

In the morning, the companions decided to delay exploring for the gateway and rest until they were all back on their feet. All of the companions were stiff and badly bruised from their recent battles.

A few days later, refreshed and invigorated, the group exited the bank at dawn to quietly ride their purring bikes through the still streets. Their packs and bedrolls were strapped across the rear fenders of the vehicles, lessening the load of equipment each carried, and making driving a lot easier.

The metropolis looked exactly the same, but when they swung by the department store to check the sec droid, they found the remains of the machine were gone, and every window in the building was smashed, the sidewalks littered with torn merchandise. Parking the motorcycles a short distance from the store, Ryan and J.B. did a quick recce of the structure and found the interior had been completely trashed, clothing ripped to pieces, ceiling fixtures busted, display cases toppled over and mirrors cracked.

"This kind of destruction wasn't done by a sec droid," Ryan said, using the Steyr to touch the mutilated form of a mannequin. There were teeth marks on the torso, and the head had been crushed into lumpy plaster.

"Got to be an ape," J.B. said, indicating a pile of droppings near an empty rack of candy bars.

"At least one," Ryan agreed with a scowl. What a pesthole this burg was becoming—spiders, sec droids and now the apes were here. The predark city was a treasure trove of supplies, but protected by an army of inhuman guards.

"This is a bad spot to get trapped," J.B. said, stepping over a clothing rack, the steel pipes bent and twisted. He had a feeling that something was real pissed about not finding any norms here.

"Agreed. Let's go," Ryan ordered softly, the SIG-Sauer and Steyr sweeping the darkness outside the range of the lanterns for any movement.

Staying alert, the two men took turns covering each other, one walking while the other stood still, until they backed out of the store into the sunny street. Even then, the men didn't holster their blasters until among the other companions.

"Hunters are here," Ryan said, climbing onto his machine. Tucking the Steyr into a gun boot strapped to the frame, he twisted the throttle and the big engine kicked into life.

"Robots and gorillas, behold the alpha and the omega," Doc rumbled, his frock coat billowing in the morning breeze.

"Think they're hiding on the rooftops?" Dean asked, craning his neck to look skyward. Nothing was visible above them, except for the patchy clouds, irregular breaks in the storm layer giving brief glimpses of azure blue behind the fiery rads and chems.

"More likely they're in that park we passed," Krysty said, flipping her hair over a shoulder. "Animals always return to the familiar, and that's the only greenery we've seen so far on this mesa.''

''Avoid there,'' Jak said, sitting at the handlebars in front of Doc. Experimentally, the teenager spread his legs to stand over the bike, and was pleased with the lack of pain from his ankle. Mildred was right: he needed only a couple of days' soaking in hot water. Damn odd way to heal an injury.

Just then, a window slammed shut, and something came off the ledge. The companions crouched and opened fire, blowing the plummeting object into dirty shards, the remains of the flowerpot crashing onto the back seat of a powder-blue convertible parked at the curb.

''Could have been the wind,'' J.B. said, sounding uncertain.

''Mebbe,'' Krysty replied, swiftly reloading her revolver.

''Not going to take the chance,'' Ryan said, revving the bike. ''Let's get out of here and find someplace where we can talk. Start moving.''

Traveling a few blocks, the companions took a corner and braked to a halt in the middle of a deserted intersection. The location gave them a clear field of fire in every direction, and they could see anything coming their way long before it arrived.

''Okay, before we go hunting for the gateway, we better get more supplies,'' Ryan ordered, tapping the fuel gauge on the handlebars. Less than half a tank. ''Shine is a priority.''

Wisely, the others agreed. The department store had been low on vodka. They needed to find a well-stocked liquor store.

''And additional ammo,'' Krysty stated. ''Only a

couple of rounds for my Webley, and about the same for the Smith.''

"Here," Dean said, passing the woman a fistful of .38 cartridges. "I'm fine. Still have eighteen rounds for the Weatherby."

"Thanks."

"No prob."

"Watch for bars, taverns, any place with booze," Ryan said, driving away slowly. "And stay sharp. We're gonna need a lot more than a fistful of ammo to stop another sec droid."

Keeping to the middle of the streets, the companions began driving a spiral pattern around the city blocks, slowly expanding the area covered until finding a liquor store in the middle of a street lined with outdoor restaurants. The front door was unlocked, the shop open for business, and the people raided the shelves and storage room, obtaining enough vodka to fill their tanks. Always on the prowl, J.B. found a double-barreled shotgun hidden under the counter, but the weapon was empty, and no ammo anywhere. Some peaceful shopkeeper intended to use it as a prop to scare away robbers.

"Triple-stupe bastard," the Armorer snorted, disgusted by the sheer stupidity of the deceased owner. What good was a blaster you couldn't use?

On the way out, Ryan paused to break open the cash register and check the money in the till. He carefully scanned the bills, then he tossed the paper aside and departed with the others, leaving the register drawer open for the insects and mice to harvest as bedding for their nests.

Krysty noticed him inspecting the money and nodded. Smart man.

None of the pay phones on the sidewalks had a Yellow Pages book, only a short chain attached to ragged pieces of faded paper. But a nearby video store had a phone book behind the counter, and Ryan carefully turned the brittle pages to search for the address of a gun shop. Strangely, there were no listings for military supplies or gunsmiths, only a sporting-goods store, which they determined was located a couple of blocks to the east.

Arriving at the location, five of the companions stayed astride their bikes at an intersection to stand guard while Ryan and J.B. walked along the middle of the street. The dark shops were lined with dead neon signs, placards in the windows announcing January sales. A few cars dotted the curb, and a police sedan was parked at a sharp angle in front of a sleek roadster, but immutable time had reduced both cop and criminal to powdery bones on the black asphalt.

The sporting-goods store was closed, an iron grille in place across its window and door. Normally, that wasn't a problem, but unfortunately there was a broken key jammed in the lock of the grating. J.B. tried for a while, then pronounced it hopeless unless they used plastique. Holding their small supply of C-4 in reserve, Ryan checked the pawnshop across the street, the classic three brass balls hanging from a post announcing the honored profession. Pawnshops often carried weapons and ammo. The main window was coated with black paint on the inside, making it impossible to see if there were any blasters on display inside. Were the owners trying to hide from the rampaging mobs? But this city had died at the instant of skydark, and there had never been any crowd of starving people to loot the stores. Curious.

But luck was on their side. The steel grating before the establishment was drawn aside, and J.B. easily picked the lock on the door. Taking the point position, Ryan started to open the door when he stepped on something hard.

Instantly, the man froze. Only recently, he had encountered a land mine, and since then he was extremely wary of stepping on anything. His heart pounding, the man glanced at the sidewalk and slowly tilted his boot to see underneath. The lump proved to be only a small blob of congealed silvery metal on the concrete. As the puzzled man glanced around, he noticed the source of the puddled steel and felt cold adrenaline flood his body.

"Hey, Albert!" Ryan called out in forced casualness. "Get the bikes over here so we can load them easier."

Caught by surprise, the startled companions looked hastily around for the source of the danger. If any of them used a name that began with the first letter of the alphabet, that meant they were in an ambush. But from where? The streets were empty.

"Aw, push your own damn bike," Dean shouted, working the lever of the Weatherby while it was still in the boot. "That ain't my job."

With an elaborate sigh, Ryan took his hand off the door latch. "Come on, Adam," he said to J.B. "Sooner we start, the sooner we're done."

"Yeah, yeah, I hear you," the Armorer agreed, faking a smile, and the man ambled along the street until reaching the intersection.

"What's wrong?" J.B. asked out of the side of his mouth, as they climbed onto the bikes.

"Droids. It's a trap," Ryan said urgently, thumbing

the ignition button to start the big Twin-V engine. "We have to get out of here fast."

Making as little fuss as possible, the companions rolled away on their bikes while nervously watching the pawnshop until they were a good block distant.

"Far enough," Ryan ordered, halting the bike. "I want you all to see what we almost walked into."

"Trip wire?" Jak asked, holding the Colt Python.

The Deathlands warrior shook his head. "Lot worse than that. Going for the door, I stepped on some congealed steel," Ryan said. "Seemed odd, so I looked around. There's a reason why the grating of the pawnshop was open. To chill us. Damn near succeeded, too."

"Those crafty bastards," Krysty said, squinting into the distance. "Look at that."

Pulling out the telescope, J.B. located the store and scanned its front, searching for something subtle he had missed before. The man spotted it when he came to the lock on the open grating. "Dark night," he muttered. The mechanism was gone; there was only a smooth hole in the grating where the lock should be located, the surrounding metal discolored from severe heat.

"That was done with a laser," J.B. said, passing the Navy brass to the others. "A droid is in that store, waiting for us. Mebbe more."

Accepting their word on the matter, Mildred waved off the telescope. But Doc took his turn with the long-eyes. "I wager the machines also placed the broken key in the lock of the sporting-goods store to divert us to their trap."

"Tricky," Jak agreed, cracking his knuckles. "Okay, what do?"

"Last time it took a hundred rounds of ammo to stop one of those things," Krysty said, loosening the Webley in her belt. "Could be a dozen in there. Two dozen! We need better weapons."

"More than that," Ryan stated, flexing his hand above the SIG-Sauer in its holster. "We need to go someplace the droids haven't thought of yet. Gun shops are obvious sources of ammo, police stations, too. Bet a live round the droids are waiting for us at both."

"Navy base is a rad crater," Dean offered, unbuttoning the flap that covered the breast pocket of his shirt. During their rest, the boy had sown the pocket into sections to hold the long cartridges for the Weatherby for easy access.

"Banks are useless," he continued. "There isn't anywhere else. Not for what we need."

"Weapons were considered unnecessary at a vacation resort," Mildred said, working the bolt on the Thompson and slinging the weapon around her neck. That way the rapidfire was instantly available, but out of the way enough for her hands to steer.

"I'm pretty sure we can find more ammo," Ryan said, wheeling the bike around. "But first we need some distance to cover our tracks."

As the motorcycles raced away, the tiny bell above the entrance to the gun shop gave a musical tinkle as the door swung open a crack, and a small video camera extended to track the progress of the departing humans. Then, just as smoothly, the lens retracted and the door closed, leaving the street to appear peaceful and empty for the next visitors.

TEN BLOCKS LATER, Ryan turned toward the west and slowed. Checking the street signs, he took a few turns until reaching a residential section, brightly painted pink apartment houses, interspaced fast-food restaurants and strip malls.

"What about a courier company? They'd have some weapons," Dean suggested, bumping over a manhole cover.

Ryan glanced at the boy. "Never thought of that before," he admitted. "Good idea, but they wouldn't have anything we could use against the machines. Just some handcannons, mebbe a few shotguns, but no big ordnance."

"What we need is a Finnish 20 mm ATR," J.B. stated. "Plus a shit load of shells. That'd send those droids to the junkyard."

"Gun collectors?" Jak suggested, arching around an open car door.

"They'd have the blasters, but no ammo," Ryan said, checking the street. "There, that'll do."

"A recruitment station?" J.B. asked as they turned into the parking lot of the strip mall. Set between a vegetarian sandwich shop and an insurance agency, the small store was brightly decorated with American flags and printed inducements to earn valuable college tuition by joining the military service of your choice.

"This is why I checked the money in the liquor store," Ryan said, parking his bike. "Wanted to make sure this was still American territory and that there would be a recruitment center."

"Won't be any blasters there," Dean grumped.

"Good, that means no droids," Ryan said, going to the glass door. A bell tinkled as he walked inside. "We're here looking for maps."

"Maps?" Jak stated, blocking the door with a folding chair. "What for?"

"The location of the National Guard armory," Ryan said, going to a file cabinet and rifling the top drawer. "A lot of phone books don't list the address of the armories in case of riots. Just the phone number. Also, makes them harder for enemy outlanders to find. Ah, got it."

Going to a desk, Ryan cleared the top with a sweep of his arm and began unfolding the old map. "But these recruitment posts often do training at the armory," Ryan finished, gently smoothing out the wrinkles. The yellow paper tore, and he moved with greater care.

"These things are from my time," Mildred said petulantly, softly touching the remnants of an American flag hanging from a tarnished brass pole. "I have no knowledge of this."

"You loot enough ruins, you find these things out," Ryan muttered.

"There it is," Krysty said, stabbing the map with a finger. "Near the big lake. Good thing we have bikes. That's twenty miles away."

"Hope that's still on the mesa," Dean said. "Could have fallen off when it rose."

Using only fingertip pressure, Ryan folded the crumbling map as carefully as possible, then placed it inside his shirt. "Let's find out," he said, heading for the door.

AN HOUR LATER, the companions were traveling along the bypass of the city, skirting a canal that was broken in two, the jagged bottom sticking over the side of the mesa like the teeth of a saw.

The day was becoming hotter as the tropical sun rose in the sky, muted thunder rumbled defiantly as the climbing orb burned holes through the orange-and-purple storm clouds. Stretched across the eternal storm were the fuzzy black lines of altocumulus clouds, the dense plutonium vapors resembling prison bars, making it appear as if the whole world were in jail—a dire penitentiary that the prisoners themselves had set on fire for no sane reason.

Banking the bikes to follow the endless curve of the bypass, the companions slowly circled the predark city. There were very few cars on the roadway, which seemed odd until they drove past a Mack truck hanging out of the side of an apartment building. When the neutron bomb aced people and electronics, the speeding vehicles had sailed off the bypass from simple inertia. Maneuvering closer to the berm, they could see countless wrecks in charred impact craters spaced irregularly along the suburbs below the elevated bypass.

Rich with the smell of sulfur, the wind blew through their hair, and the companions kept a watch on the quivering gauges of their motorcycles as they settled in for a long drive. The armory was on the other side of the metropolis, many miles away.

Faded white billboards flashed, and gradually the bypass began to move away from the culvert. Soon the roadway was cutting between rows of low buildings only eight or ten stories high. Mountains of concrete and steel compared to almost any ville, but were mere foothills in comparison to the monolithic giants of downtown.

"Triple red!" J.B. shouted, throttling down his

bike, both hands holding the handlebars steady as he savagely braked.

Fighting his bike to a halt, Ryan said nothing as he studied the obstacle blocking the roadway. A huge spiderweb stretched between two of the low buildings, the bottom level of the thick strands only a couple of feet off the smooth concrete.

Fat white blobs dotted the precise geometric expanse, a few cawing like condors, one sounding like a weeping man, another thrashing wildly as the occupant of the cocoon still fiercely struggled to escape.

"Poor bastards," Mildred said. "Spiders eat their prey alive. It's saving them for later."

Dean raised the rifle and started to aim at the weeping cocoon, then paused. They didn't have a lot of rounds, and if they had to fight the giant insect, this single round could make the difference between running and getting cocooned. Reluctantly, he lowered the longblaster and tucked it back into the boot. Just then a weapon fired, and the human-shaped cocoon jerked once, then went still as a crimson stain spread across the silky material.

"I think there's enough clearance for us to walk the bikes under the web," Ryan said, working the bolt on the smoking Steyr and sliding it back into the gun boot.

"It's going to be tight," J.B. said, removing his hat and stuffing it inside his jacket.

"We could burn our way through," Dean suggested, nudging the satchel full of Molotov cocktails, the firebombs silent from the layers of protective padding between each bottle.

"And the smoke would tell everything in the city where we were," Ryan said, stepping off his bike, but keeping a hand on the throttle to keep the engine from stalling. The timing had to be off, or maybe there was blockage in the jets, because the bike was beginning to run a little rough. He'd have to keep a watch on that problem.

Pausing before the complex arrangement, he could see the main cables that anchored the web were thicker than a man, slimmer ropes connected each cable and small strands no bigger than a soup can closed off the sections of the web, making it impossible for anything to escape. A masterpiece of nature, the spiderweb was beautiful and bone chilling. From a distance, the web had appeared old and dirty. This close they could see the shading actually came from the thousands of tiny winged insects coating every strand.

Approaching the colossal web, Ryan glanced straight up the side and quickly looked back down at the road. The sheer size of the web gave him a rush of vertigo. Probably wasn't as bad for the folks with two good eyes, but for him the dizzying effect was strong.

The bottom strand stretched across the roadway at waist height. As he tilted the bike far enough over to roll it underneath, the engine began to sputter, the carburetor flooding from the steep angle. Quickly, he adjusted the throttle to keep the engine going as he stooped low and scuttled under the death web. Ryan was almost past the white net when something tugged on his hair. With blinding speed, he drew the SIG-Sauer and turned, ready to fire. In relief, the man saw the tug came from some of his long hair stuck to the web. Holstering the blaster, he pulled out the panga and cut himself loose, letting the web keep its small trophy of hair.

Reaching the other side, he gratefully righted the motorcycle and rubbed his scalp to ease the sting. The purring of the other bikes got louder as the vehicles were pushed by the riders under the obstruction. Regrouping on the far side, Doc and Mildred were both rubbing their heads, both obvious victims of the web, and Krysty's animated hair was coiled so tightly to her scalp she appeared to have a curly crew cut.

"Made it." Dean sighed, getting on his bike, gunning the engine a few times to clear away any excess shine puddled in the carb.

Doing the same, Ryan watched in approval. The boy knew machines. With each companion teaching the boy what he or she knew, Dean was getting good lessons in survival.

"Gaia save us, it's here," Krysty whispered, drawing the Webley.

A hundred yards down the road ahead of them, the spider was crawling off the roof of a radio station and onto the roadway. Standing twenty feet high, the bulbous torso of the mutie was striped like a tiger in yellow and black. The bristly head was oversized for the body, indicating possible intelligence, and its huge ruby eyes were perfectly stationary, making it impossible to tell in which direction the monster was looking.

Instincts honed from a hundred battles flared within the man, and Ryan reviewed their situation with lightning speed.

"Follow me," he ordered in a normal tone of voice. Climbing onto the bike, he started to roll forward so slowly, that he needed to drag his boots along the road to keep the vehicle upright.

"Slow as possible," Ryan added, staying in motion. "Nothing that big can change directions quickly. We get close, then hit the gas and roar right past the motherfucker on the berm."

"And drop a few of these in our wake," J.B. said, easing a gren from his munitions bag.

"Got any Willy Peter?"

"Nope."

"Damn. Then use whatever you got," Ryan said.

Turning toward Dean, the man gestured at the web. "Give it something to worry about aside from us."

The boy nodded and retrieved a Molotov from the padded saddlebag. Holding it ready to throw, he watched as the rest of the companions began creeping forward on their bikes, boots dragging. As the spider began to start toward them, Dean quickly ignited the oily rag tied around the neck of the bottle and smashed it on the concrete at the middle of the web. The Molotov crashed into a fireball, blue flames licking at the thick strands.

Keening loudly, the giant spider rushed for the blaze, and the companions separated to roll past the huge mutie. As they came alongside, they each drew weapons but nobody fired or made any sudden moves. A pungent wave of putrescence followed the creature as it scuttled by, the reek of honey sweetness and rotten meat almost making them gag.

Once past the norms, the spider dashed for the precious web. Crackling loudly, the flames were commencing to burn through the lower cable, the silky ropes above charring badly. In frantic haste, the spider crawled onto the web, snipping lengths free with its mandibles. In only a few moments, a ragged patch of smoking material fell to the ground, and promptly burst into flames, the silky material sending off greenish smoke.

Now angling its head, the insect keened again in a lower tone and crawled off the web to charge toward the departing norms.

"Move!" Ryan shouted. He twisted the grip on the handlebars to the last stop, and the Harley lurched forward.

As the rest of the companions hit the gas, gray smoke poured from under the spinning rear tires until they caught, and then the machines shot forward. But the spider was only fifty yards behind, and closing fast. The Harleys were slowly building speed, but so was the spider.

Shifting to the highest gear, J.B. pulled the gren and used his teeth to peel off the safety tape. Grabbing the pin with his other hand, the Armorer yanked it loose and tossed the HE charge at the oncoming creature.

"Shotgun them," he ordered, wheeling to the other side of the bypass and dropping another. "No groupings!

A rain of grens arched over the companions to hit the concrete road, and bounce toward the spider. Moving with incredible agility, the mutie dodged the pattern of spheres and was past the first gren when it detonated. Zigzagging, the spider nimbly maneuvered past the grens, the rest exploding in ragged order, throwing out great clouds of black smoke to mix with the green fumes of the burning silk.

The friends fired a flurry of rounds at the mutie as it snapped its mandibles at the rear bike carrying Jak and Doc. The LeMat boomed twice, but the .44 miniballs did no visible damage to the creature.

Spitting curses, Ryan pulled out a gren and started to slow, attempting to reach a position where he could drop the gren and ace the mutie, but not Jak and Doc.

As it tried again, Doc fired the LeMat steadily until realizing that the creature was dropping farther behind with each passing second. In triumph, the old man gave a shout in Latin as the beast began to fall behind the motorcycles, and then receded into the distance.

SLIDING BACK into formation, the companions reduced their speed and put a couple more miles under their tires before they stopped watching for the mutie.

"Need an armored tank to chill that thing," J.B. stated grimly. "Something that size would toss an APC around like a kitten."

"If it caught the APC," Doc offered.

"Armored personnel carriers are not famous for their speed or durability," Mildred said, allowing herself to breathe once more. "The best would be an Apache gunship with heat-seeking Sidewinder missiles."

"Any chance we might find one of those at the armory?" Dean asked.

"Could be a lot of choppers there," his father said, watching the temperature gauge. "But that's not a wag you can operate by guessing, like a tank or PT boat."

On the horizon, the southerly volcano belched forth a tremendous black cloud of ash, laced with geysers of white steam. A minute later, the roadway trembled, and the companions fought to control their shaking bikes.

"By gadfrey, I think an eruption is imminent!"

Doc said, slowing his bike. "Mayhap we should take the next exit ramp and abandon this expedition."

"Relax, that was just a pressure quake," Mildred shouted as the vibrations began to lessen. "The volcano is balancing itself."

"No danger?" Dean asked, trying to watch the bypass and the volcano at the same time.

"Not until the lava arrives," Ryan replied. "And then it's too bastard late."

The bypass continued for a couple more miles, then started to bank inland toward a wide highway. Only the pillars that supported the ancient skyway still stood, topped with wild twists of iron rods, and the broken ends of steel girders. The beltway that once encircled the metropolis was gone, reduced to piles of rubble on the ground.

Slowing, Ryan gave a sharp whistle as he rolled along the side of the roadway, craning his neck to look at the buildings and stores below. There were plenty of signs along the berm, but the wind and weather had reduced them to blank steel rectangles carrying no more information than a dead man's eyes.

"Military wags over there," Krysty announced, pointing.

Set in a small park, near a dried lake, was a stout granite building with a curved roof and a massive concrete wall. A garage stood with its doors swung up, a collection of assorted civilian vehicles in the parking lot. An iron-spike fence topped the massive wall, and the only entrance in sight was closed with a steel gate and a large guard kiosk. But only half of the enclosed area was present. The edge of the mesa cut the rest of the location in two, the leafy tops of trees visible over the rim of the cliff. The thick jungle stretched for miles to the base of the live volcano.

"That's got to be it," Ryan said over the purring engines.

"Half of it's gone," Dean complained. "All this way for nothing."

"Might as well see what we can salvage," J.B. said, removing his hat and straightening the brim. "Even an old 60 mm recoilless rifle would give us enough punch to remove the spider and the droids."

Taking the ramp, the companions braked to a halt and were forced to walk their bikes onto the sloped grass to get past a bad crash. Several cars had plowed into a military half-track embedded into a bus full of tourists. The grinning skeletons in swimsuits had been brutally crushed under the tonnage of the military wag.

"Tourists heading for the beach," Mildred muttered, an unexpected lump in her throat. "Poor bastards."

"Hell of a crash," Ryan agreed, stepping onto his bike. "Good thing they were chilled already."

Mildred blinked. "What was that? Well, yes, they would have to be, from the neutron wave," she reasoned aloud. "First they died, then they crashed."

"Unless they knew the war was coming before anybody else," Krysty said, steering her motorcycle through a clump of weeds to reach the street.

"Not possible," J.B. agreed, pausing to clean a few tiny bugs off his wire-rimmed glasses, squashed trophies garnished from the lengthy bike trip.

"Verily, not a soul knew the sword of Damocles was falling," Doc whispered, so softly that nobody else could hear the words. "Except for the fools who cut the string themselves."

Chapter Fifteen

That section of the mesa had been hit hard by the concussion from the aerial blast of the neutron bomb. Most of the structures were smashed flat, the overpass lying on the ground in jumbled piles of broken concrete and rust-eaten steel girders.

Squeaking loudly, a battered sign for a gas station swung over a blackened pit that reached for half a block. At the bottom, rats splashed in a rain pool, eating something vaguely cat shaped. Wrecked vehicles were scattered everywhere: crashed into trees, through store windows and piled into mounds of corroding metal.

"They set off the neutron bomb down here," Ryan said, "to chill everybody on the island, but to not damage anything downtown."

"Mebbe there's a gateway there," Krysty said, running stiff fingers through her flowing hair. "Not exactly good news."

"Why not?" Jak asked bluntly.

"If there's a gateway downtown, then why did the whitecoats travel a hundred miles to a different island to build another gateway and jump from there? Why not use the device here?"

"Because they couldn't," Ryan stated. "That's the only possible answer. We just have to figure out why they couldn't, and then fix the problem."

"If we don't?" Dean asked, pulling the bike over a curb and onto the sidewalk.

"Have to," his father answered grimly.

Broken glass sparkled on top of the twisted car wrecks, and nobody spoke as the companions carefully walked the motorcycles down the debris-filled ramp. Ryan, Krysty and Doc each caught their long coats on sharp metal, and finally removed the garments to stuff them inside saddlebags. The day was warm, and there seemed little chance of acid rain. They would take the chance.

Reaching the ground, they uneasily surveyed the area. Potholes dominated the paved streets, weeds lined the cracked sidewalks and not a window was intact, windblown leaves piled high inside the stores and homes. In ancient days, this had been a nice section of town, but the residual rads from the nuked Navy base and the concussion of the neutron bomb had changed that. Clusters of tiny red eyes watched them pass by from the sewer drains, and fat crows sitting on a sagging roof shared something bloody and stretchy.

Suddenly, a humanoid figure moved past a broken window. Ryan caught only a glimpse of prehensile fangs and clawed hands before it was gone.

"We got company," he said gruffly, drawing the SIG-Sauer. "In the ruins, one o'clock."

"Droids," J.B. said with certainty, squeezing off the pistol-grip safety of the Uzi so it was ready to fire. "The damn things followed us!"

"That was no machine," Krysty answered, thumbing back the hammer of the Webley. "Something else."

"Stickies?" Mildred asked, dumping the spent

rounds from her ZKR revolver and quickly thumbing in fresh ones. This was the first chance she'd had to reload since the spider. The physician had tried doing it on the moving bike, and stopped after dropping a live round.

"Not unless this breed has a mouth and fangs," the redhead said, listening to the sounds of the desolation around them. "It more resembled one of the People."

"Shitfire." Mildred frowned, closing the ZKR. Those blasted blood drinkers had been tough to chill. Of all the humanoid mutations encountered in the Deathlands, the New England vampires had been the most vicious, and the most devious.

"'Iron bars and stone walls do not a prison make,'" Doc rumbled, checking the load in the LeMat. "But suffice, they shall, for a repository of destruction."

"Let's get our butts in the armory," J.B. suggested.

"Jak, Dean, you're on point," Ryan ordered, and started across the street for the predark fortification. As the only companions without bikes to push, the teenager and the boy were the best choices for the job.

Showing barely a trace of a limp, Jak moved to the left with both of his blasters drawn. Dean went to the right, the Weatherby rifle appearing huge in his young hands.

As the group moved along the bumpy sidewalk, shadowy figures shifted positions in the decaying house, but none rushed the norms. Ryan hoped the muties knew what blasters could do, and were too afraid to risk an attack. Dangerously low on ammo, the companions couldn't afford even a brief firefight.

If the National Guard armory was empty, he had no idea what they could do next. Returning to the pirate ville to steal weapons would be madness. This was their best, perhaps their only chance.

There were too many potholes to safely ride the bikes, so the companions turned the machines off to save fuel, and walked the vehicles through the maze of depressions, always keeping one hand on the handlebars and the other filled with a blaster.

Reaching the front gate, the companions stood guard while J.B. checked the lock. A plump rat scurried along the top of the wall, but they withheld chilling the rodent. Dean threw a stone and missed, but the animal ran away in fright.

"Well, we're not getting in this way," J.B. finally announced, stepping from the gate and tilting his fedora. "This kind of lock can't be forced. We've got to blow it."

"Thought so," Ryan growled. "But it was worth a try."

"I could climb over," Dean offered, studying the bars of the gate, "and pull the lever in the kiosk. Easy."

"Gate's electric, not mechanical," his father stated, pointing to the exposed power cables. "Without power, it still wouldn't open."

"We could all climb over," the boy insisted.

Ryan thought about the suggestion. "Too risky," he decided. "We're going to need the bikes to carry ammo."

"Then blow the lock," Krysty said, almost firing as something large dashed from one crumbling house to another.

"Plas make lot noise," Jak pointed out succinctly,

his hands crossed at the wrists to support the heavy Magnum blasters. ''Gonna attract stuff.''

''We could recce the ruins,'' Mildred suggested hesitantly, shifting her hold on the Thompson. ''Find some mattress to muffle the sound of the explosion.''

''Nobody goes in those houses,'' Ryan stated grimly. ''I'd rather ask a baron for mercy.

''Besides,'' he added softly, feeling things watch their every move, ''the muties already know that we're here.''

J.B. rummaged in his munitions bag. He extracted a piece of C-4 and molded the claylike charge into a small wad the size of a walnut.

''Ten seconds,'' he called, stabbing a timing pencil into the plastique and breaking it off in the middle.

Quickly, the companions retreated. There was a muffled bang from the lock and the gate flew open, leaving a contrail of smoke in its wake as it loudly crashed against the brick wall.

The companions waited to see if there was any response to the noise, but only the faint noises from the jungle below could be heard, along with the ever present sheet lightning and thunder from the tortured sky.

Leaning against the wall, Jak stayed on guard while the others rolled the bikes through the gate. Dean went to the kiosk and raised the striped wooden beam blocking the entrance. As the motorcycles rolled by, he noticed that inside the kiosk skeletons were sprawled on a table covered with playing cards and matchsticks. Lucky bastards never knew what hit them.

Then a shot rang out, and the companions spun with weapons raised.

"They attacking?" Krysty demanded, taking a step.

"Not anymore," the teenager stated, walking backward into the compound.

On the street, something hidden in the weeds made a guttural noise and went still. Inside the ruins, skulking creatures retreated to the safety of the darkness, one of them consuming a squealing rat that was not long from dead.

"Mayhap I should stay here and sound a ballyhoo if there is trouble," Doc offered, pulling the spare Webley from his belt and thumbing back the hammer, only to ease it down again. Unlike the LeMat, the Webley was double action and didn't require setting the hammer as a prerequisite to firing. The scholar suddenly realized that differences between the two weapons might be confusing in a fight and cost lives, so he decided to dispose of the Webley at the first chance.

"We stay together," Ryan stated with the SIG-Sauer drawn, climbing on the Harley and pressing the ignition button. The bike purred into life.

"Dean, close the gate. Bind it with some rope, a belt, whatever you got."

"Done," the boy said, shouldering the longblaster.

Under the watchful blasters of the others, Dean pulled out his bowie knife and cut away the power cable leading to the defunct motors for the gate, then used the insulated wiring to bind the entrance shut.

"That'll hold," he said, dusting off his hands.

As the boy climbed onto the saddle with his father, Jak slid behind Doc and the companions rolled along the wide expanse of the cracked tarmac for a hundred feet before reaching the warehouse. The asphalt of the parking lot was badly cracked, stunted weeds growing in the cracks.

Braking to a halt for a brief consultation, Mildred served as the anchor with her rapidfire, while Ryan and Krysty drove a recce around the building. When they were gone from sight, J.B. went to the front door of the warehouse and studied the complex locking mechanism.

"Nobody about," Krysty reported, returning from around a corner of the warehouse and braking next to the other bikes.

A few moments later, Ryan appeared from the opposite side. "Loading dock in the rear," he added, spreading his legs to support the purring machine. "But the doors are bigger and look even stronger than the front."

"Which are also locked," J.B. reported. "Electronic keypad, palm reader and ID card necessary. Going to take a lot more C-4 than I have to open that slab of steel."

"And the rear doors are stronger?" Doc asked incredulously.

Ryan nodded. "Like a bank vault."

"Any windows?"

"None."

"So let's try Occam's razor," Mildred said, glancing at the small building with the flagpole in front. "Maybe the keys are in the main office."

"Worth a shot," Krysty agreed, turning off the engine.

Leaving Doc to guard the bikes, the others took the pressurized lanterns and walked over to the small building. On point, Ryan found the screen door locked, but the inside door was held open with a rubber wedge. Rain blown in through the screen had destroyed the front room, the chairs and carpeting reduced to rags, the legs of a dark wooden table bleached gray.

The lanterns were lit, and, cutting a slit in the screen, Ryan released the latch holding the outer door in place and entered the dim building. Immediately, he was assailed by the stink of dust and mildew, the smells as familiar to him as blood and cordite.

Spreading out, the companions found nothing of interest in the waiting room, and started along a short hallway. Side doors led to a file room, a bathroom and finally to a large office with tarnished gold lettering stamped on the mahogany door. The name shown was Major Eric K. Thomas, Commanding Officer.

Kicking the door open, Ryan immediately fired and the sheet of paper fluttering off the desk jerked as the 9 mm round punched through to slap into the wall. Entering the room, the Deathlands warrior picked up the spent brass from the floor and cursed at himself for wasting a round.

Gray sunlight filtered through the grimy windows to poorly illuminate the CO's office. In the corner was a water cooler streaked by mineral deposits on the inside. Next came a line of red leather chairs that had been badly nibbled by mice, the foamy cushions tufting out randomly. The walls were heavily decorated with framed diplomas and commendations, pictures of family and friends, each so badly tilted that a few were hanging sideways. Near a green metal file cabinet was a sofa blanketed in cobwebs, and a vid camera hung at the distant corner of the ceiling where it could cover both the door and the windows.

The door to a private bathroom was ajar, and dominating the room was a tremendous oak desk, topped with a sheet of greenish glass. A skeleton was slumped over the desktop. Tiny bits of blue fiber and tarnished metal sticking to the collar bones seemed to imply that this was an officer of some kind, possibly the CO himself. As the companions started searching the office, puffs of dust were raised from every step on the crunchy carpet.

"Stinks in here," Mildred said, wrinkling her nose, setting the lantern on a convenient coffee table. The covers of the magazines showed smiling politicians, sleek cars and skinny women in bikini swimsuits that looked painful to wear.

"Smelled worse," Jak stated, going through the file cabinet.

As with most offices, the key to the cabinet had been left in the lock, to be removed at the end of the day. But the end had come sooner than expected and the files were completely accessible. The teenager found a dried-out bottle of Scotch whiskey in the bottom drawer, along with a couple of Western novels and a rat who had made a nest by chewing the documents into shreds.

Defensively, the rodent hissed and snapped at the intrusion. Without an expression, Jak flipped his wrist and the rat fell over dead, its head neatly removed. The neck stump pumped out a gush of red blood, soaking the books and making the pulp paper swell to twice its original size.

Interrupting the search, a window rattled as a boom sounded from outside, closely followed by two sharp whistles. Holstering their blasters, the companions relaxed and returned to their task. Whatever the trouble was, Doc had handled it alone.

"Found the warehouse ID card," Dean said, pulling a plastic card from a battered wallet, then glanced at the open door. "Same name as the base CO."

"Keep it," Ryan said, standing in the middle of the dusty room, his arms crossed. "Could come in handy."

"At least it means we're on the right track," J.B. said, going through the top drawer of the desk.

Krysty made a rude noise as she lifted a ring of keys into view and started going through them one at a time. The lock on the warehouse was large and shaped like the letter *H*. A Vishi, or something like that. One of the few locks J.B. said nobody could trick or pick. He often joked that a sledgehammer was the best way through a Vishi.

Not helping in the search, Ryan stayed where he was and continued to carefully study the furnishings of the room. Something was out of place here, but he just couldn't put a crosshair on what was wrong.

Then he spotted it. Hung on the wall behind the desk was the classic unfinished portrait of George Washington. There was nothing obviously suspicious about the picture, and Ryan had to look twice before finally realizing it was the only thing hanging on the walls that was still perfectly plumb. This close to the volcano, the base had to have received thousands of miniquakes from pressure vents over the decades.

"There's a wall safe," Ryan said, going around the desk and pushing the office chair of bones out of the way. The deceased commanding officer tumbled to the carpet and was kicked aside, but the bones rolled under the desk. Even in death, the officer refused to relinquish his post.

Running his fingers along the frame, Ryan thought that the portrait was nailed in place, until he touched a release switch on top and it swung away from the wall on squeaky hinges. Set in to the concrete wall was the pebbled armor front of a small safe. It was regulation size, with the standard numbered dial and lever.

Ryan stepped out of the way and let J.B. sweep it with his compass.

"No mag fields," he said, tucking the compass into a pocket. "If it's boobied, I can probably bypass the trigger."

"Mebbe we shouldn't bother," Krysty said, beating the dust off her clothing. "Safes are usually cleaned out."

"Not always," J.B. replied, pressing an ear to the steel door and closing his eyes to concentrate on the task.

Artfully, he rotated the dial twice to zero, then began slowly turning the dial listening for clicks. Less than a minute later, J.B. twisted the handle and began pulling out wads of papers marked Top Secret.

"No warehouse manifests," Ryan said, glancing at the paperwork before tossing it away.

Triumphantly, the Armorer withdrew a small wooden box. Forcing the lock with a knife blade, it sprung open to show red velvet lining with irregular indentations, spaces for a dozen keys, but only four were in place.

"Front gate," J.B. said, reading the tags, "main office, fuel pump...loading dock!"

"Bingo." Mildred grinned.

Leaving the office, the companions started toward the last warehouse. Blaster in hand, Doc waved in passing, a shoe resting on top of a crow, feathers strewed across the parking lot.

From the jungle, Ryan could hear a mixture of animal noises and glanced at his rad counter. The needle was near the redline and climbing steadily as they approached the rear of the warehouse. Any higher and they would have to cancel the recce or risk getting rad poisoning. That was a bad way to get aced, just about the worst.

Staying as close to the brick building as possible, the companions crept along the loading dock, the concrete ramp extending from the warehouse at shoulder height. On the dock were three rust-streaked metal doors and a wire fence closing off the dock itself. To the left was a set of stairs leading from the parking lot to a door alongside the dock, but those were also enclosed by wire fencing, this time topped by what was probably once concertina wire. Only the endless coil of razor blades had disintegrated from exposure to the elements, and nothing remained but some reddish-brown stains on the fencing.

"Dark night, it's hot here," J.B. said, checking the rad counter on his lapel.

"Which is why we're not going to waste time with lock picks," Ryan stated, firing the SIG-Sauer at point-blank range. The padlock blew apart, and the man hastily dragged off the chain holding the gate closed.

Rushing into the enclosed area, the companions climbed the stairs and breathed a sigh of relief as the rad counters eased their ominous clicking. The warehouse had to be at the very edge of the rad field, mere yards making the difference between lethal and livable.

At the top of the stairs, J.B. fired the Uzi and shattered the door lock. Instantly, a loud siren cut the stillness of the air, and the companions covered their ears, momentarily stunned by the power of the alarm. But a few moments later, the siren faded away completely.

"Impressive," Ryan commented, uncovering his ears. "The damn thing still worked after a hundred years."

"Just a fluke," J.B. retorted, pushing open the door with his rapidfire.

Just like in the city, the companions held their breath while out poured a rush of dry lifeless wind. Impatiently, they waited until fresh air had a chance to circulate inside.

Then Ryan gave it an extra couple of minutes, just to be sure. Sometimes, the corpses in the sealed buildings rotted in a strange way, maybe from the rads pouring through the walls, and the bodies filled the air with sickness. He'd seen strong men begging to be chilled only hours after entering a sealed structure.

When Ryan deemed it safe, he took the lead and entered, J.B. and Krysty close behind. In the bright illumination of the pressurized lanterns, they could see the three huge doors of the loading dock to their right, and straight ahead was a large open area with the floor sectioned in yellow stripes. A forklift stood mutely near an oil drum whose top was littered with foam coffee cups and a large thermos. Clothing and shoes lay in disarray on the polished concrete floor, obviously disturbed by small scavengers.

"Any rads?" Dean asked.

"We're clear," J.B. said, setting his lantern on top of the oil drum. A startled beetle scuttled out of the thermos and spread its wings to fly into the rafters.

A cargo elevator filled one wall, the panels closed, the controls dark. The door to a stairwell stood alongside, yellow lines on the floor marking its swing pattern, obviously to prevent folks from getting hit by the opening door.

"'Safety First,'" Krysty muttered, reading a sign on the wall.

Straight ahead, a long central corridor stretched to the far brick wall, both sides of the passage with large doors marked in alphanumeric sequences.

"Damn predark codes," Ryan snorted, resting the stock of his longblaster on a hip. "These storage units could be filled with shoelaces for all we know."

"Got to open each," Dean said, walking his lantern closer to the first door. The portal was veined metal, unblemished by the passing of the years. If there was a lock or hinges, they were nowhere in sight.

"How the hell do we get in?" he asked, annoyed.

Jak went to a toolbox lying near the forklift and returned with a sturdy pry bar. "Got key," he said, proffering the tool.

"Hey, what was that?" Krysty asked, swiveling. The woman stood in a crouch, with her blaster searching for a target. "Sounded like...well, like popcorn."

Mildred scowled. "What makes a noise like that?"

"Nothing I know of," Ryan said, lifting a pressurized lantern high to see the rafters. Nothing moved in the shadows, and overhead there was only the bare iron rafters, some moist water pipes for the fire-control system and the silvery insulation wrapped around the electrical conduits.

Krysty listened intently, but the noise was gone.

"Rain on roof?" Jak asked, looking upward. "Mebbe birds?" There was no skylight in the warehouse, and no windows to see outside, only a hooded ventilation fan in a steel cage. The building was a fortress offering no easy way for thieves to get inside.

Slowly, Krysty shook her head. "Can't say exactly what it was," she murmured uneasily. "But definitely not rain."

Ryan went to the rear door and glanced outside. "No sign of anything," he reported. "Might have been a fan moving from the breeze of us opening the door."

"Mebbe," Krysty agreed reluctantly.

"Hear anything now?" Mildred asked, listening herself. There was only the hiss of the pressure lantern to be heard.

"Nothing," the redhead said, easing her stance.

"Good. Let me know if you hear it again," Ryan said.

"Bet your ass," Krysty muttered.

Going to the first storage room, J.B. checked for traps, and Jak stabbed the pry bar into the jamb. The teenager gave a heave, something snapped loudly and the door slid sideways. Mildred raised the lantern to see, and there was only bare floor inside the storage unit.

"Empty as a stickie's pockets," Ryan growled, lowering his blaster.

"Sure hope this isn't a bust," Dean added.

"Funny," Krysty said, wrinkling her nose. "Now I smell horseradish."

Mildred spun from inspecting the corrugated walls

of the unit. "You sure?" she asked urgently, sniffing hard. "God no, please, not that."

"I smell it, too," J.B. said, puzzled. Horseradish, he'd smelled that before in a predark ruin many years ago.

Retreating a step, Krysty pointed at the baseboard of the wall. "Look!"

With a burbling hiss, thin yellow fumes began to rise from disguised vents, the vapors becoming thicker and stronger in irregular swells.

"Gas!" Ryan cursed, covering his face with a sleeve. "Everybody, out of the room!"

Dashing into the central passage, J.B. shoved the door shut, but the fumes seeped past the jamb, swelling and expanding to sluggishly fill the passageway completely. From the rafters, a beetle tumbled down to hit the floor near a twitching mouse, lying on its side. Blisters were already forming over its furry body.

"Mustard gas!" Mildred spit, backing away fast. "Don't let it touch you!"

"This way!" Jak commanded, heading for the exit.

But as the companions tried for the loading dock, the swirling yellow fumes were already waist high there, sealing off any possible escape in that direction. Retreating to the far end of the central passage, Ryan and the others put their backs to the brick wall. Steadily increasing in volume, the deadly mustard gas was swirling like a living thing, slowly filling the passage in random spurts. The reek of horseradish was becoming overpowering, their eyes painfully tearing, and breathing was becoming torture.

Pulling out a canteen, Mildred splashed some water

on her face, then soaked a handkerchief and held it to her mouth.

"Make masks!" she ordered, passing over the container.

"This stop?" Jak asked hopefully, coughing hard.

The physician shook her head. "Wet masks will only buy us a few minutes. We're dead meat unless we get out of here right now!"

"Vents must not be working correctly," Ryan said, his voice muffled by the wet rag.

"Only reason we're still here," Krysty agreed, gasping for breath.

"I'll stop it," Dean growled, pulling a Molotov from his bag. Igniting the fuse, the boy threw the bottle at the expanding death cloud. In a crash, the cocktail roared into a fireball, but as the poison gas touched the flames, they dimmed and diminished in size until winking out of existence.

"Goddamn it," Mildred cursed. "Fire is useless. There's no free oxygen to feed the flames." In desperation, her mind raced to recall chemical formulas. Did she have anything in med kit to use as a counter agent for mustard gas? Truthfully, the physician wasn't even sure there was a counteragent effective against the lethal war gas.

Slow and steady, the yellow fumes moved along the passageway, getting inexorably closer.

"Got to find another way out of here," Ryan said, running his hands over the brick wall. The concrete between the bricks was flush to the surface, leaving nothing for them to use as chinks to climb to the roof.

"Blow the wall!" Dean shouted, his chest heaving.

"Wind would only bring the gas on us faster!" J.B. shot back.

"Other wall!" Jak urged, pointing down the passage.

Turning, Ryan thrust a hand into his pocket. The teenager meant blow open the loading bay doors and vent the gas out the front. Brilliant.

Pulling grens, Ryan and J.B. whipped a couple of HE spheres through the mustard gas. Moments later the charges violently exploded, but there was no change in the growth of the poison vapors.

"Dark night, it didn't work!" J.B. raged.

Snarling, Ryan pulled another gren. "Do it again!"

"No, cover your faces!" Krysty commanded, pulling out the Veri pistol. Aiming for the ceiling, she yanked the trigger and the signal gun thumped in her grip, her last flare launching on a sizzling column of colored flame.

Chapter Sixteen

Streaking away, the signal flare slammed into a steel rafter and exploded into a blinding flash of colors. Almost instantly, there was a gurgling hiss and water began to sputter from the fire sprinklers lining the vaulted ceiling. As the brackish fluid began to rain upon the swirling poison, yellowish water started running along the concrete floor and into the rusty drains.

Tearing and coughing at the pungent reek of horse-radish, the drenched companions held wet handker-chiefs and covered their faces. Incredibly, the cloud was getting smaller, the deluge of water diluting the gas and washing it away. But the volume from the sprinklers was already slowing, what little water had remained in the century-old feeder pipes depleting rapidly. Now, the military warehouse was fighting it-self, the two defensive systems locked in mortal com-bat. Long minutes passed with the floor vents spitting out tiny gasps of mustard gas while the sprinklers pitifully drizzled their dwindling supply onto the reeking death mist.

Then without warning, the vents became silent, the chem reservoir completely drained. But designed to extinguish a warehouse full of burning munitions, the fire sprinklers still sputtered out the occasional burst of water. In growing relief, the companions watched as the mustard-gas cloud slowly thinned away, even diminishing in density and height, until only faint wisps floated over the puddled floor.

Dean started to remove his rag and Mildred stopped him. Patiently, the group waited for the sprinklers to cease operation, and there was no longer any sign of the lethal gas. Soaked to the skin, Ryan decided to be the first and hesitantly lowered his damp cloth to chance a sniff. The warehouse smelled like a stagnant pool, but without any trace of horseradish. Carefully, the Deathlands warrior did so again, then drew in a full deep breath.

"Clear," he announced, tossing aside the rag. "Good thing you had a flare."

"And that mustard gas is a soluble toxin," Mildred said, blinking rapidly. "How did you know?"

"Didn't," Krysty replied, pouring some more water from her canteen into a palm and smoothing down her stinging hair. "But there didn't seem to be anything else to try."

A drop of water fell from the overhead pipes, landed with a splat on the protective hood of a lantern and hissed away into steam. Dean moved the lantern to a peg on the wall.

"Damn smart move," J.B. said, shaking the moisture from his Uzi, the bolt and wire stock clacking softly. "Going to remember that trick."

"Try running first, lover," Mildred said, squeezing out her sodden sleeves. "If this had been VX or M-55 nerve gas, we would have been chilled before the first drop of water fell."

"VK chills even faster," Ryan growled, using stiff fingers to brush back his crop of dripping hair.

"How know that?" Jak asked.

Exchanging glances, Ryan and J.B. didn't reply.

There were many secrets in the Deathlands that they
would never talk about. What they knew about nerve
gas was one of the biggest.

"I'm going to open the door," Dean said, wrinkling his nose at the remembered stink, and headed
for the exit.

Splashing through the shrinking puddles, the companions reached the loading dock and forced open the
three doors. A warm breeze moved into the warehouse, carrying the rich fragrance of the jungle, flowers, fruit and the heady aroma of living green plants.

Leaving wet footprints on the apron, the companions walked outside and Ryan gave two short whistles. A single long whistle answered from around the
corner, telling them Doc was fine, and Ryan whistled
back, informing the old man they were also fine.

Drying off in the weak sunshine, the companions
let the warehouse air out while they cleaned blasters.
Nobody spoke for several minutes, thinking about
how close they had come to death from the trap, and
knowing that they were soon going to go right back
inside and try again.

"Where there's one trap," J.B. said, wiping off the
lenses of his glasses, "there'll be more."

"I don't doubt it," Ryan said. "We'll each take
turns opening the units, and at the first sign of any
more gas, we leave fast."

"Still need ammo," Dean reminded him succinctly, exchanging the wet clip in his Browning for
a dry mag from his jacket. The water from the sprinklers had been tainted with rust and scum that could
cause a jam. Best to take no chances.

"We'll get some," his father replied. "If not here,
then at police headquarters. There should be a SWAT

room, and a vault full of blasters. The cops used to keep the vault locked to make sure nobody could get their mitts on the weapons. But that just means they were sealed safely away from the corrosive sea air of the island. Could be everything we need.''

''Only reason we're here was because of the droids,'' Krysty reminded him, fanning her shirt to make it dry faster.

Dean frowned. ''The machines will be waiting for us there.''

''Mebbe,'' Ryan agreed. ''So we'll go in through the roof. They won't expect that.''

''Who the hell would?'' J.B. said, walking back into the warehouse. Stopping at the fifty-five-gallon drum, he gathered the foam cups and stuffed them into his munitions bag. Those would help a lot if they had to firebomb the droids.

Leading the way, Ryan returned to the row of storage units, the smooth floor only damp in spots by now. The puddles had flowed into the drains and gone somewhere else.

''Stay here. Me first,'' Jak said, reclaiming the dropped pry bar and walking past the open unit to the next door.

The teenager easily snapped the locking mechanism with the pry bar, then gave the door a shove and ran for the loading dock as the door slid aside. Silence ruled the warehouse, the vents remained quiet and no swirling clouds of yellow hissed into the corridor.

''Seems safe,'' Mildred ventured, sniffing carefully.

They proceeded warily to the second unit until the companions glanced inside and found it as empty as the first. There were a few candy-bar wrappers on the floor, and faded inventory sheets attached to a clipboard hung from a nail on the wall. Nothing else.

Resolute, Ryan took the pry bar and went to the next unit only to find the same thing. It was starting to look as if the place might be empty, but there was only one way to know.

"Why was there such a strong smell of horseradish?" Krysty asked, accepting the pry bar and starting on the end unit of the row. "Mustard gas made from horseradish?"

"Don't know for sure," Mildred said, gesturing vaguely. "Could be. I know that VX gas is made from meat tenderizer. Read that in a newspaper."

"They used to put nerve gas on food?" Dean asked in shock.

"Sort of," Mildred said hesitantly. The complexities of the predark world were a bitch to explain sometimes. "In a powder form it's harmless. Only deadly when it's stabilized as a gas."

With a loud crack, Krysty broke open the door and checked inside. "Empty," she reported.

She passed the pry bar to Dean, who went to the next unit, muttering something under his breath about insane whitecoats.

An hour later, the last door was ripped open and the companions stared at yet another empty storage unit, scraps of wood and packing material floating in tiny puddles from the earlier deluge.

"Nothing again," Dean said, marching into the room, brandishing the steel bat as if physically challenging the storage unit to produce supplies. There was a calendar on the wall showing the month of January 2000 and something, the final year blurry from the sprinklers. The days were checked off up to the twenty-first.

He turned away in disgust. They already knew the date of skydark. There was nothing to be learned here.

"Come on," his father said, turning to leave. "Still got the next level to check."

"And if that's cleaned out, too?"

"Then we try for police headquarters," Ryan replied. "We know the droids will be waiting for us, but there should be lots of blasters and grens in the SWAT vault. Those are often airtight."

Passing by the elevator, Krysty paused for a moment, straining to hear the popcorn sound again, but she couldn't hear anything unusual. Maybe the popping had something to do with the gas? Made sense.

Without electricity, the elevator couldn't move, so the companions went straight to the door for the stairs. Looking over the portal with a lantern, J.B. decided it was clear of traps and pulled it open. Inside, wide concrete steps edged with steel led down into the darkness.

SIG-Sauer in hand, Ryan took the point, with Krysty right behind holding the lantern high. That left the man's hands free, and cast both of them in the shadow of the bottom of the lantern. That would make them a difficult target for a sniper to zero in on. Ryan really didn't think there was anything alive in the predark building but the mice and beetles feasting off the ancient moldy paper.

Cobwebs festooned the handrail, and Ryan's combat boots rang on the metal strips supporting the steps. Nothing he could do about that but stay icy. The steps took a turn at a landing, and he stepped over a couple of limp uniforms lying alongside several rusted beer cans. He snorted at the sight, and deliberately stepped on the soldier's uniforms. Just a pair of goldbricks caught forever shirking their work.

Two more landings later, the stairs ended on terrazzo floor, a duty roster posted by the only door. There were no signs of any boobies, so he tried the handle. The door was unlocked, but swung open only a few inches before hitting something solid on the other side. Ryan tried reaching through the slim crack, but his muscular arm was too large. He threw his weight against the door, and it merely yielded another inch.

"Let me try," Krysty offered.

Giving her space, Ryan moved out of the way, and the woman squeezed her arm through the crack. For a brief moment, Krysty thought something brushed against her bare flesh, then she found the obstruction and traced its outline with her fingertips.

"It's a forklift," she said, extricating her limb. "Must have run wild like the cars on the bypass when the nuke went off."

"Those things weigh a ton," J.B. snorted.

Turning, Ryan placed his back to the door, then put a boot onto the cinder block wall across the landing. Lifting his other boot into place, the man heaved against the blockage, and the door began to scrape along the floor, hinges squealing in protest.

Placing aside their weapons, Krysty and J.B. joined Ryan and the trio forced the stubborn door open another foot, the forklift shuddering from the sideways motion. Suddenly, the door swung open all the way and the machine toppled over in a strident crash, the noise echoing through the blackness. Expecting this, Ryan dropped a boot and stopped himself from falling, then stood and spun with his blaster out. Krysty and J.B. were already in that position, studying the room beyond in the light of the pressurized lanterns.

The bottom level of the warehouse was filled with open wooden crates bearing military identification codes. Excelsior stuffing was strewed about in piles a yard deep, the broken tops of the crates dashed into corners. Empty plastic pallets lay on the cold terrazzo floor, tangles of steel packing straps coiled into wild formations. Foam packing pellets covered the floor like snow, and everywhere lay sheets of gray cushioning foam bearing the cutout silhouette of weapons, handcannons, longblasters, rapidfires.

"Shitfire," J.B. muttered as they walked through the vast piles of litter. "Been looted."

Bending to pick up the top of a plastic box, Ryan couldn't read the military code set in raised lettering, but he knew the distinctive shape.

"LAW rocket," he growled, tossing the lid away. "Just what we needed."

"Looks like the soldiers took everything," Krysty said, trying to see what lay beyond the range of the lanterns. The mounds of trash and packing material seemed to extend forever. How big was this level of the armory?

"Not everything," Dean said, lifting an M-16/M-203 combo assault rifle into view. Brushing away the foam packing peanuts, he inspected the weapon, working the bolt and opening the breech of the 40 mm gren launcher fitted underneath the M-16 machine gun.

"Just fine," the boy announced, tilting it against the wall. "Just needs ammo."

Grabbing a large wooden crate that was lying on

its side, Ryan flipped it over and laid the M-16/M-203 on wooden slats.

"We start here," the man directed, glancing around. "If they missed one blaster, there could be more buried in the rest of this crap. J.B., stand guard, the rest of us rummage through the trash."

"Better stay in a group," Krysty said, surveying the acres of garbage. "Or else we'll only end up going over the same ground."

"Like hunting land mines," Jak said, squatting on the floor, stabbing a knife into the plastic foam and bubble wrapping. "Only now want find."

Going to their hands and knees, the companions started shifting the ancient litter, running stiff fingers through the mounds of pellets and carefully pulling apart the sharp strands of steel packing strips. Mildred cried out, lifting another M-16/M-203 combo from the rubbish and placing it on top of the crate next to the first longblaster. Shifting a pallet, Jak pulled out a belt of 40 mm shells that had slid underneath. In a pile of foam pads, Dean found a repair kit, and mixed into a heap of used tape Krysty located two empty ammo clips, and then two more.

Time passed as the work slowly progressed. Many times the people grunted as slivers of wood stabbed their questing fingers, or the steel straps sliced across knuckles, but the hunt neither paused nor slowed. The piles of trash reached more than six feet high in some spots, and they went through every bit, watching for individual rounds. A single HE gren was found and added to the small pile on the crate, then a battered Claymore mine in questionable working condition. Next, came a windfall as an entire box of timing pencils for C-4 was discovered, but no plastique itself.

Reaching the far wall, the companions took a short break, then started digging their way back, now tossing the litter into their original path. This made the work a lot easier, and their speed increased. But nothing was found on this pass, or the next.

Grabbing a sturdy fiberglass crate, Ryan tried to lift it aside, but the container seemed stuck to the floor. Kicking a clear area around the crate, the man saw that the lid was still screwed in place, the sides intact and undamaged. Drawing the panga, he used the tip of the blade to remove the screws, then cut away the security tape sealing the lid in place.

"Find something?" Krysty asked, looking up from the floor, her hair peppered with foam bits.

"Tell you in a sec," Ryan replied, carefully pulling out handfuls of stuffing until finding a huge plastic case buried in the center. In spite of its size, the case wasn't very heavy, and Ryan lifted it from the nest of packing to place it gingerly on the floor.

"I know that box," J.B. said from across the room.

Ryan undid a latch. "So do I," he said, and swung open the case to expose a mint-condition M-1 A military flamethrower. The burner and louvered hose shone with protective gel, the twin tanks satin smooth under the camou paint job. Checking the main crate again, Ryan found canisters of condensed fuel and a charging unit for the pressure tank mixed in with the flamethrower. Excellent. This was old tech to the man. The Trader liked to use flamethrowers in battles. They were fearsome weapons that often made raiders leave, thus saving lives and ammo. Ryan and J.B. could repair the things in their sleep, and both men knew how to walk a burner and not get scorched by the splash.

"This will do," Ryan said and closed the case to search through the rest of the crate. There was nothing more inside, so he ferried the flamethrower over to J.B. and continued the garbage hunt. A few more of those and they would be back in business.

An hour later, the tired people reached the starting point and broke for a fast meal of granola bars and beef jerky while J.B. finished his inventory of the meager finds.

"From the grease trails and fuel stains on the floor, I'd say the National Guard stored their wags down here," Ryan said, biting off a chew of jerky. "Lots of Hummers, a few trucks and a couple of APC wags, Bradleys from the tire tracks. The soldiers loaded them with the blasters from storage and drove away."

"To where?" Dean asked.

His father shrugged. "Where did all of the troops from the redoubts go? Nobody knows."

"And they just tossed the trash down here as they unpacked the weapons," Krysty added, unwrapping a stick of gum and popping it into her mouth. "Must have been in a hell of a rush to leave the area."

"Which was lucky for us," Mildred observed. "We found quite a few working weapons accidentally disposed of in the trash."

"And some that are worth shit," J.B. said, joining the group and tilting back his hat. "Want the bad news first?"

"Nothing good?" Jak asked, wiping his mouth on a sleeve, then screwing the cap on his canteen.

"Some," J.B. admitted. "We have an M-60 with no ammo. A hundred rounds of 30 mm shells and no blaster they'll fit. Got ten blocks of 4.5 mm caseless ammo, which I wouldn't give as a gift to a stickie.

There's two shotguns with bent barrels, four M-16 longblasters with dented receivers, six Stinger guided missiles without a launcher tube or radar box, not that the circuits would have worked anyway after the EMP of the nuke.''

None of the companions smiled at the information.

"Now the good news,'' the Armorer said, turning to walk along the line of four crates covered with military hardware. "We got a flamethrower with ninety seconds of fuel. Six M-16/M-203 combo blasters, nine usable clips and a thousand rounds of ammo. Plus, twenty assorted shells for the 40 mm launchers. Ten grens, two of them smoke charges, one Claymore land mine with a broken timer, but I can jury-rig something for that, a hundred timing pencils, a 4-shot LAW rocket with one live round, and an Armbrust with five HE rounds, only one of which is usable. Plus a ton of assorted small-arms ammo, more than we could ever carry.''

"Got the bikes,'' Dean reminded him, going closer.

"More than even they can carry.''

The boy nodded. "Good.'' His Browning didn't really have much of a punch, and Dean was thinking hard about getting a second blaster, something with more power. However, the Weatherby weighed ten pounds. He wanted something lightweight, but with maximum chilling capability.

"Was hoping for more,'' Ryan said gruffly, standing. "But it should do. Everybody take an M-16/M-203, I'll haul the flamethrower.''

Each of the companions took their fill of ammo for their personal weapons, filled their pockets with grens and draped themselves with the new blasters.

Taking his share, J.B. then went to help the man

with the straps and tapped the pressure gauges to test the needles.

"Should have thirty-two, three-second bursts," the man warned. "But it might only be half that since the pressure valve was sticking and we don't know if that's a true reading."

"Say fifteen. So at short range, forty-five seconds total," Ryan finished. "Good enough for the droids. Don't know about the spider. That last mutie fought for a long time after we set it on fire."

"No prob." Jak pulled shut the 40 mm gren launcher of the M-203, and slapped a clip into the receiver of the M-16. Then with a scowl, the teenager pulled the clip and primed it first by rapping it against the wall, then sliding it into the weapon.

"Triple-stupe design," he muttered.

Mildred grunted in agreement. "Give me an AK-47 any day," the physician said, yanking the top bolt on the blaster. "Or an Uzi. Something reliable."

"Blast, I can't carry all of this," Krysty said, and laid down the Webley. "We'll have to make two trips."

"Better save the .44 bullets for Doc," Ryan suggested, tugging the body harness of the flamethrower into place. "Mebbe we can finally get him to abandon that antique and keep the other Webley."

"Hope he's okay," Dean said, changing the subject. He knew only one person was needed to guard the bikes, and with the gates closed the parking lot should be secure. But the National Guard base was cut in two by the cliff, and anything could have climbed onto the mesa and caught the old man from behind.

"He fine," Jak stated confidently, stuffing a box of

.357 ammo into the pocket of his jacket. "Hear shot if trouble."

Closing her eyes, Krysty tilted her head for a moment.

"Curious," she said, frowning. "There it is again."

"Doc?" J.B. asked, stuffing the Armbrust into his backpack.

Pensive, the redhead turned slowly. "No, it's that soft popcorn noise again."

"More gas?" Dean demanded, looking about for any signs of yellow smoke.

"I hear it, too," Ryan added with a frown, tucking the vented wand of the flamethrower through the chest straps and drawing his handcannon. "Seems to be coming from the elevator."

"We never checked that," Mildred said, pointing the double barrels of her M-16/M-203 in that direction. "If the soldiers sent the trash down here with the elevator, then anything could be in there."

"Making popcorn?" Jak asked, puzzled.

"Or mebbe something walking on bubble wrapping," Dean suggested.

"Droid?" Jak asked skeptically.

"Damn near anything," Ryan said. "Triple red."

Quickly, the companions assumed positions behind the mounds of rubbish.

With his Uzi in hand, J.B. walked to the elevator to listen for a moment, before placing a hand on the lever of the elevator door.

"Open it," Ryan directed, leveling the fluted muzzle of his weapon.

Grabbing the handle of the cargo elevator, J.B.

pushed up the gate, the action making the bottom half drop from sight.

Inside the lift was a towering stack of wet wooden crates piled high on a plastic pallet identical to the one used for the *Pegasus*. The sides of the boxes were soaked with an oily residue that was dribbling onto the metal floor. As each drop struck, it detonated like a firecracker. The irregular sound was vaguely reminiscent of making popcorn.

"Dark night," J.B. gasped, going motionless at the sight. "Everybody freeze. Don't move. Don't move a goddamn muscle or we'll be blown to bits!"

"Dynamite," Ryan said between clenched teeth. "Nuke-shitting hell, that's got to be four or five tons!"

Lifting a leg, the Armorer awkwardly untied his left boot and slid his foot out, then did the same with the other.

"Remove your boots and walk to the stairs in your socks," he ordered in a whisper. "Make no sudden moves, and for fuck's sake don't drop anything. Take whatever you're holding. Nothing more."

"But the ammo..." Mildred began.

"Leave it," Ryan said, tying his boot laces together and slinging them around his neck to keep his hands free. "That old dynamite is sweating pure nitro. We got to go, and fast."

"Come again?" Dean asked.

J.B. felt a trickle of sweat run down his face as he moved for the door to the stairwell. "Dynamite was just nitro in some sort of inert packing—fuller's earth, sawdust, anything would do. But over time, the nitro can seep through the waxy covering of the sticks and ooze on the outside in droplets."

There came a crackle of tiny explosions from the ground of the elevator.

"And then it explodes whenever," the boy said hoarsely, suddenly understanding.

"Damn straight. Why the fuck it didn't detonate when I yanked open the door, I have no idea. But if it goes off now, there wouldn't be enough left of this armory to stuff into a spent brass round."

Gently placing her sock-clad feet on the terrazzo floor, Mildred stared at the stack of crates on the pallet. "Anything we can do?" she asked, licking dry lips.

"Leave," J.B. said, tiptoeing toward the exit. "And then run for our lives. That elevator is a bomb just itching to go off."

Easing out of their boots, the rest of the companions started slowly creeping toward the stairwell. Making a small detour around a crate, Dean reached out to snag the shoulder strap of the Armbrust rocket, then kept moving.

Turning off the preburner of his weapon, Ryan scowled at the action and promised he would have a stern talk with the boy about obeying orders in emergencies.

Crossing the few yards to the stairs seemed to take forever, every retarded motion excruciatingly slow. But finally they were inside the stairs, their socks patting on the hard steps as the men and women ascended at glacial speed. Finally reaching the ground floor, they risked moving faster and dashed across the damp floors, the yellowish moisture stinging their feet through the Army socks.

"Landing dock is closer," Mildred suggested.

"Fuck that. We'd have to jump to the ground," Ryan said harshly. "Use the stairs."

Easing out the back door, they quickly traversed the stairs and through the gate in the fence to finally reach the parking lot. Not wasting a moment with their boots, the companions dashed around the building in their stocking feet and raced straight for the bikes pell-mell.

Standing near the collection of motorcycles, Doc arched an eyebrow at the companions' unusual appearance.

"Salutations all!" he rumbled with a smile, then noticed the stern expressions on their faces. In remarkable speed, the old man was on his bike with the engine running, as the others arrived.

"Droids?" Doc asked, revving the engine.

"Sweaty dyno," J.B. said, climbing onto his bike. "Tons of it."

"Saints preserve us," the old man muttered, as Jak climbed on behind him.

Rolling to the gate, Ryan slashed the rope holding it closed with his knife and the iron grille swung away to crash into the brick wall. The companions flinched at the noise, but when nothing happened, they rolled the bikes onto the street and drove toward the on ramp of the bypass.

"A little distance more and we'll be safe," Ryan said over the purring motor.

"Sure hate to leave those blasters," Krysty griped, maneuvering around the maze of potholes. "But we had no choice."

"None," J.B. said, watching the ruins. Things darted about in the shadows, but none dared to emerge and challenge the norms on the street.

The entrance ramp proved to be clear of wrecked cars, and the motorcycles zoomed up the sloped concrete to the bypass without any trouble. Soon, the companions were streaking away at their best speed, the purrs of the engines rising to throaty growls.

"Gate open," Jak said. "Muties recce warehouse."

"Let them," Ryan snapped, leaning into a turn. "The blast'll only attract more muties and give us some breathing room."

Bright light flashed behind the companions, and a rumbling roar grew to staggering proportions, then faded away. Seconds later smoking debris rained from the sky. A burning tire hit the roadway directly in front of the companions and rolled along with the bikes for a few yards before veering away and disappearing over the side of the elevated bypass.

"Now let's go find that gateway," Krysty shouted, her Army-issue socks pressed tight to the checkered rider pegs. The woman tried not to think what would happen if her unprotected foot slipped and brushed against the rushing surface of the roadway. "And get the hell off this island!"

Black hair streaming in the wind, Ryan shot her a look. "Agreed," he muttered, sagging a little in his seat from the array of weaponry strapped across his body. "We'll stop in a couple of miles, and look for a place to stop and check over our weapons."

"And boots," Jak added, shifting his bare feet on the floorboard of the fancy Harley.

"What about the spider?" Dean asked, the tube of the Armbrust rocket sticking over his shoulder like a samurai sword.

Keeping a tight grip on the handlebars, Ryan

pumped the throttle. "Since we know where the bug is, we'll take the off-ramp just before its web," he said. "Then get back on the bypass after we go underneath."

"Sounds good," the boy agreed.

"And if not," J.B. added grimly, "we got the blasters to chill a dozen of the big muties."

"If these junkyard weapons work," Mildred stated, leaning over the handlebars as if urging the machine on to greater speed.

Chapter Seventeen

All of her eight legs dancing nimbly, she turned to inspect the new trap.

It was perfect. A few inches off the ground was a sturdy line of her best silk that stretched across the flat river of black stone. When the two-legs came back riding their not-alive animals over the line, they would fall down and get very hurt. Maybe even break the not-animals and make the two-legs drop their thunder sticks. That would make them completely helpless. The tiny killers had great speed, but no agility.

Then she would swing up from under the strip of land that did not touch the ground and pounce on them in surprise. The giant female had never done such a thing before, but her ancient instincts said the trick always worked. Soon it would have the two-legs wrapped tightly in cocoons, stored food for the children when they were born. Except for the little two-leg that threw the orange beast that damaged the web. That one she could plant her eggs into, and let the infants consume the two-leg alive when they were born.

Placing her legs with care, the giant spider walked over the edge of black stone river and swung underneath. Settling comfortably into place, she locked her legs into position and settled in for the hunting sleep where she would rest, but not dream. Always ready to instantly attack in any direction. It was the greatest talent of her race—infinite patience mixed with ruthless cruelty.

Time passed—how much was impossible to say—then a soft purring sounded from below her. The spider snapped open her segmented eyes and stared at the tiny two-legs racing away below her on their not-animals. They had detoured around the trap! Impossible! Intolerable!

Without pause, she squeezed out a thick strand of silky material from her spinnerets and released the hold of her legs on the sky-river. The strand held her weight as it should, and she descended toward the two-legs as fast as possible. A short distance from the ground, she released the spinnerets and fell the rest of the way, her tremendous weight easily balanced on her eight strong legs.

But the two-legs were already ahead of her, the not-animals moving at an unbelievable speed. She roared in anger, but the noise didn't make this food freeze in terror as it did the jungle cats and four-arms. Some of the two-legs looked backward at her and made banging sounds, tiny pinpricks of pain stabbing into her chest.

Staying level, she charged at the defiant food, her flashing limbs carrying her easily over the broken ground and oddly shaped stone eggshells. She roared again and snapped her mandibles, feeling her heart pound as the blood beat quicker through every vein. To chase and kill! This was the greatest pleasure!

But the not-animals were too fast, and she angrily slowed as they purred up the sloped stone to the sky-river of black stone disappearing from view. Raging fury formed in her mind, and she hissed long and loud at the escape. Twice! Nothing had ever gotten away twice before! A blinding rage to kill flooded her mind, and she raised quivering antennae high to begin stroking the air. Mixed into the thousands of smells around her nest, there was the strong reek of the not-animals lying in a stream along the ground.

Checking to make sure her egg sacks were strongly attached to her abdomen, she dashed forward at killing speed to follow the invisible river of odors, knowing that eventually it would lead her to the defiant food. Time didn't matter. She could sit in a trap forever, or chase a prey for even longer. Soon enough, she would drink their blood, saving the withered flesh for the precious eggs.

"THINK IT'LL COME after us?" Dean asked, glancing over a shoulder as they rolled along the bypass.

Keeping a tight grip on the handlebars, Ryan shrugged in reply. His engine was still running a little hot, but that shouldn't be a problem now that it had had a long rest.

"At least it can't camou like that big bastard in New Mexico," J.B. said with a frown.

"How's the fuel?" Ryan asked, tapping the gauge. He wasn't overly worried about discovering that this spider could perfectly copy anything it was near and disappear. The creature fought at White Sands was a different kind of mutie from this hairy brute.

Krysty looked down. "About half a tank," she replied.

"Same here," Mildred answered, swerving to avoid a pothole. Every bounce made her collection of bags and blasters slam into her. The physician knew she had to be covered with bruises by now.

"Less," Doc said. "But then we are carrying a double load."

After checking the rearview mirror, Ryan studied the city on either side of the elevated roadway. There were mostly homes and strip malls below, the monoliths of the downtown skyscrapers miles distant. Nothing clearly dangerous was in sight, and his sweaty feet were constantly slipping off the floorboards. Time for a break.

"Let's find someplace to stop and refuel," Ryan ordered, carefully maintaining a steady course on the bike. Any sudden move on his part made the fuel in the flamethrower tanks slosh about, the weight shift threatening to topple the bike.

"Rest stop up ahead!" Krysty said.

"That'll do. Follow me in," Ryan commanded, gently slowing the motorcycle.

Blank signs announced the turnoff lane, and the companions rolled along the macadam strip into the rest area. With weapons in hand, they stayed on the vibrating bikes and closely scrutinized the vicinity. Bisected by the access road, the rest area was a half circle of forested land, packed with an untamed bramble of wild trees and thorny bushes. The public washroom was a sagging ruin of bricks and exposed pipes, with birds nesting in the exposed stalls. However, there was plenty of open area around the cracked parking lot. Nothing could come close without their seeing it in plenty of time to react.

"Seems clear," Krysty said, turning off the bike and listening as the engine went still.

Turning off their motorcycles, the rest of the companions stood and gratefully stretched their backs. On a horse, the strain was in the thighs; on a bike, it was the lower back that got stiff.

Dropping their packs, longblasters and bags, the friends tossed away their filthy socks and pulled on fresh dry pairs taken from the department store, then pulled on their boots.

"Better," Jak grunted, stomping the ground. The teenager had been wary of making a sharp turn on the bike, afraid he would stick out a leg to brace himself and lose a foot. First lesson he ever received in riding a predark bike was that the road hated riders and wanted to chill them every chance it got. After a few mishaps, the youth soon learned that was sage advice.

Arranging the mixed collection of weaponry on the ground, the companions distributed the blasters and ammo evenly. J.B. stuffed his M-16/M-203 into the gun boot lashed to the frame of his motorcycle, keeping his regular weapons about him, the LAW rocket launcher sticking out of the saddlebags. Since it was almost out of rounds, Mildred put the Thompson into her bike's boot and draped the M-16 combo over the handlebars. The physician preferred the accuracy of her ZKR over the spray-and-pray firepower of rapidfires. Slinging the M-16/M-203 over a shoulder, Krysty then shifted her revolver to the middle of her belt for easy access. Doc did the same with his weapon, the LeMat holstered at his hip, the Webley jutting from his belt.

"Behold, and tremble in fear," Doc rumbled, adjusting his numerous blasters, "at the modern Gilgamesh."

Switching positions, Jak took the driver's position

on the Harley so that he could put his assault rifle into the gun boot, the slim Armbrust hung across the back of his jacket. He was unfamiliar with the stealth projectile launcher, but the instructions were printed on top and the operation was fairly simple.

"We got plenty of ammo, but save the 40 mm grens for the droids," J.B. instructed, filling a pocket with 12-gauge shells for the M-4000. The bent shotguns in the trash had been fully loaded, and he managed to salvage all of the cartridges.

"Better keep the Weatherby handy, son," Ryan suggested, tucking the Steyr into the gun boot. "We got enough firepower with the M-16s. Could use some decent penetration."

"Gotcha," Dean replied, packing the M-16 combo into the saddlebags strapped over the rear fender, along with their extra food and spare ammo. The plastic stock stuck almost straight up alongside the roll bar.

"Pressure is good," Ryan said, checking the dials and igniting the preburner in the vented muzzle.

"You sure that thing will work?" Mildred asked, making room in her med kit for the one spare clip for her M-16. The single 40 mm round was already in the M-203 launcher, primed and ready to fire.

"Time to find out," Ryan said, hefting the weapon and walking away from the others. "Stay clear in case she blows."

"Got you covered," J.B. said, raised a small CO_2 fire extinguisher from the Harley's repair kit.

Bracing for the expected recoil, Ryan triggered the spray. The weapon bucked in his grip, sending a fiery lance of burning chems thirty feet down the old pavement.

After a full count of three seconds, Ryan released the trigger and closely watched as the flame collapsed, then checked the dials. Pressure was good, no blockage in the jets, an even dispersal.

"Trigger sticks," he said, resting the hot barrel on a shoulder. "But other than that, works fine."

Placing away her own CO_2 extinguisher, Krysty walked to a railing, her cowboy boots crunching on the loose gravel.

"Food, ammo, fuel," she said, looking out over the expanse of the predark metropolis. An acrid breeze from the distant volcanoes ruffled her long crimson hair, the filaments recoiling from the traces of sulfur in the wind.

"Now we just have to find the gateway," she finished grimly.

"Gonna be tough," J.B. agreed, extending his Navy telescope and studying the tall buildings on the jagged horizon. The gateway could be hidden anywhere in the city. The basement of a store, a second-story bedroom, inside a bank vault. Anywhere.

"Needle in fucking haystack," Jak grunted, thumbing fresh rounds into his Colt Python. The Ruger was packed into the saddlebags, where it was going to stay. Having too many weapons, was almost as dangerous as having not enough. Almost.

"Indeed, my young friend, what we ardently need is a native guide," Doc stated, standing on the berm, pressing loose rounds into an empty clip for the M-16. When finished, he slipped the mag into the receiver and worked the bolt. "But where can we locate a Chingachgook for us to play Hawkeye?"

"Are you sure it was science and philosophy you

taught,'' Mildred demanded in irritation, ''and not classic literature?''

''Quite definite, madam,'' Doc replied. ''But there is no more noble a pursuit for both heart and mind than spending time with a book.''

''Fireblast, we have a guide!'' Ryan said suddenly, returning to the group of bikes. ''We're looking for a gateway, and there's sec droids in the city.''

''They're the guards,'' J.B. realized aloud. ''Shit-fire, that's got to be right. Why else would they be here?''

As she turned away from the cityscape, a smile crept onto Krysty's face. ''You're going to use the droids,'' she said, ''to find the gateway.''

''Tell me a better plan,'' Ryan asked, turning off the preburner. The tiny blue propane flame winked out immediately.

Removing his glasses, J.B. polished off the bugs dotting the lenses. ''Wish I could,'' he said, sliding the frames back on his face. ''Sure as hell don't want to drive along every street and look in each building. That'd take months, years mebbe.''

''A robotic stalking goat,'' Mildred muttered, tucking a lock of beaded hair behind an ear. ''Could just work.''

''Count on it.'' Briefly, Ryan cast a glance at the clouds overhead. The descending sun filled the fiery clouds with a profusion of colored lights, the sheet lightning slashing tortured rainbows across the polluted sky.

''Let's get moving,'' he said, climbing onto his Harley. ''There's still a couple hours of daylight left. That can work in our favor.''

"Going to the department store," Dean stated confidently, getting on the saddle behind his father.

"Pawnshop," Ryan corrected, pressing the ignition button. "That's where we know the droids were waiting to ambush us. But instead, we're going to hit them. Hard and fast."

"Just hope we don't chill all of them," J.B. said, starting his own bike. "That would ruin everything."

WITH THE FRONT window painted over, it was quiet and cool in the ancient store, and the three droids stood patiently behind the front counter, hidden in the growing shadows.

The glass panels had been removed from the display cases to make the collection of rifles and handguns more readily apparent. That was an established procedure to distract looters and prevent retaliatory strikes, before the droids could eliminate the invaders.

Something scurried along the baseboard, and a droid swiveled its belly-mounted weapon to shoot. There was no noise or muzzle-flash from the odd device, yet a wide section of the wooden baseboard was torn apart, splinters flying everywhere, and the tiny body of the mouse was reduced to bleeding hamburger.

The other droids noted the kill in mechanical precision and returned to their long vigil. The norms should have arrived many hours ago. There had definitely been activity at the front door early that morning, but the norm males had departed, claiming to return posthaste with vehicles to ferry away the weapons in the store. The minicomps operating the droids now could comprehend that was nontrue information, and such a trick wouldn't be allowed to occur again.

The 1 mm HK needlers of the droids would annihilate as many of the norms as possible upon the next confirmed sighting. Not again would they wait and attempt to kill the entire group in a single volley. For the sake of expediency, efficiency would have to be overlooked in favor of simple force. There was certainly enough fuzzy logic in their programming to handle such a change of tactics.

The loud crash of the front window was the only warning the trio of droids got before a thunderous explosion engulfed the front of the store, shards of glass flying everywhere. Even as the machines rocked to the buffeting of the concussion, two more blasts ripped the floor apart, making the ceiling collapse as a wave of chemical flame washed through the predark establishment.

Rushing through the billowing smoke, two of the dented droids reached the sidewalk and swept the area for viable targets, their needlers silently sending out probing waves of death. Cars jumped as the barrage of 1 mm needles punched through chassis and engine, every window along the entire street shattering under the arrival of the deadly depleted-uranium, hollow-point slivers.

But there was no reaction to the attack from any of the buildings—no screams of pain, sounds of running footsteps or even return fire from primitive flint-locks. Just the sounds of tinkling glass, and the growing crackle of the fire inside the destroyed building.

A few minutes later, the third droid stumbled from the burning pawnshop, its silvery hull badly dented and dragging a damaged limb behind.

Gathering close, the three machines conversed for a microsecond, the masers from their vid cams strobing as they exchanged binary information. Then the damaged droid limped around a corner, and the other two went back into the raging inferno of the pawnshop to wait in the thick smoke for the expected arrival of the norm looters.

Chapter Eighteen

On the roof of a movie theater situated on the opposite corner from the pawnshop, J.B. lowered the mirror he had been using to watch the street below and nodded.

"It worked," the Armorer whispered, tucking the plastic square away for safekeeping.

Also lying prone on the rooftop, Krysty, Mildred and Jak quietly finished reloading their 40 mm gren launchers and started crawling for the fire escape attached to the rear of the building.

Reaching the ladder first, Krysty dropped her weapon over the side, then slid down the iron railing of the ladder, her gloved hands becoming hot from the friction before she reached the ground. As she stepped away from the fire escape, Ryan handed her back the combination blaster he had caught just as Jak arrived. Doc was next, and finally J.B. landed.

"One droid," the Armorer reported. "Bad leg, moving to the west."

"Go," Ryan ordered brusquely to his son.

Revving the purring engine, Dean drove off on the motorcycle. Rolling out of the alleyway, he took a sharp turn onto the side street, watching carefully for the damaged machine. Dean knew the droids had the ability to walk along the sides of the buildings, but hopefully this one couldn't do that with a damaged leg. If it could, this whole gamble could go sour, and they'd be back to square one trying to find the gateway.

Coasting to a stop at an intersection jammed with rusted cars and overturned buses, Dean throttled down the muffled engine and peeked around both corners. Only a block away, he spotted the machine limping down the middle of the left road, traveling between the line of dead vehicles. Retreating slightly to be less visible, Dean watched as it went past the next intersection, then took the following right turn.

Pursing his lips, the boy gave the call of a desert eagle, and the rest of the companions rolled into view with their bikes bristling with weaponry. Holding up two fingers, the boy gestured to the right, already moving after the slow machine.

Soon the others were in hot pursuit, zigzagging their bikes between the ancient cars, avoiding the potholes and open manholes. In passing, Ryan noted that the rims of the manholes weren't ringed with rust. So somebody had been checking the sewer systems very recently. Maybe those corpses on the vista outside the metropolis weren't the only pirates to get past the jungle apes.

Straight ahead, Dean darted into an alleyway, and Ryan followed close behind, trying to catch up with him. Increasing their own speed, the companions reached the father and son moments later just as they were going by a group of lizards tearing apart the bloody corpse of what appeared to be a large bat.

"From the sewer?" Krysty asked, swerving to the far side of the alley.

"Makes sense," Mildred answered, keeping her blaster pointed at the reptiles. "Bats love tunnels."

"And hate the sunlight."

"Leave darkness food," Jak said hesitantly, the soles of his combat boots tapping the ground to keep the slow-moving bike upright. "Or something scare out?"

"Those manhole openings are too small for a droid, or an ape," Ryan declared, pulling the vented wand from the straps across his chest and resting the muzzle on the chrome handlebars. "But just right for people."

Using his butane lighter, the Deathlands warrior ignited the propane preburner of the flamethrower and drove one-handed, the other supporting the wand and hose of the flamethrower.

As the motorcycles cut through the rear of a gas station, the alleyway ended on a major boulevard divided by trees on a grassy median. Checking both ways, neither Ryan nor Dean could see a sign of their prey. The road was clear for blocks in either direction, only a few scattered vehicles stalled in the street, none of them large enough to house even a single droid.

"Either it's hiding, waiting for us to leave," J.B. said, flexing his hands against a cramp, "or the base is somewhere close."

"Could be there," Dean suggested, pointing with the Browning.

Catercorner from the intersection was a large plaza, floored with colorful ceramic tiles and some weird metallic structure standing fifty feet high.

"Busted?" Jak asked, staring at the towering maze of coiled steel dotted with hundreds of tiny rectangles.

"That is the double-spiral of a DNA helix," Mildred explained. "The basic building block of life."

The teenager frowned. "Supposed look that?"

"Yes."

He snorted. "Damn."

"Blessed Mother Gaia," Krysty said softly, her hair flaring out in response. "Look at the middle building!"

"Well, I'll be nuked," J.B. muttered, removing his fedora, only to replace it again. "There it is in plain sight!"

Fronting the tiled plaza were three great buildings of chrome and glass set in an equilateral formation. Alongside the faded name of each mirrored monolith was their corporate logo, just an artistic squiggle designed to be attention catching. But the logo in the middle got the full attention of the companions.

"That's the symbol we found written in blood," Ryan said grimly, "in the gateway when we arrived here. This is where the chilled whitecoat was trying to tell us to go."

"Or avoid," Krysty said warily, revving her engine. The machine shuddered once, then smoothed out again. "We were never sure which it was."

"I'm betting on directions, not a warning," J.B. said, studying the rooftops along the intersection and plaza for snipers.

Nervously, Mildred clenched and unclenched her hands. "Somewhere inside there is a gateway," she said softly. "The way out."

"No sign of any droids," Ryan added gruffly. "But that doesn't mean they're not here. Waiting for us."

"Let them come," Dean stated, working the bolt on the Weatherby to chamber a massive .460 round.

With Ryan in the lead, the companions drove their bikes openly across the boulevard trying to draw fire, poised to feed the hungry engines fuel and race to safety. But nothing occurred as they bumped over the curb and parked the vehicles behind the glittering DNA statue. Sliding off the bike, Ryan drew his blaster and gave cover as Jak paused, then sprinted for the front door. Nearing the portal, he dived over some scraggly hedges and rolled behind a marble pillar. Pausing again to listen for any response to his presence, the teenager leveled his M-16/M-203 and checked the interior of the building through the low-power scope built into the assault rifle. Nothing seemed to be moving inside the plush lobby and foyer. Raising a fist, Jak spread his fingers once, and now he and Ryan gave cover as J.B. crawled to the front door on his belly, only to find the heavy glass door unlocked.

Shoving a spent brass cartridge under the lower hinge, the Armorer jammed the door open and Ryan raced inside, the preburner of his flamethrower illuminating the dim interior with an eerie blue light. Taking position behind a cigarette machine, Ryan surveyed the area, his nerves keyed to battle pitch. But nothing stirred among the ancient furniture. The carpeted lobby was dark beyond the wash of sunlight from the glass walls in front, the air oddly scented with dust.

The one-eyed man whistled sharply, and the rest of the companions charged into the office building, quickly spreading out to find cover. Doc was the last, and as he dashed into the lobby the door abruptly swung shut and locked with an audible click.

Instantly, the companions shifted positions and started wildly firing their weapons, the rounds from the Uzi and M-16 tearing up the carpeting and walls.

Just then, the ceiling tiles swung apart on disguised hinges and a pair of robotic blasters dropped into view, the tiny barrels hissing death. Only a blur in the air, the crisscrossing lines of 1 mm rounds stitched across the lobby, chewing a path of destruction along the carpeting, tearing apart tables and chairs until hitting the front windows. The slim needles slapped into the resilient Plexiglas, becoming solidly embedded in the clear plastic.

Standing from behind a newspaper dispenser, Ryan hosed a 3-second spray from the flamethrower at the closest needler, the lance of fire brightly illuminating the interior. Dripping flames, the weapon gave only a short burst then shorted out, the burning housing crackling with bright electric sparks as the barrel slumped toward the floor. Ryan turned to get the second needler, and saw it was already trashed, torn to pieces under the combined fury of the chattering Uzi and M-16 rapidfires.

Warily lighting their pressurized lanterns, the companions placed the lamps in different locations before starting to move forward. Immediately, three droids rose from behind the reception kiosk and flashed their lasers, the scintillating beams slashing across the lobby to explode the precious lanterns and plunge the area into darkness. But that lasted only a split second as the puddled oil from the smashed reservoirs touched the glowing metal wicks and ignited into pools of fire. Stubbornly, the droids lasered the spreading oil, and seemed confused at the lack of response from the flames.

Counting to ten under his breath, Jak rolled behind a cigarette machine, yanked the Armbrust off his back, prepared the one round, then stood and fired.

The triple lasers stabbed into the predark dispenser, melting deep holes into the machinery as the Armbrust made a crack like a .22 pistol, and a blizzard of plastic flakes mixed with nitrogen snow vomited from the aft end. There was no flash from the muzzle, no contrail or fiery exhaust to mark the path of the AP projectile as it left the tube. The round crossed the lobby at subsonic speed and broke apart in midair, a hellstorm of steel fléchettes arriving to tear the kiosk and the droids apart.

Vid cams utterly annihilated, hull riddled, the blind droids tottered about on their buckling legs, hydraulic fluid pumping from the legs like greasy blood. The lasers flashed again, but only hit the front windows, searing brownish spots in the dense material. Using the ten-second recharge lag, the companions stood and cut loose a concentrated volley from their assorted rapidfires. The incoming barrage savagely pounded the droids until they toppled over to loudly crash onto the tattered kiosk.

Small fires dotted the lobby, the charring carpet giving off thick clouds of smoke. Returning to the bikes outside, Mildred and Jak got the extinguishers, while Krysty and Doc beat out the flames with their coats. If the building went up, there was no way they could find the gateway.

Going to the rubble of the kiosk, Ryan prodded the droids with the SIG-Sauer to made sure they were aced, then pumped a few rounds into their exposed circuitry just to make sure. The armored sheeting of the hull warped apart, CPU and circuit boards shattering easily under the 9 mm rounds.

In short order, the fires were under control. Assuming the position of guard, Ryan stayed at the kiosk with the flamethrower ready as the rest of the companions did a quick recce of the first floor. They came back in only a couple of minutes.

"Nothing," J.B. reported, walking from the shadows rear of the lobby. "Just an elevator bank and a big cafeteria. A lot of people worked here."

"Like to know what it was they did," Ryan growled, going to the office directory hanging from the ceiling above the kiosk. Unfortunately, the bullets from the rapidfires had slammed the board pretty hard, punching dozens of holes through the material and knocking off most of the letters. Only a cryptic scrambling of names and departments remained. Totally useless.

"Okay, we do this the hard way," Ryan said, trimming the preburner and lowering the pressure on a feeder valve. "We go floor by floor. Stay tight, and ace anything that moves."

"No prob," Jak agreed, tossing aside the Armbrust and swinging around his M-203 to work the arming bolt.

"Droid!" Dean shouted, and hit the floor, throwing a gren toward the bathroom.

Slipping out of a men's room, a droid strode into view as the sphere bounced along the floor and detonated. The blast lifted the sec machine off the ground, slamming it against the marble wall. Broken to pieces, the droid fell back to the carpet, sparking steadily from a dozen short circuits.

Pulling both handcannons, Doc leveled the Webley and triggered a single thundering round, the .44 slug blowing open the armored hull protecting the minicomp. Then he fired the LeMat, the massive miniball punching through the CPU and smashing it into a million pieces. The sparks ceased abruptly.

"We've got to move fast," Ryan stated, lowering the vented muzzle of his flamethrower. "These things are gonna be on our ass every step of the way."

"Which direction, basement or penthouse?" Krysty asked, removing a spent clip and slapping a fresh mag against the stock of her weapon before ramming it into the receiver.

"Penthouse," Ryan answered promptly. "If nothing else, we'll have a good view of the city from up there. That might be helpful."

"Agreed."

Heading for the stairwell, the companions braced for another ambush, but the stairs proved to be clear to the next level.

"The programmers probably have the machines set to protect the elevators first," Mildred guessed as they swept through the array of office cubicles filling the second floor. "Places like this always have emergency generators for the mainframes in case the city power grid went down."

There was nothing on the second floor except for some rats, and the third floor was merely vacant conference rooms, as large and empty as the graves of giants. The fourth floor was strictly maintenance. However, the fifth had carpeting once again, the wooden doors elaborately carved, and old paintings in gilded frames adorned the plaster walls. A glass-topped mahogany reception desk was set in a small alcove with several plush wing-back chairs set nearby.

"Protoculte Bio-Medical Corporation," Ryan said with a frown, reading the name in brass, or maybe gold, letters on the front of the reception desk. "Anybody know what that means?"

"Most certainly, it is a polyglot of classic and antiquarian Latin," Doc said, placing the strap of the M-16 combo around his neck to distribute the weight more comfortably. "It roughly translates as 'wondrous new science.'"

"Don't like the sound of that," Mildred muttered, lifting a business card from a cut-crystal stand embossed with the company logo.

Scowling, she threw it away. "Might have guessed—this is a damn genetics firm. The kind of idiots who play with DNA to make juicier apples whose blossoms poisoned bees, and bigger cows that freeze to death in summer."

"And biological weapons for the government," Doc suggested.

"Exactly."

Krysty and J.B. paused in the alcove to check the desk, while the rest of the companions continued onward. Branching hallways cut the level into a maze of offices and rooms. Walking slowly along the main hallway, Ryan passed a guard station with a pile of loose clothing and bones behind a waist-high Plexiglas barrier. Bending, he rummaged through the clothing, but found nothing.

"Was hoping for an ID badge," he remarked, wiping off his palms on his fatigue pants. "Might have made the droids leave us alone, but no luck."

Suddenly, a loud thud sounded from behind, and the companions spun about to see a gorilla clawing at the window. Furiously, the mutie beat on the Plexiglas window with three fists, but the bulletproof material wasn't affected in the least by the savage pummeling. Baring its fangs, the creature pulled back and threw itself at the norms only yards away. The window bent a little, then popped from the frame, throwing the beast to the floor.

Swiveling his bulky weapon, Ryan gave the gorilla a short burst from the M-1 A, the burning spray engulfing the creature completely. Its fur ablaze, the ape shrieked insanely and charged the companions, clawed hands of fire reaching for the hated tormentors.

Retreating a step, Ryan doused the gorilla again, filling its screaming mouth with the burning spray. Temporarily beyond pain, the gorilla bellowed a roar and beat its chest, a living nightmare still struggling forward through the fiery flow.

Working the bolt on his longblaster, Dean pumped a couple of rounds from the Weatherby into the creature, geysers of blood exploding from its back. Out of grens, Jak stitched it with a wreath of tumblers from the chattering M-16, the slugs peppering its hide. The beast staggered backward and tumbled out the broken window. A flaming meteor, the howling animal plummeted to the hard street five stories below and hit with a resounding wet smack.

Tiny patches of flame dotted the hallway carpeting from the spray of the flamethrower, and the companions moved away from the destroyed corridor, a stiff breeze outside the gaping window sucking out the putrid fumes rising from the melting carpet.

"How find us here?" Jak demanded, removing the half-spent clip and slapping in a full mag. Spent brass littered the carpet, flecks of gold lost amid the complex art deco pattern of the delicate weave.

"No way it could," Ryan said, waving the wand

to disperse some of the unburned fumes from the injector. "It must have been here for the same reasons as the droids, standing guard."

"Apes outside the city, droids in the streets, a cafeteria that could feed a hundred soldiers." Mildred glanced around the hallways. "What in hell were scientists doing here that required that much protection?"

Dean started to answer, when Doc interrupted.

"Excuse me, but where are J.B. and Krysty?" the old man demanded, glancing about.

Shocked, the companions quickly looked around, but the two were nowhere in sight, the long hallway behind them clear all the way to the elevator bank and dark stairwell.

Chapter Nineteen

Snarling in rage, Krysty triggered another burst from her M-16 into the Plexiglas wall, the slugs slapping into the soft material and staying there.

The moment J.B. broke open a locked drawer in the desk, the transparent barrier silently descended from the ceiling to seal them off in a heartbeat. They shouted for the others, and fired rounds into the walls and ceiling, but the companions walked away, obviously not hearing a thing.

"Same as the windows downstairs," she cursed, working the bolt to clear a jam. "Must be some kind of a burglar trap."

"Millie says folks were allowed to chill thieves in the predark world," J.B. muttered from under the desk. "Stupidest thing I ever heard of...ah! Found it! There's a hidden button down here."

"Mebbe it opens this," Krysty said, tapping the barrier with the rapidfire. "Press it, quick."

"Have already," the man replied. "Anything happen?"

"Nothing."

An annoyed grunt. "Shit! I'll try different combinations. One long, one short, two in a row. Let me know as soon as it moves."

"Gotcha."

Suddenly, Ryan and the rest of the companions ran

into view. Stopping before the sealed-off alcove, they
stared at the Plexiglas shield. Ryan asked a question,
but Krysty touched her ears and shook her head. Understanding that vocal communication was impossible, the one-eyed man frowned and stepped closer,
looking at the slugs embedded in the plastic material.
Reaching in a pocket, he withdrew a gren and gestured her to move away.

"The others are back," Krysty said, moving behind
the desk. "Ryan is going to try a gren."

"Good," J.B. replied, getting out from underneath
the desk. "I wanted to use the Claymore, but trapped
in here the concussion would have pulped us both
flat."

In the hallway, the companions started making a
pile of furniture to help contain the blast of the gren,
when Krysty noticed one of the elevators down the
hallway open its doors. Standing inside the lift was a
droid, its belly needler swiveling in search of prey.
Nobody in the hall seemed to notice the arrival of the
elevator and continued working to free their trapped
friends.

"Ryan, droid!" Krysty screamed, firing her M-16
in the direction of the approaching machine as a
warning.

The impact of the 7.62 mm rounds into the barrier
had to have made some small noise because Ryan
looked up in time to see the droid crawling from the
elevator. Without hesitation, the man triggered the
flamethrower, the burning lance washing over the machine in a hellstorm of liquid destruction. Blinded by
the flames, the droid cut loose with its needler, the
slivers tearing apart the pile of furniture as wood
chips and stuffing exploded into the air like confetti.

Dropping to a knee, Dean assumed a firing stance and triggered the Weatherby, a foot-long tongue of flame erupting from the longblaster. The droid jerked from the brutal impact of the heavy slug into its armored hull, the needler going wild, hosing the deadly slivers into the ceiling, chewing the tiles into dust.

Webley and LeMat booming, Doc hammered the machine with miniballs and bullets from his twin .44 handcannons. Then, past the flaming droid, the other elevators opened and two more droids strode out. Any view of the companions blocked by the flames and furniture, the machines turned their lasers on J.B. and Krysty. The Plexiglas wall became spotted with brown patches from the hits, and soon they couldn't see what was happening on the other side. But as Ryan sent out another spray, the reinforcement droids swiveled about and marched over the burning wreckage of their fallen brother, lasers stabbing through the swirling smoke.

"Bastard button summoned the sec droids," J.B. spit, forcing his hands away from the Uzi. His friends were fighting for their lives only a foot away, and there was nothing he could do to help them with the barrier solidly in place.

"There has to be another way out!" Krysty shouted, looking at the walls and ceiling. She sent a burst from the M-16 into the ceiling, blowing away the tiles to expose a sheet of prestressed concrete. The alcove was as solid as a bunker.

"Got an idea," J.B. said, grabbing hold of the desk. Groaning with the effort, he flipped over the massive piece of furniture and it crashed to the carpet, throwing business cards, phone and computer helter-skelter—but also exposing a column of bundled wire extending from inside a hollow leg and going into the floor.

Quickly, the Armorer slashed the wires and scraped the ends clean to start twisting all of the bare copper together. A minute passed in tense silence while the man worked feverishly, the soundless battle in the hallway only visible as flashes of light in the dense smoke and fumes.

A bright spark snapped as J.B. twisted in the last wire, and a large section of the alcove wall behind them broke apart to expose a shiny steel door. The wheel lock turned by itself, and with a hiss of hydraulics, the armored portal swung aside to reveal another room deeper in the office building. Without pause, Krysty charged through the doorway, desperately trying to find another way to reach her friends.

Stainless-steel walls and floor announced the next room as a surgical laboratory of some kind, the ceiling a complex array of pipes, cables and wiring. A glowing panel of white plastic illuminated several X-ray negatives clipped to the frame showing the details of human anatomy. Several locked cabinets stood alongside a line of operating tables, a curved bank of comp controls facing the tables from the far end of the lab.

Spotting a second door, Krysty headed that way but slowed for a tic as she realized the X-ray negatives were of pregnant women, their unborn babies resembling tiny brains equipped with ropy tentacles. The woman barely had time to react to the sights when flashing lights danced across the control boards. Suddenly, her M-16/M-203 was seized by a mechanical arm from the ceiling, the robotic claw yanking away the weapon with enough force to break fingers if she hadn't released the rapidfire.

"Warning," a soft voice chimed from a hidden speaker. "Security breach, level one. Weapons in the surgery. Repeat, weapons in the surgery. Automatic recovery of test subjects in progress."

Instantly, the ceiling became alive with mechanical arms, clacking and snipping, a rain of rust heralding the limbs as they extended for the startled woman.

Standing in the open doorway, J.B. randomly sprayed the entire ceiling with his Uzi, the 9 mm rounds ricocheting off the servomotors and guide rails to ricochet down onto the operating table and the control consoles. Burning sparks flew everywhere, the overhead lights flickered and the robotic arms began to wildly thrash about, smashing open the cabinets and spilling out scalpels, forceps and other healing instruments indistinguishable from primitive implements of torture.

Drawing her S&W .38 revolver, Krysty fought a rush of panic as she dodged an arm tipped with rapidly spinning blades. In cold precision, a robotic limb clamped around her upper arm and lifted the woman off the floor. At point-blank range, Krysty fired her .38 into the assembly of gears, to no effect. The predark surgical droid was made of the finest alloys, much tougher than the soft lead slugs of her revolver.

The limb began rolling along the ceiling, and Krysty wildly fought to break free. With her feet off the ground, she couldn't even summon her special strength because she would still be helpless in the iron grip of the computerized machine.

"Patient reacquired," a speaker crackled. "Prepare bed six."

At the end of the line, an operating table's curved restraints snapped open, and water began trickling along the blood trough to flush away the excess flesh.

The lab was going to harvest her! Now icy panic hit Krysty, and she fired the last two rounds trying to disable the table. The slugs zinged off the bare steel, leaving gray streaks from the lead but nothing more.

Frantically shooting his way across the lab, J.B. tried to reach the redhead, but the gyrating arms made that impossible. A clamp lurched for his throat and the man ducked, the pincers crushing his fedora instead.

"Subject two is male," the speaker announced. "No ID. Terminate at once."

Trying to reload the Uzi, the Armorer was forced to dive for cover under an operating table as metal rods tipped with spinning drills and spinning bone saws thrust from converging directions. His disappearance seemed to confuse the equipment for a moment. Slapping a fresh clip into the Uzi, J.B. then swung around the M-4000 and blasted the ceiling with steel fléchettes. Hydraulic fluid began spurting from a cut hose somewhere, and two of the arms dropped to the floor.

Charging through the gap in the rods and snaking cables, the Armorer reached the control console and emptied the scattergun into the keyboard and dials. Half the board went dark, but the ceiling-mounted machinery still continued to function. Dark night, the bastard things had to have reserve capacitors! Those would weaken and fail eventually. But not soon enough. Krysty was already suspended over the operating table, kicking and jerking to avoid the clamps.

Putting another long burst into the active section of

the control board, the man reached inside and began pulling out handfuls of wiring. But a reflection in a dark monitor made him drop low as a metal claw slammed into the console exactly where he had just been. J.B. felt the passage of the metal through his hair and, staying on the floor, he began firing the Uzi at anything coming his way.

Grabbing an animated cable trying to encircle her waist, Krysty hauled herself higher into the ceiling and managed to rest an arm on the guide rails. This eased the pain of the tugging clamp attached to her other arm and gave her enough time to fumble in her pocket for a gren. J.B. was far enough away to make the explosive charge safe to use. Unfortunately, a telescoping rod slammed into her hand and the gren fell to the floor, rolling out of sight beneath the tables.

Swearing, Krysty desperately pulled out her knife and rammed the blade deep into the spinning gears of the clamp holding her prisoner. Instantaneously, the robotic limb stopped moving, the resulting jerk throwing her free. Krysty landed sprawling between two of the steel tables and dived for cover beneath another table closer to the open doorway. As fingering ceramic rods and ferruled cables quested for her location, the woman pulled out a fistful of rounds, dropping most of them as she quickly reloaded the revolver. Her dropped gren was nowhere in sight, so Krysty darted from table to table, firing at anything that moved. She had to reach J.B. Covering each other's back, they could make a stand and shoot their way out of there. Fighting alone, each of them stood little chance of survival.

Something moved on her right, and Krysty stopped herself from firing at J.B. at the very last second. He shoved the loaded shotgun at her, and in unison they blasted the hellish nest of flexing machinery nonstop.

Something exploded outside the lab, and the cables slowed their relentless attack. Seizing the moment, J.B. slapped the damaged Claymore mine on the console and stabbed in a timing pencil where the timer used to be. As he reached to snap off the pencil, all the robotic arms festooning the ceiling reached for the couple, slapping aside weapons and pinning them helpless. Barely able to breathe in the crushing iron bonds, J.B. and Krysty struggled madly but were still dragged toward the waiting tables.

Somewhere the speaker crackled with static. "Unauthorized personnel secured," the monotone voice reported to its dead masters as a spinning circular saw came straight for Krysty to harvest the unborn mutie. "Commence primary procedure."

A deafening staccato filled the lab as numerous rapidfires peppered the ceiling with hot lead. Then Ryan hosed the control board with chem flames, filling the air with the reek of condensed fuel and propane. As the liquid fire seeped into the controls, sparks flew from the switches and dials, monitors shattered and the Claymore detonated.

Louder than a shotgun blast, the directional explosion blew a tremendous hole in the console, and the rest of the board went dark. Abruptly slowing their motions, the rods and cables soon ceased to move, the serrated edge of the rusty saw indenting the shirt over the woman's taut stomach.

Rushing to her, Ryan grabbed the machine limb in his fist and ripped it from the ceiling, then cast away the filthy surgical tool.

"You okay?" he demanded anxiously, looking for any wounds.

"Just bruised," Krysty replied, picking up her revolver from the floor. Pieces of wiring and IC chips were scattered everywhere, hydraulic fluid dripping from above to form red puddles on the steel floor, then trickle into drains.

"That explosion was you folks trying to get in," J.B. said, unraveling a length of cable from around his waist.

"Blew a hole in the floor above," Mildred said, passing him the dropped Uzi. "But getting to the next level took longer than expected."

Expertly, the Armorer checked the rapidfire for damage before draping it over a shoulder. "More droids?"

"Not anymore," Doc boasted, grinning with his oddly perfect teeth. "We came, we saw, we conquered."

"Thank you, Jealous Caesar," Mildred snorted.

Stooping under a table, Dean retrieved the M-16/M-203 and took it to Krysty. "Here you go," the boy said. "But I don't think it's going to work anymore. That barrel is pinched shut."

"So I see," the redhead muttered, and removed the half-spent clip from the rapidfire before laying the weapon aside. The M-203 was intact, but without grens the launcher was just deadweight.

"Take ammo," Jak suggested, holding out a hand.

Krysty tossed him the mag, and the teenager tucked it into a jacket pocket. Scavenging through the debris, the companions spent a few minutes recovering the rest of the fallen weapons and sorting out the ammo.

"What is this place, anyway?" Dean asked, walking around the destroyed laboratory, the Weatherby cradled in his left arm, his right hand resting on the checkered grip of his Browning.

"Nursery," J.B. muttered, straightening the brim of his crushed hat before returning it to the accustomed position. "Check those X rays. The babies look just like the mutants inside a Firebird. I saw one when the bus crashed and a rocket broke apart."

Crossing the room, Mildred removed one of the film negatives from the darkened panel and held it to the flickering ceiling light. "Merciful God," the physician whispered, her expression turning ugly. "If this was inside a normal female, then these aren't muties, but genetically altered human children."

"Breed on purpose?" Jak demanded, resting a boot on a broken section of the control board.

"So it would seem."

"Why?"

"Most likely to replace comps," Ryan said, frowning. "The EMP blast of a nuke fries electronics unless they are heavily shielded. Shielding no missile can carry and fly. But these whatever you call them would still be able to guide a missile to the enemy."

"Pervs," Jak declared, as if that settled the matter.

"Yeah, even stickies protect their own young," Dean added. "The whitecoats here must have been triple fruit-brained."

"Merely ruthless and greedy for a fat government contract," Doc rumbled hatefully. "I have dealt with the ilk of such dastardly men before in a similar abattoir."

Walking across the lab, Ryan stood before the second door. "Anybody check this?" he asked, gesturing at the bare steel portal with the flamethrower.

"Never had the chance," J.B. said, ambling closer. "We got jumped the minute we entered the lab."

Taking a stance, Ryan aimed the flamethrower. "Do it now," he directed.

Getting out his tools, J.B. got busy, but the metal door wasn't locked and was free of traps. Proceeding inward, they found the next room was a small office with tall windows overlooking the downtown shopping center and theater district. On a bentwood hat rack hung a white lab coat, with the artistic symbol of the Protoculte Corporation on the right breast pocket. A sofa stood near a compact bar, the array of bottles thick with dust on the shelves in the corner. Some sort of a multicolor chart covered the remaining wall situated alongside a Spartan desk of three chrome legs supporting a thick sheet of tinted glass. There were no drawers or files for documents, just a slim briefcase-size comp with a beige mouse on a plain pad. The power cord and phone line were wrapped in a silvery tube that went across the glass and down a chrome leg to reach an outlet. A black leather chair stood behind the desk; some bronze coins lay on the dark cloth seat.

"Still warm," Mildred said, turning the machine around and checking the ports. The CD drawer was empty, but a red diskette was sticking out of a slot, the writing on the label faded with age.

"Pity," the woman said, returning the disk. "When we blew the power to the lab, we killed the computer. This might have told us where the gateway is."

"No fix?" Jak asked, inspecting one of the bronze coins. It was a token of some sort. Odd.

"Not without a power source."

"How about this?" Dean asked, walking in with the nuke battery from a droid in his hands.

"That should have enough voltage," Mildred said. With help from J.B., she wired the battery to the surge protector, and when she hit the switch, the screen began to glow and the device loudly beeped.

"We're in," Mildred said, watching numbers and weird lines of coded text scroll by as the old comp sluggishly booted.

"How can this thing work?" Dean demanded curiously.

"Building must be shielded against an EMP blast," his father said as the laptop gave a flourish of trumpets and a picture of a busty girl in a very skimpy bikini appeared on the screen. "Same way the redoubts are."

"Called a Farraday Cage," J.B. explained. "Sort of an electric fence against mag fields."

Jak blinked. "That work?"

"Better believe it. But a Farraday uses a shitload of power. Megavolts to protect even a small house."

"Think the location of the gateway might be in a file?" Krysty asked pointedly, watching over their shoulders.

"No," Ryan replied sourly, turning the device around for them to see better. There were no icons on the wallpaper of the pretty blond girl at the beach. "The files have been erased."

Sliding into the chair, Mildred took the laptop. "Erased or deleted," she said, bringing up the wastebasket and checking the contents.

"Success," she announced, restoring the files. "Nothing marked redoubt, gateway or anything like that yet. Ah, a word processor program. Let's see if any text files are still listed.''

Using the mouse, the physician shifted the cursor and double-clicked on the icon of a book only to have a pop-up screen appear demanding a password. Typing clumsily, the physician tried several of the most common passwords getting no results.

"Fuck this," Ryan said, standing erect. "There's a million passwords he could have used. This is a waste of time."

"Just a minute," Mildred said, lifting the mouse pad to check underneath. There were several alphanumeric sequences on a yellow sticky note, and she tried the longest. As the woman hit Enter, the password screen went away and the word processing program began to expand.

"We're in," Mildred reported, typing steadily.

Rubbing his cheek with the edge of a hand, Ryan grunted in reply. "The idiot wrote down the password?"

"Lots of folks used to do that," she admitted sheepishly, having done the same thing herself at the hospital. "Corporate security always keeps changing the passwords, and so folks write them down somewhere convenient to not forget."

Reviewing the text files, there was still nothing marked redoubt or gateway, so she shifted to the disk and brought up a large file marked "important."

"Okay, the man who worked in this office had the National Guard haul the supplies from the armory to this building," Mildred said, compressing the broken sentences and random words. "Then had his technicians carry it to the redoubt."

"Where is it?" Ryan demanded.

Mildred shook her head. "He doesn't say yet. This is very badly typed with no spelling whatsoever. I wonder if he was dying, it's so muddled. Ah, here's something. He also shipped all of the live 'pilots,' he calls them, to Maturo Island. It has nothing of military importance, so his children should be safe there. God-damn son of a bitch actually calls the poor muties his children!"

"The whitecoat is aced," Krysty said gently. "His crimes have been paid for."

"Not enough for me," Mildred argued.

"Why gateway redoubt here?" Jak asked frowning. "Broken?"

"Cave in," the physician reported hesitantly, as if unsure of the event. "Apparently six technicians died trying to dig through the rubble before the scientists decided to leave and assemble the gateway as far away from this island as possible."

"Strange to go when they were so close," Dean said, standing at the doorway to keep watch on the laboratory.

"Hurry it up, Millie," J.B. warned, holding the power cord attached to the battery. "These wires are red-hot, and are gonna burn out any sec."

"Doesn't matter," Mildred said, turning off the comp without any preamble. "That was the lot. The rest of the disk was blank."

"If they had the supplies relayed here by the military," Ryan said, thoughtfully rubbing his chin, "then a bunch of whitecoats moved it to the redoubt—it has to be very close. A couple of blocks at the very most."

"And underground," Krysty added. "I'd say the basement here is the logical place to start looking."

"Just a second," J.B. said and left the room. He returned in a few moments with a handful of metallic disks.

"Subway tokens," the man said, spreading the items on the desk. "The secretary's desk was full of them."

"And here, too," Doc said, lifting a similar disk from the black chair.

Going to the window, Ryan yanked away the curtains and looked at the city. An ivy-covered helicopter was parked on a rooftop, cars filled the streets, stores and restaurants abounded and only a block away was a subway station.

"Less than a hundred feet away," Ryan stated resolutely. "Let's go."

As they departed, Krysty noticed a nasty smell in the air of the lab, but paid it no attention. The companions were already in the lobby and heading for the exit when the smashed equipment in the medical lab burst into flames, the electrical fire following the overheating wires into the walls like fuses on a bomb.

Chapter Twenty

"Do it," Colonel Mitchum commanded, and placed the folded piece of leather into his mouth. He was sitting on a park bench, his pants cut off above the knee, and the wound in his leg was now only a shiny smear of cauterized flesh. The sec chief was breathing hard, trying not to think about what was coming.

Nodding assent, the sec man lifted the orange-hot poker from the crackling campfire and touched it briefly to the bullet wound in the man's shoulder. Flesh sizzled at the contact, and Mitchum went stiff, his eyes distending as he throated a scream muffled by the thick leather filling his mouth. His big hands grasped the predark bench, tendons swelling in his arms and neck as he rode out the wave of pain.

As the branding iron was removed, a mix of shine and water was splashed on the glassy scar, and Mitchum only grunted at the minor stinging it created. Sweat was trickling off the sec chief as he pulled the leather from his mouth and gulped in fresh air.

"That did it, sir," a corporal stated, tossing away the red-hot metal rod. "No more bleeding. That wound is healed."

Grabbing the jug of shine and water, Mitchum drank a healthy draft and poured the rest over his face and body, then wildly shook his head like a dog in the rain to remove the excess. Anything could be endured, if it brought Ryan under his blasters.

The climb up the side of the mesa had been pure torture to the sec chief with his bad arm and leg. But the bodies of the shot Hunters left by the outlanders had left a clear trail to the top. The first sec man crawled to the top with a rope around his waist. Once he was secure, the man dragged up the rope with a tow cable attached to the end. The cable from the winch at the front of the Hummer had been just barely long enough to wrap around an outcropping, but then the stripped wag winched itself to the top of the mesa. After that it was easy, and the rest of the wags soon followed.

From the cliff, Mitchum had been able to see the beach fronting the valley. Out in the ocean, a score of PT boats darted about, launching Firebirds and torps at the fifty enemy windjammers. Huge clouds of black smoke from the thundering pirate cannons blew across the water, blocking the view of the raging battle. Then for a moment, the air was cleared and the legions of wounded men splashing in the red water could be seen. Many seemed to be attacking the ocean with their blasters and knives, and Mitchum could only guess that the sharks had arrived, attracted by the battle. More than one man gushed blood from his mouth as he was crushed by something below the surface. Often, a friend or shipmate would then fire a blaster into the dying man to stop the hideous screaming. At any moment now, he had expected a Deeper to arrive, and then all of the fools would die unless they joined forces to repel the sea mutie. No way that was going to happen.

Thankfully, some of the peteys had unloaded Hummers before the pirates arrived, or else Mitchum would have been stranded. He'd been down to his last wag and less than a pound of black powder when the relief ships arrived with fresh wags, weapons, Firebirds and, hopefully, a way home. The ville of the pirates was beaten, but the street fighting went on. Damn pirates never knew when to quit. He might have admired the trait in a sec man, but in a pirate it was damn annoying.

"Sir!" a sailor cried, charging around a corner. "Look there! A skyscraper is on fire!"

Standing awkwardly, Mitchum squinted toward the downtown area. True enough. From the middle of a glass skyscraper, black smoke was pouring from the broken windows of the fifth floor. Flashes of light appeared within the flames as something exploded. A lance of flame extended from a window, seeming to push out something metallic with lots of legs that promptly dropped from sight.

"Found you," Mitchum growled, brandishing a fist smeared with his own blood. "Time to get aced, traitor."

Turning, he limped toward the Hummers, checking the revolver in his new shoulder holster. The branding iron had cauterized the wounds closed, but the pain still slowed him like chains on a slave.

"Everybody in the wags!" he shouted, stiffly getting behind the wheel of the lead Hummer. "The outlanders die today!"

Grimly, the sec men and sailors grabbed their blasters and climbed into the armored machines, preparing for battle.

LEAVING THE Protoculte building, the companions stayed alert as they headed across the plaza for their bikes. Halfway there, Ryan cursed and swung up the flamethrower, but withheld fire.

"Droid!" he shouted as the machine appeared from behind the towering DNA sculpture. But Ryan eased his hand off the trigger. He couldn't use the M-1 A; that'd only burn their transport.

Its long legs stepping high, the droid strode through the parked bikes as its laser pulsed. Firing the SIG-Sauer, Ryan felt a rush of heat past his face on the blind side as the rest of the companions separated and attacked. The M-16 rapidfires chattering steadily, the noise punctuated by the telltale booms of the Weatherby and Colt and Webley, the friends kept on the move, never giving the machine a stationary target.

Incoming lead peppered the machine, and the laser started to pulse once more when the crystal lens was shattered by a 7.62 mm tumbler. As the energy weapon winked out, the companions charged to finish the job at close range. Bullets tearing it apart, the damaged machine tried to run, to dodge, then climbed into the complex rigging of the DNA sculpture for protection. But once the droid was clear of the bikes, Ryan hosed the artwork with a chem storm of flames.

Dripping fire, circuits sparking, the droids still tried to escape, but as its onboard systems overheated and shut off, the machine fell from the sculpture and landed on the parked bikes. The crash sounded louder than doomsday, pieces of fender and windshields flying into the air.

"Good thing the machines are old and slow," Krysty said, reloading her revolver as she looked around the plaza. "We wouldn't stand a mutie's chance in a rad pit against a fully functional droid."

"Mebbe." Shuffling among the wreckage, J.B. lifted a fuel-drenched seat from the jumble of steel and rubber only to toss it away. "Son of a bitch did this deliberately," he growled.

Exchanging clips, Mildred agreed. "It's probably in its programming to destroy the transport of the enemy as a last action."

"Two still okay," Jak said, righting a Harley. He pressed the ignition and the engine purred to life.

"This one is okay, too," Mildred added, starting her bike. The rpm were low, and the engine had a slight ping now, but it still operated.

"Okay, scav what you can, pile it on the two," Ryan directed, black smoke from the burning sculpture rising high into the stormy sky. "The rest of us walk from here."

"Only a couple of blocks," Krysty said. "But we better stay sharp."

"Razor," Jak agreed, climbing onto the motorcycle.

After gathering what intact supplies they could and retrieving their backpacks, the companions started down the ancient boulevard, watching the alleyways and rooftops.

Suddenly, Krysty turned and fired, a small lizard sitting on a garbage can blew apart, the bloody gobbets smacking against a stone wall. A block later, Dean triggered the Weatherby, the corner window on a second floor shattering on both sides from the arrival of the big grain .460-caliber round. From somewhere inside the building came the chest-thumping roar of a gorilla.

"Hot pipe, missed him," the boy stated, fumbling in his pockets for more ammo.

But the search became more intense, and soon the boy realized he had lost count and was out of rounds for the longblaster. Scowling, he draped the weapon over a shoulder and pulled out his Browning Hi-Power, racking the slide to chamber a cartridge.

Cradling the softly hissing flamethrower, Ryan made no comment as they approached the subway station, his every sense strained to the limit. Obviously a converted train station, the white brick building stood two stories tall, with an impressive face for the tourists. A row of slit windows skirted along the overhang of the red tile roof.

"That would make a good fort," J.B. observed, adjusting his glasses. Then the man stopped dead in his tracks to start firing the Uzi in controlled bursts.

"Twelve o'clock high!" he shouted over the stuttering roar of the deadly rapidfire.

Heads swiveled, and there was the mutie spider crawling over the building. The beast paused on the top of the roof to spread its mandibles wide and hiss loudly.

"Run for the door!" Ryan ordered as he triggered a long arching spray into the sky, aiming a lot higher than the oncoming mutie.

As the companions raced for the entrance to the station, the stream of burning fuel shot across the plaza and descended in a fiery rain upon the creature, its stubbly hair instantly igniting. Keening in pain, the creature danced madly about, snapping at the fire on its back.

Charging after the others, Ryan rejoined his friends at the entrance to the station, J.B. already busy at the lock. Jak and Mildred had parked the bikes nose to nose and were stripping off the saddlebags; Dean and

Krysty were taking everything they could with them, while Doc stood guard.

Putting his spine to the wall, Ryan started sweeping the flamethrower back and forth, establishing a growing half circle of flames on the plaza before them. Before he was done, the spider arrived and tried to cross the field of flames, but the heat forced it temporarily back. The mutie keened again and tried another section only to be repulsed once more.

"Open the bastard door!" Ryan commanded, sending another lance of flame at the beast. The gauges were nearly empty, the pressure flickering at registering zero. One or two more sprays and the M-1 A would be empty. He'd have to make each burst count.

"Can't. Locked from the inside," J.B. answered, pressing on the door. It opened a crack, exposing the thick steel chains wrapped around the handles on the other side.

"Blow it!" Mildred commanded, emptying a clip into the giant insect. As the rapidfire cycled dry, she dropped the heavy blaster and drew her ZKR. That had been her last clip for the M-16.

"Prep the LAW," Krysty shouted, carefully placing the shots of her Smith & Wesson for maximum damage.

"No room," Ryan said, sending another spray across the ground to maintain the fire wall. "We're too close! The back-blast would blow us apart."

Stepping close to the fire, Doc braced for a recoil and fired the M-203. The short weapon thumped, sending a 40 mm shell straight into the shoulder of the beast, the blast splattering out gobbets of flesh, and a limb fell off. Staring at the ghastly wound pumping blood, the mutie screamed, backing away from the norms. Ryan sent off the final arc of flame, coating its head for as long as he could until the spray sputtered and cut off.

Hitting the buckle on his chest, Ryan shrugged and the spent weapon dropped to the ground. Then he grabbed the harness and heaved it into the flames.

"Cover!" he yelled, going to the ground.

A heartbeat later the pressurized tank blew, sending out a death shroud of shrapnel. Hot steel zinged off the ground, slammed into the closed door, knocked over both bikes and ripped a long gash across the bulbous back of the spider, blood gushing in an emerald torrent.

Unexpectedly, there came the sound of heavy-caliber rapidfires, squirts of blood spitting from the side of the howling mutie. Squinting against the dying flames, Ryan could see Hummers full of sec men rolling down a wide flight of stairs on the plaza, the .50 cals throwing death at the creature. Then a line of rounds stitched the front of the train station, shattering the pretty white bricks.

"Mitchum." Jak cursed, then slapped the used clip into the M-16. The nuke-shitting blasters would have lasted them for months in the Deathlands. Was there anything on these stinking islands that wasn't trying to chill them?

"Let us welcome him properly," Doc announced, opening the breech of his M-203. "Any more 40 mm shells?"

"Only had six," Ryan replied, pulling the pin on a gren and throwing it at the oncoming wags.

The HE sphere hit the ground and bounced twice, going over the lead military wag and exploding on the hood of the second. The windshield vanished and the crew inside the Hummer screamed, clutching their ripped faces. Without a driver, the wag veered away from the other vehicles. Cutting across the plaza, it slammed into a fountain and spilled out the corpses, its hood buckling and the horn coming on to blare an endless monotone warning.

Standing, J.B. swung around the shotgun and gave the door two strident rounds of fléchettes. The wood blew apart, and the portal swung open on creaking hinges.

"The bikes," Dean began.

Ryan shoved the boy forward. "Leave them!"

Rushing inside the building, the companions spread out behind the rows of pillars supporting a mezzanine. Shafts of sunlight streamed in through the slit windows along the top, filling the interior with crisscrossing beams of light. Rows of wooden benches badly consumed by beetles filled the open area, phone booths and ticket counters lining the side wall. At the far end was an iron grating, similar to the ones on the downtown stores, completely sealing off the stairs and turnstiles beyond.

"There's the entrance," Krysty said, pocketing the spent shells and quickly reloading.

"Save your grens," Ryan suggested, holstering the handcannon and bringing out the Steyr. "We may have to blast through."

Watching through the doorway, they could see the horribly wounded spider attack the Hummers, slamming the nearest one onto its side.

Supplies and men tumbled onto the ground, the spider triumphantly raising a screaming norm in its mandibles and slowly closing the pincers, the hoary chitin slicing the victim in two. The body fell away, and the spider charged at the next military wag, tendrils of intestines dangling from its segmented mouth. Its thick legs stomped two more men flat, and Sergeant Campbell was lifted cursing from a Hummer. The spider shook him the way a dog did a rat to snap its neck. But the sec man lived and fired a flintlock pistol directly into the eye of the creature before it cut him in two. His legs fell away, but his wide leather belt got caught on the mandibles and his torso flopped loosely about until the beast shook it free.

The concrete of the plaza was becoming dark with spilled blood, and most of it was human.

Chapter Twenty-One

"Fire!" Mitchum ordered, and a Firebird was launched from the pod of his wag.

Spiraling in fast, the rocket slammed deep inside the creature and came out the other side before exploding. The soft bulk of the spider didn't offer enough resistance to set off the warhead. Mortally wounded, the insect grabbed a Hummer in its mandibles but was unable to lift the heavy wag.

Flintlocks discharged steadily, and the battle zone was becoming smoky with the fumes of spent black powder, but the sec men raked the beast with their rapidfires, then put two more Firebirds into the gore-streaked mutie.

Taking advantage of the distraction, Ryan and J.B. returned to the broken door of the train station and surveyed the outside battle. The spider was clearly dying, and soon Mitchum would concentrate his attention on the station.

"Spider is losing," J.B. stated.

Ryan checked the SIG-Sauer. "Gonna be after us next."

"We could hide in the tunnels," J.B. went on, firing a few rounds at the busy sec men. One clutched his throat and fell over, crimson blood gushing between his fingers.

"Mitchum would only run us down with the Hummers," Ryan said, squeezing off shots with his silenced weapon. Two more sec men fell. Then a flurry of machine-gun fire ripped up the doorway, and the men retreated behind the brick wall.

"Our best bet is to stop them here," Ryan continued, "then go hunt for the redoubt."

Several miniballs hummed through the open doorway.

Sticking out the Uzi, J.B. triggered a short burst. "Yeah, I'm sick of running away, too," he growled.

Holstering the blaster, Ryan held out an empty hand. "Give me that launcher," he said brusquely.

Shifting his bag and packs, J.B. passed over the boxy 4-shot weapon. "Only got one," he reminded him.

"That'll do." Ryan pulled out the arming pin for the remaining rocket and moved away from the doorway to take a position behind some benches a few yards distant.

Then the man assumed a firing stance, but with the wrong end of the launcher pointed toward the broken doors.

"What's he doing?" Dean demanded from behind a pillar.

"Chilling two birds," Krysty replied, cocking back the hammer on her blaster. "Get ready, here they come."

With the roar of a diesel engine, a Hummer crashed through the double doors, the armored fenders slamming the remains of the doors aside and removing most of the jamb. Ignoring the vehicle, Ryan triggered the launcher. Instantly, the LAW rocket shot away from the front on a column of fire to streak across the station and strike the iron grating. Designed to kill tanks, the shaped charge blew the barrier apart and sent a shotgun charge of shrapnel hurtling down the sloped ramp beyond.

At the same moment the rocket launched, the back-blast erupted from the aft end of the boxy weapon just as the second Hummer appeared in the doorway. Holding the weapon steady, Ryan let the sec men drive their vehicle through the fiery exhaust, shattering the windshield and beheading the driver. The sec man standing at the .50 cal was ripped away from the blaster and went flying, leaving an arm behind. The rest of the crew was buffeted by the searing-hot gases, the flesh scalded from their faces. Completely out of control, the Hummer cut a swath through the benches to the sound of splintering wood and crashed into a ticket counter, a whirlwind of ancient paper engulfing the dying men in an impromptu blizzard.

Tires squealing, the third Hummer banked away from the doorway, and J.B. riddled the crew with his Uzi as they drove by. Expertly, the wiry man rode the chattering rapidfire into a tight figure eight, the copper-jacketed 9 mm rounds tearing the sec men apart like rag dolls.

Meanwhile, the companions stayed hidden behind the pillars and rattled the first Hummer as it drove around inside the station. In short controlled bursts, Doc emptied his M-16, chilling the driver. As the rest of the sec men started returning fire with their flint-locks, Krysty rolled a gren under the armored wag. Her aim was good and the sphere detonated under the front of the military wag. The explosion flipped the nose, and, impelled by their speed, the wag flipped over to crash onto the marble floor and slid for several yards.

Pinned underneath, the trapped sec men cursed and beat their fists on the steel plating as the smell of shine from the leaking fuel tank got stronger. Then Dean hit the wag with a Molotov and the vehicle was engulfed with flames, the curses changing into shrieks of terror as the fuel ignited and spread toward the crumpled pod full of Firebirds.

"Gonna blow!" Jak warned through cupped hands.

Realizing their plight, Ryan and J.B. tossed away the launcher and raced past the burning Hummer to rejoin the others and head quickly down the ramp into the subway tunnel. Hopping over the turnstile, they rushed to the edge of the departure platform and looked quickly around for any indication of the redoubt. The only illumination was a weak shaft of reflected sunlight coming down the ramp. Nothing unusual was in sight. Soda machines, benches and pay phones dotted the long platform. On the walls of the tunnel, a vista of mosaic tiles depicted people playing on the beach, the picture gently sloping into a high vaulted ceiling.

"What now?" Mildred asked.

Before Ryan could speak, the whole station shook under the trip-hammer blast of the detonating Firebirds. The titanic concussion blew down the ramp like a hurricane and knocked the companions off their feet. Too close to the edge, Mildred was thrown off the platform to land sprawling across the predark train tracks with her face resting on the third rail.

Gasping in horror, Mildred recoiled from the contact, braced for death, only to remember there couldn't possibly be any power flowing through the rail. But trained responses were hard to break. In her time, even this brief a contact would have been utterly lethal, the dreaded third rail carrying more hard current than a federal penitentiary's electric chair.

"Got to find the redoubt," Dean said, starting to light the pressurized camping lantern.

Ryan stopped the boy. "No lights," he ordered, withdrawing into the darkness.

Heart still pounding, Mildred rose stiffly and shuffled into the stygian darkness beyond the shaft of sunlight pouring down the stairwell.

Then bright lights filled the ramp, and a Hummer bumped its way through the twisted ruin of the grating and rolled slowly down the sloped ramp. Then it surged with speed to ram through the turnstile and screech to a halt at the edge of the platform.

"Over there!" a voice cried out, and the .50 cal started chattering, the big slugs ricocheting everywhere in the confines of the tunnel.

Moving fast, the companions took cover in the darkness of the subway tunnel, splashing through the ankle-deep water and kicking the rats out of the way.

The parallel beams of its headlights washing along the tunnel, the military wag rolled to the edge of the platform, and Mitchum set the brakes but kept the engine running.

"Think we can make that?" he asked aloud.

The corporal at the .50 cal scowled. He really wasn't sure about anything after seeing the obliterated Hummer lying in pieces in that blast crater upstairs. Damn outlanders were trickier than an old baron, and meaner than a two-headed snake.

"Don't know, sir," the corporal replied honestly. "Might bust an axle. But we could winch a wag down."

"And give them a wag to escape in?" the colonel muttered. "Fuck that. We'll stay here."

Suddenly, lights flashed from the ramp and the second Hummer rolled to the platform and parked along the first. But not so close that if one exploded, the other would also be destroyed. The sec men had learned the hard way to be wary of the one-eyed outlander and his crew of coldhearts.

"Orders, sir?" the driver of the second Hummer asked softly.

The private standing at the .50 cal nosily worked the bolt on the massive rapidfire as a preparation to fire.

"Stay where you are and shoot anything that moves," Mitchum commanded, removing the predark revolver from his shoulder holster and stepping from behind the windshield. The sec man stood there for a while listening to the sounds of the underground passageway before speaking. As long as he stayed behind the headlights, the beams should blind anybody out there to his exact presence.

"Ryan! I know you're there!" Mitchum shouted, the words echoing into the darkness. "Surrender, and I'll make your death quick and painless! That's a promise!"

There was no reply.

"Fight me, and it'll take you weeks to die!" the colonel shouted, losing his patience. "And your bitch will be the first to get aced!"

There was a distant cough as if somebody were clearing their throat to speak, then a 9 mm round ricocheted off the fender of the armored wag, missing the sec chief by less than a prayer.

"Chill the fucker!" Mitchum roared, fanning the

tunnel with his handcannon. The twin black-powder machine guns chattered to life, filling the tunnel with a hellstorm of hot lead.

Keeping close to the tile wall, Ryan placed the shots of his SIG-Sauer, then switched to the Steyr and better accuracy. Most of the companions were ensconced in similar locations, blasters banging away as they tried for the headlights. The triple-stupe sec men couldn't hit what they couldn't see, but the moment Mitchum thought of using the high beams this battle would turn against them. Privately, Ryan had hoped Mitchum would be stupe enough to try to lower a wag to the tracks. Then they would take it out with their last few grens and the fight would be equal. But the man was too smart, or too cowardly to risk a direct assault.

Sliding in a fresh clip, the Deathlands warrior heard something deeper in the tunnel, then ignored it as the sound got fainter in the distance. Krysty and Dean were moving slowly along the opposite sides of the tunnel, exploring the wall with their hands, trying to find the entrance to the redoubt. Unless the whitecoats used a subway train to move the supplies, the redoubt was right here, hidden somewhere in the dark, maybe under the very gravel they were standing on. But there were no more clues from the dead Protoculte whitecoat. They had to find it by themselves, or get flatlined. That was all there was to the matter.

Just then, the .50 cals stopped firing and four brilliant beams of light filled the tunnel with blinding illumination, trapping the companions in plain sight. Diving to the ground, they took cover in the shallow pools of dirty water, rats scurrying over their bodies as they crawled backward trying to reach the darkness again. The .50 cals raked the ground, the muzzle loaders adding their firepower to the incoming barrage.

Then a gren bounced along the train tracks from deeper within the tunnel. The sphere stopped near Ryan, and he saw the handle was still wrapped in electrical tape. A gift relayed from Krysty. Reaching out, he tried to reach the gren, but the heavy slugs from the sec men were hitting everywhere and Ryan was forced to duck low again. He tried once more and got a bullet through the hair.

Fireblast! This was triple bad. They were trapped and the next step by Mitchum would be to launch a Firebird and blow them to hell, guided by the tiny pilots in the warheads.

Now they were going to have to try to run for it. Never a good plan, and confined in a tunnel it was damn near useless. But the one-eyed warrior knew to never surrender, never give up. Life wasn't neat and orderly. Folks made mistakes, got lucky breaks. One lucky break was all they needed. Just one.

Working the bolt to clear a jam in the Uzi, J.B. glanced overhead and saw the ceiling was coated with sleeping bats, thousands of them. They were safe from the blasterfire because of the angle, but maybe he could do something about that.

"Doc, cover me," the Armorer shouted, switching weapons.

Without pause, the old man dropped the Webley and fanned the LeMat, the smoky discharge of the weapon making a dense cloud of gray fumes in the air.

Immediately, J.B. stood and swung up his shotgun to pump all four shells at the sleeping night flyers. The blasts from the 12-gauge scattergun echoed louder than thunder, and the bats awakened, screaming and squealing. A few took flight, a couple more, then dozens.

Understanding the plan, Ryan whistled loud and sharp, once long and two short, and everybody froze motionless. This was exactly the type of situation they had created coded whistles for, when you couldn't yell out a warning without letting the enemy know your plans. And the companions never needed to keep their intentions secret more than right now.

The bats wheeled about over the companions, confused and angry, unable to comprehend what was happening. Then they noticed the sec men who were continuing to fire their blasters, all the while shouting and cursing over the engines of the Hummers. Attracted by the noise and lights, the bats poured along the tunnel in a river of wings.

"Shitfire!" Mitchum cursed, covering his head as the bats arrived. "Shoot these freaking things!"

The .50 cals fanned death down the tunnel, dozens of riddled corpses fell to the tracks, but the night flyers swarmed over the warm sec men, getting tangled in their hair and clothing. The warm hoods of the Hummers were coated with the creatures, the headlights blocked by the leathery wings. Darkness enveloped the Hummers.

"Launch some Birds!" Mitchum ordered, crushing a wiggling bat in his bare hand.

"We can't!" a sec man cried, slapping the bats aside with his blaster. "They'll only hit the bats and detonate yards away. Mebbe right in the pod!"

"Then gut them!" the colonel snarled, drawing a machete and slashing the winged rodents apart.

Knives were used to hack the animals off, but the

smell of blood only excited them more and a feeding frenzy began. The tiny fangs first ripping open the flesh of their own dead, then the humans were next and the screaming really began.

Chapter Twenty-Two

"Now's our chance," Ryan said, standing from the puddle and starting down the tunnel.

Muddy and wet, the companions quietly hurried away from the broiling firefight between the sec men and bats. The high beams were only a flickering glow blocked by the multitude of angry bats. They couldn't see Mitchum any more than he could them. How long the condition would last was another matter entirely, so they moved fast.

"Over here!" Krysty shouted in the gloom.

Following the sound of her voice, Ryan found her and his son standing before a plain steel door set into the tiled wall. A burnished plate listed it as Access 9 Sewer Pumps. The companions gathered close as J.B. picked the lock in the dark and pulled the door open.

Inside was a small antechamber, closed off by the standard black metal entrance to a redoubt. The alloy was smooth and unmarred, without handle, hinges or keyholes. Just smooth steel. Searching along the sides, Ryan found a small steel plate set into the wall and eased it aside to find an armored keypad. Quickly, the man tapped in the entry code.

As the nuke-proof portal slid ponderously aside, the companions rushed forward, only to stop as a strong smell of ozone filled the antechamber.

"Fireblast!" Ryan cried out, shoving the others backward from the door.

Then the first wisps of crackling white fog flowed into view. A wafting tendril touched the barrel of Jak's M-16, dissolving the predark steel, leaving only a hollow nubbin sticking out from the frame.

"Fuck!" Jak cried, throwing the useless blaster at the fog. The rapidfire went into the mist and vanished.

Retreating into the tunnel, the companions could only watch as a swollen expanse of gray-white fog flowed out of the redoubt. There was no true surface, but its bulk was impenetrable, forever moving and alive with countless tendrils of mist. Heaving as if taking deep breaths, an eerie glow emanated from its core, casting the tunnel into ghostly blue shadows.

Half of the companions had never seen such a thing before, but they clearly remembered the horror stories told by Ryan, Krysty, J.B. and Doc about the incredible monstrosity, the ultimate guardian of the redoubts. Sometimes the underground bases were patrolled by sec hunter droids or comp-operated weapons systems for protection from invaders. But only an occasional redoubt had ever had this hellish bastard of science and insanity.

The companions fell back before the fog, and it pulsed from the redoubt, expanding and swelling in size to fill the tunnel. A bat on the ceiling screamed at the sight of the thing, and tried to fly past the glowing fog. A tendril of mist caressed the animal in flight, and it was gone, only the bloody tip of a wing tumbling down to splash into a puddle between the railroad tracks.

"Beware of the Cerberus," Doc rumbled softly, the

LeMat and Webley held steady, his arms crossed at the wrists to support the heavy handcannons.

The fog seemed to react to the sound of his voice, almost as if it recognized the old man. Then a .50 cal crackled around the corner, and the fog abruptly paused, unable to decide between the two groups in the stygian tunnel.

"Keep nice and slow," Ryan growled, a hand on his blaster. "No sudden movements or it'll strike."

"Let me try something," Dean said, unbuttoning his shirt pocket.

"Do nothing!" his father ordered sternly. "Only weapon that can kill this are implo grens."

"Don't have any," J.B. said, shaking his head. The man held both the Uzi and the shotgun at the ready, even though he knew they would be useless against the living death cloud.

"Maybe we can outrun it," Mildred suggested, feeling very small and defenseless before the colossal fog. "Trick it somehow and then double-back and slip inside. No way it could reach us past the nuke-proof door."

There was a sense of intelligence about the creature, and she wondered if it could actually understand their words, or if it was merely responding to the tone of their voices, as a dog would.

Billowing endless, the fog started toward the companions, but another barrage of blasterfire from the sec men made it reconsider.

"Trick this? Not a chance," Krysty said, moving away from the creature. Her hair tingled from its proximity, and her skin seemed to crawl as if alive with static electricity.

Holding the last gren, Ryan pulled the pin and

dropped it at his boots. "No way we can reach the redoubt now," he said grimly. "We can't kill it, or even harm the bastard thing. So when I drop the gren, run down the tunnel and don't stop. If anybody makes it to the surface alive, head for the bank. We'll meet there."

"We return to the city of the gorillas," Doc stated, holstering his piece as a prelude to running, "yet a fighting chance for life is better than none."

"Get ready," Ryan said. "On my mark."

Pushing his way past the adults, Dean walked straight to the towering Cerberus and held out a small plastic rectangle.

Instantly, the fog pulsed toward the boy but then stopped, and a single thin tendril extended to brush over the mag strip on the B12 identification card from the corpse on the crashed Hercules aircraft.

Just then, bright light bounced along the walls of the tunnel and a Hummer drove into view, Mitchum at the wheel with a revolver in his hand. His face was in ribbons, blood everywhere, the dead bodies of his crew hung off the armored war wag, clusters of tiny bats still feeding off the nutrient-rich life fluids of the corpses.

"You fucking bastards are gonna pay for this!" the colonel screamed, spittle spraying from his mouth as he fired the blaster.

Suddenly rushing forward, the mist split apart and flowed around the companions, leaving them undamaged in its midst. But they were surrounded, unable to move in any direction.

"Smoke wouldn't hide you!" Mitchum screamed, firing his revolver into the swirling banks of glowing fog.

Oddly, the bullets didn't seem to reach the outlanders even though they were only fifty feet away. Slamming on the brakes, the sec chief climbed into the back and grabbed the .50 cal, only to notice the ammo belt was gone, completely used up in the fight against the bats. Shitfire!

Clambering into the rear of the Hummer, the colonel lit the main fuse for the Firebirds and swung the pod at the companions. Instantly, the fog surged forward. One by one, the Firebirds launched and punched into the cloud to simply disappear.

"Impossible," the sec man muttered as the fog flowed irrevocably over the military wag. The headlights dimmed and a strange stink of lightning filled the air, making it hard for Mitchum to draw a breath.

"This can't be happening!" he screamed from within the confines of the shapeless fog. Still launching, the Firebirds left the pod and their exhaust winked out, the impotent rockets falling to the ground and breaking apart, spilling their precious cargo of black powder.

As the cloud began to thin around them, Ryan raised the Steyr to try to chill the sec man, but it was too late. Already the clothes were dissolving off his body, then his skin began to sag and melt away, showing the network of muscles and veins. Gurgling horribly, the dying man swung the pod about, still valiantly trying to chill his inhuman attacker even as his organs slid from his torso and piled at his feet, white bones appearing within the raw, red flesh.

The cloud was gone from around the companions as Mitchum's bloody skeleton toppled over, knocking the pod to swivel about and point straight up. The last couple of Firebirds slammed into the roof of the tunnel to violently explode, broken tiles and concrete debris raining upon the companions. J.B. pulled Mildred out of the way of a falling slab of concrete, and Dean cried out as a chunk of ceiling hit his hand, knocking the card into a puddle.

"Hot pipe!" he shouted, sucking on the minor wound while rummaging about in the dirty water with his other hand. "Where the hell is it?"

As if understanding the words, the Cerberus cloud billowed about in a circle and started hastily for the companions.

"Get inside!" Ryan commanded, starting for the steel door.

"But the card!" Dean cried out, splashing in the muddy water.

His father grabbed the boy by the collar and hauled him erect. "No time. Leave it!" Ryan commanded, pushing his son toward the open doorway.

Tendrils of fog were already snaking along the ground as they piled into the alcove. The armored portal of the redoubt had automatically closed, and Krysty hurriedly punched in the code to open it. As before, the massive truncated door ponderously slid aside, and the companions squeezed through the widening crack to get inside.

The door was still opening when the main body of the fog arrived before the outer doorway. Throwing the gren into the tunnel, Ryan then fired from the hip, the slug hitting the wall behind the door, the ricochet slamming it shut with a loud bang. A heartbeat later there was an explosion, and the door shook, fumes seeping around the edges. Then the fumes began to coalesce and pull the weakened barrier away from the jamb, static electricity crackling over the warping sheet of metal.

"Molotovs!" Ryan shouted, and Dean rummaged in his shoulder bag for the firebombs.

Doc was already at the interior keypad, tapping in the access code to try to make the redoubt door close faster. But the armored slab didn't increase or diminish its speed. Slow and steady, it reached the far wall, paused and began the journey back home.

Flicking her butane lighter, Mildred started igniting the greasy rag fuses and the companions crashed the Molotovs into the alcove, the combined bottles building a raging conflagration that overflowed into the redoubt. Jak added a pint of whiskey he had taken from the department store. The flames soared as the materials ignited, and the companions waited breathlessly to see if the door would close before the death cloud breached the bonfire.

The opening between the black metal door and wall was only a foot wide when the first tendril writhed out from the dying flames. The companions poured hot lead into the narrowing crack, but still more of the fog pulsed into the redoubt when the door finally slammed shut. The piece of the Cerberus lashed about wildly as if in pain, then began to dissipate and vanished from sight.

"Safe." Mildred exhaled, slumping against the wall. Warm currents from the life-support system were already carrying away any trace of the cloud or the firebombs. The replacement air was dry and flat, tasting of iron and antiseptically clean, the floor vibrating with a faint hum of powerful machinery. The overhead fluorescent lights were bright, with only a few dark tubes in the fixtures, and one flickering as it struggled to stay active.

"The hell we are," J.B. cursed, backing away.

Faint wisps of cloud were seeping through the hairline cracks around the massive portal.

"Mat-trans chamber," Ryan ordered, working the bolt on the Steyr to chamber a fresh round.

Heading down the zigzagging antirad tunnel from the front door, the companions burst into the garage of the redoubt. The area was packed solid with the materials and supplies from the National Guard armory—vehicles, Bradleys, trucks and a dozen Hummers. Crates of weapons, explosives and blasters were stacked to the ceiling. It was the wealth of the predark world.

"Implo grens!" J.B. cried and went straight to the case. The other companions assumed defensive positions and watched the mouth of the entrance corridor for any sign of the approaching fog.

"Well?" Ryan snapped after a few seconds.

"Almost got it," the Armorer grunted, struggling to rip open the packing case. His knife slipped and hit the floor, skittering away.

Jak gestured and handed him another.

"Move it, John!" Mildred shouted, pointing as the first tendril of the Cerberus cloud came sneaking around the corner.

"Buy me some time!" J.B. cried, stabbing a knife into the resilient plastic. Flakes chipped away with every blow. In just a couple of minutes he'd have the grens they needed.

"Pray tell, with what?" Doc retorted hotly, both hands busy reloading his Civil War blaster.

"Try this!" Dean said, throwing the last Molotov.

The tendril retreated a bit from the small blaze, and Ryan looked over the assortment of military hardware for an answer. There was enough here to conquer the world, but nothing was primed and ready. In five minutes they would be safe, in an hour unstoppable. But they had only moments before the cloud would be here. They needed something right now.

"The lantern!" Ryan said, and grabbed it from Krysty to smash the pressurized lamp on top of a sealed wooden crate carrying the alphanumeric sequence for thermite grens. The wick ignited the oil and the flames climbed high, burning into the wood.

"Time to go," Ryan ordered, stepping into the maze of crates. "Take the stairs. The elevators might not be working."

"Just another couple of secs," J.B. grunted, hacking away at the stubborn wood. There was already a hole in the top of the crate, and he could see a piece of an implo gren. It was only inches away. The Armorer tried to shove his hand into the opening, but it was too muscular. The splinter stabbed his flesh, making the hand slippery with blood and he forced it in deeper, a fingertip brushing the handle of the deadly high-tech gren.

Grabbing the arm, Mildred pulled the man away from the crate. "We have to go now, John," she shouted, firing her revolver at the approaching fog.

Blood dripping onto the floor, J.B. glared in raw hatred at the packing crate, then grabbed his Uzi and started off at a run.

Almost every redoubt was built along similar designs, and this was a configuration the companions knew by heart. Dodging through the crates, they reached the stairs and jumped down the steps. As they reached the third level, they plowed out of the stairwell and charged for the mat-trans chamber.

Slamming open the door to the control room, they saw that the comps and monitors were operating normally. Going to the chamber, Krysty opened the veined door and everybody raced through. The last one in, Ryan saw a wisp of fog snake into the control room.

"It's here," he stated, then hurriedly closed the door and sat quickly on the floor.

As always, the mat-trans unit waited patiently a few moments for a destination code to be pressed into the keypad. When nothing was entered, the machine commenced to activate a random jump.

Static electricity began crackling in the air as wild lights sparkled. Slowly, a swirling mist began to cloud the chamber, twinkling lights like tiny stars shooting through the material of the floor and the companions themselves. Only yards away, Ryan saw the door begin to dissolve under the arrival of the Cerberus fog. Seconds counted now.

The lights grew in numbers and brightness until they were immersed in a swirling galaxy of flaring novas. The universe vanished, and the companions fell through the floor into infinite nothingness, and beyond.

Epilogue

A hundred miles away, Lord Baron Kinnison was driving his Hummer through the farmlands of his island, heading for the sulfur mines to review the torture status of some slaves, when a powerful quake shook the land.

"What the fuck was that?" he demanded, braking the military wag to a fast halt amid the young green plants.

Sitting beside the obese norm, the Lady Deirdra Kinnison looked up in terror, every fiber of her being jarring in warning. Without a word, she scrambled from the vehicle and started running toward the nearby ocean.

Utterly confused by the strange behavior, Kinnison scowled at the woman when another quake shook the mountain range and the dormant volcano erupted.

Hot ash and smoke thundered from the ragged peak, the noise so loud it became silence to ruptured ears. Fiery balls of burning sulfur spewed from the mountain, then the side of the range cracked open wide and out poured a river of molten lava.

Spitting curses, Kinnison started the wag and twisted the wheel to escape even as a soft gray snowfall of pumice ash fell to blanket the ground. The Hummer traversed only a few yards before the tires slipped in the loose material. Baron Kinnison stomped on the gas pedal, pushing it to the floor, but the engine rattled and died, the air intake completely clogged by the thick ash.

The bandages around his face acting as a natural mask, the fat man struggled from the wag and waddled hastily away, his heart pounding savagely in his laboring chest. Again and again his boots slipped in the swirling ash, and he finally went sprawling as a sulfur ball crashed nearby and the explosion tossed him away, a broken, bleeding lump of flesh. His smashed body racked with agony, Kinnison could only lie there weeping as the ash slowly covered him. Another tremor shook the island, and then the ground beneath the man yawned open wide. Helpless, the baron fell into the crevice and landed on a sluggish river of lava. Instantly, his hair vanished, his bandages caught fire, as the heat seared into his cracking bones. Saturated with jolt, the baron stayed alive for long seconds, his body sizzling until the intense heat boiled his blood and the fat man burst apart in a gory spray.

Ripping off her new dress, Deirdra continued to sprint for her life, the terrible heat of the lava flow announcing its arrival right behind her. The mutie could feel her hair singe off, the very clothes on her back beginning to smolder. But icy adrenaline poured into her veins and the woman dashed forward with renewed strength, her velvet slippers pounding against the hot soil. The killing heat diminished slightly as she pelted across the grasslands, leaping over small bushes and a dry creek. Yes! She was going to make it! She was going to live!

Reaching the cliff, Deirdra simply threw herself over the edge and arched her body into a diving position as she knifed for the life-saving water below.

She was still falling when a vent from the volcano vomited red hot lava into the sea and the shoreline began to furiously bubble from the stygian geological exhaust.

She barely had time to cry out before she plunged into the boiling ocean, her death scream overwhelmed by the roiling fury of the erupting volcano.

James Axler

OUTLANDERS®

TOMB OF TIME

Now a relic of a lost civilization, the ruins of Chicago
hold a cryptic mystery for Kane. In the subterranean
annexes of the hidden predark military installations
deep beneath the city, a cult of faceless shadow figures
wields terror in submission to an unseen, maniacal god.
He has lured his old enemies into a battle once again for
the final and deadliest confrontation.

*In the Outlands,
the shocking truth is humanity's last hope.*

Readers won't want to miss this exciting new title of the SuperBolan® series!

DON PENDLETON's

MACK BOLAN®

A DYING Evil

THE TYRANNY FILES

BOOK III

The deadly hunt began in the United States, as an escalating series of terrorist incidents were linked to neo-Nazi fanatics calling themselves Temple of the Nordic Covenant. Each time, Mack Bolan had been there to thwart the temple's grisly agenda for global dominance and to minimize the spill of innocent blood. But now the temple is going nuclear. On the frozen frontier of the South Pole, it will be determined whose vision—Bolan's or a madman's—will prevail.

Available in September 2001 at your favorite retail outlet.